EX LIBRIS

VINTAGE **CLASSICS**

STELLA GIBBONS

Stella Gibbons was born in London in 1902. She went to the North London Collegiate School and studied journalism at University College London. She then worked for ten years on various papers, including the *Evening Standard*. Stella Gibbons is the author of twenty-five novels, three volumes of short stories, and four volumes of poetry. Her first novel *Cold Comfort Farm* (1932) was an immediate success and won the Femina Vie Heureuse Prize for 1933. Among her works are *Nightingale Wood* (1938), *The Bachelor* (1944), *Westwood* (1946), and *Starlight* (1967). She was elected a Fellow of the Royal Society of Literature in 1950. Stella Gibbons died in 1989.

ALSO BY STELLA GIBBONS

Cold Comfort Farm
Bassett
Nightingale Wood
My American
Christmas at Cold Comfort Farm
The Rich House
Ticky
The Bachelor
Westwood
The Matchmaker
Conference at Cold Comfort Farm
Here Be Dragons
White Sand and Grey Sand
The Charmers
Starlight

STELLA GIBBONS

Enbury Heath

VINTAGE

3 5 7 9 10 8 6 4 2

Vintage Classics is part of the Penguin Random House group
of companies whose addresses can be found at
global.penguinrandomhouse.com

Penguin
Random House
UK

Copyright © Stella Gibbons 1935

Stella Gibbons has asserted her right to be identified as
the author of this Work in accordance with the Copyright,
Designs and Patents Act 1988

First published in Vintage Classics in 2021
First published in the UK by Longmans, Green and Co. in 1935

penguin.co.uk/vintage-classics

A CIP catalogue record for this book is available from the British Library

ISBN 9781784877194

Typeset in 10.75/13.25 pt Bell MT Std
by Integra Software Services Pvt. Ltd, Pondicherry

Printed and bound in Great Britain by Clays Ltd, Elcograf S.p.A.

The authorised representative in the EEA is Penguin Random House Ireland,
Morrison Chambers, 32 Nassau Street, Dublin D02 YH68.

Penguin Random House is committed to a sustainable future for
our business, our readers and our planet. This book is made from
Forest Stewardship Council® certified paper.

MIX
Paper from
responsible sources
FSC® C018179
www.fsc.org

To
Gerald and Lewis

The characters in this story are fictitious.

Children of the same family, the same blood, with the same first associations and habits, have some means of enjoyment in their power which no subsequent connections can supply.

MANSFIELD PARK.

CHAPTER I

Hartley Garden had been a bad man but a good doctor, and he was much loved in Enbury Fields. A crowd half a mile long attended his funeral. It stopped the trams on their way up to Enbury Heath, and filled his youngest son, Francis, with a gloomy pride.

His only daughter, Sophia, sat looking out of the window of the first car behind the coffin, but she was not seeing the crowd; she was staring up at the pale blue sky over the Heath and the six delicate dark birch trees on the top of Minister Hill. The trees were bare, because it was January; and thin snow lay on the roofs.

Enbury Fields is in North London. A long ascent rises from Tottenham Court Road and soars until it ends in Minister Hill and in the little valleys and hillocks of Enbury Heath. The funeral was now crawling up this long hill on the way to the cemetery at Northgate; and the crowd pressed round the cars, staring at Francis and Sophia and wondering why Harry, the other brother, was not there.

'Don't show proper feelin', does it, not turnin' up for 'is dad's funeral?'

'Oh, all the young ones are the same nowadays. They don't none of them show proper feelin's, if you ask me. Look at 'er jumper. Pink. She might 'ave put on a black one; it wouldn't 'ave killed 'er.'

Sophia, in fact, was thinking about her jumper. She was wondering whether she ought to have taken Uncle Preston's advice, bestowed on her yesterday over the telephone, and bought something black. It was true that she had only five shillings in the world until Friday afternoon, and today was Wednesday, but she could have borrowed the money; anybody would have lent a person a pound to buy a black jumper to wear at their father's funeral. That was just what had kept her from asking anyone; that, and the fact that she was not sorry her father was dead. Why should she wear mourning?

But she was miserable; so wretched that she was sick and frozen with misery; and at the same time she felt callous and flippant. She could not cry, even from shock.

This was the second funeral in six months, and funerals are shocking affairs. Their ritual, the blend of vivid nodding flowers and grand words, and the unbearable facts of loss and corruption, strikes on the nerves without mercy. Sophia knew the routine of a funeral by heart; and thought that never again could she bear to go to one, even if it had been the funeral of Harry or Francis.

The first funeral had been that of her mother, whom Sophia loved better than anyone in the world. Mrs Garden had died from a stroke, and the forces which brought it upon her had gathered during the twenty years of ceaseless worry, fear and unhappiness that had been her married life.

Sophia, whose character and upbringing combined to make her a merciless judge, considered that her father had murdered her mother as surely as if he had shot her through the heart; and that was why she was not sorry that he was dead.

'Sophia ... er ... Sophia ... !'

Uncle Preston, who was sitting opposite her, had been trying to attract her attention for nearly half a minute, but she refused to hear him. She did hear him with her small pretty ears, but she was not listening with her mind. She was longing to be walking alone over the Heath, kicking at the snow and staring up at the still, brown trees.

'Uncle Preston is trying to tell you,' suddenly said Francis in a loud, sarcastic, trembling voice, 'that your petticoat's showing.'

Sophia, trying in her turn to be as infuriating as she could, slowly moved her head round until she was staring at Uncle Preston's prim, anxious face.

'Your dress, Sophia. It seems to be caught up ...'

Sophia slowly looked down at her legs, which were decently veiled in black lisle stockings at one and eleven pence a pair. The rather grubby hem of a white petticoat showed below her skirt. She slowly drew her dress over it, and turned away to the window once more.

Now they had left the crowd behind, and the three cars had stopped crawling; they were smoothly climbing Greenride Hill, and between gaps in the houses and trees London could be seen, dim in the winter haze of the valley. Sophia was glad to be getting near the Heath. She hated Enbury Fields, and never wanted to see it again.

She glanced at Francis. He looked as stony, grim, white and exhausted as she did. He was sixteen and a half, five years younger than she, but this afternoon he looked at once very young and very old, and frighteningly like his dead father. Darling Francis, she thought, he's hating it. I expect he'll be sick afterwards. Oh, I am so hungry. I wish I'd remembered to buy some breakfast last night.

She had been living alone for the six months since her mother died, in a room near the Heath on her salary of three pounds a week; and she had so many things to think about and to arrange that she often forgot to buy her breakfast. This failing infuriated her, for Sophia liked eating and looked forward to mealtimes.

She had left her father's house two days after Mrs Garden's funeral, and had not seen him from that time until the morning when she saw him in the coffin. Aunt Maxine and Uncle Preston, his sister and brother, thought this action of Sophia's a shocking one. They would probably go for her about it after the funeral.

They would also go for Francis, who had approved Sophia's action, but who could not imitate it because he was still at school; and if Harry had been there they would have gone for Harry, too. Buoyed by a pleasing conviction that it was impossible for them to be in the wrong, they never hesitated to go for anyone.

Sophia thanked her stars that he was not there, because Harry, who was twenty, was a gentle, peace-loving, romantic sort of cuckoo, and not grim and slightly sardonic like Francis and herself.

Sophia stared out of one window; Francis stared out of the other. Aunt Maxine, who sat opposite Francis in her natty mourning suit, studied Sophia's profile and wondered if she ever thought about boys, and if she was having a love affair with anybody? There's no fun in her, thought Aunt Maxine regretfully; she would have liked Sophia to think a lot about boys and to be having a very exciting love affair which she would discuss in minute detail with her Aunt Maxine. Sophia was an unnatural sort of girl. Why, when Aunt Maxine was Sophia's age, she was a regular little pepper pot; couldn't keep her off the boys. And Sophia *ought* to be a pepper pot, lord knows, with poor Hartley for a father! As for Francis, he'd never break hearts with a nose that size, and Harry was a softie. The beauty of the family, but undoubtedly a muff. Why, at his age, most young Frenchmen were running several women.

But Uncle Preston, now that he had made Sophia pull her skirt modestly over the hem of her petticoat, had stopped thinking about poor Hartley's children. He was a great one for modesty, even in times of family crisis; but now he was worried about the will.

Who would get what? Marriot, the family's solicitor had kept very quiet about the will. No one knew anything. Everyone was pretending not to care a bit, but everyone was also teetering with excitement and trying to find out what everybody else knew, and this, added to a natural feeling of relief at Hartley's death and a strong desire to interfere with any imprudent arrangements which might have been made on their own behalf by his three children, made the occasion as inwardly exciting as it was outwardly sedate. Certainly, Sophia and Francis were the only people present who felt sick with shock and frozen with the accumulated misery and memories of years.

The car stopped. They were in the cemetery; and Sophia and Francis, while getting out of the car under the eye of Uncle Preston, observed to their dismay a number of persons who were even more repulsive in appearance than Aunt Maxine, Uncle Preston and the cousins and sisters-in-law and things occupying the other cars. These were lurking uneasily among the tombstones.

Years of miserable family life had compelled Sophia, Harry and Francis to practise a method of communication which they fondly believed could not be observed by grown-up people.

It consisted in twisting the mouth as far on one side as it would go, and then talking through it. Harry said that this was how convicts talked to each other in prison; and Sophia's comment had been that such a method was therefore peculiarly suited to use by the young Gardens.

It was this method which they now adopted, in discussing the tombstone lurkers.

'My god,' said Francis. 'What are they? They look like troglodytes or something. Surely they can't be relations?'

'Must be. Or perhaps they're patients? A lot of them sent wreaths. There was a lovely one from old Fanny.'

'Oh well, she would. She's been in love with Father for years. I saw her in the crowd round the surgery door when the coffin came out, roaring like a town bull. Oh lord, I'm so hungry.'

'So am I. Never mind, darling; if we can get away together afterwards we'll go off somewhere and have some food. I feel so queer; all unreal, as though I were looking at everything through a sheet of glass.'

'That's nerves,' said Francis wisely. 'My legs are trembling, and I feel sick.'

'We are a pair, aren't we? Never mind; we've got each other. I wish Harry were here.'

'I don't. He'd loathe it. He was fond of Father, you know.'

'Shall we go to Celia's party tonight? I know it seems awful to go to a party on the evening of your father's funeral, but I'd rather like to; I feel so awful, and I want to forget about things and just not care about anything.'

'I've got to get back to school. I'd rather – and besides, even if I stayed, Uncle Preston wouldn't let me go to a party.'

'Blast Uncle Preston.'

'Shut up, he's looking at us.'

Sophia stared at her prayer book during the ceremony in the little chapel, and did not look up until the great coffin was swaying out through the door on the shoulders of six men, and the mourners turned to follow it.

It held the body of a huge man, which had been full of a terrifying vitality and a pitiful weakness. It was buried in wreaths of dark red roses, violets, daffodils and carnations from a woman who had loved him and delicate stiff tulips. The sacrificial flowers at funerals are invariably called 'beautiful flowers,' as though flowers were not always beautiful, even on a coffin. But these flowers ... Sophia fancied that their colours burned with triumphant life. They sprang from wreath, cross, spray, like transparent flames, as though drawing their strength from the great body in the coffin.

She followed with the others out into the fresh afternoon air, and saw it lowered into the grave.

Her mother lay there.

She forced her mind from the thought.

Rain began to fall before the clergyman had finished reading the service, and Uncle Preston put up an umbrella which he held over Sophia and Francis. Francis occupied himself, during the last few moments of the ceremony, by edging away from the umbrella until he stood bareheaded in the rain, his glasses misty with steam. He stared sternly into the distance with large pale blue eyes, and wished the beastly business were over. Once his hand went to his inner breast pocket. It was all right. What he had carried for three months was still there, safe and hidden.

The earth was sprinkled, the sexton moved forward and the crowd of relations broke up and turned away.

They stood in little groups under their umbrellas, peering at each other through the rain, hurrying forward to shake hands eagerly and to remind each other that the last time they had met was at poor Mildred's funeral; that must have been a good eleven years ago.

Most of them began by looking critically and disapprovingly at Sophia and Francis, who stood a little apart, but soon they got so interested in exchanging gloomy reminiscences and telling each other that there were not many of us left now and wondering mournfully whose turn it would be next and asking how was Auntie Bessie's catarrh and was poor May any better and what had become of poor Stanley, that they forgot to look carpingly at Sophia and Francis.

Sophia and Francis took the opportunity to stroll a few yards off and examine a tombstone.

'What a crew,' murmured Sophia, with her head on one side and a gentle, pensive expression on her face as she surveyed the stone. 'Francis, I can't help wishing we had just one decent relation. Suppose we'd come here today, and there had been an absolutely unknown first cousin, just back from Vienna – very tall, well dressed, with a sense of humour, knowing all about music and very well read. Think of it! The relief!'

'He'd be only one more person to try and boss us about. There're quite enough as it is.'

They were wandering slowly, aimlessly in the direction of the avenue leading to the gates. No one looked round at them.

Uncle Preston and Aunt Maxine were now haranguing the relations, and telling them that of course they must all come back to the surgery and have a little something. But the cousins and widowed sisters-in-law and distant connections hesitated; they did not wish to appear too eager to have a little something. They were coy; they must be persuaded.

Auntie Loo, Uncle Preston's wife, saw Sophia and Francis escape. She saw Francis's school overcoat and cap Sophia's worn tweed suit and beret, fade among the weeping trees, the tombstones and the fine rain, but she did not want to pluck at anyone and raise the alarm. Poor little things, she thought, it's hard on them. Let them run away, if they want to. And she looked placidly at Uncle Preston, and thought out a plan for dealing with his distress when he should discover the absence of Sophia and Francis.

Sophia and Francis broke into a run. Down the avenue they ran, between the tombstones, the rain beating in their young faces, on their way to the gates.

When they were seated in the little single-decker bus which runs between Northgate and Enbury Heath, Sophia began to feel apprehensive. They ought not to have run away. There would be a simply frightful row.

Her bursts of bravado usually ended like this; for her courage was of the long-suffering rather than the aggressive kind. Her usual manner was cold and rather severe, and strangers often took her to be an efficient young woman of decided views and character, with a good opinion of herself. But this manner was not due to these qualities at all, but to her extreme concentration on whatever matter she might have in hand.

She had to concentrate because, if she did not, her mind went flying off into dreams. The first lines for poems, airs of music, calm or violent memories, went floating through her mind in a delightful medley, and asked to be followed, and she looked solemn and severe with the effort of not following them.

When she acted rashly, she followed the beckoning of the images and the music in her mind, and temporarily forgot to concentrate on reality. In that moment of relaxation, disaster usually befell her. The folly once committed, she realized what had happened and became penitent and alarmed.

Francis said that he did not care if there was a row; he had had just as much as he could stand of Uncle Preston, and if the old fool didn't like it, Sophia knew what he could do. 'They all treat us as though we were still wearing bibs,' said Francis fiercely, 'and I'm not going to stand for any more of it.'

They got out at the Turpin Arms, which looks out over the wide wooded expanse of the Heath, and walked down the steep High Street to their favourite Primrose Café; two thin, white-faced, dangerous-looking young creatures. Evening was falling rapidly now; the glimpses of London between the little old houses on the hilltop showed it glittering with lights, and the street lamps here, high over the city, swung in the rainy wind and scattered purple light on the wet pavements.

CHAPTER II

They felt better as soon as they began to climb the stairs which led to the upper dining room. The room was warm and quiet, with a rosy little fire dancing in the basket grate, and no one else was there. Downstairs a party of noisy Jews laughed with their girls, but up here there was no sound except the flutter of the flames.

Sophia and Francis dragged off their caps and coats, and piled them on a chair, and sat down at the table nearest the fire. Sophia saw herself in the old spotted mirror over the mantelpiece, between the advertisements for Kaola and Spearmint which were stuck into its sides. She looked so drawn, so white, with her fair hair dull and ruffled and her lips pinched, that she hardly knew herself.

'Don't we look awful?' she said, in the queer unreal voice which she knew was her own, but which for the last few months, she had been able to hear talking as though it had been the voice of a stranger.

Francis turned and looked at himself. An expression of distaste grew on his face.

'I do hate my nose,' he said, and rang the handbell for the waitress.

When she came, they were sitting with their elbows on the table and their chins sunk in their cupped hands, in silence. It was Molly, their own waitress. They cheered up a little when they saw her, because she was so pretty, and they always instantly responded to anything pretty. Also, they knew her, and her presence made them feel less alone, less cut off and isolated in an unfriendly world.

'Two steak and chips, please, and jelly and cream to follow. Two rolls and butter and two coffees,' said Francis, fixing Molly with a firm but flirtatious eye.

'Cream's off,' said Molly, smiling.

'Just our luck. Custard? All right. That'll do. And could you hurry them up, please, because we're simply ravenous.'

Molly promised. Francis wanted to tell her, when she came back with the food, that they had been to their father's funeral that afternoon, but Sophia said no, he was not to.

'She wouldn't understand. She'd get all shocked because we're sitting here eating, instead of lying at home on our beds roaring our eyes out. Then we'd have to explain why we aren't sorry, and that would take hours and be such a bore. I hate explaining things.'

'I don't. I rather like it, except when I have to explain to Uncle Preston. My god, it took me nearly twenty minutes this morning to explain Harry's letter. He wouldn't believe they wouldn't let Harry come, and I couldn't show him the letter because Harry called him an old fool in it.'

'Wouldn't they really let him come?'

'No. They couldn't get another man to do his part at such short notice, and besides, I don't think they believed he really wanted to get off to a funeral. I believe they thought he wanted to get up to town to see a girl or something like that.'

'It does sound a bit queer.'

'Hasn't he got an understudy?'

'He says not. He says the chap who was supposed to be understudying him has been so busy shifting scenery that he hasn't had time to learn his part. But he's coming up to hear the will read, next Sunday.'

'Oh ... another ghastly family gathering,' said Sophia, drinking hot coffee with her mouth full of steak and chips. She was enjoying her supper, and felt a little better. 'Do you think I need go? I'm sure Father hasn't left me a ha'penny. The family's favourite indoor sport is Leaving Sophia Out of the Will. Grandpa did, and Uncle Oliver did. I bet you Father has, too.'

'Father used to be jolly fond of you.'

'I know ... until I showed him what I thought about the way he treated Mother. (Oh damn! Now I suppose I'm going to cry again. I do nothing else. Have you got a hanky?) And then, of course, I wasn't musical, which was another death blow to his hopes. (Oh damn! I'm *sick* of crying.)'

But she had to put down her knife and fork, and cry, all the same. Francis carefully put the saucer over her coffee, to keep it warm, and patted her hand sympathetically until she was better. Despite his grim and sarcastic air ('very unpleasant in so young a boy. A most unfortunate manner' as Uncle Preston said) he was very affectionate, sensitive and kind, and liked petting his sister, whom he dearly loved.

'Thanks; I'm all right now,' said Sophia, blowing her nose. 'I shan't go to Celia's party. I shall ring up and tell her I'm going home to bed.' She began again on her steak and chips. 'Francis, what are you going to do now, darling? Shall you go back to school? Oh dear, there's so much to do and arrange ... I feel it will never get straight ... Do you want to go back to school?'

'No. I want to leave. I've been wanting to leave for two terms now. I feel so much older than all the other chaps—'

'So I should think. You've had enough to make you.'

'Helping to put your father to bed when he's drunk makes you grow up. You know, Sophia, the one thing I dreaded, all the time I've been at Northgate, was that he'd come up to Founder's Day or a match or something, drunk. I used to go about in a blue funk on match days until everything was over and I knew he couldn't come.'

'Oh, darling – don't. He wouldn't have done that. He was pretty bad, but not so bad as that. He was proud of us, in a queer sort of way.'

'I don't know. You know Harry can't save a penny of his salary, and spends it all on clothes. Well, that's Father's fault. You remember how he let Harry go up to Northgate so badly dressed, in his first term, that he was jeered at by all the chaps.'

'Beasts, they must be,' said Sophia, rubbing her eyes childishly with her fists and yawning.

'No, they weren't. They were just stupid, that's all. They thought Harry's patched trousers were funny, and I suppose it was funny – only we can't be expected to see it. But he's such a nice chap and so charming that they all got to like him after a bit, and forgot about his clothes.'

'But Harry doesn't forget, does he? Oh, Francis, the harm Father did! Twenty years of misery for seven or eight people, just because one man was a brute!'

'All the same, I used to feel sorry for Father. He wasn't happy in spite of all those women and dashing money about—'

'That Mother ought to have had—'

'—and having everything his own way. Now he's dead, everything feels flat, somehow.'

'That's because you're tired out. So am I. I couldn't feel another thing, not if I was given a hundred pounds. I can't see properly and I ache all over.'

'You'd better go off home to bed, dear.'(Francis often called Sophia 'dear,' in a sober grandfatherly manner.) 'I shall ring up Uncle Preston to let him know I'm all right, and then I'll go back to school.'

'Won't you be miserable, darling? I wish you could come back with me, but there's nowhere you could sleep.'

'Oh, I shall be all right. Old Squitters is very decent; he won't let people bother me tonight. And I'll write to you in Prep time tomorrow, and we'll see each other on Sunday, and Harry will be there, too.'

And Francis suddenly grinned, his thin sensitive lips parting to show small white teeth. He looked for an instant like a fierce young wolf.

'What's the joke?'

'Oh, nothing. I was thinking about Sunday, that's all.'

They were wearily putting on their things again, Francis patiently holding Sophia's coat while she poked ineffectually for the armholes. She was an extraordinarily clumsy girl, and was always bumping into things and bruising her thin skin, turning her ankles over, and nearly falling in front of lorries. She used to defend herself by saying that Shelley fell over things, too, and look what a poet he was, but this scarcely relieved the apprehensions of her friends.

When they got outside they found it had stopped raining, and was a beautiful windy night. Arm in arm they walked slowly up the steep hill to the Turpin Arms, where Francis would catch the little bus to Northgate School, which was halfway to Northgate village.

Sophia had the strange feeling that they were alone in the world. The rain had driven people indoors, many of the shops were already putting up their shutters, and the High Street was almost empty. It was too early for cars to be going past on their way down to the theatres, and the crowds coming back from shops and offices were indoors, and just beginning on their well-earned suppers.

Slowly, slowly, with bent head and lagging feet, she climbed the hill, leaning on her brother's thin, steady arm. He was a few inches taller than she, and she had the comfortable sensation of leaning on him spiritually as well as physically. She wished that Harry were there to take the other arm, and then there would be the three of them, climbing the long, dark hill slowly but surely together. Her dear, dear brothers! A wave of love for them flowed into her mind, and she pressed Francis's arm.

'Tired, my dear?' asked Francis. They were at the top of the hill. The fresh glimmer of dancing water came to them from the Oval Pond, opposite the bus stop. On either side of the Don's Mile the dark Heath dropped away in sweet miniature valleys, thinly sewn with may trees and birch, with sleeping swans on its little pools and the grass on its hillsides wet with rain.

'Here's the bus. Goodbye, darling, I'll write.'

Francis dropped both his hands on to her shoulders and kissed her firmly, then ran over to the bus. She saw his stern young face for a few seconds, while he fumbled in his pockets for the fare, and then the bus's lights dwindled down the Don's Mile. Too late did she remember that she had forgotten to borrow from him, and that she had only five shillings till Friday.

Oh well, thought Sophia, too tired to be anything but philosophical, I shall borrow from Celia, and if she hasn't any, I shall ask Mr Piper to advance me some. He will. And, already soothed by the darkness, the freshness and silence all about her, she set off dreamily across the Heath on her way home.

Sophia liked being alone so much that often, when she came home from a walk with her cheeks cool yet glowing from the pressure of a west wind and her eyes filled with pictures of moving boughs, the uplifted faces of flowers, and the dance of water, she felt guilty. Everybody was so kind and so pleased to see her back again, everybody asked so placidly whether she had had a nice walk; and there she was, returned like a prisoner from his one day's leave on parole! – having enjoyed herself more, so much more, than she could ever say, and remembering with a start how nice, interesting and affectionate the stay-at-homes were. For two hours, not a thought of the nice, interesting, affectionate ones had crossed her mind.

What did cross it? Nothing coherent. She was too busy inhaling smells, listening, recovering her balance when she tripped (which was, as we know, frequently) and looking.

Now, as she went home across the Heath, she looked up at the huge amber clouds which were rolling quickly, in toppling mountains, over the blue-black sky. Tiny stars glittered between the dun vapours, dimmed, were gone. She could not look at the clouds and also see where she was going, so she walked into a good many puddles and got her ankles splashed and her shoes loaded with mud. Halfway down Willow Hill, she sternly pulled herself together, turned to the right, and left the Heath for the pavement and the security of Church Avenue; she reminded herself that she would have to clean her shoes tonight, and dry her stockings. There was no point, none at all, in getting them wetter than they need be.

When she got to the house she began to walk quietly, and she crept down the area steps to the tradesmen's entrance which she used as her own front door.

She did not want to meet her landlady, Mrs Parr.

This was not because Sophia owed back rent to Mrs Parr. It was because Mrs Parr, being a natural and primitive female, was extremely interested in births, marriages and deaths, and in the ceremonies attached to them. Sophia was not very natural or primitive; even her passion for being in the open air was unlike the passion of a primitive human being for stuffiness, enclosure and cosiness, and she was rather bored by the ceremonies which thrilled Mrs Parr.

She did not want to be waylaid by Mrs Parr and have to tell her all the dreary details about the funeral.

But she need not have worried. Mrs Parr was out. Just round the corner, at the Walley Memorial Hall, a Jew who had escaped from the Nazis was telling an audience of indignant Enbury Heath residents about his experiences; and thither, in pleasant anticipation of hearing about some atrocities, had gone Mrs Parr.

Sophia soon discovered that Mrs Parr was out, and with a feeling of relief and peace, she went into her room and shut the door.

The room had a miserable dark blue wallpaper and looked out over a paved stone yard and a towering row of houses at the back, but Sophia had arranged one or two of her battered treasures on the mantelpiece, and at the end of the paved yard grew four young poplars whose tops she could see moving against the sky when she lay in bed, so she quite liked her room. And in any event, she never minded her surroundings much, so long as she could arrange things and keep them tidy.

She dragged off her cap and coat and fell on to the bed, with her legs hanging over the side so that she could kick off her muddy shoes.

Presently, she thought, I must go and telephone Celia about the party.

But it was so quiet in her room, the bed was so soft, the pillow so cool. The gas stove burned with a comfortable glow, and she was so tired.

It was lovely to lie quietly on the bed. Next to walking in the air, she liked it better than anything in the world. In bed, in the open air, she marshalled her forces for dealing with events and people when she came back again into the solid world.

She had not drawn the curtains. They hung, straight and dark blue, on either side of the black window, and between them shone square gold lights from the houses at the back.

I must go and telephone.

First one shoe, then the second, fell to the floor with enormous thuds. She curled her feet up under herself. Not a sound, except the humble hissing of the gas stove; blessed peace, silence, softness.

I ought to put out the light. I must go and telephone ...

Dear Francis. I hope he got back safely. Harry. Mother ... She turned her cheek deeper into the pillows, with a weak little sob. Darling Mother ...

She was asleep.

CHAPTER III

Some authorities on child psychology say that the most important factor in the bringing up of a happy, well-balanced and normal child is a serene background. They recommend routine and calmness, a life as orderly as that of the solar system, with Father and Mother shining like the sun and the moon amidst the obedient planets, and keeping the frightening darkness at bay with their tender light.

Others recommend a more exciting method which suggests, rather than the solar system, the Chelsea Arts Ball taking place in a birth control clinic; but it is doubtful whether even this second school of thought would approve of the way in which the young Gardens had been brought up.

For they had not been brought up at all.

They were in the immortal position of Topsy, which is not such a comfortable position as some admirers of Self-Realization would have us believe. A weed on a rubbish heap grows up in grand, unrestricted freedom and may be very comfortable, but the children of a bitterly unhappy marriage, who have had ample chance to develop as they please, are profoundly uncomfortable.

Weeds may wander, but children need authority, guidance and answers to their questions, because children have souls which can develop, and weeds have not.

The wild, free-weedy system of upbringing had a really good try-out on the young Gardens, but the results would scarcely have pleased one of the advocates of the New Freedom.

Were they sane, gay, balanced, kind, and capable of managing a series of experimental love affairs with gallant yet tender ease?

They were not. Sophia judged the visible world very harshly and liked nothing better than to escape into her private world of dreams. As for love, she hardly thought about it; and normal girls of twenty usually think about it a great deal. Harry was so calmly sure that his beauty would win him fame and the worship of thousands of girls that *he* never thought about hard work and perseverance. Francis liked to dramatize his feelings and feel fierce and lone-wolfish; he enjoyed disliking people, especially relations. And all three were as moody, sensitive and quick-witted as show cats; they had hardly any of the virtues which would fit them for citizenship in a brave new world.

But these were small faults compared with their lack of standards.

All their short lives they had seen gentleness oppressed, beauty ignored, and order thrust aside in favour of chaos. The most beautiful object in their daily lives had been their mother, and her life had been a bondage to misery. They all reverenced gentleness and beauty, and Sophia had already resolved that she would try to mould her own life to include these qualities, but the daily spectacle of the apparent *powerlessness* of virtue had sunk deeply into their minds.

They took it for granted that life should be ugly and harsh, as more fortunate children assume that life is delightful. They intended to escape from that harshness in time, if it were possible, and to enjoy themselves in their own way, but they did not rebel against the misery of their home life because they were inured to it, and even found some of its aspects funny. Pope's bitter saying about the monster who is endured, pitied and embraced was true of the young Gardens and the cruelty of life. They grew up surrounded by it, and therefore could not utterly avoid absorbing its taint.

Sophia was the most fortunate of the three, because she was a child of love and hope. She grew up in the wreck of hope and the slow, strange living death of love, but because she was conceived in love, she was the happiest of the three, and she never forgot it.

'Mother was happy when she had me, so that's why I'm a happier person than Harry and Francis, and so I've got to look after them. They haven't had a fair chance,' she decided, when she was about twelve years old.

She took a natural delight in beauty and order. This is one of the finest gifts which a human being can possess; next to the gift of faith, it bestows more joy on its possessor than any other. Sophia accepted the existence of vice without a feeling of horror, but it bored and annoyed her because it usually upset order and spoiled beauty.

This calm acceptance of the ugliness of life, and a painful nervous instability, were the worst results which environment and heredity had so far produced in the young Gardens. It was surprising, in the circumstances, that all three were not much nastier than they were; but the good qualities which they had inherited from their mother helped them to be courageous and to find laughter where one would least expect it to be; and on the whole, Sophia and Harry and Francis were likable.

But while there is life there is always hope; and Aunt Maxine, Uncle Preston and the rest of the relatives did not despair (though of course they all said how dreadful it would be if it happened) of seeing poor Hartley's children go to the dogs as poor Hartley had done. These indiscreet prophecies fostered the natural dislike which the children felt for their relations, but also made them determined, in a bored sort of way, *not* to go to the dogs as your poor father did.

The elder Gardens were always prophesying woe, woe. They dearly loved a bit of excitement, but they disapproved of the usual healthy means of obtaining it, and were therefore

compelled to fall back on family rows, dramatizing their emotions, deploring the probable fates of Sophia, Harry and Francis,
and woe, woe-ing; and, heaven knows, there was usually something to woe, woe about, for the family came of an unusually
passionate and vital stock, born to rows and trouble.

Old Acton Garden, who died three years before the children's
father, had been a violent Irishman, a doctor who had married
his gentle first cousin Mary, and fathered three boys and a
girl – Oliver, Hartley, Preston and Maxine.

His strong passions had been held in check, not by reason,
but by forces which have come to be called 'typically Victorian,'
though it is doubtful whether they are so. He bound his demons
down with chains of fear, respect for convention, and his deep,
inborn sense of the wickedness of the instincts. A violent love
of beauty in all its forms dwelled in him side by side with this
sense of guilt; he was particularly moved by the loveliness of
women and by the power of music.

He suffered considerably from this deep conflict in his spirit,
and so did his two elder children, Oliver and Hartley. Their
sufferings looked out from their eyes, the large bright grey-blue
Garden eyes, which in Hartley were lightened to the green of
the sea on an April evening; and the natures of both brothers
were so twisted, difficult and unhappy that their father never
ceased to thank Providence that Maxine and Preston, though
they were nervous and moody enough, were not quite so impossible as Hartley and Oliver.

Oliver's life, which ended when he was nearly fifty, was a
long and sullen frustration in work and in love. He had been
drowned while staying in Cornwall with his family, and his
old father had ever afterwards tried not to think that he might
have committed suicide. He was certainly unhappier as he grew
older, and had begun to drink heavily.

Fortunately for his wife, she was extremely stupid and the
suspicion did not occur to her. When he died, her natural, com-
monplace cheerfulness bubbled up, and she began to enjoy her
life. For twenty years all her little ordinary pleasures had been

spoiled by his silences, angers and sudden disgusts, and by his contempt. She had been at first fascinated by him, then afraid, and finally impatient and indifferent; and though of course it was dreadful that poor Oliver was dead, things were certainly much pleasanter now that he was.

Oliver's life had been dull and bitter; Hartley's had been terrible.

The violence in the elder Garden men called for its complement, a yielding weakness in women. They married gentle, small women whose lives they made miserable, but Hartley came against an unfamiliar quality when he chose Ethel Parry for his wife. She was a small dark girl, pretty as a cherry or a little red rose, and she had a sense of humour.

None of the Garden men had; and neither had poor Auntie Grace (Uncle Oliver's widow) and poor Uncle Tom, Aunt Maxine's husband, who was dead. Auntie Loo had one which she carefully suppressed, and it was said that Grandmother Mary had had one, but she died long ago and none of her sons liked to recall that Mamma used to laugh at them when they got into tempers. Mamma's memory, naturally, was as solemn as it was sacred.

But Ethel's sense of humour was part of her saneness and her natural wisdom. Even twenty years of being married to an unhappy neurotic could not kill it; she passed it on to her three children and it helped to save them from becoming 'typical Gardens.' They hated the thought of becoming typical Gardens worse than anything in the world, and refused to admit that there were some fine qualities in the Gardens, who had superb vitality, were adventurous and responded with quick ardour to beauty. When ageing second-cousins-twice-removed tottered up to Sophia and announced, after peering at her, that she was 'exactly like her poor father, isn't she, Preston?' Sophia became coldly furious and stunned the well-meaning women by saying brusquely, 'I'm sorry to hear it. I don't want to be.' And she and Francis envied Harry because he looked like their mother.

When Sophia first heard of the girl who was born under a dancing star, she thought at once of her mother, who had, for weapons against a terrible existence, humour, courage and faith in the hidden goodness of life.

Mrs Garden had no wealthy and powerful relatives to help her to get a divorce, even if she had wanted one. Her family consisted of two or three small, merry, very affectionate people like herself, who were alternately amused by, and terrified of, the large passionate Gardens with their solemnities and their appetite for rows. The Parrys kept out of the way; but sometimes Mrs Garden would slip down to visit them at Portsmouth, where they had lived for many years, and as soon as her little unmarried sister opened the door, and held out loving arms to her, she would step for a few hours into her happy girlhood again, and almost forget the monotonous misery which lay in wait for her in London.

Yet she did not want a divorce, because, despite her husband's cruelty and the strangeness of his nature, and the unhappiness of their life together, she loved him still, and he loved her.

She was the symbol of his lost youth which had been so full of superb promise, and together they had brought three children into the world. Of course they still loved one another, though they could never have been happy together. Fairy and ogre, they were chained together in their terrible bondage. They could not escape, and would not have done so even if they could, for they were bound by love.

But Sophia, the merciless judge, did not realize this until both had been dead for many years.

Her father had his full share of the Garden conflicting strains, Acton's fierce passion and Mary's timidity.

He was a most unhappy man, whose very great energies needed more outlet than his work as a doctor in a slum could give them; yet the timorousness and lack of self-confidence which he had inherited from his mother prevented him from turning his powers into satisfying channels.

He was ambitious, but his ambition sprang from vanity, and when it was not fed by achievement, it turned sour and increased his misery. He did not possess the concentration and aptitude for hard, persistent study which would have burnished his gifts, and brought him social and professional success. On every side he was thwarted, and he threshed insanely against the nets woven by his own most unfortunate character.

Yet his gifts were great. In the practical execution of his work he excelled. He worked like a demon, building a large practice of patients who loved him as much as they feared him, in the heart of a miserably poor and crowded district; and during the twenty years of his work there he saved many hundreds of lives by the exercise of his brilliant gifts of diagnosis and surgery. He let in light, sunshine and a fierce humour into the wretched rooms where his patients lived.

They called him the Fresh Air Doctor, because fresh air was what he most often prescribed. He realized the curative powers of light and sun some time before they became part of the stock-in-trade of clinics and general practitioners in very poor districts and he insisted, with oaths, on his patients sleeping with their windows open.

Sophia used sometimes to ride on his rounds with him when she was a child, and she could remember in later years how, when his small cheap car appeared at the top of the street, windows would fly up all along its squalid length. 'Open the winder, quick! 'Ere comes Dr Garden!'

The demands made on his vitality by hard physical work were great, but still it ravened for more power, beauty, life – he did not know what would satisfy it, and still the feminine streak of weakness kept him chained in the slum, a lion in a tiny den. He turned to intrigues with coarse or sentimental women to find release; and as he grew older and dimly realized that he would never escape from his own nature and the life to which it bound him, he turned to whisky and drugs.

He knew that his life was horrible, but it never seemed quite real to him. He never grew into an adult with a man's mature realization of the awful brevity of life, and the necessity for shaping it.

He always had, in the depths of his suffering spirit, a belief that suddenly, without effort, the enormous load of work, misery, frustration and drink would roll away; and leave him happy, in a clear radiant world filled with the sound of Wagner's music and the smell and colour of dark red carnations, which were to him the symbols of perfect beauty.

Mrs Garden shared this belief. He felt it as a bound Titan; she felt it as a miserable but brave child. Neither of them was capable, however, of working to secure this world of which they dreamed, and both died in the full tide of mingled misery and secret, irrational hope.

Mrs Garden was forty-eight when she died, and her husband was eight years older. He only lived for six months after her death; and during that time he changed.

Perhaps her death wounded his spirit in some secret place which had been untouched by his other women, or perhaps he felt that his youth had died with her. Whatever it was, he changed. Though he did not stop drinking, he became gentle and quiet, and when heart failure killed him one evening in three minutes, in the interval between seeing two patients, all his relatives and women felt that he had been cheated out of a last, and a genuine, repentance.

Sophia did not feel this. She decided that six months of pensive grief did not atone for more than twenty years of bullying and unfaithfulness and cruelty, and that was why she was not sorry (so she grimly told herself) that her father was dead.

But when she was older, and growing wiser, she would sometimes meet at a dinner party a distinguished elderly throat specialist or a surgeon, who would stare at her as though he had been introduced to a ghost and say at last: 'Surely you must be Hartley Garden's daughter?' And then, after a pause filled with vivid thoughts, 'You're very like him ... I was up at Bailey's with him, you know. Very like ... yes, he was a brilliant man, your father. He ought to have been in Harley Street with his gifts, but he didn't take care of himself. A great pity. Yes ... it's a really astonishing likeness. You might almost be Hartley, looking at me.'

And Sophia, who no longer resented her likeness to her father, would add a little to the pity for him and the understanding of his nature which had begun to grow in her heart.

But for many years she could not forgive him for the way in which he had allowed his three children to grow up.

He would not send them to school because he thought that this would make them 'ordinary,' and he despised ordinary people. He was proud of their strongly marked personalities and their precociousness, and he wanted to develop these qualities under his own eye.

When Sophia was ten, the three children were handed over to a governess.

She did not stay very long; and neither did the nine other governesses who took her place between Sophia's eleventh and thirteenth birthdays.

They had a habit of departing in a hurry at the end of a few months, either in tears and very insulted about something and glad to be going, or else in tears and darkly hinting at an undying devotion to somebody and begging to be allowed to stay.

It was Sophia who discovered that her father made love to the governesses. She saw him kneeling at the feet of Miss Leadlay, through the sitting room window which opened on to the back garden. He looked very handsome, and he was evidently pleading with Miss Leadlay to kiss him or something.

Sophia was much shocked. Reluctantly she conveyed the information, decently veiled in hints, to Harry and Francis. They were not very much interested, but they were rather jealous of Sophia because she had seen their father, so to speak, in action, and they had not. Apart from this passing regret they found the situation amusing.

Sophia did not. She knew that it made her mother very unhappy, and when each new governess came she would ask in her prayers, which Mrs Garden had taught her, that the governess might stay and everything might be all right.

But it never was. Of course some of the governesses stayed longer than others; Miss Strudwick, who was plain, good and kind, stayed for nearly a year, but in the end she went too, in tears, because Dr Garden told her that the children had learnt all that she could teach them. In truth, she left because Dr Garden did not want to teach her anything.

Then came Miss Vereker. Her departure resulted in the children being sent, at last, to school.

Miss Vereker tried to kill herself one quiet sunny afternoon, because Dr Garden had become bored by their intrigue.

He was out on his rounds, the little boys had gone for a walk on the Heath with their mother, and Sophia, who was at this time thirteen years old, was sitting on the landing which led up to the attics, reading Thomas Moore's *Lalla Rookh*. Miss Vereker crept sobbing out of her bedroom and down to the dispensary, where she took enough veronal, she hoped, to kill herself.

Sophia, who had observed the sobbing and creeping with much disgust from her perch on the stairs, found her an hour later on the sitting room floor, unconscious. It was Sophia who fetched the cook and the parlourmaid and suggested that they should carry Miss Vereker upstairs to her bedroom.

Sophia and the two servants knew exactly what had happened and none of them felt sorry for Miss Vereker. The servants thought that my lady had been asking for trouble and had got it, and Sophia thought that Miss Vereker, of whom she had been rather fond at first, was a silly tiresome nuisance and that it would be rather a good thing if she died. But she never forgot the picture that the two servants made, slowly climbing the stairs with the big, unconscious girl swinging between them.

Miss Vereker did not die, but she very nearly did, and her parents had to be sent for at once to come from Cornwall; and there was a terrible fuss. There were people crying and shouting all over the house, and the children were packed off to stay with Aunt Maxine whom they disliked intensely.

This ended the regime of governesses. The boys were sent to a preparatory school and Sophia to a cheap but excellent day school where she was extremely miserable, because a spoilt, arrogant, lazy and precocious child naturally cannot be popular with, or even accepted by, ordinary and properly brought up little girls.

School set a barrier of shyness between the three young Gardens, formerly united in an unspoken but deep alliance. Yet mutual unhappiness and fear had forged the alliance so strongly that nothing could break it, and they had not been together for one day of the holidays before they rediscovered the fact that they were happier in each other's society than in any other, except that of their mother.

When those four were together, they spun a delicious web of frail gaiety and laughter that neither memories of the past nor apprehensions for the future could spoil.

Sophia and her mother had the same lively fancy and both could tell stories; they could spin like two spiders by the hour, capping each other's absurdities with wilder and wilder flights until the big bed in the attic, where the boys slept, shook with the weight of the four who sat curled on it and their helpless laughter.

How they laughed, stuffing pillows into their mouths to muffle the sound, an unfamiliar one in that house of slamming doors and sudden shouts of anger!

Harry's fair face, so like his mother's lovely dark one, was crimson with laughter, and all his curls would bob as he shook, and thin little Francis would sit silently rocking, with tears of laughter rolling down on either side of his big freckled nose, and Sophia, perched astride a pillow with her arms waving and her hair on end, would gabble on and on and on, only stopping to shriek with uncontrollable laughter at her own mad flights of invention.

Once Dr Garden came up unexpectedly and found them.

He opened the attic door very quietly, hoping to catch them before they knew he was there.

But before his hand was on the door, they heard his deliberate stealthy footsteps. The laughter stopped. He opened the door to see four quiet, stilled faces looking up at him. Mrs Garden drew Francis into her arms.

'What's the joke?' asked Dr Garden, softly looming over them in his full height of six feet and two inches.

'Nothing, Hartley ... I was just sitting with the boys before they went to sleep. Did you want me? Were you calling?'

'You seem to be enjoying yourselves,' he said, still looking down at them.

'Oh ... nothing ... only a silly story of Sophia's.'

'Sophia never tells me stories,' he said, sneering. And he turned and lumbered downstairs.

'Oh Mummy – he's mizzerable! Quick – run after him!' implored the tender Harry, and Mrs Garden, after hastily tucking them up and kissing them, went anxiously down to soothe, if she could, her monster.

'Daddy always spoils things,' whispered Francis to Harry, just before they fell asleep.

'Poor Daddy. He's mizzerable,' said Harry. 'Never mind, I love him.'

Sophia and her brothers did not make many friends at school because they were afraid to ask people home to tea lest there should be a row, or Dr Garden should come in drunk. Sophia suffered the most from this situation, because people liked her in spite of her severe appearance and self-opinionated manner, and she was often asked to tea by other girls, and had to refuse because she knew that she could not return the hospitality she received. She could not help making one or two friends, but she did not ask them home to tea.

'My people are unhappily married,' she would say sternly, staring straight ahead of her straight nose, and the friend, much embarrassed, would mutter 'Rotten luck,' and be devoured by speculation.

Francis suffered in the same way; but Harry accepted invitations as his royal right, and never bothered about asking people to tea in his turn.

'Chaps hate going out to tea, anyway,' he would say mildly, looking at the shocked Sophia and Francis with beautiful eyes of clear blue-green. He was very popular at Northgate, the big school to which he and Francis went after they left their preparatory school, because he was good at games, modest, and gifted with natural charm and a delightful sense of humour. He had a talent for writing light verse of the kind which schoolboys like best, and his physical beauty charmed the eyes as much as his good nature and nice manners pleased the social sense.

Sophia and Francis were proud of him, but in a troubled fashion. Francis used to say, 'The old chap hasn't got a very strong character, you know,' and Sophia would reply firmly, 'Yes; we've got to look after him,' and so they did.

The years at school seemed endless yet they also seemed to fly. Matters at home grew very much worse. Dr Garden was hardly ever sober; and their mother was often ill with terrible headaches and attacks of vomiting. Sophia could hardly bear to think when she was older about her mother's last years; the memory was too painful.

Life was divided sharply into the white of the pleasant time which she idled away at school (for she was extremely lazy, and not clever) and the black of the awful time spent at home, comforting her mother, standing up to her father in one of his rages with her knees trembling under her, and the infuriating tears of anger coming too soon to her eyes and reducing her to speechlessness.

When she was eighteen she left school.

She had no talents except one for writing, and by this she proposed to earn her living. She had no dreams of going off into an attic to write novels. She wanted to be a journalist, and earn enough money to take her mother away from her father, and get her brothers started in decent jobs.

She felt a huge weight of responsibility; sometimes the thought of it ground round in her head until she felt confused and half insane. There was no one in the world to whom she could turn; no kind, rich, sensible older person. She thought of the Garden relatives as melodramatic silly people who were worse than useless in a situation like this, and her mother's relatives, though she loved their gentleness and humour, were poor and afraid, and she thought of her brothers as children. It's all on me, she thought. I must do it all.

But the forces which had been gathering for more than twenty years were, naturally, too strong for her. Some months after she left London University, where she had taken a course in journalism, she got a post as editorial assistant in a newly established Canadian news agency, at a salary of three pounds a week; and believed that, at last, her plans could go forward. She put two pounds of her first week's salary into the Post Office, and went about with her chin set very firmly, walking on air.

On the day that she had saved twenty pounds her mother died.

She had not believed that it could happen. Her mother had been like her own right hand or like the daylight itself; it was impossible to think of life without her. All meaning seemed to leave life, except when Sophia walked among the birch trees on Enbury Heath and their beauty comforted her. She was too stunned to mind much when Francis, much disturbed, wrote to tell her that Harry, who had left school some time before, had gone out on tour in a repertory company run by one of Aunt Maxine's shady friends; Aunt Maxine had flattered him into believing that he would be a West End star, with his looks, in a year.

'Father didn't try to stop him going. He's drinking a bottle of whisky a day,' wrote Francis. 'He seems very miserable; I think he misses Mother.'

And the pressure of unceasing grief, of having no adored little mother to work for and rescue, of being utterly alone and feeling ill and strange, and knowing that her father was drinking himself to death, wretched because she would not see him – the pressure of these things went on, grinding into Sophia's spirit. She did not feel like a real person, but like a ghost who worked, walked in the woods, and cried silently, hopelessly for hours at night.

But one day Uncle Preston telephoned her at the office to tell her that her father was dead; and the pressure went away, at last.

Grief stayed, and the strange ghostlike feeling, but with her father's death the last link with the terrible old life seemed to snap; and she felt clear and free.

Twenty-one years had ended; she was just twenty-one years old, and there was a new world in front of her, waiting to be entered and conquered.

Francis and Harry had this feeling, too.

They were like three people who have been fighting their way through a fierce storm of wind, rain and thunder, for many hours. And suddenly the storm is over, a hush falls, they stumble into a quiet lamplit room and close the door. They stand staring at one another in silence, wearily wiping the rain from their faces, too tired to speak. But their bright eyes are eager with questions as they stare round the room. How quiet it is! Is everything really over – really ended at last? What's going to happen now?

CHAPTER IV

Uncle Preston was extremely annoyed when Francis rang up at eight o'clock that night to announce that he was all right. Uncle Preston was tempted to say that he did not care whether Francis was all right or not, but he did not say so, because he always tried to forgive people and never to say anything disagreeable or honest, no matter how badly people behaved to him or let him down.

So all he said was:

'Oh, is that you, Francis? Rather *odd*, my dear boy, was it not, *to disappear* this afternoon in the way you did? Not very *considerate*, was it, to all your friends and relations? Several people asked after you; old cousin Clara (she was a *Mumford*, you know, you must often have heard your poor father speak of the *Mumfords*) wanted to see "Hartley's youngest boy." Yes. Yes. Eh?'

'I didn't say anything.'

'She was *very disappointed*. Quite upset. Eh?'

'Sorry ... I mean, was she? Oh.'

'Yes. Your Aunt Maxine, too. She wanted to have a little talk with Sophia. I thought Sophia did not look at all *well*. Aunt Maxine ... eh?'

'I said – I'm sorry I must cut off now, Uncle Preston. My housemaster wants to see me.'

'Of course. Yes. Well, I am glad to know you are all right, my boy. *Get a good night's rest.* It will do us all good. Eh? Well, goodbye ... Goodbye. *We shall all meet again on Sunday*, for the reading of the *Will*. I shall see you then. Well, goodbye, Francis, goodbye.'

'Goodbye,' said Francis. And after he had hung up the receiver, he added under his breath 'Cissie.'

Uncle Preston went pattering back into the sitting room where Auntie Loo sat mending his socks.

He felt more cheerful; he was looking forward to Sunday when they would all meet again.

There was nothing Uncle Preston liked better than all meeting again. If he had had his way, the family would have all lived in one enormous house in the middle of a desert, where there was no one else for them to meet, and seen each other every day. Nothing upset him more than a family row. When one occurred, which was every five weeks or so, Uncle Preston could not rest until he had rung up everybody and told everybody how dreadful it was, and collected everybody's opinion about it. He would then patter round to see the two chief persons concerned and try to get them to make it up. He usually succeeded; because, much as the Gardens loved quarrelling, they loved not being bothered by Uncle Preston even better, and they gave in out of sheer weariness. (Not from boredom; no Garden was ever bored by family affairs.)

Auntie Loo was pleased to see him looking happy. She was fond of him. Sophia had discovered this and had amazedly reported it to Francis.

They had never taxed her with it (for another of their precocious qualities was a spidery, delicate, scarcely-daring-to-breathe tact in dealing with the feelings of people they cared for) but perhaps Auntie Loo suspected their amazement. For on one occasion, after Uncle Preston had been more than usually maddening, and had gone out of the room to fetch something, leaving the three young Gardens sullen and quiet, Auntie Loo had said, suddenly but placidly, 'You mustn't mind your uncle, my dears. He means kindly, you know...'

'Of course. Oh yes, Auntie Loo,' said three voices, polite, breathless, eager. And Auntie Loo added, as though this explained something, 'I knew him as a young man, you know.'

'Ghastly he must have been. I expect he played the harp and pressed seaweed,' said Harry afterwards, when they were alone.

'I like the harp. It's my favourite instrument,' Francis had said firmly.

'Who was that, dear?' Auntie Loo now asked, neatly weaving her needle in and out. Uncle Preston loved being asked about things.

'It was Francis. He just wanted to tell me that he was all right. It was *very inconsiderate* of him, I think. He should have rung up before; I have been worried about them; quite worried about him and Sophia ...'

'Perhaps he couldn't get to the telephone, dear. Schoolboys don't have much time to themselves, you know.'

'They would *surely* have given him permission, if he had *explained* the whole matter ... But there, let's put it out of our minds. Pouf! Away you go!' and Uncle Preston made the gesture of one who poufs something out of his mind and smiled a martyr's smile at Auntie Loo. 'He is all right, and that's all that matters. We mustn't expect young people to realize how much older people feel things, must we? It's only natural. And after supper I can write to Cousin Clara Mumford and tell her that they are all right.'

'Yes, dear. I am sure she will want to know. Are you ready for supper now, dear?'

'Just as you like, dear. I am ready if you are ... but I think that perhaps I had better just telephone to Maxine to let her know that the children are all right. Yes. Dear me, how chilly the hall is!'And then, as there was no reply from Auntie Loo, who had gone into the kitchen to superintend the preparations for supper and could not hear him – 'Loo! Loo-ie!'

'Yes, dear?' Auntie Loo came placidly out of the kitchen along the corridor and out into the hall. 'Did you call, dear?'

'I only said that the *hall* is very *chilly.*'

Auntie Loo looked round the hall as a warhorse might look round a battlefield.

'It is rather, isn't it, dear? What do you suggest?'

'Why, an oil stove, of course,' said Uncle Preston, at once testily and triumphantly. 'The very thing. An oil stove is cheap, easy to work, gives out an *excellent* heat, a really *fierce* heat, and the newest kind do not *smell*. Yes. What do you say?'

'That's a *very* good idea. I'll order one from Batwick's tomorrow,' and Auntie Loo, who had been subterraneanly at work putting the idea of the oil stove into Uncle Preston's mind for the last three months, and overcoming his objections to smell, expense and dirt by a masterly policy of silence, went back to attend to the fish pie.

It is fortunate that the telephone cannot transmit smells as well as sounds; if it could, it would certainly have conveyed to Uncle Preston the smell of Aunt Maxine's flat.

His own small, neat house in Forest Hill did not smell; Auntie Loo saw to that. Aunt Maxine's flat in Earl's Court smelt a great deal. Aunt Maxine did not mind because she did not notice. She had too many other things to think about.

Aunt Maxine had been on the stage. She had played second leads in musical and straight No. 2 companies (for she had a bit of a voice, and more than a bit of a figure) in the palmy days before the War, and though she was not now likely to make a crashing comeback (for her age was fifty-two, her charms were ill preserved and she had neither personality nor intelligence) she clung to the stage with affection. As the saying is, she took an interest.

All her friends were on, or off, the stage; she frequented those small snack bars in the back streets round Leicester Square where stage people meet to eat waffles, and she faithfully read the *Stage* and the *Era*. She seldom missed queueing for the pit on an important first night. She spoke of Marie and Gertie, of Noel and Cedric, and she belonged, rather surprisingly, to two dreary clubs, which performed dirty plays with no entertainment value on Sunday evenings. But no; when it is remembered that Aunt Maxine looked at life from a severely biological angle, her adherence to the Restoration Society and the Sunday Night Circle is not so surprising.

Aunt Maxine lived on four hundred pounds a year, which had been left to her by her husband, a successful stockbroker who had been killed at Mons but not before he had saved money. She had a very nice time; except that her cats and her friends were always dramatically betraying her and letting her down, Aunt Maxine had not a serious woe in this world, and what woes she had she thoroughly enjoyed, so no one need feel at all sorry for Aunt Maxine.

She was a ruin, but a handsome one who wore its dark hair wound into a suspicious sort of egg round its head and rows of curls on the forehead, and could still flash a pair of large blue-grey eyes; the fine Garden eyes, eager and full of light. Her figure was quite square, as Late Victorian figures often are, and her chest stuck out like a shelf. She bought clothes of the kind that other would-be smart women buy, but the minute she put them on they looked queer. It was partly the egg and partly the shelf, and partly just being Aunt Maxine.

The stockbroker husband was rumoured to have been madly in love with her. Perhaps, in those strange days before the War, Aunt Maxine had been subtle and fascinating, eagerly drinking in life with her big eyes as she hung on the stockbroker's arm in a lace blouse and a big hat loaded with roses. No one knew for certain. Aunt Maxine referred to the stockbroker as Poor Tom, and always with an intonation as though he had been very lucky to get her, and perhaps he thought that he had.

When the telephone bell rang, Aunt Maxine was having a passionate scene with Beatty, her latest cat.

Beatty had been naughty. So had Soo-soo, Woodles, Lovey, Whiskey, and all the other cats which Aunt Maxine had rescued from the gutters and a fate worse than death; that was why Aunt Maxine's flat was in the state that it was. Naughtiness was the one thing, Aunt Maxine was telling Beatty, that she could not put up with. Beatty might steal the milk, sleep on the bed, be sick in the bath and Aunt Maxine would understand and forgive. But naughty – no. And Aunt Maxine with a cigarette hanging from one corner of her mouth which dropped ash all over Beatty, gathered Beatty up to the shelf in a passion of reproof.

Beatty, looking very bored, stayed there with her eyes screwed up and a yard of creamy white stomach hanging down, ending in two stiff, protesting feet.

The telephone bell rang.

'Blast, who's that?' said Aunt Maxine, but she looked pleased. She loved people to ring her up, and the longer the conversation, and the more involved, the better she liked it.

'Oh … oh … Maxine, it is I. Preston. *Preston.* Yes. I thought you would just like to know about the *children.* Yes. Eh?'

'Little devils. What have they been up to now?' said Aunt Maxine good-naturedly. Old fool, silly old woman, thought Aunt Maxine, unaware that, of the two, the children preferred Uncle Preston's squeamishness to her coarseness.

'Oh, nothing. Nothing, I hope … that is, unless of course you have *heard anything new?*'

'I haven't heard anything. They never ring me up. No one ever does, unless they want something. What about the children? I thought Sophia looked pretty seedy. Girls of that age often do. It's a tricky time, the early twenties … shouldn't be surprised if she's in love. I was, at her age. But *you'd* never get it out of her, if she was; a man's no good at talking to girls. I've been meaning to have a talk to her for some time … might get her to come for a long weekend, p'raps … do her good.'

'A very good idea, Maxine. Excellent. *We must all see more of each other now poor Hartley has gone.* And the children, too; it is very bad for them to be too much alone. After the *will* is read on Sunday, we must talk things over. Yes. The children will have to *live* somewhere, of course … I just thought you might like to know that Francis rang up a few moments ago, to say that he and Sophia are *all right.*'

'Did he say why they cut off like that? I thought it was damned queer.'

'No ... no ... now I come to think of it, he *didn't*. Very odd, running away like that. *Very rude*. I told him so. I said ...'

Aunt Maxine, with her eyes half shut and the corners of her mouth turning down with boredom and cigarette ash all over the shelf, listened for two minutes, and then cut in with— 'Nothing more about the will, I suppose?'

'Nothing more. No news at all. I must say that I think it a little unfriendly of Marriot to be so secretive about it. After all, he does *all* our business ...'

'Must make a damn' good thing out of it, I should think. I know he does out of me. And Grace told me she had an enormous bill in from him the other day. Can't remember the figures, but it was something enormous. Well, I don't suppose poor Hartley will leave much. That North woman will probably get the lot.'

Mrs North was reigning favourite at the time of Dr Garden's death.

'Dear me ... I hope not. That would be ... really, that is *quite* a new idea. I must telephone Marriot tomorrow and try to find out ... really, his secretiveness is absurd. You don't really *think*, Maxine? Surely not ...'

'Shouldn't be at all surprised.'

'Well ... really ... this has quite upset me. I must talk to Looie. Dear dear, there is always something ... Well, goodbye. Goodbye. We shall all meet on Sunday at the Surgery. Goodbye.'

' 'Bye.'

Aunt Maxine, who did not at all think that Mrs North would inherit Dr Garden's money, but who enjoyed alarming Uncle Preston, hung up the receiver and looked at the clock. In twenty minutes 'It Happened One Night' would be showing at the Regal, just up the road. Aunt Maxine cast a look of perfunctory inspection, which ignored smell, over her stiff sitting room with its orange and black decorations and framed Kirchner girls and artificial marigolds in tall glass vases, and then she put out the gas stove and the light, smacked Beatty and locked her in the scullery and went off to see 'It Happened One Night'.

She did not expect that her dead brother had left her any money, and she did not particularly want any. That was a virtue in Aunt Maxine; she was not greedy. She was very pleased with her income, smelly flat and recreations.

If she was not left anything in Hartley's will, she would naturally protest loudly to Preston, Grace and Loo, but she would not really mind.

Let's hope the children get what there is, she thought, walking quickly up the dark street towards the cinema. There can't be much because Hartley could never save a ha'penny and he spent such a lot on his women, and there was no money in the practice, anyhow. The practice will be sold, I suppose, but who'd want to go and live in Enbury Fields and kill themselves with hard work among a lot of dirty, ungrateful devils? If the children get a few hundreds each, they won't come sponging on us ... not that I'd grudge it them if they did, poor little beasts. They haven't had much of a life. No fun. Poor Ethel ... poor Hartley ...

Aunt Maxine, with big bright eyes reflecting the brilliant electric lights at the cinema's entrance, went in to see 'It Happened One Night'.

CHAPTER V

At three o'clock on the following Sunday afternoon, Sophia was sitting on the stairs by the surgery front door, waiting for Harry and engaged in her favourite occupation of doing nothing.

A pane of clear glass was let into the woodwork over the front door, and through this she could see part of the slate roof of a house opposite. It looked like a narrow dark road, going up a hill into the white sky, and she was staring up at it with much pleasure and imagining exciting places to which it might lead. She had discovered this piece of roof when she was six years old, and never grew tired of watching the imaginary road and thinking about it.

The house was quiet, for once, because it was Sunday afternoon. It was a tall, narrow dark house with creaking stairs and a basement kitchen in which lived rats, which Sophia used to feed in defiance of her father's orders, and black beetles of which she had an almost mystic horror, as though they were symbols of everything evil in the world.

At the back there was a tiny square of bare earth, in which grew one tree of dark lilac; and there was a crumbling and dirty old wall round it, over which the Garden children used to hang on their stomachs, gossiping with the children of the caretaker who looked after Pusey's Piano Factory. The gossiping, like feeding the rats, was strictly against Dr Garden's orders, because Sophia, Francis and Harry were supposed to be a young lady and young gentlemen, and the little Motts were not.

The Surgery was an unhappy house. So many miserable and violently ugly events had happened in it that they had soaked the walls and staircases in an atmosphere of oppression and terror. Even unimaginative people felt this atmosphere, though they sensibly explained their sensations by pointing out that the house was dark, old, and overlooked by Pusey's Piano Factory, which was ninety feet high and built round three sides of a long stone courtyard, and they added that the noise was shocking.

There were the trams and motor buses which ran past the little *cul-de-sac* in which the Surgery stood, and there was the sawmill in Pusey's Piano Factory which began screaming at seven in the morning and did not stop screaming until six at night; and there was the endless subterranean humming of hidden machines inside the factory, which made an unchanging background for the shriller sounds.

It need scarcely be said that the young Gardens found the factory a delightful and romantic place and liked nothing better than to escape over the spider-haunted, boot-scuffed wall into the stone yard for a game with the young Motts. The rooms were covered with dents and scratchings which were scars of family rows.

There were two banisters missing from the hall staircase, near the bottom; Dr Garden had torn these out in a fit of fury one night. On a cupboard door in the basement dining room there was a long, glancing scar; that was made when he had thrown a table knife at their mother; and a small hole in the cloudy glass window between the dining room and the kitchen, marked where he had hurled a plate at the housemaid – the same girl who now sat in the kitchen, red-eyed and silent because he was dead.

The children were rather proud of these marks than other-wise and used to point them out to shocked visitors, but as they grew older they perceived that such scars were causes for shame rather than pride, and tried not to look at them.

It was really not very surprising that Sophia wrote poetry about objects which were as different as they could possibly be from the objects which made up life at the Surgery, Enbury Fields.

Francis was upstairs, moving among the assembled relatives like a hypocritical butler, offering condolences and enquiring after their healths and storing up their surprised but grateful answers to relate, with sneers, to Harry and Sophia later.

The relatives had an awful fascination for Francis. He hated them but he could not leave them alone. Thus, when Sophia suggested that he should sit on the stairs with her and wait for Harry, he said no, he thought he would stay upstairs with the old fools instead, or else there was sure to be a ghastly fuss.

Sophia, knowing his peculiar little ways, had said that he was quite right. It was always best to be prudent, and suck up when you could. And she had sighed, for she herself was not much use at sucking up or at being prudent, adding hastily, 'Not that you suck up, darling. *Somebody* has to spy out the land and find out what they're thinking about things and what they're likely to do; then we can be warned in time.'

Aunt Grace, Uncle Oliver's widow, came out on to the upper landing, peered over at Sophia, and called her a funny girl for liking to sit down there in the cold. There was a gorgeous fire in the sitting room. Hadn't Sophia better come up?

'I'm all right, thank you, Aunt Grace. I'm waiting for Harry.'

'You look very cold, dear. Quite blue. And do you know you have a hole in your heel? – the left one. Won't you just pop into the bedroom and let me catch it up for you? You must look neat, you know. It's very important for a girl; I'm always telling Angela so. Men don't like untidy girls.'

'I don't want them to like me.'

'Now, dear, I'm sure you don't mean that. It's just silly. All girls want men to like them; and surely you want a home and dear little children of your own?'

'Not particularly, thanks.'

'Oh come, dear, I'm sure you do. Angela does. She's so sweet about it.'

Beastly little nim, thought Sophia; and made no reply. Conversations with Aunt Grace had a curious way of plunging immediately into the profondities. She came out on to the landing to ask if you would come upstairs, and in a few sentences you were arguing with her about whether you wanted any children or not. It was certainly very odd.

Sophia said firmly, 'I think I'll stay here, thank you, Aunt Grace,' and with a sigh and a 'Just as you please, funny girl,' Aunt Grace went back into the sitting room.

It was now a quarter past three. Harry was extremely late. The will was to be read at half past three, and Harry had half promised to be there for lunch at one o'clock, with the family. Where could he be?

A little later the front-door bell rang, and she flew up to open it. It was not Harry but Mr Marriot who stood there, not studying his reflection in the plate with 'Hartley Garden, M.D., M.R.C.S., L.R.C.P.' on it, but looking disapprovingly sideways at a tram which was just rushing and clanging past the end of the alley. He's thinking what an awful place to live in, and he's quite right, thought Sophia.

'Ah ... goodafternoon, Miss Garden. Very dull, isn't it? Looks as though we might have a fog this evening. Well, we've been spoilt, I suppose; it's been such a mild winter on the whole, hasn't it? How are you? How is the famous "job" going?'

'Very well, thank you, Mr Marriot. Will you come upstairs? Everybody's there ...' and she led him away before he could ask if Harry was there too.

Mr Marriot, who possessed a strong imagination and a heart which he quietly controlled, did not permit himself to have violent feelings as a rule, but he really detested the Garden family. If they had not been a source of income, he would have refused to act for them. But there were so many of them, and they had to be acted for such a lot that it would have been very foolish to decline their business. But he detested their talkativeness, their melodrama and their extraordinary, their almost unbelievable, ignorance of the manner in which ordinary persons conducted their affairs. Whenever he heard the phrase about seeing through a glass darkly, or the one about seeing men as trees walking, he was reminded of the manner in which the Gardens looked at life.

As for Sophia, her mind flung itself passionately on to Mr Marriot, as it did on to every person she knew, trying to imagine what it would be like to *be* him, to look at evening clouds with his small, dim eyes, to live in a large, comfortable, well-run house at Brixton, and be dreaded by an office in Cannon Street, and have an invalid wife.

But it was no use. She could never feel herself properly inside other people's minds. She could only stare and stare, absorbing details with her long greenish-hazel eyes under their black eyelashes, until people muttered after she had gone, 'Heavens! how that Garden girl stares!' and Harry, when accompanying her on a walk, would nudge her and say fiercely '*Sophia!* Don't *stare!*'

She had only just come down again when the bell rang. This time it must be Harry. She flew up, and flung open the door.

'Darling, how late you are!'

There he was, with a soft hat cocked impudently on one side, an amiable smile, a muffler of checked silk which was a present from some girl or other, and a taxi just driving away in the background.

'Hul-lo, darling!' said Harry very affectionately. 'All right, are you, darling? Where's the old Deedle? Is he all right?' The Deedle was a pet name for Francis.

Sophia perceived immediately, with some dismay, that Harry had been out to lunch with someone. Nobody who had a strict sense of justice could have said that he was tight, but neither could they have said that he was sober. He was rosy, smiley, loquacious and amiable, and the fact that he had twice called Sophia 'darling' in his first sentence only confirmed her fears. In fact, he was in that pleasant state which may be described as the better for liquor.

'He's all right. He's upstairs with everybody else. And Mr Marriot's here, too; they're only waiting for you. I think you'd better go up.'

'All there, are they? All right. Right you are. I say, I'm frightfully late, aren't I? I've been having lunch with old Edward,' and he began to follow his sister up the stairs. 'Marvellous lunch.'

'And how is Edward?'

'He's marvellous ... Going to be in Hensatt's new show. So is Emily. God, she's marvellous. I bought her some red carnations.'

'Good,' said Sophia, opening the sitting room door with her mind in a whirl of pleasure in Harry's arrival, dismay at his condition, and a dryly malicious anticipation of what the relatives would say.

Harry stopped on the threshold, and made a gay ceremonious little gesture of greeting, mocking yet friendly.

Dearly beloved aunts and uncles, I'm a bit tiddley, said the little gesture.

It was a kind of parody of the Fascist salute, much favoured by the young in England and America during that year. In its transportation from Italy and Germany it had lost severity, shape, and a hint of austere terror lying in wait behind it, and had been gently worked upon by American gaiety and English casualness until it was a ghost, a mere faint echo, of its Continental original.

It was nevertheless exotic enough to affront the assembled elders, with the exception of Aunt Maxine, who was so pleased to see her handsome nephew that she was in the mood to forgive anything. She soon gathered that he was a little merry, and became more full of admiration than ever.

Francis came forward and took his brother's arm. At the first glimpse of Harry's charming face, he knew. He muttered 'Steady, man,' grimly out of the side of his mouth and Harry immediately assumed an expression of tender anxiety, willingness to serve, and funereal solemnity. The change was too abrupt to be convincing, and did not improve the situation.

'Well, Harry, you're very late. Very late indeed. We expected you about half past two, didn't we, Looie? Didn't you say something about being here for *lunch?*'

'Sorry, Uncle Preston. The train was late. Fog on the line.'

'Well, well, it can't be helped. Now, Mr Marriot, don't you think perhaps we had better begin? It is nearly a quarter to four. Yes, now that Harry is here I see no point in waiting further, do you, Maxine? Yes, of course. Now I suggest that we all sit *down*. Harry, are you cold? Sophia! You look quite blue, my dear; you had better come to the fire, near me.'

Everybody – Aunts Maxine, Grace and Loo, Uncle Preston and the three children – arranged themselves comfortably on the old chairs of blackest oak and worn crimson leather, beauties which Dr Garden had picked up in an antique shop some eighteen years ago, and which Sophia had known and loved since she was a child.

The Surgery contained much old and beautiful furniture and china which he had collected; he had a flair for recognizing such things.

It always seemed strange to Sophia that she could hate the Surgery itself, yet love the oak bookcase carved with Adam and Eve and wreaths of black apples and leaves, the two little footstools embroidered with beads in the shape of baskets of flowers, the two bronze storks from Japan which stood on the sitting room mantelpiece; and above all the little painting on wood of a dark girl in a Greek dress patterned with a red key design, who was holding out an apple in her gentle, olive-coloured hand. Sophia thought of her as Nydia, the blind girl in *The Last Days of Pompeii*, and loved her very much.

Mr Marriot had gone to the table which stood between the two windows, and now stood facing the room, resting his fingertips lightly on its surface. He waited until the rustlings and other tiny sounds had stopped; then he coughed and said mildly and a little nervously, staring down at the table:

'I shall not keep you very long; there is not very much to say. As you know,' here he lifted his eyes, and looked round

impersonally at his intently listening audience, 'Dr Garden was
very much distressed, naturally, at Mrs Garden's sudden death.
Naturally. After the funeral I approached him more than once
on the subject of making a new will, but I could not get him to
do so. He wrote to me a week after her death, instructing me
to destroy the will in her favour, but he did not want to discuss
the matter of a new will at all. In fact, on the last occasion
when I mentioned it to him, by letter, I had a very strongly
worded reply' (here Uncle Preston and Aunt Grace exchanged
looks and Aunt Grace compressed her lips, shook her head, and
looked down severely at her shoes; Harry's lips, to the horror of
Sophia and Francis, could be seen to form the words 'Atta boy!').
'Very strongly worded indeed. So I decided to leave the matter
over, for the moment, until the shock of Mrs Garden's death
should have been – er – softened by time; and then open the
subject again. Unhappily, Dr Garden died before I could do so.'

He paused, and coughed again.

Sophia happened to glance at Francis. He had turned extremely white and was sitting straight up in his chair, staring
at Mr Marriot. She saw that his knees and hands were trembling, and wondered what on earth was the matter with him?
He can't care about the beastly money, she thought; who wants
it, anyway? Then she glanced at Harry, who was also staring
at Mr Marriot with his head on one side and an expression of
sentimental interest on his angelic face. Sophia doubted if he
were taking in a word of what was being said.

She felt uneasy and on the defensive as she always did when
surrounded by a lot of Gardens. Their personalities were too
strong; they oppressed her. But she remembered that Keats
had written of himself, 'When I am in a room with people
... the identity of everyone in the room begins to press upon
me, so that I am in a very little time annihilated,' and she felt
comforted because a great poet would have understood how
she was feeling.

'Therefore,' went on Mr Marriot, 'Dr Garden died
intestate.'

Harry, who was sitting at the back of the room next to Francis, leaned across to his brother and whispered, looking interestedly at the carpet:

'What's intestate mean?'

'He means Father didn't make a will,' hissed Francis, staring straight in front of him. 'Shut up.'

'But—'

'All right. I know. Shut up.'

'Under the new law regarding intestacy,' went on Mr Marriot, 'the estate of a person dying intestate is divided equally between the nearest of kin. In this case, therefore, Dr Garden's estate will be divided into three portions for Miss Garden and her two brothers.

'I think it only fair to prepare you by telling you' (he was now speaking more directly to the three children) 'that there will not be very much. Your father borrowed heavily on his insurance policies (strongly against my advice, I may say) some eighteen months ago, and consequently they will be of little value. There are also debts; quite considerable debts. When these are paid, I am afraid there may not be so much as a hundred pounds in cash between the three of you. But there is, of course, the practice. I do not know what your plans will be, but I presume that you will sell the practice, together with the contents of this house and your father's car. The practice should realize quite a handsome sum, perhaps as much as three thousand pounds. That may seem a very large amount to you' (his tone became a little dryer as he observed an expression of awe on Sophia's face. He was surprised, but cynically pleased, to discover that this odd-looking girl did, after all, respect money and care for it. It was the first sign of humanity he had so far observed in her), 'but I assure you that it is very little, as money is judged and used today. Even if it were most carefully invested (which I presume that it will be) it would not bring in enough for any one of you to live on in security, much less in comfort. And there is always, of course, the possibility that you may not find a purchaser – though, in view of the flourishing condition of the practice, I may say I think that is unlikely. I think, and I hope, that you will find a purchaser quite easily.'

His speech was over. He made a movement as though to sit down, glancing half-enquiringly round the silent room.

His glance became fixed on Francis. Francis had stood up. He was very white and shaking. He said in a loud, drawling, melodramatic tone which only Sophia knew was meant to be quietly impressive:

'Mr Marriot. Just a moment. I've got something rather interesting here.'

And he held out a small, folded paper.

Everyone turned to stare at him except Harry, who, with his arms folded, was staring down at his shoes. Uncle Preston was heard to mutter 'T-t-t!'

But Mr Marriot's dislike of the Garden passion for melo-drama rose to the occasion. He certainly looked a little startled, but he said, with just the right amount of elderly impatience:

'Well, what is it? I am afraid I cannot see it from that distance. Will you kindly bring it over here?'

'Certainly,' said Francis, twisting his mouth on one side, and he slowly made his way to the front of the room, in a satisfactorily complete hush. Bless him! he *is* enjoying himself, thought Sophia, as he brushed past her, but he's wishing he hadn't said anything, too, and I suppose that's Father's will. Bang goes my share of the practice ... I bet you.

Mr Marriot took the piece of paper, unfolded it, read it, read it again paying particular attention to the date at the top and the three signatures at the bottom, while Aunt Grace and Auntie Loo exchanged the wildest of glances with Aunt Maxine, and Uncle Preston sat and glared at Francis, who was looking down over Mr Marriot's elbow at the piece of paper, resting his shaking fingers on the table.

'Well,' said Mr Marriot, looking up after what seemed an extremely long pause, 'this seems to be Dr Garden's Will. It is very short, but quite legally correct, and properly dated, signed and witnessed.'

His face was as expressionless as he could make it. He was very annoyed indeed, deeply angered by the dramatic manner in which Francis had produced the will, by this fresh evidence of Dr Garden's disdain of his services as a lawyer and advice as an old acquaintance, and above all, by Francis's concealment of the will for so long. For it was dated September 3rd, a good four months before Dr Garden's death. The miserable boy must have been carrying it round in his pocket for all that time, telling nobody about it, and enjoying the joke in a perverse, morbid way which was most unsuitable in a lad of sixteen, but quite in keeping with the Garden temperament. And how the boy must have laughed to himself when he, Arthur Marriot, confessed that his attempts to get Dr Garden to make a fresh will had been snubbed!

However, the will must be read. He stood up again clearing his throat, and said:

'The will, which appears to be written upon a leaf from a prescription pad, is quite in order. It is dated September 3rd, 1934, and it says simply, 'I leave everything I possess to my eldest son, Harold Hartley Garden.' It is signed in full by Dr Garden, and witnessed by M. E. North and George Bailey.'

Mr Bailey, thought Sophia. Mr Bailey, the pale, tubby, little dispenser who made up the medicines in his damp little cavern smelling of chip boxes and iodine, behind the big waiting room. Mr Bailey had been very fond of her father; he had worked for him for fifteen years, and knew how to keep a secret.

And Mrs North, the red-haired beauty with the large eyes and thin lips, was also fond of Dr Garden and knew how to keep a secret, though her period of service had not lasted for fifteen years, and had been stopped by death.

The elders were too distressed and outraged at Francis's behaviour to say a word. They all looked towards Mr Marriot as sheep towards the sheepdog; they seemed to feel that the affront had been aimed at him, and he must therefore administer the reproof. Their turn would come later; like anything, it would.

But all Mr Marriot said was:

'Well, this alters matters considerably, of course. It means that your eldest brother inherits everything ...'

'But that won't make any difference,' said Harry suddenly, looking up. 'I shall split it with the others just the same.'

He resumed his shoe staring. He was no longer merry and elated, but quite sober, and looked pale and distressed; he was wishing that the old Deedle hadn't written to him suggesting this plan a few days ago.

It would have been much more sensible to destroy the will, as he, Harry, had suggested four months ago, when Francis first told him about it. He did so hate fuss, but Francis rather enjoyed it.

'That is generous of you,' said Mr Marriot disapprovingly, 'and shows a fine spirit. May I ask,' turning to Francis, 'how this document came to be in your possession, and for how long you have had it, and why you thought fit to conceal its existence from everybody?'

'Father told me not to tell anyone about it,' said Francis defiantly. 'He said people were too fond of trying to run him. He wrote it one evening, after surgery, when Mrs North had come in to see him, and we were playing poker with her and Strang. (Strang was a railway porter that Father liked; he used to play cards a lot with him.) He wouldn't sign it, so Father called in Bailey and made him sign it, instead. And he gave it to me (I was home for the weekend) to take care of, and said I was to hang on to it, and not tell anyone till he was dead. That's all.'

'I see. And why did you not inform your uncle, or one of your aunts, or even your sister of the existence of the will, as soon as your father was dead?'

Francis said nothing. He had his reasons, but they could not be aired here.

'Well, well, it does not matter,' said Mr Marriot. 'It is a little irregular, and I consider that you have behaved in a peculiar, not to say impertinent, manner. But no harm is done. No harm

at all. I am delighted to see that your father reposed so much
confidence in you. Mr Garden, I must now congratulate *you*,'
and he turned to the unhappy Harry, and held out his hand.

Immediately afterwards, he went. He declined Auntie Loo's
invitation to stay to tea; he was too angry, too ruffled, to endure
half an hour more in that black and crimson room, surrounded
by Garden faces and listening to Garden comments while he
ate toast and strawberry jam. Better, far better, to miss tea and
speed back to Brixton, to an early supper, to the yet unread
Observer and the sympathetic voice and eyes of his dear wife.

Sometimes vivid pictures haunted his imagination.

On his way home in the Tube one came; he saw the black
and crimson room in winter, dimmed with greenish fog, the
doctor scribbling the will under the eyes of the red-haired
woman and Strang (playing cards with a railway porter – no,
it was impossible! Mr Marriot had never seen the fellow in the
flesh, and he simply could not visualize Strang at all), the little
dispenser bending over the table to sign; and the pale, thin
young Francis, scornful and yet honoured by the responsibility,
carefully folding the leaf from the prescription pad and putting
it away in his pocket.

He saw it all; he had had glimpses of Mrs North and Bailey
and other parasites of the family from time to time, in his legal
dealings with them; and the picture was real to him as a page
from Dickens, whose books he loved.

That's it, he thought, forgetting his anger for a second in
pleasure at having made a discovery. They are not like real
people at all; they are like people out of a book. A mad, twisted
book.

CHAPTER VI

The door closed on Mr Marriot.

Instantly Aunt Maxine turned to Francis—

'Well! You're a sly one, I must say! Carrying it about all those months and never saying a word to anyone ...'

'Now, now, Maxine; remember it was Hartley's *wish*, it was our brother's *wish* that no one should be told. It is hard, I must say; it is rather hard that Hartley should have shown such mistrust of everyone. And *why, why*' (lamented Uncle Preston in a loud whisper, with a tactful glance in the direction of Harry, who was gloomily slapping his pockets and staring round the room in search of a match, with a cigarette cocked between his lips), 'why leave it all to *Harry*? Most unfortunate ... most unjust. Francis, my dear boy, why did you not confide in me or in one of your aunts? Why did you wait until today, and then bring it out in such an odd, such an *abrupt* way? It has been a great shock to us all ...'

'Tea will be here in a minute, dear,' said Auntie Loo, over her shoulder; she had turned her back on the room and was drawing the heavy crimson curtains to shut out the lowering evening.

'I'm sorry,' said Francis, not looking at all sorry, but sulky and bored.

'It was so selfish, Francis,' said Aunt Grace, plunging in with a voluptuous splash. 'So selfish. Such a shock for us all; so

57

unexpected. It was not a *manly* thing to do. I am sure none of the fellows in your form at school would have done such a thing. I don't know what Angela will say when I tell her. She will be so disappointed and hurt—'

Francis's expression did not change at this prophecy, but Harry and Sophia exchanged frightful grimaces, indicative of contempt and loathing. Sophia, who had not said a word since the explosion, now got up and slipped out of the room. She nearly cannoned into tea on the landing, which was being carried up in sections by the red-eyed parlourmaid, Lily.

She went down to the shabby room next the Out-Patients' Department, dialled a number, and waited until a sleepy voice said, 'Hullo?'

'Oh, Celia, this is Sophia. Look here, can the boys and I come up and see you? There's been a frightful fuss about the will.'

'Yes, of course. Have you been left anything?'

'What do you think! Harry's got it all, only there isn't anything, really.'

'Oh, dear.'

'Is there anything to eat in your house? We're rather hungry.'

'Only cold potatoes and bacon and eggs, and a sixpenny Lyons' cake.'

'Oh, well, we'll bring something. Goodbye, darling.'

She went upstairs again, to find the elders uneasily settling to the tea table like vultures on to a carcass, while Harry and Francis stood intractably in the background. Uncle Preston was saying—

'But that is not a *reason*, Francis. I can quite understand your respecting your father's wish that no one should be told until after his death. You were quite right, of course, to obey him. But after he was dead, my boy, surely you must have felt a *wish* to confide in some older person?'

'I'm sorry. I've said I'm sorry ...' said Francis, his voice rising a little towards the end of the sentence. He stood quite still, staring at his uncle.

'Come and sit down and have your tea, Francis,' said Auntie Loo. 'You can help me hand the cups down, if you will, dear.'

Auntie Loo, as the sanest and most comfortable person present, had naturally taken her place in front of that symbol of comfort and sanity, the teapot (at which, incidentally, passionate and lofty souls are far too ready to sniff).

But Sophia said brightly, coming in with her beret swinging from her fingers, 'I'm frightfully sorry, Auntie Loo; I'm afraid we can't stay to tea. A girl I know just rang up to say that her mother is expecting us. I thought she might. The mother, I mean. I half promised this girl we'd go when I saw her yesterday. I'm awfully sorry.'

'Oh dear, what a pity. Never mind; you mustn't disappoint your friend's mother,' replied Auntie Loo placidly, glancing up at Sophia with small but very bright eyes, which were neither placid nor unobservant. 'And the boys, too?'

'I'm afraid so. I'm frightfully sorry.'

'Oh, Sophia! It's too bad. You can't go. You must telephone your friend's mother, and say you're very sorry, but there are important matters to be discussed here, which must be settled,' said Aunt Grace. 'It's too bad of you children; you're always running off on your own affairs. We never see anything of you, you naughty ones,' and she playfully shook Sophia's bony young arm.

'Sorry, Aunt Grace.' Sophia dutifully showed her teeth. 'But they aren't on the telephone. Eleanor had to come out to the call box in the fog, to telephone.'

Harry and Francis still in the background, had assumed the expression which Sophia called 'our cheese look.' Their faces looked as much like two sections of Empire cheese at eightpence a pound as human faces can look. Nevertheless, Harry had picked up his coat and hat, and both had sidled nearer to the door.

'It's very tiresome, Sophia. Very annoying indeed,' said Uncle Preston. 'Just when there is so much to be settled. Where does this friend live? Could you not come back here this evening?'

'At Mill Hill, I'm afraid, Uncle. Rather a long way out. It's foggy, too.'

'And I've got to catch the 9.50 back to Wolverhampton from Paddington,' said Harry suddenly. 'There'd hardly be time.'

'No, no, I suppose not. Well, it is extremely irritating. Very annoying indeed. There are endless things to be discussed, and arranged, which cannot be settled unless the three of you can talk them over with Mr Marriot and myself. However, there is no hurry. No immediate hurry, that is. How much longer has your tour to run, Harry?'

'About three days, if we're lucky,' said Harry gloomily.

'How's that? Aren't you doing well? I thought old Budgy could get away with anything?' said Aunt Maxine sharply. 'His companies used to do so well.'

Harry shrugged his shoulders and muttered that the competition from the cinemas was pretty fierce, and there were other things, too, against their being a success. He included old Budgy among these, but did not say so.

'I suppose, then,' pursued Uncle Preston, 'you're likely to be back in Town quite soon?'

'Jolly likely, I should think.'

'Ah ... well, I shall expect to hear from you as soon as you arrive, and we will arrange a meeting. And if your tour lasts longer than you anticipate, possibly Mr Budgett would give you permission to come down for a *long* weekend, and then we can really *discuss* matters and get things *settled*.'

'Rather,' said Harry, smiling enthusiastically.

And by the simple process of beginning to kiss everybody the three fobbed off further questions and enquiries, and managed to get downstairs and out of the front door.

The plate with their father's name on it, which had been bright when Sophia had admired herself in it at lunch time, was already dulled by the creeping fog. The evening was still and heavy, full of the deadened distant voices of children playing in the streets. The trams were already lit; their yellow lights rocked past, and the sky was deepening with foggy twilight.

'I don't feel like trams,' said Francis, and just at that moment by great luck a cruising taxi rolled past the end of the alley. It was most unusual to see one in that slum; they raced towards it, and stopped it. Sophia told the driver to go to the Ivy Bush, in Northgate Ride, and then she would tell him where to go from there.

The instant they were in the cosy dark cavern of the taxi and travelling away from the Surgery, Francis burst out, 'Look here, I'm frightfully sorry about today. I never thought it would be split up between us three, you know; I thought the relations would probably get a lot, even if Father had died intestate. That's why I didn't tell anyone. I wanted to see their faces when I popped up with the will, and did them out of their little legacies. It's rather rotten for you, Sophia; you don't get a bit.'

'Well, neither do you,' retorted Sophia. 'And I don't see what else you could have done, really; except that I rather wish you hadn't put old Marriot's back up; he was furious. As far as the relations were concerned, it fell a bit flat.'

'It was jolly good,' said Francis, beginning to laugh. 'Uncle Preston's face was a sight.'

'Are you awfully fed up, Sophia?' asked Harry, anxiously, 'It won't make any difference, you know. If we do manage to sell the practice, I shall split it up between us. Of course, if we don't, there won't be anything.'

Sophia considered for a few seconds, staring out of the window at the dingy little houses which they were passing.

'No,' she said at last. 'Not really fed up. I've never had any money that I haven't earned, and it would have been nice to have had a little bit that was really my own and hadn't had to be worked for. To buy things, I mean, and really have some in the bank. That's what I should have liked; something saved, in case anything awful happened. But it can't be helped. Besides, I can always earn money. Not lots, but enough to keep me going.'

'How do you know?' asked Francis; this boast seemed to him, as such remarks do seem to people who have never earned a half-penny by their own work, an amazing piece of self-confidence.

She shook her head.

'I just know it, in the same way that I know my eyes are green and I like walking. I bet you I'm right. You see.'

'Well,' said Harry. 'If we don't sell the practice, we shall be in a ruddy mess, because the old Deedle and I don't feel we can always earn money, and bloody Budgy's tour looks like going bust any minute. He's made a second cut in salaries. I'm getting two pounds now. I ought to be home for good in another week, I should think.'

'I think I can earn money,' announced Francis. 'Not always, like Sophia says she feels she can, but I do feel I can earn. I'm going to leave school and get a job.'

'*Angel!*' said Sophia, suddenly kissing his nose and knocking his spectacles on one side. He accepted the kiss graciously.

'Do you know why Father left it all to Harry?' asked Sophia.

'Oh, it was after he'd had a row with me,' said Francis. 'He said I was always trying to run him, one night when we were at Frascati's. He didn't say anything about you at all. I think he was too fed up even to talk about it – your never coming to see him after Mother died, I mean. I didn't take any notice; he was drunk, anyway, and didn't know what he was saying. But next time, when North came in, he told her she was just in time to witness his new will, and he wrote it there and then.'

'Wasn't North sick?'

'Oh, I think she was, a bit; I expect she hoped she'd get something, but he shut her up when she said wouldn't he think it over. Bailey and Strang thought it was rather rough on you and me; they said so, after he'd gone to bed.'

'I hate Strang. Soapy beast,' said Sophia, meditatively. 'So you've had it all this time?'

'Yes.'

Neither Sophia nor Harry said, 'I wonder Father trusted you with it,' because the thought did not occur to them. Some element in Sophia's silence, her bent head and gaze fixed on her folded hands in their shabby gloves, struck Francis; and he said awkwardly,

'You aren't hurt that I didn't tell you about it, are you, dear?'

'Well, I am, but only a very little bit, and I shall soon get over it so don't worry. I'm not easily hurt. At least, I should be only I'm so terrified of getting like Uncle Preston.'

'My god, yes,' said Harry feelingly, and added, looking out of the window into the fog, 'I say, where are we going?'

'To see Celia,' explained Sophia, 'Oh, bother, I promised we'd take in some food, and now we've gone past Eddy Creab-the-Notorious-Gangster; I never noticed.'

'Eddy Creab would be shut anyway, it's nearly five o'clock, and I'm not hungry,' said Harry.

'I know, but the Deedle and I are; we were too afraid and polite to eat much lunch. Never mind, we'll eat everything Celia's got; she can always have bread and marmalade for her breakfast; she likes it.'

Eddy-Creab-the-Notorious-Gangster was their name for an old woman who kept a little general shop in Enbury Heath, which she never seemed to shut except for two hours on Sunday afternoons. Her shop was a proper village store, which sold everything from tinned salmon to packets of cauliflower seeds, and Celia and Sophia had found it very useful in their ill-organized but regal housekeeping, until the awful day when Eddy Creab had refused to trust Celia (whom she had known since Celia was a child of six) for a halfpenny.

Celia was terribly insulted and had sworn she would never enter Eddy Creab's shop again; and the faith of the young Gardens in Eddy Creab was much shaken by this incident, although they continued to buy things from her.

She was called Eddy-Creab-the-Notorious-Gangster because she had adenoids and when she asked you if you wanted any cream today that was what it sounded like. Eddy Creab sounded exactly, the Gardens thought, like a notorious gangster, and that was how they referred to her. They could never remember her real name, which was written over the shop.

The taxi came to four shillings. Sophia and Francis deplored this, but Harry said, feeling in his pocket, 'Never mind, we've got three thousand pounds,' and for the next year he was to act comfortably on this assumption.

But Sophia was not feeling at all comfortable, as the three walked up the narrow lane between old cottages to Celia's house. At the other end of the lane she could see a darkness, which she knew was the Heath, chilly and silent and smelling of sodden leaves under the heavy fog. Celia lived in one of the two old villages of Enbury Heath, which had been isolated hamlets a hundred years ago. Now wide roads ran past them, leading to sprawling new suburbs, but if a walker turned aside down any of the tiny lanes in Enbury Heath he came to weather-boarded houses, cottages, and gardens with old trees which had scarcely changed since Keats looked up at them.

Sophia was feeling uncomfortable because, though she loyally tried to suppress the thought, she was conscious that of the three Harry was the least likely to make a prudent use of a possible three thousand pounds.

Celia opened the door to them.

She was a little, fair person with a face of angelic and noble beauty, which filled painters and sculptors with an immediate desire to translate the planes of her cheeks, her benevolent brow, full throat and long eyelids into their own medium. She was Sophia's closest friend. They were united by indolence, delight in beauty, a strong and rather ironical sense of humour, and a fundamental seriousness of temperament, but Sophia was bossier and more severe in her judgments than Celia. Also, Celia was quite alarmingly attractive to young men, in whom she took a tender and maternal interest, while Sophia tended to drive them away with snortings and an ironical manner.

Celia was the youngest of three Irish sisters, with whom the young Gardens used to play on the Heath when they were all small. The two elder had married and gone to live abroad, and Celia lived on alone in the little house which belonged to her widowed mother. Mrs Carmody liked to pay long visits to the sisters and their families, and Celia, who was nineteen, seemed to be perfectly happy taking a vague course at the School of Economics, comforting young men, and living on Lyons' cakes and fillet steak, so her mother did not have a conscience about her.

Celia was as Irish as she could be, in the dreamy, sweetly sleepy, time-ignoring Irish way, not the brilliant, firework way, and her odd life suited her very well. She always behaved as though she had a hundred years to live and would be young until the very end of them, so why should she hurry or complain? This was restful to Sophia, who detested bustle, though she was often compelled by Fate to be a bustler herself. She deplored the fact that the keynote of Celia's nature was the desire to love and to give, but recognized that this was so, and that nothing could alter it.

Sophia and Celia kissed one another, and Harry, with a matchless air of ease, also kissed Celia. It was the first time he had, but no one would have thought so, judging by the easy way his lips found her cheek. She raised her eyebrows a little and smiled, but said nothing; after all, she had known him since he was four.

'Hullo, Celia,' said Francis, with reserve and they all went through to the drawing room, which looked out at a little winding garden, opening on to the Heath.

There was a fire here, and a large comfortable old sofa pulled up to it, and the curtains were drawn. A crumpled copy of that well-informed but dreary and alarming journal *The New Onlooker* was on the sofa, with Celia's huge horn-rimmed glasses. Harry nearly plumped himself down on them; they were just rescued in time by Francis.

'I do wish you wouldn't read that miserable paper, Celia,' said Sophia fretfully. 'Beastly depressing rag; no wonder you're always in a ferment about the tariffs and pacifism and Fascism and all the rest of it.'

'I like to keep abreast. So ought you; I wonder you ever manage to do your job. You never read the papers, and you never know what's going on anywhere.'

'When I don't know, I invent,' said Sophia superbly, pushing herself deeper into her comfortable chair.

'I suppose your job *is* quite safe?' Harry asked her. 'I mean, are they likely to sack you at a minute's notice?'

'*No one* is safe in Fleet Street,' replied his sister, quoting old Mr Burrows, who worked in the news agency where she was employed, 'Anyone's likely to be fired at any minute. *No one is indispensable.* But Mr Piper seems quite to like me. He says I've got a real nose for news, and later on he's going to let me try doing some short articles for Canada – not just re-writing, I mean. I'm to write them entirely.'

'Will he pay you extra?'

'I expect so. He's very kind. He said it would be pocket money for me and I could buy silk stockings with it.'

'I expect he's after you,' Harry said, looking at his sister with interest.

'Oh, surely not! Oh, I shouldn't think so for a moment. He likes Miss Candy, his secretary, much better than me; she's so pretty – rather like a canary, you know; wears a bright yellow jumper and always talking in a high, sweet, birdy sort of voice.'

'Sophia, you are extraordinary,' said Celia. 'You never seem to think anyone admires you.'

'Well, usually they don't. Not like that, anyway. I'm far too severe, and I put people off by laughing at them, too.'

'One day you'll meet someone who won't be put off.'

'Well, that will be very nice. I shall like it,' she said simply; and then was silent, as were the others.

They were all a little languid, the three young Gardens because they had spent an exciting and exhausting afternoon, and Celia because she had been lazing by the fire for three hours, half-asleep, but rather distressed about the Polish Corridor.

No one felt inclined to rush into a gossip about the will. Harry was now a little embarrassed because his inheritance seemed to cut him off temporarily from his brother and sister; Francis was suffering from a reaction after his dramatic *coup* earlier in the afternoon, and did not want to talk, Sophia felt saddened and very worried. They had hardly any money, no home except the hated Surgery, no parents. What would become of them?

Celia's manners were too good even in the presence of her three oldest friends to permit her to ask questions when they obviously did not feel like talking. So the four sat in comfortable silence, with the smoke from Celia and Harry's cigarettes going straight up into the air, and the quiet ticking of the clock and the fluttering of the fire making a soothing little duet.

At last Harry said: 'Celia, would you mind awfully if I had a bath? It takes fourpence to have a proper bath in my digs and a chap must have a bath every day, and so it comes rather expensive. Would you mind?'

'Of course not. The geyser's just been mended again. Do you know how to work it?'

'Not if it's an electric one. It is, isn't it?'

'Yes. I'll come and show you.'

'And I'll sit with you while you're having it,' said Francis, who liked Celia but thought that she was too bossy for a girl, and was rather afraid that Harry might fall in love with her while they wrestled together with the electric geyser.

He and Harry were very fond of sitting with each other and gossiping while they had baths; the custom dated from the days when they were so small that Harry had been told to watch Francis wash himself, and see that he did not drown while their mother or nurse went out of the room. Then they floated celluloid swans or played rafts with the soap; now they talked about girls and Edward Sweeting or boxing; but gossiping in the bathroom was still one of their favourite pastimes.

'I'll get some supper and it will be all ready for you when you come out. We'll have it by the fire; only don't be too long, because if you've got to catch that train you must leave here by nine, and it's nearly half past five now, and you mustn't go out just after a bath, you'll catch cold,' said Celia leading the way to the bathroom.

The boys shut themselves in, and the room soon became full of steam and the steady murmur of their voices, while Sophia and Celia went down into the old basement kitchen, where there were deep cupboards and a stone floor, but an elaborate and terrifying electric stove.

Sophia, having asked if she could help and been told no, sat on the kitchen table and stared down at her slender ankles and rather large muddy brogues, swinging them slowly to and fro, while she told Celia about the will.

'I *do* think your father was a *swine*, darling, if you don't mind my saying so,' observed Celia gently, at the end of the tale; the ugly word came with odd effect out of her beautifully shaped lips. 'Fancy not leaving you a thing.'

'It isn't that – so much,' said Sophia, still staring down at her shoes, 'I don't mind Harry having it a bit, really. It's just that ... well, Celia, I don't want to be a beast about Harry, and disloyal, only I do rather wonder if he was the most sensible one of the three of us to leave it to? You see, if we sell the practice and get all that for it, we shall be really quite rich, for a bit at any rate.'

'You'll be able to have a lovely time,' said Celia, who had as much money sense as a caterpillar.

'I couldn't have a lovely time if I thought all the money was being wasted and dwindling away when it ought to be properly invested. If we do get it, Harry ought to let Mr Marriot invest it for us.'

'Well, perhaps he will. You must try and persuade him.'

'Oh, I'm quite sure he wouldn't. He and Francis are like Father in that way; they get quite livid and crazy at the very idea of anyone trying to 'run' them, as Father used to say. I have to be awfully careful not to try and boss them, though they're really fond of me, I think ... I'm so *terrified* of getting like Aunt Maxine and Uncle Preston, always poking about and interfering and trying to alter people. It would be too awful to get like that, and perhaps have Harry and Francis stop caring

about me. I couldn't bear it. And yet, at the same time, I do
so want them to live orderly lives.'

'You all ought to live together,' said Celia, skilfully turning
the frying potatoes, 'then you could. Live orderly lives, I mean.'

'Oh, that would be lovely!' said Sophia, staring at her with
a transfigured face. 'I never thought of that. Do you think we
could? If we pooled our money, and Francis got a job, and
Harry got one too, in town? (Edward would help him, I expect
... he knows everybody on the stage, and it hasn't spoiled him
a bit, being such a success. He still likes Harry and Francis
just as much ...) I could keep house for them, and perhaps in
a year or two we could afford a maid; a proper one, I mean,
not like the ones at the Surgery who always fell in love with
Father and had to be sacked. Do you really think we could?'

'It would be a bit of a sweat, I expect, getting away from
your relations, but I don't see why you shouldn't, if you all
stick together. Of course, if you sold the practice at once it
would be much easier. Oh, Sophia, it would be lovely! You
must come and live near me. I expect Mother would let you
have the Cottage, if you asked her; it's to let, you know, and I
am sure she would rather you three had it than some ghastly
person who would break all the windows.'

But Sophia hardly heard the end of her sentence; she jumped
off the table (twisting her ankle and nearly overbalancing as
she did so) and seized Celia by the arm.

'Celia! *not* the heavenly little cottage in the Vale, with the
panelled sitting room? It's too good to be true! She wouldn't
let us have it, would she? Besides, we haven't any furniture ...
and in any case I'm sure it's too nice ever to happen.'

'You could buy some of the Surgery furniture, if Harry
decides to sell it later on. I don't know about rent; of course,
it's furnished now, and she could let it for about four guineas
a week, but she wouldn't want anything like as much as that
from you; we've known you for such ages – and then you
wouldn't want it completely furnished. Oh, Sophia, of course

you must live there! We'd have such good times! Let's write to Mother tonight!'

'I must ask the boys first,' said Sophia, suddenly grave, 'I can't go behind their backs, and they might not like the idea at all; I'm not sure whether they want to live orderly lives. But it would be wonderful if we could; we've never had anything but disorder and rows and misery. I love peace and quiet. I feel I want years and years of peacefully going to work every day and coming home to a cool quiet house smelling of flowers, and writing poetry ... The Cottage is on the Heath, too! Could we have a dog, do you think? And I could go for walks with no shoes on before breakfast. But we must wait. Everything's in too much of a muddle now; it wouldn't be fair to ask your mother to let us have the cottage and then find we couldn't afford it after all ... But it would be marvellous, wouldn't it? And then, even if the boys didn't like the idea of an orderly life, just at first, perhaps I could persuade them to – without getting too much like Uncle Preston, I mean.'

'I'm sure you could, darling,' said Celia. 'Will you carry the Lyons cake?' and she added rather severely, 'Those boys *ought* to appreciate you more, Sophia. You do a *lot* for them, you know. They don't appreciate you *half* enough.'

Meanwhile, Harry was lying luxuriously in a very deep bath, with his beautiful face crimsoned by the steam and his dark hair curling with the damp, and saying in a lordly voice to the admiring Francis, while he tried to turn off the cold tap with his toes –

'My dear man, I shan't save a farthing of it. Not a farthing. I shall give you five hundred, and perhaps Sophia five hundred (she's got a job, so she's not so badly off) and I shall just blue the rest. We'll blue it together. I hate the beastly money. It was all earned from diseases and people dying, and who wants it, anyway? You wait. We'll have a good time. We'll have some marvellous parties ...'

It would seem that there were grounds for Sophia's doubts about her brothers' wish to lead an orderly and peaceful life.

The rest of the evening passed away very pleasantly, for
everybody was soon full of fried potatoes, hot tea, and egg,
and warmed by Celia's big fire. The girls said nothing about
the cottage scheme, and the boys did not mention Harry's
regal plans for disposing of the three thousand pounds, so
no arguments or boring discussions about money took place.
They talked a little about the will, but soon the subject lost
its freshness, and they did not want to discuss it any more.

Perhaps this is one of the major differences between the
young and the old; the young so quickly accept a strange event,
assimilate it and cease to wonder at it, while the old, intent on
chewing the last drop of savour out of that endlessly savoury
bone, life, go on discussing an event for weeks and weeks. At
nine o'clock that night the red sitting room at the Surgery was
still steadily humming with the voices of Uncle Preston, Aunt
Maxine and the rest, Talking It Over, but the three children
and Celia were already, in their minds, eagerly pressing on
towards the next event.

To Sophia that event was to be the securing of the cottage
by some vague and splendid means, and the settling down of
herself, Harry and Francis, into a life of orderly and pleasant
routine. Her passion for order, shape and beauty was still only
half recognized by herself, and it fought constantly with her
instinct to idle and day dream and suck in impressions without
delivering judgment on them; and the conflict weakened both
instincts.

Nevertheless, the shaping and ordering instinct was an
extremely strong one; and what secret wisdom made her conceal its strength from her brothers?

She did not know; but she knew that if she wanted them to
lead the life with her that she planned, she must never, never
try to 'run' them, nor let them think she was.

So it would all be extremely difficult, because she was dreadfully bored by the intrigues and the subtle 'managing' of obtuse
males, which the feminine woman is supposed to enjoy so much.
It was so much easier to Sophia to tell a person plainly what

she wanted them to do, and, if they would not do it, to go
away and manage as best she could by herself. She found long
talks about people's motives, actions and probable reactions the
most boring experience within her range, and as for 'managing'
human beings, as though they were tame animals, that shocked
her sense of humanity's dignity.

And after all, who was she to impose her ideal way of life on
another human being? It suited her very well, but for someone
else it might be all wrong.

Wearily, curled up on the comfortable old sofa, she turned
her mind away from wrongs and rights, wills and brothers and
cottages; and began to think a poem over to herself, staring
into the fire.

For Harry, the next event was to be the securing of the
three thousand pounds, and a deliberate plunge into a good
time, with the help of theatrical friends, who had just initiated
him into the meaning of this phrase.

Harry seemed to have been affected the least by their home
life; this was because his manner was gay and charming, and
he seemed to have a happy temperament, but actually the years
of fear and insecurity had wounded him more deeply than they
had wounded his brother and sister. He was a gentler person,
who lacked the fighting instinct of Sophia and Francis; and
the angry sounds and the terrifying anticipation of blows and
unknown horrors which haunted his childhood had given him
a true soul wound; a painful sense of inferiority hidden deep
under his gay, easy manner.

He thirsted for gaiety, crowds, noise and admiration to lull
his own sense of insecurity. The idea of responsibilities terrified
him; he wanted to escape from them, and to forget the ugly
noises, shames and endless fears of his childhood. Sometimes
he could hint at this state of mind to Francis, who loved him
and whom he loved, but not easily or often, because he scarcely
realized what was the matter with him.

And Francis had made up his mind that the next event for
him would be a girl. It was jolly humiliating to be sixteen and

have no girl; all his friends had girls. He did not yearn over the vision of this mythical girl, nor prostrate himself before it. She was going to do the prostrating, not he. With that quiet determination to be cock of the flirtatious walk which was to serve him so well in later years, and which was to please so many young women who were tired of being allowed to do just as they liked, the precocious Francis sat in front of Celia's fire, sunning himself in the imaginary but lovely eyes of a cheerfully submissive Girl.

Not one of the three said a word about the events which they were anticipating. Even so united a family had its natural and stubborn reticences; and it may be that in pondering over their plans for the next few months, Sophia, Harry and Francis felt a tremor, a murmur of ancestral voices prophesying war, for their dreams of the kind of life they meant to lead were certainly rather different.

Of course the position of the three was not so friendless and unfortunate as Sophia chose to think.

If she had put herself frankly under the protection of her uncle and aunts, confessing that she felt lonely, miserable and frightened of the future, they would most certainly have comforted her and confided to her the plans which they had discussed for the children's welfare. They might not have understood precisely how she felt, and they might have been patronizing and fussy, but kind they would certainly have been; they were not monsters, despite their love of melodrama and their lack of humour. They only awaited confidence and signs of youthful desire for guidance from the children.

But this was just what Sophia would not make, and the boys never even thought of making signs. They stood as firm and reserved as three annoying Japanese images, and all the plans for their good had to go on behind their backs.

In the course of Talking It Over that same evening Uncle Preston, who was the senior partner in a small but prosperous firm which imported French chalk and minerals, suggested that he might be able to find employment for Francis in the offices of a larger and more prosperous firm which also imported French chalk and minerals.

'What a life for a boy!' said Aunt Maxine, lighting her eleventh cigarette since supper. 'Shut up in an office all day, never seeing a girl from week's end to week's end, no fun! Much better let me find him a job on the stage, like Harry. That's the life for a boy! No money in it, of course, nowadays; everything's gone phut since the War, but it doesn't do youngsters any harm to rough it a bit.'

'Surely Francis has roughed it enough for the time being,' quietly said Auntie Loo, who was knitting in a corner, as far away from Aunt Maxine's cigarette smoke as she could put herself. 'He looks very thin and pale, I thought. So does Sophia. Poor little things! I should say they wanted time to look round a bit and lots of fresh air and sleep, not "roughing" it. Couldn't you find a place for Francis with Pettitt & Sons, Preston? It would be so much better for him to be under your eye.'

'H'm ... I doubt it. I doubt whether that would be *wise*, Looie. Pettitt's nephew came to us last Easter, you may remember, and we have had some trouble over him. Complaints about favouritism and overtime ... yes. Very irritating. No, I think on the whole that if I *could* approach Graby & Bryant, it would be better. Much better. Of course it would be only a *very* small post at first with a nominal salary ...'

'Addressing envelopes, I suppose, at fifteen bob a week. My god ... ! and Cissie Montague is going out on a year's tour in March with a Number One Company of "The Love Liar." She'd start him at three-fifteen if he showed promise. She's got a heart of gold, that woman has ...'

Uncle Preston informed Aunt Maxine with patience and dignity that in the offices of Graby & Bryant the addressing of envelopes was not entrusted to a junior, and went on, 'I must talk the matter over with Marriot and see what he thinks. I presume that the *next* thing to arrange will be the sale of the furniture and the car. Then there will be a little money for the children to go on with, while they are waiting for a purchaser for the practice, and there will of course be additional sums from the practice itself. I shall suggest to Marriot that he should take care of the money and make Harry a small weekly allowance. Undoubtedly that would be best, while we are waiting for probate to be proved.'

'And where is Francis to live, and what's he going to live on?' demanded Aunt Maxine, 'I suppose they can't live here, if the stuff's going to be sold, and he can't live on fifteen shillings a week anyway, can he?'

'Some arrangement will have to be made, of course, about Francis,' snapped Uncle Preston, coughing pointedly as his sister lit another cigarette. 'I cannot think of *everything* at once, and I must say that so far I *have* had to think of everything that has been discussed. You don't seem to *realize*, Maxine, how *important* it is to get the children settled.'

'Dear, isn't it time we were thinking of getting along?' said Auntie Loo, coming out of her corner with her knitting rolled in a neat sausage and stabbed with two steel needles, like a vampire in a German legend. 'It is nearly a quarter past ten, and I'm sure Grace and Maxine must be tired. We shan't be home, you know, until well after eleven.'

This broke up the meeting, and everyone discovered that they were too tired to say anything more on the subject of the children's fate except Aunt Grace, who confided to Auntie Loo on the way downstairs that she had always dreamed of Francis being a writer, a great writer. He used to write really quite clever little stories when he was ten, all about hunters and snakes and elephants, and then he wrote such good letters! Aunt Grace would have liked to be a writer if she had had time. She had always been told that she wrote such good letters, too. Had Looie ever seen any of Francis's letters?

'He never writes to me,' said Auntie Loo, going carefully down the slippery steps into the fog in the wake of Uncle Preston and the umbrella. 'Boys don't get much time, you know.'

And as she busily pulled her bunchy coat round herself she suppressed, as she had suppressed numberless times in the last thirty odd years, a thought which had come into her mind, like a sad, dim bell tolling, of her own little boy who had died when he was three years old.

'A great writer,' said Aunt Grace sentimentally. 'Such a wonderful life, I always think. Such opportunity for doing good.'

Auntie Loo looked at her. What a goose Gracie is, thought Auntie Loo, nodding in placid agreement with the goose's remark.

CHAPTER VII

Harry's prophecy came true. Bloody Budgy's company was told it could go home, if it had the fare to do so, on the Saturday morning following the reading of the will, and Harry came back to London on Monday in the car of a middle-aged widow with whom he had made friends in Wolverhampton, thus saving his fare.

The widow wanted to go on being with Harry when once they got to London, but he disposed of her; and went to a telephone box and called Edward Sweeting, who lived some few miles out of town.

Emily, Edward's new and lovely wife, answered the telephone. She told him that Edward would be away playing football until late that evening, but that Harry must come down and stay with them until he could find a job.

'Oh, I say, that's marvellous of you, Emily! But are you sure it's all right? Sure the beloved old figure in the shabby dressing gown won't be butting in or anything? I expect I could go and stay with one of my tatty old aunts or something, you know.'

'God, you don't want to do that,' said the far-off but clear and fashionable voice of Emily, who combined the delicate colouring and appearance of a Dresden china figurine with the tenacity and discipline of a Roman legion on the march. 'You come down here to us; we'd love to have you.'

So Harry went off to a snack bar called Pip's to have a bite before catching a train to Taplow, where the Sweetings lived.

He was thinking gratefully what bricks Edward and Emily were.

Edward came of a theatrical family whose members had played in England since the 'fifties of the last century; he was five or six years older than Harry, a dark, slender and gifted young man, whose recent success had been partly due to talent and hard work, and partly due to his passion for the stage, which made him restless and unhappy unless he was acting.

It is doubtful whether anyone can succeed in any profession or art without this passion for their work. Unfortunately the passion does not always guarantee the success, but it is fairly safe to say that the success never comes without it.

The two young men had first met when they were playing in a repertory company some months ago. It had been Harry's first job, while Edward, who had the excellent habit of taking any job that would give him experience and increase his range in acting, had had many, but they got on very well together from the word Go, because both were romantic and just a little bit silly under their veneer of men of the world, and they had the same beery and lowbrow sense of humour.

Both were solemn and almost religious on the subject of Keeping Fit, and both laughed at themselves for being so. Sophia used to say that they Kept Fit to drink more beer; they used to pant away on horrible exhausting runs and walks, and then undo all the good they had done themselves by falling into a pub and drinking beer until they were quite distended.

When Edward left the ill-paid job in the repertory company to take up his first part in the West End of London, he did not forget Harry. He got on with alarming quickness. A second important part followed the first, and he earned enough money to marry one of Mr Hensatt's loveliest and most slender Young Ladies, but still he liked to creep round pubs with the amiable Harry, and to laugh at ingenuous beery jokes. He liked Francis too, and Sophia, though he thought she was a bit severe and clever.

She for her part was very grateful to him because of his unfailing kindness to Harry.

She knew well that her own standard of looks and grooming fell dismally below the awful purity and loftiness of Edward and Harry's standard; and sometimes this depressed her, but she sensibly decided that, however well groomed they were, the girls admired by Edward and Harry could not write poetry. Meanwhile, she got on very well with Edward, who often told her she ought to be more romantic and not so intellectual and cold. He said that if she were more romantic it would be much better for her poetry. He and Harry, warm-hearted and easily beguiled souls that they were, frankly admitted to being very romantic indeed.

It was a nasty jar to Harry to see Aunt Maxine sitting in Pip's eating egg mayonnaise, with a perfectly frightful and rather fat blonde friend in a silly little red hat. He darted back, but too late.

'Harry, hi, here, here (it's my nephew, Harry Garden, been out with Bloody Budgy – *that* must have gone phut, I suppose) here, where are you off to? Come and lunch with us. Miss Van Veek, my nephew, Harry Garden.'

Harry at once felt so sorry for Miss Van Veek's peroxide curls and sagging jaw line that he came across to their table immediately, with his delightful smile, and made himself charming to both the ladies.

He had now been long enough on the stage to get over his first foolish and irrational supposition that anyone who was on the stage would sometimes want to talk about anything else but the stage; so he prepared himself to answer, in the minutest detail, all Aunt Maxine's questions about the personnel, misfortunes, salaries and final collapse of Bloody Budgy's tour.

But as well as having been an actress, Aunt Maxine was a Garden, and an aunt: and she suggested, at the close of an enthralling account of the row between Tessie Ashfall and Barner Brabazon, that Harry should telephone Uncle Preston and let him know that he was back in town.

'Oh, Maxine, need I?'

'I know it's a bore, my dear,' said Aunt Maxine, delighted at not being called 'Aunt,' 'But it would be good policy, I think. Your Uncle Preston is the most irritating man I know, but he means well. He's an old maid, but he means kindly. I think you'd better 'phone him, really I do.'

Harry promised that he would; and got away by saying that he must get it over before he caught a train into the country.

'Where are you off to, naughty boy?' enquired Aunt Maxine playfully, 'Weekending?'

'Rather not; no such luck! Going down to the Sweetings for a few days; old Edward, you know.'

He made his 'goodbyes' charmingly, and both women watched him swing out of the café with his two big suitcases and his hat becomingly cocked.

'Good looking, isn't he?' said Aunt Maxine, looking proudly after him.

'My god, what a pair of eyes,' said Miss Van Veek, who had been silently watching Harry while he talked, 'I suppose he's got a string of girls as long as your arm. Got a cigarette?'

And they began to talk about the stage again.

Harry's arrival in London made it possible for matters to advance quickly. Uncle Preston made his nephew see that he must come up from Taplow the day after his arrival in town to talk over the sale of the furniture at the Surgery, the future of Francis and many other questions; and accordingly Harry came and spent a portentous hour with Uncle Preston and Mr Marriot in the latter's office.

The two elder gentlemen succeeded in persuading him that they should act, until he came of age in six months' time, as his trustees. No official trustees had, of course, been appointed by Dr Garden's will; and the Public Trustee therefore would officially control Harry's funds, such as they were. But Mr Marriot pointed out that it would be convenient if he, Mr Marriot, should be in a position to advance Harry sums of money from time to time. It would be an excellent idea if they were advanced at regular intervals, say quarterly. They could be repaid later, from the takings of the practice or from its sale.

Harry agreed amiably to this suggestion. Too amiably, if Uncle Preston and Mr Marriot had but known. He had every intention of letting Mr Marriot advance him sums, but not quarterly. Whenever he felt like having sums, Mr Marriot could advance them. That would be a much better plan. But he said nothing of his decision to his elders. He had already learned that it is wise, if you have a plan which people may dislike, not to mention it until absolutely necessary.

Then Uncle Preston suggested that either Harry or Francis or both should train for the medical profession. There was a flourishing practice waiting for them, which could be managed by a reliable locum while they were training; and they could live at the Surgery. This would be the obvious thing to do, said Uncle Preston.

'Oh, I say,' said Harry mildly, 'I don't think we should like that at all, you know – god, no.'

'Why not, my dear boy? A most interesting profession, and there is the house all ready for you. It is surely the obvious plan.'

'I don't think the old Deedle and I want to be doctors. It would be such a grind. And the old Deedle loathes the Surgery. So does Sophia. They don't ever want to see it again. It's a tatty sort of hole, you know.'

'It could be redecorated and refurnished.'

'Wouldn't make any difference.'

Uncle Preston put forward sensible arguments, refusing to admit that such painful things had taken place in the Surgery that no person with any sensitiveness or memory could wish to live there. He would not talk about this. He deplored the life of his dead brother, but always refused to discuss it or to admit to anyone that it had been anything worse than 'sad.' And perhaps his verdict was just.

But Harry, with the obstinacy which gentle people alone can command, refused even to think about being a doctor.

He said that diseases, blood and death not only made him feel sick; they bored him. The Deedle was bored by them too. So was Sophia. All three of them only wished to forget the house in which they and their mother and father had been wretched, and to sell the practice upon whose earnings they had lived; and the elders at last had to let him have his way. They hoped that he would change his mind later.

Harry was not depressed by the uncertainty of his prospects. He appeared to think that money would fall from some comfortable source. This source, had Mr Marriot but known it, was Mr Marriot. At least, Harry saw it as Mr Marriot for the next few months, and after that, he imagined they would sell the practice, or that something would turn up.

It was arranged that Mr Marriot should deal with the firm of agents who were to try and sell the practice, and act for Harry.

The problem of Francis was then discussed. Harry was able to tell them with authority that Francis did not want to stay on at school and matriculate, because Francis had told him so during their talk in the bathroom on the Sunday evening following the reading of the will.

As for Francis's wanting to go into Graby & Bryant's, he could not say. He thought that it would be quite a good idea if old Francis didn't mind being stuffed up in an office all day. Upon hearing this, Uncle Preston and Mr Marriot both said, in a kind of Greek chorus, that it was not a question of what Francis wanted; it was a question of what Francis would be exceedingly lucky if he got. Did Harry *know* how many boys would be leaving school at the end of the term, and how small a proportion of the number would be able to find posts? '*Posts*,' said Mr Marriot, pushing out his lips over the 'p' as though he saw so many thousands of lucky boys safely tied up to solid, newly painted little white wooden ones.

Harry sat listening with a careful, polite expression of attentiveness on his charming face. The expression hardly changed during the hour's discussion; Mr Marriot had a fleeting and despairing impression that Harry was taking in very little that was being said, and Mr Marriot was quite right.

Harry was wondering how soon he could get away from Uncle Preston and meet Edward at the Golfing Green Club, and thinking that perhaps the old Deedle would not be quite so cut off from girls after all, even if he did go into Graby & Bryant's, because even in old Marriot's ghastly office, he had managed to catch the eye of two quite pretty typists or something; and he was also wondering when he might ask Mr Marriot to advance him some money on the three thousand pounds? He had three pounds, thirteen and sixpence at the moment, but that would not last long.

Despite Harry's wool gathering, Uncle Preston and Mr Marriot managed to settle one or two of the more important problems during the hour. It was now the third week in January; the auction at the Surgery was fixed for the seventh of February and it was agreed that Uncle Preston should approach Mr Graby about an opening in the firm for his nephew.

They all agreed that, if Francis did not wish to matriculate, there was no point in his doing so, though Mr Marriot pointed out that he would have a slightly better chance of getting a post in a good firm if he did so.

'By then he'll be eighteen. Getting on,' said Harry, who shared with his brother and sister a feeling that they were all three pretty old.

'Nonsense,' said Mr Marriot, austerely. 'One must take the long view in these matters.'

But Harry and the absent Francis had their way about Matric.

As for the practice, that vague, but so-important entity, that fluctuating source of income, it was decided that a non-residential locum should be installed. Dr Casey, who had occasionally helped Dr Garden when the pressure of work was overwhelming because of an influenza epidemic or some other cause, would do very well.

He lived on Greenride Hill, some ten minutes' walk from the Surgery, he knew the work and the patients knew him. He was already installed there, keeping things going, because most fortunately he happened to have been doing a fortnight's work with Dr Garden at the time of the latter's death, and Uncle Preston had asked him to stay on until affairs were more settled.

'The patients don't like him,' observed Harry. 'He's a boring old beast.'

'He has been extremely useful to us all,' reproved Uncle Preston. 'Without him, the situation would have been very awkward indeed; yes.'

'Well, they don't like him, anyway. They used to tell Father so. They liked Father much better. I bet you they won't come to see old Casey nearly as often as they did Father. You see.'

'That remark opens a rather disturbing possibility,' said Mr Marriot, glancing at the clock and wishing that his tea and biscuits would come in; he felt in need of comfort. 'The value of the practice – of any practice – is, of course, a fluctuating one. It depends upon size and stability. In the case of your father, Mr Garden, there is no doubt that his personality, and that alone, kept it as large as it was at the time of his death. I am afraid that there is a possibility that the size of the practice may decline abruptly, now that people can no longer rely upon your father's attentions. That means, of course, that we must try to effect a sale as quickly as possible.'

'Rather,' said Harry.

He was glad to think that people had liked to see his father. Whenever he thought about his father, pity came into his heart. He had loved him and in a way which he could not explain looked up to him. Sophia and Francis were coldly angry with his father's memory; he could not feel thus.

He knew, of course, that his father had been a bad man, who had brought his children up in a way that would make life difficult for them. But he could not resent this when he remembered his father's vitality, his power to charm, his sudden bursts of useless generosity, his beautiful soft singing voice which used to delight Harry when he was a little boy and which came so strangely from the throat of such a huge man, his power to make the piano sing too, gently and sweetly, as though the notes loved the touch of his blunt short fingers. Harry abruptly turned his mind from memories.

And then, because it was four o'clock, Mr Marriot's tea and three small, severe ginger biscuits were brought in, and Uncle Preston and Harry declined to share them with him, and the interview was over.

The two went out into the lit winter dusk of Cannon Street.

Harry, of course, managed to find a taxi, as he would have done if suddenly dropped in the midst of a Tibetan steppe, and was borne away to meet Edward Sweeting, waving cheerfully at Uncle Preston who was very cross because he was planning a nice tea with a poached egg and more discussion about family affairs.

He ate it miserably by himself in a Lyons, wishing that Looie were there to listen to him.

He was extremely worried about the children. It was very irritating that Harry and Francis refused to be doctors. It was irritating that they wanted to sell the practice, when they might have put in a locum indefinitely and kept the practice's earnings as a steady income. And it was more than irritating, it was alarming to hear from Mr Marriot that the practice would not bring in much money while they were waiting to find a buyer for it.

Enbury Fields was such a poor district that most of Dr Garden's patients could not afford to pay more than one and sixpence or half a crown a visit; and when the salary of Dr Casey and the dispenser, and the rent, and other expenses had been paid, there would not be much money to repay to Mr Marriot what he would advance to Harry. And the value of the practice would decrease too. It was all most worrying.

Dr Garden was not on the Panel. He had refused to be. He had resented the Panel and suspected it as an attempt to 'run' him by the Government. He said that he gave twice as much attention, care and intelligence to a patient because he was not expected to do so by any bloody Government, and though the comfortable, regular cheques from the Panel which other doctors had may have tempted him, he would never change his views. These Panel cheques would have made a much more handsome income from the practice, and Uncle Preston was sorry that they were not coming in.

Well, he thought (carefully wiping a soft piece of toast round the plate so as to gather up all the runny part of the egg), Harry would have to be economical, that was all. He, Uncle Preston, would have to keep a most watchful eye on the three children and see that they did not grow extravagant, or get into debt. There would be much to do, much to arrange. There always was.

He finished his tea with a sigh, and wished again that Looie were there. She had a most soothing presence, like a quiet little cosy fire, or a cup of tea when you were tired. Uncle Preston did not compare her to these comforts, but that did not prevent him wanting her presence.

He went home to Looie; and that evening he did all that could at present be done. He telephoned Aunt Maxine and gave her a long, detailed and pessimistic account of the afternoon's talk with Mr Marriot. He telephoned Aunt Grace, and did the same kind office for her. And he wrote to the headmaster of Northgate, and told him that Francis would leave at the half-term, or before if necessary.

And the boy's fees would have to be paid, too. There was no end to the spending of money, the planning and botheration and anxiety.

The family then settled down, as much as it ever did, to wait for the sale.

It was held on a Saturday afternoon at three o'clock, so Sophia could have gone to it if she had liked, but she did not go.

She had only twenty pounds in the Post Office, for she had stopped trying to save money as soon as her mother died, and she was going to hang on to this nest egg and treat herself to

a holiday abroad in the summer; or perhaps it might be useful
if one of the boys got ill or into debt. Anyway, she was not
going to spend it at the Surgery auction sale. Also, she dreaded
seeing Mrs North, who was sure to be there, and who hated
her and was so jealous of her that the feeling broke out in a
terrifying, sneering, snakish insolence which made Sophia's
heart bang and her legs tremble.

Nor was she sure if she wanted some of the Surgery furniture
in the cottage – (if they secured the cottage!). It would remind
her of horrors; horrors would come winding out of the shining
black oak like dark smoke. She would have loved to buy the
little picture which she called Nydia, and the seamed old yellow
table under which the boys and she used to play when they
were all small, but it was no use; she could not afford to bid,
she was afraid to go; and so she walked to the Vale instead,
to look at the Cottage.

So far, she had only hinted that they might perhaps live
together to Francis, who received the suggestion with surprise
but with flattering pleasure and excitement, and had promised to
sound Harry about it. And then, on the advice of Celia, Sophia
had written what she described as a manly and straightforward
letter to Mrs Carmody, who was staying with her eldest daughter
at Rapallo, explaining her circumstances, prospects and desires;
and now awaited, in an interesting mixture of hope and anxiety,
Mrs Carmody's reply.

So events had been put in train; undoubtedly she had made
moves towards securing the cottage.

Oh! if only they had the three thousand pounds!

The Vale was a cluster of old houses on the Heath, near a
large pond where swans sailed and little boys fished, sitting
among the thick stems of the water willows. The houses stood
amid tall, old trees; and the dark branches were printed against
the faded, yellow weatherboarding of the houses; blue smoke
came calmly out of their midst. A road shaped like a Y ran
down into the Vale. It was so steep that in frosty spells, Celia
said, horses could not get down it. It did not look very steep

today, but no doubt Celia was right; she and her mother had
spent last winter in the Cottage, and she ought to know.

The right branch of the Y-road went down to the pond, past
the only six slummy houses in the Vale; the left branch went
past the Cottage and led to a steep part of the Heath, where
may and lime trees grew.

The Vale had no tiny general shop, because it lay only ten
minutes' climb from Enbury High Street, but otherwise it was
a village, pleasantly isolated and proud of itself, its ramshackle
charms, its two large houses and old gardens, and the fact that
Leigh Hunt had lived in one of the houses; but there were
heated local arguments about which one.

The Vale was a delightful place in which to live; and not
the least delightful part of it to Sophia, the Londoner, was the
fact that London lay spread away, away, as far as the eye could
sweep, below the Vale; looking between the gentle trees like
a lulled monster in a vision, with half its cruelty gone. She
never grew tired of looking at its smoky beauty. She did not
want to live down there; she enjoyed escaping every evening
from the monster and climbing her green hill of refuge, but
she delighted in its unending variety, power and pure romance,
and loved to lose herself in a maze of dreams about places to
which she had never been, such as Alperton, Stoke Newington,
Highbury and New Cross Gate. She knew, of course, that if she
did ever go to these places she would find there trams, fried
fish shops, big cinemas and small newsagent tobacconists, but
that did not make the places any less romantic to her.

The Cottage was wedged between a house that was just a
little bigger than itself, and somebody's back yard.

It was an extremely small cottage, whose door, which was
painted blue and was half a window, opened directly save for
a worn little stone step on to the street. There was another
window to the left of the door, and two windows on the second floor above; and that was all. The cottage was only two
storeys high, and it was painted a mild shade of yellow, which
had deepened in fog and rain to the hue of parchment.

All the windows rattled and let in draughts, and sometimes when they were pushed up in a certain way a sound like a note on a distant and mysterious gong came from inside the place where the sashline was; Sophia was always hoping to hear this.

The side of the cottage overlooking somebody's backyard was made of brown weatherboarding with a tiny window set in it, and there was a roof of purple slates crowned at one end by a huge, brick chimney, looking much too big for the little house to support.

The Cottage did not look aggressively romantic, nor picturesque. It was about a hundred and forty years old, and as it was joined on to the back of one of the big houses where Leigh Hunt was supposed to have lived, it is possible that a workman or perhaps a groom attached to the big house may have lived there. Mrs Carmody, who also owned the alleged Leigh Hunt house, had filched a bit of its larder to make a bathroom for the cottage (you could see that it had been the angle of a passage; it was a very odd shape indeed), but really no one knew much about the Cottage.

It was called The Cottage, The Vale, Enbury Heath. An odd, self-contained, lovable little house, thought Sophia, who was one of the people who fall in love with places as well as with persons, and rather more easily; just big enough for the boys and me, and looking over gardens running sideways on to the Heath, full of bare fruit trees, and the golden lettering of 'Meuxwell's Ale' on the side of the Vale Arms, at the end of the slummy alley. An independent, sturdy-looking little house, thought Sophia, and at Easter we shall be able to see the Fair Ground from the bedroom windows ... if we get it, that is!

This sobering thought reminded her of the sale; she sighed, and wondered how it was going and who had bought little Nydia? It was nearly four o'clock; the low, bright winter sunlight had left the Vale in shadow half an hour ago, and was lingering on the high ridge of the Don's Mile, which overhung the Vale and stole much of its light in the late afternoon. The golden letters on the Vale Arms glittered against the pale blue sky, the low roar of motorcycles rushing along the Don's Mile came peacefully to Sophia as she sat on the inviting step of the Cottage, with her beret for a cushion, and dreamed.

Presently she thought she would go up to the pond on the edge of Wrenwood, an estate which had recently been added to Enbury Heath, and try to see a water rat. They came out when it was getting dark, and once she had played peep-bo with one there, the rat looking round a tree root every three minutes or so to see if she had gone away yet, and Sophia, delighted and silent, staring at him with all her eyes and refusing to go.

She walked off, dragging her feet through the withered winter grass and enjoying the fresh cold smell of the evening.

But when she got to the pond she found that someone else was there before her. She heard a confused noise of barking, splashing and whining and a human voice before she came round the curve of the trees, and did not like what she heard; the noises were ugly, and the voice too loud, and the evening was so frozen, exquisite and still that she resented any loud sounds. She began to feel annoyed before she saw what was happening, and when she faced the still expanse of water backed by the hazy brown and deep purple of water plants, she blazed into rage.

She did not hesitate, but marched straight up to the young man who was setting a bull terrier on to the terrified moorhens and demanded loudly, 'What the hell do you think you're doing?'

The young man, who was leaning over the railing, urging the dog into the water, spun round at once; Sophia saw a dark, foreign, dapper face and two big, dark eyes, which just for a flash, were afraid. But when he saw that the bold questioner was only an angry young woman in a shabby coat and no hat, he looked amused and angry instead, and said, in a light voice coloured by some unfamiliar accent 'Who the hell are you to ask?'

'Never mind who I am; how dare you set your beastly dog on the moorhens? Call him off, can't you? Oh, look, he's got one! *Call* him off, you can be fined five pounds for this, if a keeper catches you! Here, here, boy,' she made a very funny attempt to whistle through her rage, extending her fingers and snapping them. 'Here, here, good dog ... if you don't call him off, I'll—' and she looked wildly for something with which to hit the young man, who was laughing.

She could see nothing that would do for a weapon, and so she went straight at him with her fists clenched, eyes wide open and staring with rage and her short fair hair blowing back.

He backed before her, saying something in a foreign language, and then, 'All right, here, hi, keep off! I'm sorry – I'll call him off! Here, Brandy, good boy! come here, sir. Brandy!'

Brandy stopped splashing among the reeds and reluctantly came back, swimming through the icy water, which streamed away on either side of his pink, split mouth. A moorhen was still twitching among the broken reeds, with two little claws, the colour of yellow-green water plants, sticking straight out in front of it.

'There!' said the young man. 'Bad dog! How dar-r-re you, sir. *Bad* dog!' (and then something in the unknown language again). 'You *bad* dog!'

'You needn't blame the dog. He wouldn't have gone for them unless you'd let him,' said Sophia, turning to go.

Her feelings had been so near the surface for the last few months that the slightest display of emotion brought maddening tears, and she now turned her back in order to hide them, wishing that her heart would stop racing, her legs shaking and her stomach churning.

'Well, it was like your impertinence to interfere,' he said. 'What business was it of yours? Trying to hit a perfect stranger! You're mad, I should think.'

'Oh, go to hell,' muttered Sophia, and walked away, while the young man, carefully talking to the dog to show that he was perfectly in control of his nerves and temper, strode off in another direction.

Sophia, stumbling through the twilight and crying in a choked angry way, gradually grew calm enough to grin reluctantly. She was still extremely angry about the moorhen, but the young man had looked so frightened when she flew at him, and she had so thoroughly upset his dignity that she felt she had not come off so badly. Beastly dago, she thought; he looked like a tailor's dummy with that awful little moustache ... never mind. I shouldn't think he'll set his beastly Brandy on moorhens again in a hurry.

She was, however, so soothed by a rich tea at the Primrose Café and a calm perusal of a copy of that morning's *Daily Mail* which someone had left on her table, that she felt capable of telephoning Uncle Preston about half past six to ask him how the sale had gone?

Apparently it had gone rather well. Nothing of course had fetched anything approaching the amount which it was worth. That was only to be expected. Times were bad. Nevertheless things had not gone so badly. Not badly at all. 'How much?' asked Sophia baldly, trying to hold her breath, because she disliked the stuffy smell of the telephone booth.

Well ... Uncle Preston had not, of course, the exact figures by him; he was in the middle of tea when the telephone bell rang; no, of course it did not matter at all, he just wanted Sophia to understand why he had not the figures by him.

'But, Uncle Preston, you must have some idea?' insisted his niece. 'Don't you even know about how much?'

Well, Uncle Preston hardly liked to say. It was not easy to be definite. He thought he might go so far as to say that things had not gone so badly, and then, of course, there was the *car* to be sold ...

'Does Aunt Maxine know how much?' demanded Sophia, 'I'll ring her up, I think, and ask.'

Oh, there was no need to ask Maxine, none at all. He believed, though of course Sophia must realize that the figures were not *exact*, that the sale had realized about a hundred pounds. There had been one or two dealers there who had taken a fancy to some of poor Hartley's bargains. The sitting room chairs had sold very well, he believed, and the little table inlaid with fruits in coloured woods ... perhaps Sophia remembered it?

'A hundred pounds. That's pretty good, isn't it? Uncle Preston, I suppose you didn't notice who bought a little painting on a wooden panel. Quite small. It was a girl holding out an apple ... I only wondered.'

Uncle Preston, as it happened, did chance to notice what became of that little painting. Er ... Mrs North ... she was there ... she bought it, quite cheaply, with one or two other small things.

'Oh ... thanks. I just wanted to know, that's all. Thanks awfully, Uncle Preston. Goodbye.'

She hung up the receiver.

A hundred pounds; that was quite a lot of money. But Nydia the gentle and dark-eyed, holding out her sweet apple of tranquil wisdom for the tired world to taste – Nydia had been sold to a stupid and malignant woman. I'm a coward, thought Sophia. I ought to have gone, and bought her myself.

But when she got back to her room, prepared to spend the evening in bed with a book, she found a letter with an Italian stamp and she forgot Nydia and everything else in the world as she tore it open.

Like the flap of most painfully important letters, the flap of this letter was sealed down too tightly and too close to the top, so that it took the wildly impatient Sophia much longer than it should have done to get it open.

Yes, it was from Mrs Carmody. Yes, they could have the Cottage unfurnished or semi-furnished for thirty-five shillings a week, and Celia could be their landlady, receiving the rent in trust for her mother every Saturday. They could have it for a year, to see how the plan worked, and then, if it worked well (and we don't get behind with the rent or bust things, thought Sophia), the lease could be renewed, possibly at a slightly higher rent.

Mrs Carmody was an old friend and an extremely kind one, but she did not buy expensive cottages on Enbury Heath for fun: sooner or later, they must begin to be profitable. Sophia knew enough about rents in Enbury Village to know that, just for the first year, they would be getting the Cottage at a bargain rent. She felt solemn with gratitude. She could have sung with joy and relief ... and at the end of a year, they might have the three thousand pounds and be able to afford the slightly higher rent.

Now she had to telephone two or three people, and write a letter.

This must be done at once – before supper – before something awful had time to happen and spoil everything – the ground that had been seized *must* be consolidated and mapped.

She slapped her pockets to be sure that her keys were there, grabbed her handbag, and ran out again into the foggy blue night. She stopped at a shop on the way down to the telephone, bought a penny stick of chocolate and got eleven pennyworth of coppers with which to feed the telephone. She would probably need all these and more, for she was going to tell Uncle Preston about the cottage.

CHAPTER VIII

The nearest telephone box stood just inside the dreary, grimy, badly lit and romantic entrance to Enbury Heath Station on the L.M.S., and as she went into it she hoped that one of those seedy but pugnacious little men who always seem to want to use telephone boxes would not come and grimly plant himself outside, taking out his watch, tapping with his pennies on the window, mouthing at her, and otherwise urging her to hurry and finish her conversation, for she intended to be in the telephone box for some time.

No little man came, with a list of probable winners or a long involved message for some Old Charlie or Old George. It was half past seven on a cold February night; everybody was eating, stunned by the wireless, or gone to the pictures; and Sophia got straight through to Harry, at Taplow, and laconically told him about Mrs Carmody's letter.

A series of Marvellous's! came over the line, mingled with the noise of a gramophone, the barking of dogs and a roar of voices. Edward and Emily were as usual having a party, and though Sophia was pleased to have Harry's whole-hearted approval of her schemes, she would have felt on safer ground if Harry had said Marvellous! a few less times and asked one or two sober questions about sleeping accommodation, living expenses, etc.; but it was no use expecting the impossible. She

must boil Harry's exclamations down into a useful weapon,
part of a solid and united front.

'Then I can tell Uncle Preston you'll want to come, and you
think it's a good plan?' she demanded.

'I think it's marvellous, darling. You tell the old fool so
from me. Marvellous! I say, darling, would you like to speak
to old Edward? He's here, just by the receiver ... Edward, I
say, Edward ...'

'Not now, thanks. Give him my love. He and Emily must
come and see us when we're safely in. Any sign of a job yet?'

'Nothing doing yet, darling. Old Edward's going to speak to
Roger Tidy about me. He's putting on a show at the Imperial ...'

'Oh well, that's grand. Very decent of Edward. Good luck.
I'm going to tell Uncle Preston now. 'Bye.'

The hapless Uncle Preston had passed an exhausting
morning in wrestling with the natural perversities of the
French chalk trade (like so many other trades at this time it
seemed possessed of a lumpish, sodden yet malignant demon
which fell upon the French chalk purveyors at every turn and
baffled them; it was easy to believe that the chalk was doing
it on purpose); an embarrassing and distressing afternoon at
the sale of his dead brother's effects, where he had been very
conscious of the handsome, shameless presence of Mrs North;
and he had a slight touch of asthma. His high tea had been
interrupted by the telephone, and when he returned to the
table the haddock, in spite of being immediately popped down
in front of the fire by Auntie Loo, had lost its first hot, smoky,
delicate appeal. The bloom had gone off the tea, and he had
been annoyed at having to tell that tiresome girl Sophia exactly
how much the sale had realized. He also disliked, he very much
disliked, having to mention that woman's name to a young girl,
to his own niece. It brought the whole sad, painful, disgraceful
business too clearly into the open.

In short, Uncle Preston had passed a very disagreeable and
tiring day.

His feelings, when the telephone bell rang for the second time to summon him from the quiet fireside, the muffled boom of the wireless and the sheets of the *Evening Standard*, may be imagined.

'Is there *no* peace, *no* quiet, *no* rest?' cried Uncle Preston, sitting bolt upright and rolling his eyes and gritting his teeth, instead of throwing down the paper and muttering, 'Who on earth's that?' as anyone but a Garden would have done, 'Who can be wanting to speak to me at this hour of the night? I cannot answer it, Looie. I am sorry, but I *cannot*. I am too exhausted. I am afraid you must go. Tell them – tell whoever it is – that I am *extremely exhausted*, and I am afraid that I cannot come to the telephone.'

Auntie Loo put down her knitting, and pattered out into the hall. Mentally, she was making a t-t-t-t-ing noise but she never so indulged herself aloud. You cannot be married to an Uncle Preston and give way to noises expressing nervous exasperation; your thunder, so to speak, is stolen from its birth.

Sophia was rather relieved to hear Auntie Loo's quiet voice, although she saw immediately that the explanations would now take longer than ever.

She plunged into them at once.

'Auntie Loo ... ?'

'Yes? Is that Sophia? I thought I knew your voice, dear. What is it? Your uncle is rather tired this evening; he has a touch of that nasty asthma. Yes ... the fog, I suppose. Such a nuisance. Is it anything important, dear? Can you tell me? and I can give him a message.'

Auntie Loo was one of the few persons in Great Britain over fifty years of age who became neither muddled, flustered nor semi-deaf when listening to facts over the telephone. She composed herself to hear what her niece had to say.

'Auntie Loo, the mother of a friend of mine has offered to let us her cottage, unfurnished or partly furnished, for thirty-five shillings a week. It's on the Heath. We all want to live

together. Harry and Francis do, too. We want to *very* much.
Do tell Uncle Preston, Auntie Loo. Say I'm awfully sorry to
bother him again, but I simply had to tell him about it, and
get permission. You see, I want to write to my friend's mother
tonight, and tell her that we'll take the cottage.'

'Hold on, dear. I'll just tell your uncle.'

Auntie Loo went back into the sitting room with a bright
look on her face which she was careful to subdue as much as
she could. She thought that this was the pleasantest piece of
news she had heard for a long time. Poor little things, no doubt
they would get into shocking muddles, but it would be very nice
for them to be together like that. Brothers and sisters ought
to love each other, and to like to live together when they were
not married. That was as it should be ... and she suppressed a
disloyal thought about poor dead Oliver and Hartley, Maxine
and dear Preston, who certainly, as brothers and sisters, had
not been at all as they should be.

She repreated the message, quietly, accurately, slowly.

Uncle Preston, who was not so intelligent as Auntie Loo,
immediately flew into a muddle.

'A cottage? What sort of a cottage? Where is it? Where's
the money coming from? What are they going to live on? I
never heard such nonsense ... ringing me up at eight o'clock
at night and asking me to settle such a thing at a moment's
notice. Just like Hartley and Oliver – no *prudence*, no *foresight*.
Is she still there? And how about the boys? Do they want to
go and live there, too? It's miles away, I suppose, in the country.
How about their fares? *Fares mount up ...*'

Auntie Loo waited for a lull, and sailed neatly in with –

'What shall I say to Sophia, then, dear?'

'Tell her that I am very displeased. Very displeased *indeed*. I
must talk it over with *Marriot*, and then I must see the *cottage*,
and then I must talk to *Graby* about *Francis*, and then we will *see*.
I *cannot* be rushed into things in this way. I *will* not. Sophia is
exactly like Hartley – he was always so *eager*, so headstrong ...'

'Perhaps, dear, you would like to talk to Sophia about it to-morrow, when you are less tired. Suppose I ask her to telephone us about lunch time? or say at half past twelve?'

'Well ... yes ... possibly that would be best. I can say nothing until I have seen Marriot and talked it over with him. *Nothing*. But perhaps I can tell Sophia best myself tomorrow. Yes. Tell her, please, to telephone me tomorrow no later than half past twelve. And say that I am very much upset, very agitated—' and indeed, he was beginning to breathe in short, distressing gasps, a sight which made Auntie Loo's face lose its bright look.

After the message had been given, Sophia, chilled and impatient, said pleadingly – she so longed to talk to someone kind about the cottage – 'Don't you think it would be lovely, Auntie Loo, if we could?'

And Auntie Loo, even though she knew that Uncle Preston could hear every word from where he sat by the sitting room fire, replied clearly and firmly, 'I think it's a splendid idea, dear. Very good indeed; and I hope everything will turn out for the best, so that you can all live together for as long as you want to. That's how brothers and sisters should be.'

'Thanks awfully, Auntie Loo! You are kind!' said a surprised, grateful young voice at the other end of the line, and having agreed to telephone her uncle at half past twelve the next morning, Sophia rang off.

Uncle Preston said no more about the cottage for two hours, much to Auntie Loo's relief, for this was a good sign. Silence, accompanied by an intent perusal of the newspaper meant that Uncle Preston, instead of letting his nervous system take charge of his views about the cottage, was allowing his common sense to do so. Auntie Loo knitted a jumper in placid silence, broken by occasional dry little laughs at the jokes made by a comedian on the wireless. 'Very comical; quite amusing,' said Uncle Preston, at half past nine; but then they turned the wireless off because somebody was going to give a talk on 'Mice', and

Auntie Loo did not want to hear anything about them, nasty dirty little things.

'What do you think of this cottage idea?' asked Uncle Preston at ten o'clock, sipping his Mil-koko and looking at Auntie Loo over the top of the glass. His large round pale grey eyes were still a little irritable, but they expressed a desire for a second opinion.

'Well, I think it's quite a good idea, really, dear,' replied Auntie Loo, carefully flattening her voice and expression. 'Of course, there will be a lot to be discussed and arranged first. It would never do to let the poor little things do anything in a hurry. But it would really be an advantage, Preston, to have them all in one place, under your eye, instead of scattered all over London, as they are now.'

'But miles away! in the country! expensive fares!'

'Not in the country, dear. On the Heath, Enbury Heath. So convenient for Sophia's work and for Francis, too, if Mr Graby can have him. And then if Harry could get into a play in the West End, it would be *most* convenient! They would all three be so comfortable together; and it would be a more economical way of living too, because all their money would be going into one household, instead of three separate ones. And it would give Sophia a little training in housekeeping as well.'

'Grace said something about wanting Francis to go and live with her and Angela,' said Uncle Preston, looking at his counsellor over the top of the Mil-koko cup. 'Eh?'

Auntie Loo compressed her lips, in the renowned and expressive manner of Mrs March, but she said nothing rash. She knew quite well that that silly goose of a woman, Gracie, hoped that Francis would get engaged to his cousin Angela; it would be so romantic. They had played together, she used to remind them, as tiny tots; and conveniently forgot that Francis's idea of playing had been to pour sand into Angela's shoes and butt her in the stomach because he hated her.

He still hated her, with the yawning, bored hate which is not a disguise for an unwilling admiration. Auntie Loo knew that all the children hated Angela, who was so pretty, so feminine, so bright and so good at sewing and games; but she would not distress Uncle Preston by saying so. She saw that he suspected Grace of vague but troublesome designs which might lead to family quarrels, and so she lulled his fears.

'Oh, I don't think Grace really meant that, dear. I expect she just spoke without thinking; she has a very kind heart, but I don't think she would really like it at all, if we suggested it to her.'

'Maxine wants Harry to go and live with *her*', muttered Uncle Preston, his voice becoming lower and more depressed as the Mil-koko sank in the cup, and endless vistas of disagreements, rebellious refusals and surprised resentments opened before his tired eyes.

A prolonged pause.

'I hardly think that would do, dear, do you?' mildly enquired Auntie Loo, who had been knitting very quickly during the pause, so that her needles flashed and flew like tiny spears.

'Bless me, no. Of course not. Out of the question,' said Uncle Preston briskly, draining his cup to the last rich milky drop, sitting suddenly upright, and putting it firmly on the table. 'Quite impossible. Yes.'

Neither of them said why it would hardly do and was quite impossible, but they agreed about it, undoubtedly; and though no more was said that night of the children going to live in the cottage, Auntie Loo was sure that the conversation would bear the fruit which she wanted it to bear when Sophia telephoned tomorrow.

It occurred to her, as she stood plaiting her little tail of hair for bed that night, and staring mildly at her dumpy reflection in the mirror, that none of the relations had suggested that Sophia should go and live with them.

Girls, of course, were not so exciting as boys, and yet they were more of a responsibility. It was not an attractive combination. Auntie Loo, who had a soft spot for Sophia in her heart, would have hesitated a long time before she asked that large, silent, sometimes embarrassingly wild and outspoken girl to come and live at Forest Hill.

But when the embarrassing one telephoned the next day, she was delighted to find Uncle Preston almost converted to the plan.

He pointed out to her how convenient it would be to have the three children under one roof; what an advantage it would be for herself and for Francis to be near their work – if Mr Graby could find a post for Francis, that was – and how much more economical it would be to establish one household than three. Of course, he must see Mr Marriot and Mr Graby before anything could be done about moving in, but meanwhile perhaps it would be as well if Sophia wrote to her friend's mother and told her that they were *almost certain* to take the cottage in, say, three weeks or a month.

Sophia had already written and posted the letter late the previous night, but she did not tell him so.

She had rapturously thanked Mrs Carmody, promised that they would be model tenants, and said that she would write again the moment she had any definite news.

And she had prudently added that they would probably like to take the cottage partly furnished, as she, Sophia, was the only one of the three who possessed any forks or pillows or bookshelves. Francis's furniture consisted of most of the works of the late H. Rider Haggard, three silver cups which he had won at school for jumping and shooting, and a number of second-hand assegais and weapons of vaguely Oriental appearance but doubtful authenticity, which he called 'My Collection'. All Harry's possessions went round with him in two fat, battered, mysterious suitcases. They had also two sword sticks, which had belonged to Dr Garden, and which Francis had stolen one night from the Surgery soon after his father's death because he wanted them for My Collection and no one else seemed to. These treasures, with Harry's gramophone, were all they had.

Sophia hid her joy from Uncle Preston. She tried to sound sensible, grown-up and sober: and flew home to write an over-flowing letter to Francis, telling him the exciting news.

None of the children ever found out what Uncle Preston told Mr Graby about Francis, though Francis, who took a morbid interest in other people's opinions of him, made one or two attempts to find out.

Mr Graby told Uncle Preston that he would see Francis any morning at 11.0 o'clock, but a week went by after Francis left school, and still he did not go up for the interview. Harry had said to him, 'A chap must look decent when he goes up about a job,' and had persuaded him to postpone the interview until a superbly fitting new suit, ordered on tick from Harry's tailor, should be ready.

Francis spent the time at Aunt Grace's bright little house at Hendon, reading his Rider Haggard books, furiously stalking out on errands for Aunt Grace, and being icily polite to Angela when she tried to mend his shirts, which had already been adequately repaired by the matron at Northgate. Sometimes in the evenings he slipped out for a long walk over the Heath with Sophia; and they would call for Celia, get the key of the cottage, and make an exploration of their future home, planning where they would put things and soberly revelling in the cottage's charms, and deciding what furniture they would keep and which should be stored.

Uncle Preston twice rang up to ask frantically *why* Francis had not been down to see Mr Graby? and each time Francis explained that he was waiting for the new suit and hat, and Uncle Preston rang off with a warning snort.

But at last both were ready; and on a bright morning, pursued by the irritating good wishes and facetious condolences of Aunt Grace and Angela, Francis went down into the City.

Graby, Bryant & Co., Ltd., 11 Pratt Street, Monument, E.C.

He went off in a mood of deadly and pompous seriousness. His hands were wet, and he felt a little sick. He had that type of sensuous nervousness upon which sights, smells and sounds strike like bewildering blows and, unlike Sophia, whom he much resembled, he could not relieve this pressure by getting it into words and on to paper. His upbringing and environment had conspired to make him precocious; his extreme youth showed itself only in this intense seriousness tinged with melodrama, his self-consciousness, and the awful importance which he attached to every moment and every trivial event of an ordinary day.

This was his first chance of a job. It was desperately important that he should impress Mr Graby, seem at ease and yet efficient, and get it. He, at sixteen and a half, was already out in the world, taking on the responsibilities of a man, while the chaps who would go back to Northgate after the half-term were kids. They were still wearing ready-made suits and vilely fitting school caps.

He glanced at himself as he passed a mirror; and was comforted, if rather awed, by the elegance of the incredibly thin, rather tall young man in the seven-guinea suit, whose pallor, fierce pale blue eyes behind horn-rimmed glasses and satirically twisted mouth were set off by his soft hat and natty, pale skin gloves.

My god, I look about twenty, thought Francis.

But this did not stop him feeling sicker and sicker as the train drew in to the Bank.

He walked through to Monument, as he had been told to do by Uncle Preston, and came into the street, still feeling sick and beginning to feel that he would have to *be* sick.

Across the Bridge, and then to the left. He walked on quickly, noticing that there were plenty of pretty girls about; many of them were nice-looking Jewesses, for Monument is on the fringe of the East End, and its wide streets, glaring with pale light and creeping with bewildering traffic, are subject to sudden exotic invasions which make them picturesque.

Francis looked at his watch as he crossed the bridge, because he wanted, like forty other people who were draped over the parapet, to stop and watch a big boat being loaded with white sacks.

It was twenty minutes to eleven. No time to waste watching a boat which was going (so the notice above it said) to Holland. All the River broke on him from either side in its blaze of silver light, with high bright clouds piled above it, and cranes, the colour of rust, receding in procession down the wharves like the enormous, leggy, delicate Martian machines imagined by Mr H. G. Wells.

If I get it, I'll come out here at lunch time and watch, thought Francis.

It now became obvious that he must be sick, and he cursed his trembling legs and unreliable stomach. There may have been at the back of his mind an impression that his father was to blame for his present condition, but the thought never got itself expressed; he expected life to be intense, full of physical discomforts and excitement, and so it was.

He found Pratt Street, an alley running between tall warehouses made of smoky brown brick. The flaps down their sides were painted dark strawberry red, and there was dull gold lettering on windows and roofs; straw, feeding horses, and waggons and lorries were scattered down the winding length of the street. The sky, high overhead between those smoky canyons, was bright from the reflection of the river.

I'll find a quiet place, and be sick, thought Francis, slipping behind a lorry piled with more white sacks. (Most of London's heavier merchandise seemed to be hauled round in fat, white sacks.) Here he discovered a very deserted yard, closed in by warehouses, smelling of old petrol and horses in a friendly mingling.

Francis went behind a door painted the same rich dark red and was sick.

He was very sick; Aunt Grace believed in growing boys having a good breakfast. None of your grapefruit and toast for Aunt Grace.

Being sick is one of the most disagreeable of the minor human afflictions; a weakening, undignified experience which makes the eyes swim and the legs shake, and in the midst of

Francis's second spasm, a bell from a hidden church sweetly said eleven. 'Hell!' muttered Francis; and a voice just behind him enquired in a hoarse, sympathetic yet ironical tone: 'Feelin' bad, are yer, cock?'

Francis nodded, making no attempt to turn round. He got out his handkerchief and mopped himself.

'Ar … it's all this mornin' coffee, that's wot it is,' said the voice impersonally, as though passing judgment from some superior planet. 'Fillin' yer stomach up with milk and dish-water in the middle of the mornin' – what can yer expect?'

Feeling slightly better, and desperately anxious to be on his way, Francis turned round, jerking down his sleeves, and straightening his tie.

'Upsets yer, don't it?' said the owner of the voice, a fat little old man, who was sitting on an empty cask. His tone expressed some satisfaction. He was holding the early racing edition of *The Star*, and looked as though he had been sitting on the cask all his life. Yet he had not been there when Francis had come into the yard. He must have come rushing out from some lair, trundling his cask, while Francis was being sick, with the intention of creating a sensation when the boy should turn round. He looked the sort of old man whom nothing – not the Taj Mahal, nor a charge of cavalry nor Helen of Troy nor a Cup Final – could impress. 'Ar …' he would say; and wonders would wilt before the sound.

'Yes,' said Francis, too polite to ignore him, but rather nettled by his manner. He was just striding off when the old man said mildly, 'You ain't got no right 'ere, y'know, cock.'

'I'm sorry, I didn't see a notice,' said Francis, over his shoulder.

'There ain't no notice. I'm 'ere to warn people off, see?'

'Then why didn't you stop me at the gate?' snapped Francis.

'"Cos I muss 'ave a bit of lunch, I s'pose, mussn' I?' suddenly shrieked the old man, going crimson in the face. 'Oo d'you think you are – comin' 'ere sickin' coffee all over my yard and grudgin' me a bit of lunch? Be off, or I'll set the dog on yer.'

Francis did not find out if there really was a dog because he had begun to run. It was not fear of the dog; it was fear of being seriously late for his appointment.

Fortunately Mr Graby was at a directors' meeting when he was shown into the office. He had wasted another seven minutes looking for Graby & Bryant's and finally found it right at the end of the alley; it was on the left, and looked over the river.

It was a quarter past eleven when he walked into Mr Graby's room and at first he feared that Mr Graby had rushed away in a fury because he was late.

'It's all right; he's at a directors' meeting. Will you take a seat, please; Mr Graby'll be here any minute now,' said the pretty, fair child who had shown him in. Despite his elegance, his fierce air and his height, she calmly divined that he was both very young and very nervous and wanted to comfort him.

Francis thanked her, fixing her with his meaning and flirtatious eye, and she went smiling away.

The place is seething with girls!

The ecstatic thought sang beneath his apprehensions. He had seen two in the lift, giggling; one coming along the corridor, haughty; and three pattering down the stairs just outside Mr Graby's room, businesslike.

And they were all about eighteen, slender, curled and painted, pretty. The place was a gold mine, a honey hive! Oh, if only he could get the job!

He went over to the window and stared at the busy, glittering river until his eyes ached, and then he examined the specimens of mica, talc and silica on Mr Graby's table, trying hard to feel interested in them and to memorize their names and colours.

Mr Graby came in and caught him in this gratifying pose.

This interview, which loomed so thunderously on Francis's horizon, was of course only a tiny incident in Mr Graby's day, and if Francis had not been old Garden's nephew, he would have been interviewed by one of the managers.

Mr Graby did not examine prospective office boys. This act was a concession.

The words 'office boys' had been drumming a little irritably in his head for the last ten minutes, and when he came in and saw what looked like a juvenile lead bending over a tray of silica, he felt definitely cross.

'Flashy,' was the word which darted across the sensible, decent, rather hard mind which lived behind Mr Graby's red face. It had come from Hull twenty-five years ago; and it still mistrusted flash.

'Good morning. You're Mr Garden's nephew, aren't you? Sorry to have kept you waiting. I've been expecting you, though, for the last week,' said Mr Graby, brushing past Francis and sitting down at his desk.

Francis flew upright like a cobra, every nerve eager to impress, and said much too easily and eagerly, 'It doesn't matter a bit, sir. I'm awfully sorry not to have been down before. I was waiting for my new suit to be ready.'

And he glanced proudly down at himself. Surely, he thought, anyone must be impressed by the waisted elegance, the superb cling and subtle width of his new suit.

'H'm,' said Mr Graby. He looked at Francis's very pale, eager, rather arrogant face, and the words 'stook-oop' joined 'flashy' in his mind.

'How old are you?'

'Sixteen and a half, sir.'

'Just left school, I suppose? What school were you at?'

'Northgate, sir.'

'Well ... you'll have to do up parcels, sort the post in the Typing Department, stamp letters, and go down to the wharf every few days to fetch samples, and fill the inkpots and all the rest of it. Mr Faraday will tell you. Eight o'clock till six, weekdays, eight till one on Saturdays.'

'Yes, sir. I could do all that, sir. Will there be a chance to get on, sir?'

'Get on? How? Get more money, do you mean? You'll get a pound a week,' said Mr Graby, not at all impressed by this zeal. Everyone pretended to be keen when they wanted a job.

'I meant get a better position, sir.'

'There's always room at the top,' said Mr Graby, dryly and not at all encouragingly. When perplexed and irritated he often fell back on proverbs, saying them in a peculiarly disapproving voice which made people think that he had personally tested them out and found that they were all lies.

He was silent for a second or two, staring down at the tray of mica. Francis, sweating with varied emotions, glared imploringly at his face. *Oh, would he get it?*

Mr Graby, in fact, did not know whether to give him the job or not. He could get thousands of competent office boys from the Council schools. This boy had been to a public school, though not a first-class one, and was probably a snob. He might find it difficult to work under men who had not been to public schools. He had a too-easy manner, and his clothes were too smart by a long chalk (but Mr Graby shrewdly guessed that this was Francis's only grand suit). He looked bossy, bad-tempered and not very strong; his face was the colour of cheese. Mr Graby had taken a dislike to him, and was annoyed by his eagerness, and the way he had hung over the silica, trying to impress his future boss.

But after all, he could always be sacked at the end of a week if he was no good, and old Garden had hinted at some funny business at home; his father drank, or something. That might explain a lot.

'All right. Start on Monday at eight sharp. Mr Faraday'll put you in the way of things. 'Morning.'

He said this suddenly, pulling some papers towards him. They were not papers that he intended to study, and this made him crosser than ever.

The fact was, this boy made him nervous.

'Oh, *sir!* Thanks most awfully, sir!' said Francis. 'It's awfully decent of you, sir.'

'All right. 'Morning,' said Mr Graby, not looking up.

'Good morning, sir. Thanks awfully.'

Francis went, striding out of the room like youth incarnate – pompousness, earnestness, maddening spots on the forehead, elegance and adventurousness and all.

He at once rushed off to telephone Sophia.

'Dear, I've got it! Start on Monday at eight! A pound a week. He says there may be a chance for me to get on, too.'

'Francis, how *marvellous!* I say, we're really getting on, aren't we? Is Aunt Grace expecting you back for lunch, or can you come and lunch with me?'

'I've only got ninepence.'

'Never mind … I've got some.'

'And I shan't eat much. The fact is, I've been rather sick.'

So Francis may be left to the tender questions, the wonder and congratulations and the sympathy of his sister. She was convinced that Mr Graby had been impressed by his air of efficiency, and that he saw in him a future director of the firm.

CHAPTER IX

The three could hardly believe it, yet a week later they were living in the cottage.

Uncle Preston made his inspection of their new home on the day after Francis got the job from Mr Graby.

Followed by an anxious committee consisting of Sophia, Celia, Auntie Loo and Francis, Uncle Preston pattered fretfully and cautiously up and down the one flight of tiny creaking stairs, silently indicated that one of the stairs was giving way, nearly got himself wedged in the narrow bit that led from the kitchen into the bathroom, and asked where the dustbin was kept, and the coals?

Celia, who loved the Cottage extremely and resented Uncle Preston's attitude of despairing disapproval, silently opened the top half of a little red cupboard which was let into the wall of the kitchen and lo! there was quite a deep coal cellar in which stood a dustbin.

'I see ... it goes under the stairs,' said Uncle Preston. 'Now, Sophia, my dear, you must have that cracked stair repaired *at once*. If it gave way, you would fall through into the cellar and you might be *seriously injured*.'

'Yes, Uncle Preston. I'll see about it tomorrow.'

'Most unwholesome ... the dustbin in the kitchen,' muttered Uncle Preston. 'And no garden. Not even a yard in which to dry clothes. And *very* small. Much too small for three people.

One could manage to live here; *two* would be disagreeably crowded. As for *three* …'

He went across to the brick fireplace, and tapped a panel above it which looked like a little door.

'Does this open?'

'Everybody asks that,' said Celia complacently. 'No, it doesn't. It isn't a cupboard; it's just nothing.'

'Well,' said Uncle Preston at last, standing on the small worn step which led down on to the pavement. 'It's small. Very small indeed. I can only hope that you will none of you catch *fever* from living in so confined a space. Yes.'

Sophia looked up at the darkening blue sky, where ghostly white clouds like the bosoms of swans were moored. It was incomprehensible to her that anyone could find a fault with the Cottage, when it stood on the Heath, surrounded by trees, water, quietness; but older people were like that. They cared more for being comfortable than they did for anything else in earth or heaven.

'It's a pretty little place, dear,' said Auntie Loo, as Sophia shut the door, 'but I'm afraid you may find it rather difficult to run. Never mind, we all have to learn.'

And on the following Saturday, having paid the first instalment of rent to Celia and wired to Mrs Carmody, they moved in.

They had a clear windy March day for the move, which took place between two o'clock and three. Mr Cross moved them. Mr Cross kept a greengrocer's shop in one of the lanes of Enbury Village, and he agreed to transport their few things for twelve and sixpence in his unreliable-looking van.

The sky was bright, the light poured out of it like showers of jewels, everything moved and swayed, singing, rustling, whispering. Francis, sitting on the step of the Cottage waiting for Sophia to come in the van, had a delightful feeling that Uncle Preston, Mr Graby, Aunt Grace and the rest were countless miles away.

It was marvellous to be moving into their own little house (Francis was a domesticated person, despite his air of fierce elegance), where they would be able to do as they liked for the first time in their lives. And on Monday his job began! He felt, as usual, solemn with the desire that everything should go off properly, but very happy. If only he had been able to ride in the van, as well as Sophia, he would not have had a wish ungratified. But somebody had to be at the Cottage, of course, to open the door and welcome the van when it arrived after the short journey from Sophia's lodging.

He had already arranged My Collection on the narrow shelf intended to hold ornamental plates and mugs, which ran round the panelled walls of the sitting room, and it looked really impressive. This evening he would clean his silver cups and arrange them.

A sour-looking gentleman strolled past, followed by a suspicious, yellow, stiff-legged dog with a superb chest.

Both strollers looked nosily at Francis. He returned their stares with hauteur. If the gentleman had said 'Moving in?' Francis planned to reply 'No – building an aeroplane,' but the gentleman said nothing; he prowled in at the gate of a little house near by, carefully closing it after him, and was seen no more.

Here came the van, with Sophia sitting next Mr Cross's young driver and talking to him in an absorbed and friendly manner. She had no hat and her short fair hair flew about her pale cheeks in the wind.

They were discussing Communism, of which the young man disapproved. Sophia, who was beginning to dabble in its doubtful waters, was trying to defend it without making any sweeping statements; she disapproved of them. As she knew nothing about Communism her task was difficult. Mr Cross's young man had a low opinion of the Russians. His father had fought at Murmansk with the British Expeditionary Force there in 1918, and had dreadful stories to tell, which his son duly repeated in defence of his views. As a result, Sophia hopped down from the van with half of her mind in the Vale and half of it in an imaginary Russia lowering with snow, resounding with wounded cries, the horizon dark with miles of swaying pines, the unending low mutter of guns ...

'I'm glad none of the relatives are here,' said Francis, helping her to carry in a tall narrow bookshelf. 'Aunt Grace rang up to say could she and Angela come and help? I said, no they couldn't.'

'It's nice having the telephone. Where shall we stand it? On top of the little bookshelf?'

'And the table here, under the window.'

Francis put it neatly into its place. 'Did you get the leg mended?'

'No. I meant to. I'll see about it when I go to the village to get the supper. And the stair, too.'

'Doesn't it sound nice? Harry will be here about four, he said.'

'And Celia's coming to supper. I wanted her to be our first guest.'

'And tomorrow's Sunday, and on Monday my job starts. We needn't get up early tomorrow, need we? I want to arrange my books.'

'You needn't. I shall, because I shall have lots to do. Oh, Francis, the Collection does look nice! You can add to it as we go on ...'

She went upstairs with a pile of curtains.

The bedrooms had originally been one large room and had been made into two by a partition; each room had its own door opening on to a tiny landing. The well of the staircase was whitewashed, and threw clear light into the two little bedrooms, which were panelled in deal, washed over with dark stain. Their floors were of shining parquet, expensive, devilish to keep clean and easy to slip on. This had been Celia's suggestion to her mother, and was typical of the insane and grandiloquent logic of her housekeeping.

Sophia dumped the curtains, which were of a pale pink cotton striped with green and patterned with bunches of bright pink cherries, on to the bed.

She went to the window and looked out.

Sweet air, sweet spaces of the Heath busy with cheerful Saturday afternoon sounds, sweet sight of the black fruit trees in the neighbouring gardens, starry and dazzling with buds!

She was so happy that she nearly began to cry, and when she thought of her mother and wished that she could have been there with them to see the little house and to enjoy it with them, she had to rub tears from her eyes.

Her room was certainly extremely small.

There was only room for the narrow iron bedstead which Mrs Carmody was lending her, and for Sophia's battered old white dressing table which had drawers in for her clothes, and for two little hanging bookshelves. Her thicker clothes hung in a recess behind the bed's head.

But when the curtains were up and filling the room with a rosy glow, and when a spread of the same cheerful material covered the bed, and a curtain of it veiled the recess, and when the wooden boxes which Sophia had (rather badly) painted scarlet were arranged on the dressing table, the tiny room looked gay and fresh.

Sophia gloated over it. She hung out of the window, picked anxiously at minute spots on the dressing table, arranged her worn shoes in a row, refluted the curtain folds and began arranging her necklaces and handkerchiefs in the scarlet boxes, but she was recalled by the voice of Francis from the boys' room.

'Sophia! Here a minute.'

She went in, and he said impressively, 'That chap's finished and he's going. *What ought I to give him?* Five bob?'

'Good heavens, no!' she said, horrified. 'Two. Two's ample. Here … I'll give it to him. I want to thank him.'

Mr Cross's young man was waiting downstairs, looking pleasant but thinking condescendingly that he never saw such a poor turn out in his life, and yet the young lady seemed to be a young lady all right. Artists, p'raps.

'Thank you very much,' said Sophia, slipping him the two bob. 'You've been a great help, and it was very interesting hearing about Russia.'

For Russia, like a song in a minor key, was still droning at the back of her mind.

Mr Cross's young man thanked her, and backed his van away with some difficulty. She had a pleasant sensation, with his departure, that she, and Francis and Harry, were now even more on their own.

Harry arrived, as usual, in a taxi; taxis seemed to accompany him as naturally as their shells accompany snails. Out of this taxi he brought his two suitcases, two long rolls of stiff cloth that looked like rugs, and a large bunch of dark red carnations in tissue paper. Sophia and Francis were on the stairs, fixing the meat safe on to a shelf on the wall; they came down to meet him, smiling and excited, and he gave Sophia the flowers with a kiss.

'Harry, how lovely! Thank you, darling. Look, isn't it all nice? We only got here at half past two and we're nearly straight. What are those? Rugs?'

'I bought them from an Arab chap who was selling them in the West End,' said Harry, proudly unrolling the thin silky gaudy mats. 'They're my contribution to the house, and so is this.'

Sophia stared at the pack of clean green notes he held out. She had never seen so much money in her life.

'My dear, however much is there there? Where did you get it?'

'It's only fourteen quid. Old Marriot gave me thirty-five out of the sale money and the practice, and said it ought to last for a good bit. So I'm keeping twenty-one, and the rest's for you and the house. He wanted to send it to me every week, but I said I'd have the first lot in a lump; it would be more useful. He didn't want me to have it. I had quite a job to make him hand it over. My god, he's an old screw, if you like.'

'That's fourteen ... and I've got twenty in the Post Office and three a week, and Francis will have one a week and you've got twenty-five and if you get a job you'll get much more. I really think we'll be able to manage, don't you?

'Of course we shall. I can always go to old Marriot if I want a bit extra, and later on there'll be the three thousand from the practice. Oh, we'll be all right. You'll see.'

'I'd better give you half my pound, hadn't I?' suggested Francis, who had been thinking things over while he frowningly tuned his ukulele. 'Would that pay for my food and things?'

'I can't take half,' said his sister decidedly, 'because you'll want more than ten bob for lunches and fares. You give me five bob. That will help, and leave you fifteen.'

'And if you get in a mess you can come to me,' said Harry. 'My suit isn't paid for yet.'

This suit, which was Francis's most beloved possession next to his ukulele, weighed upon his conscience. He was naturally quite unaccustomed to using money, because boys are not taught this art at school, and because, like the other two, he had been brought up at home on the fearfully dangerous principle of alternate money-starvation and repletion. His father would give him an unexpected pound, and then no more money for six months, and his mother gave him what she could, but her own financial life was mismanaged in the same maddening way by Dr Garden, and she could not do much.

But from some forgotten, sober ancestor, or from some natural honesty, Francis had derived a horror and fear of debt, and so had Sophia. Neither felt really safe or comfortable unless they had a few shillings put by. As this feeling was united in Sophia with a love of wasting stray sixpences on secondhand copies of Matthew Arnold's poems, bunches of violets and icecornets or roasted chestnuts she seldom felt financially at ease; while Francis, even at sixteen, was literally tormented by a desire for silkier and richer ties, finer shirts and better cut shoes, and meant to save up savagely for them, secretive and prudent as the French housewife of fiction, and then spend royally.

Thus neither managed to save money, but so far they had kept out of debt.

Harry had as much money sense as one of the red carnations which he loved to buy for his girls. His tastes were calmly

lavish. It never occurred to him that he might save money by
not riding in taxis, treating acquaintances to double whiskies
or buying flowers for women.

Sometimes he had pounds, borrowed or earned; sometimes
he had no money at all. Neither state exalted or depressed him
... at present. He used money as he used the air he breathed,
the ground he walked on; and was adorably generous with it.

He disliked being unwashed, but otherwise he was that rare
bird, an unselfconscious bohemian. Francis and Sophia were
not. A tidying, constructive, saving little bourgeois streak ran
through their natures, and saved them from the pit of financial
misery.

'Old Bartle can wait for his money,' said Harry tranquilly
now. 'I owe him fifteen, apart from yours. He expects not to
be paid. All tailors do. God, who's he, that I should send him
any money? Old Edward says the same. Tailors deserve what
they get.'

They were comfortably assembled in the sitting room, Sophia
on the lowest stair of the tiny flight which was closed in by
a door opening into the living room, as stairs often are in old
cottages, Francis sitting upright in a fearfully uncomfortable
old wooden chair which Sophia had bought second hand for
seven and sixpence, and Harry lying on the big old sofa which
was one of the things they had kept among Mrs Carmody's
furniture.

This sofa was a beautiful shape. It was some thirty years
old, and belonged to a period when fashionable sofas and arm-
chairs did not look at once fat and brutal, like gangsters, as they
do in 1935. And indeed, it is chiefly gangsters who can afford
to buy them and to loll in them, so no wonder they resemble
their masters, just as the starved comfortless glitter of the
steel furniture suggests that it belongs to a rich, unscrupulous
psychoanalyst.

But Mrs Carmody's sofa had broad arms at either end, upon
which someone could comfortably sit when the middle of the
sofa was full, and its back had an elegant swooping curve

which always made Sophia think of a seashell. At present it was covered with a faded old red and white chintz; Sophia planned to have it covered with the same cherry-patterned cotton as the sitting room curtains.

It is possible that the heart of the gentle reader glowed with pleasure on hearing that the cottage had a panelled sitting room, but the panels were neither oak nor romantic. They might have been made of deal, but they were covered so thickly with brown paint that no one could say for certain. True, there was an authentic beam across the middle of the ceiling, but it was covered with the same paper as the ceiling.

This mongrel panelling, combined with the parquet flooring, the sternly repressed beam, the stairs in a cupboard, the modern brick fireplace and the little old door with clouded glass panels, which led into the kitchen and the bathroom, made the cottage unlike anywhere else. No one could say how beautiful! how typical of its period, how romantic, how sweet. The cottage seemed to possess a personality which was its own.

Patched, odd, undated, definitely a place in which no over-rich and ultra-sensitive person could have lived for a day, it could offer neither space nor solitude, because, if one was at home, the light in the sitting room could be seen by friends who walked past just outside; and in they would come, whooping with pleasure. If one wished to make love, one had to retreat to the bathroom or sit on the stairs with the door shut; and everyone could always hear, all over the house, what everyone else was doing and where. It also had draughts, and it did not get much sunlight except in the morning in the summer; during the day it was a little dark, because it was so low built and near the road.

Nevertheless, if the Surgery was an unhappy place, the cottage was certainly a happy one, which immediately enchanted every imaginative person who stepped into it, as well as simple sensible people.

Work stopped on the arrival of Harry. The three sat still in the pleasant, slowly darkening afternoon, with the door open and much work still to be done. Perhaps for the first time in their lives they were consciously and calmly happy. They felt at home.

At the Surgery, their places of refuge had been the small nursery, with its green, shiny walls and large cupboard which Sophia, at twelve years old, had decorated with very bad paintings of Egyptian gods, copied from a British Museum catalogue; and the landing halfway up to their attic bedrooms. But in both places they could hear the distant slamming of doors and the shouts which meant that a row was going on. There were sometimes laughter and nice times at the Surgery, because their mother had made them, but never was there that feeling of peace, security, continuity, which children, if they are to be happy, need as they need sleep and pure air.

But here there was peace. The two voices whose rising and falling had lightened and darkened their childhood would never be heard again. Already Sophia was beginning to forget the beloved inflections of her mother's voice; she tried to hear them with her mind's ear, and could not. But sometimes, when she was thinking about other things, a sentence, or her own name, would suddenly sound in her inner ear in that very voice; and she would smile and think 'Mother!'

The new alarm clock ticked loudly on the wooden mantelpiece, and the fire which Francis had lit danced in its cheerful gold; straw from the packing case lay over the floor, there was no food in the house and the beds were not made up, while respectable-looking people kept pattering past the open door and trying not to look in, and failing. Francis made shrill experimental little plucking sounds on the ukulele, and Sophia dreamed with her chin sunk in her hands; Harry was earnestly reading about football in *The Star*.

At half past four Celia strolled up and stood at the door for a second, smiling in at them with her curling fair hair lying mildly on the shoulders of an old green leather coat like the locks of a visiting angel.

The three looked up at her lazily, in smiling silence, and Harry politely swung his feet off the sofa.

It made her very happy to see her friends in her mother's little house which she loved; and because it was largely her doing that they were there she felt happier still.

'How nice it looks! Are you straight already?'

'Mercy, no. We're just idling. There's masses to do. And I'm awfully sorry to bother you, but do you think you could lend us some blankets till next week? Then I can buy some ... oh, I forgot! I've got fourteen pounds. Would I be justified, do you think, in buying some blankets? We've only got four, belonging to me. It isn't enough.'

'Of course you must buy some, Sophia, and mind you get good ones; they're an investment. Have you got any sheets?'

'Six. I had two pairs that I pinched when I left the Surgery (I thought they were 'due to me,' as The Deedle used to say) and I bought another pair at Camden Town for twelve and elevenpence.'

'Can't be any good at that price,' said Celia, shaking her head. 'Never mind, they'll do for undersheets when you get new ones. I've bought some Devonshire splits for tea. Have you had it?'

Tea in the cottage that first afternoon inaugurated the series of giant, leisurely and extravagant meals which were, for months ahead, to exhaust Sophia's pocket and leisure.

No sooner did one meal finish, with its sausages and fried tomatoes and quarts of tea, than another had to be got, with its boiled potatoes, chops and meat paste and butter and bananas and cream. There was no end to them; they went on endlessly, like the Alps in Pope's *Essay on Criticism*.

But the time had not yet come when Sophia was tired of getting meals.

'Pretty cups. Like the curtains,' said Celia, looking at the tea set for six, decorated with gaudy red cherries and gold lines on a white ground, which Sophia had bought in Camden Town. Harry pulled out the table and arranged its rickety leg with care, Francis boiled the shiny new kettle on the little gas stove in the kitchen. The curtains were drawn, the door was shut on the dark end of the afternoon. Somebody put 'Waiting For the Last Round Up' on Harry's gramophone, and a delightful mingling of warmth, cosiness, security, noise, bustle, amiability and the smell of toasting buns and fresh tea filled the sitting room.

'I'm glad Aunt Maxine isn't here,' said Francis, just as they sat down to the table. 'Or Aunt Grace or that beastly little Angela,' added Harry. 'To say nothing of Uncle Preston,' ended Sophia, lifting the teapot: and the telephone bell rang.

Everyone looked alarmed.

'I bet you it's one of the old fools; will you go, Celia, lovey, and say we're all out shopping?' implored Sophia.

Celia went to the telephone and took off the receiver. A hearty and metallic voice asked her if that was Sophia, and announced that it was Aunt Maxine, and that it was being driven over by a pal that night to look at a flat at Swiss Cottage, and that it proposed to drop in on the children and see how they were getting along.

Celia, covering the receiver, agonizedly repeated this titbit of news to the stricken three.

'A flat for who – her, or the pal?' demanded Francis. 'She isn't coming to live at Swiss Cottage, is she, god help us?'

'Tell her she can't.'

'Say we're all out; and we shan't be back till very late.'

'Don't say anything; hang up. She'll think it's a wrong number.'

'I'm so sorry,' said Celia in her drowsy voice which always sounded doubly sleepy over the telephone. 'They're all out.'

'What – all of them? I thought they only moved in this afternoon. Isn't Harry there?'

'I'm so sorry.'

'What time will they be in? I might look in on my way back.'

'Oh … not till very late, I'm afraid. They … no, not till quite late.'

'How late?'

'Oh, about half past twelve, I should think.'

'Who are you?' asked the voice rudely, like a crocodile cheated of its prey and prepared to snap at anything.

'I'm just a friend. I'm just keeping an eye on the cottage while they're out.'

'Where've they gone?'

'*Pictures!*' gesticulated Sophia, who was hanging over the telephone.

'They've gone to the pictures, I think. I'm not sure, really. I'm so sorry.'

'Well ...' said the voice, unwillingly preparing to retreat. 'It's very queer, I must say. Going out to the pictures on the night you move into a new place. Can't understand it. Well, tell them I 'phoned up. Aunt Maxine.'

'Yes. I'm so sorry,' and Celia hung up the receiver. 'Goodbye.'

'I'm sure she didn't believe a word of it,' she said reproachfully.

Everyone said they didn't care if she didn't, tea was begun again, and Aunt Maxine forgotten.

There were one or two more disturbances to jar the tranquillity of the evening's pleasures; at seven o'clock Uncle Preston rang up to ask if Sophia had had that stair mended yet, and went up in a sheet of flame on hearing that she had not; and at a quarter to nine Angela rang up just to ask if Francis would be her partner at a dance given by the local Badminton Club, and Francis, refusing to speak to her, deputed Sophia to say no he couldn't.

During these interruptions the work of getting straight went on; Sophia went out with a fourpenny-halfpenny shopping basket made of purple and green bast on her arm, and climbed the exhausting hill to the High Street, where she bought food for the weekend, and wondered as she walked dreamily under the shop lights which always seem brighter on Saturday night and among the smells of bruised celery and coffee, whether there would always be quite so much to do in the cottage? Her legs ached, her back and arms ached and her ankles turned over three times on the greasy pavements, as they always did when she was extremely tired.

But when she got home again, it was so delightful to knock at the door of this tiny house with the rosy windows, and to have the door opened by Francis and all the bundles taken from her cramped hands, that she forgot her tiredness in the thought that this was *theirs*, their home for a year at least, with all its comforts and peace.

She thought of the number of times she would open the door with her own key, at the end of a long hard day, and see the sofa, the Collection and the gramophone and the little door that looked like a cupboard but was just nothing; and she was happy.

After supper they sat on the sofa in front of the fire and Francis played on his ukulele those sombre little songs set with short curt slang words resembling nuts and bolts and screws, which he and his generation love.

Poor little jerking tunes without line or joy or hope, they dropped softly off the twangling notes of the ukulele with their own beauty. In them the lover was a sweet man but could not get a job, nor hold one down if he did, and the lass knew it, and despaired, but loved the more. None of the people in these songs had any money; they had only dreams, and who wanted those? Sometimes they expressed surprise that anyone should love so poor a thing as they were; sometimes they expressed a weak indignation because no one did.

None of them actually said as much, but one felt that consolation in the form of cocaine was waiting for them just round the corner. Snow, it is called in America; a wonderful name from that nation which coins poetry in its casual speech, unhampered by ancient literary standards; snow. Like snow it is warming if there is enough of it, and on its flakes the singer floats quietly down into the darkness.

I gotta pass your house
To get to my house ...

sang Francis softly, staring into the fire, and Harry and Celia, a little hypnotized, rocked to and fro, melted with delicious melancholy and staring too.

But Sophia, that priggish girl, moved uneasily once or twice in the dreamy dying firelight. Some bump of common sense and sturdiness in her nature disliked this musical creeping and whining and ululating, this snow-man singing. To herself, she called it 'a dreary row.' A sentimental streak in her nature could enjoy it for five minutes, and then she felt bored and ashamed and wanted something which was musically gay, firm and shapely.

A satisfied pause followed the last notes of another song of the same type; and then Sophia said diffidently, 'Do you mind if we have the little Brahms waltz? It won't take very long.'

'Oh, lord, need we have on the light? It's so nice like this.'

'I can see without it, I think.'

She found the gramophone; and in a minute the first clear, delicate and precise notes of the little waltz (Op. 39, No. 15) played by Kreisler, struck on the dark air.

It was so different from the song which had just ended that it was hard to believe both sounds could impress the ear as music. The song had been written to a formula by three extremely vulgar and rather wicked men, and the theme of the little waltz had been written by a man of genius, but the difference did not lie in this.

The little waltz sounds extremely sad. It is like a farewell which must last for ever, yet it is not despairing, because it contains order, courage, resignation, in its themes; these qualities are probably not discerned by technicians, but an ordinary listener usually detects them. The contemporary song is sad also, but with the nervous shapeless despair of the drug addict; it heels clean over, out of sight and into the last dark pit. The post-war world has got the popular music it deserves; and the little waltz by Brahms has nothing to do with it.

It is extremely odd to realize that men once naturally wrote music of this kind, and lyrics like 'Come Unto These Yellow

Sands.' It is like looking back, in an immense black cave, at the small sunlit door by which one entered.

Sophia, listening with great pleasure to the waltz, thought vaguely about these things, while Francis, Harry and Celia also listened with pleasure, and Francis remarked that it was a nice little tune. Just as Sophia was putting the record away, a peremptory scratching noise was heard at the front door.

'Aunt Maxine!' whispered Harry in horror, prepared to fly up to the bedroom.

'No, I expect it's Taffy. He always used to do that when Mother and I were here last winter,' and Celia went across to open the door.

A graceful golden-brown dog stepped inside, sneezing with excitement, his curled feather of a tail waving condescendingly. He took no notice of anyone but Celia, whom he licked with some fervour, and then went into the kitchen.

'Is he thirsty?' asked Francis respectfully.

'I don't expect so, but he always likes a saucer of water,' explained Celia, drawing some for him. He showed signs of pleasure and sneezed again two or three times as he sat down in front of the fire, but he did not touch the water.

'Does he always do that?' demanded Sophia.

'Yes. He hardly ever drinks but he makes an awful set-out if you don't put down a saucer for him.'

'I call it a piece of confounded cheek,' grumbled Sophia, who had stepped into the saucer. 'If he wants to go on coming here, he'll have to give up that trick.'

'Oh *no*, he's a darling,' chorussed the other three, patting Taffy who sat sneezing, staring into the fire, and ignoring everybody.

He sat there for a few more minutes, and then delighted them by suddenly getting up and off-handedly holding out a paw to Harry as though to say, 'Well, I must be off. 'Night.' Harry took the damp hairy paw and shook it, and Taffy went over to the door, scrabbled to be let out, and disappeared into the darkness.

That reminded Celia that she must go too, and off she went, after kissing them all good night and taking a last pleased look round the warm untidy room and her three friends.

Sophia watched her walk down the damp pavement under the feeble light of the lamp on the edge of the Heath, a small and lonely figure with hands in pockets and bare head. It occurred to her, not for the first time, that Celia was a solitary girl, in spite of one or two close friendships and her serious, maternal interest in the young men who were in love with her. She was like the little waltz; lonely, dignified, lovable, and content.

Then she turned back to her house, and closed the door on the loneliness and the night.

Harry was winding the clock, Francis was locking the window. The beds were made, and the washing-up stacked neatly on the pull-out flap in the kitchen which was used as a table, the bedroom curtains were drawn and the coverlets had been turned back by Celia, who had performed this rite for herself and her sisters ever since she was nine years old. Silence, warmth, a feeling that everything was drowsily settling down for the night filled the cottage.

Harry switched off first one sitting room light, then the second. The sinister glow of the dying fire instantly transformed the room to one in a witch's house, on whose dark, rich red air the back of the shell-sofa rode glimmering in its gracious curve.

Francis dropped the latch of the little door which closed in the stairs; and in sleepy happy silence they went up to their beds.

CHAPTER X

The economic machine is like a claw which contracts every morning about nine o'clock and pulls its victims into the places where they work, and relaxes every evening about six to release them. Their warm, variable human lives are lived outside the clutch of the claw, lopped and ruthlessly shaped so that they do not interfere with the victim's response to the contraction-and-relaxation system; and though life within the claw's grip usually insists on wriggling about and colouring the claw's scales with the rose red of love and the purple of drama in a reassuring manner, there are nevertheless some actions which it is almost impossible to perform within the claw's grip.

Sophia, for example, found it possible to write poetry during idle intervals at the Canadian News Agency (known as the C.N.A.), but she did not find it possible to make a cushion cover or to bring the bathroom shelf to the office with her and finish painting it bright blue.

The process of settling into the cottage was therefore done in bits, before breakfast and after supper and at weekends; and it was really painful to Sophia to drag herself away from the cottage at a quarter to nine every morning, when she knew that there were still so many things crying to be done and that someone ought to be at home.

The coal, for example. The firm which sold the coal simply could not be brought to believe that there existed a cottage in the Vale where no one was at home from a quarter to nine in the morning to half past six at night. It was nonsense; it was a try-on; whoever it was was doing it on purpose, and the coal firm knew better than to give way to such caprices.

So they sent coal (it was only two hundredweight, to add insult to injury, for this was all that the cottage's cellar would hold), for three days running at eleven in the morning, disregarding Sophia's frantic telephone messages, and then would send it no more.

The same difficulty occurred with the laundry, which, like some puckish sprite, some coy elf of the dells, could never say exactly at what time it would call, but preferred to pop in winsomely whenever 'the boy was down that way,' which might be at any time during the day.

Only the milkman and the postman were reliable; and Sophia, Harry and Francis got quite hysterically fond of them both because they always came at the same time, and left nice, fresh milk and interesting letters instead of dirty bits of paper, saying sullenly 'Laundry called' or prim, starchy cards announcing that a representative of the Gas Light and Coke Company had been there and, finding no one at home, had gone affronted away.

Sophia felt that she ought to have a charwoman in for an hour every day, to deal with these matters and keep the cottage looking nice. A few days after they moved in, Harry, through an introduction from Edward Sweeting, got a job at five pounds a week as assistant stage manager, with a few lines to say, in a thriller by a successful American author, which was to be put on at the Duke of Kent's theatre; and began rehearsing immediately.

This was a glorious event, but it meant that Harry would be out nearly all day, and could neither receive loads of potatoes nor make his own bed. (Sophia made hers, but that was different.) It meant more had to be done, and made a charwoman even more necessary.

The whole crew of relations from Uncle Preston to Angela meanwhile rang up almost every evening to enquire, warn,

admonish, coo and say that they simply must come over and
see the house. They were all, except Auntie Loo, hoping that
the children would make a shocking mess of the housekeeping,
and their telephone calls were in the nature of vulture-like
hoverings and anticipations over what they hoped would soon
be a carcass.

Of course, none of them knew this. They all thought they
were taking a kindly interest.

In spite of her many responsibilities at this time, Sophia
was happy.

Her situation did not include many of the things which make
most human beings happy, for she was poor, she was not in
love and had no one in love with her, she was not pretty nor
admired, she was usually exhausted from overwork and felt
vaguely ill from the pressure of her own nervous energies,
lingering grief for her mother, and from the deeply rooted
misery which had struck into her nature during her childhood.
She seldom experienced the pleasures of a theatre or a dance,
and she had not many nice possessions; her clothes were cheap,
home made and worn, and she sternly kept herself from buying
the snowy collars and cuffs, the little bottles of scent and the
elegant gloves which she wanted.

Nevertheless she enjoyed almost every moment of her day.
She had learned, at an early age, to ignore the protests made
by a tired body; this is a valuable lesson, which often serves
to develop the senses of hearing, smell and taste, and to make
them vivid, and obedient to the demands of the intelligence.
As for her eyes – what delight they gave her! ravaging a room,
a face, a landscape like buccaneers, and sending back to her
brain great loads of loot.

She liked best of all to roam about London or to go for
a whole Sunday into the country by herself on the top of a
bus. She did not think about anything; she wandered along,
falling over things and scratching her legs on brambles, vaguely
looking forward to the sandwiches she carried in a little old
camera case made of leather, and chewing a piece of grass. If

she was accompanied by a friend, she usually took a talkative one, to whom she could politely say 'Yes,' 'Indeed,' 'I should think not,' 'Oh,' and 'Did he, how odd,' without hearing more than three-twelfths of what was being related. All the friends said she was so sympathetic, and Sophia would grin, and feel a little ashamed.

Next to these aimless walks ('life-eating', she called them, when she was older and they were easier to recall than to achieve) she liked writing poetry. She had the cottage, Harry and Francis, and the pleasures derived from music, reading, flowers and trees and eating; and so she was happy.

She was not introspective. She had too many other things to think about.

Her work with the C.N.A. was definitely pleasant, and she liked it. The agency took in cables from all parts of the world which they received through another and much larger agency, whose newspaper clients were all in the United States and whose London offices, filled with large, kind Americans in their shirt-sleeves, were just across a corridor from the C.N.A.'s little dens. The C.N.A. bought the London and provincial rights of the European cables as they passed through the larger agencies' hands on their way to America, decoded them from the jerky cablese in which they were expressed, and sold them to London and provincial papers for a retaining fee or lineage rates.

This was Sophia's job, to decode some of the easier and shorter cables from time to time and to put them into bright and readable journalese, to take down letters from Mr Piper and Mr Burrows and type them, and to write up the mailers.

The mailers were news stories which were sent through the mail (or post) as distinguished from the cables which came over the machines.

They were typed on flimsy paper, in extremely curious English intended for consumption by the American public. They were sometimes written by foreigners employed by the American agency, and then the English was superb; it rocked drunkenly like a lorry on one wheel going down a one-in-three gradient, it tied itself into serpentine knots and flickered, it attempted to be arch and daring, with sickening effect.

A typical mailer dated from, say Bucharest, would begin thus:

Boris Bennoskwyz, hundred-year-old pesen from quent. Old world hill village of Pitesci in Moldavia tells startlingly of nacked danses in mountains. Paysants says Boris is returning to the old-world gods blaming for harvest. Men and young girls orgying together . . . and so on.

This she would transform into something like this:

Are the peasants of Pitesci, a small mountain-village in Moldavia, returning to the worship of the Pagan gods?

Boris Bennoskwyz, a peasant from Pitesci who is reported to be more than a hundred years old (says a message from Bucharest) tells strange stories of nude dances and orgies in which both men and women take part, which are alleged to take place in the mountains.

She often wished, in the midst of toning down the mailers, that it was possible to print them as they reached the office. 'Nacked' sounded so much more naked, somehow, when it was spelt in that way, and 'orgying together' more matey than a simple orgy.

She came to mistrust all stories from the Balkans. It was not only those reaching the C.N.A. which sounded so odd. All the Balkan stories printed by the other agencies were odd as well.

'This is slugged Belgrade, Miss Garden; be careful with it.' That was always Mr Piper's warning when a juicy mailer about werewolves or ten-legged donkeys with heads of hens came from the Balkan States. Sometimes there were stories about old women aged a hundred and thirty who had three hundred grandchildren and still made their own aprons on spinning wheels and remembered the death of Byron at Missolonghi and thought the modern girl a minx (probably they used a *stronger*

word, but like naked, it was toned down for the newspaper
columns). Sometimes there were similar records about old men
aged a hundred and sixteen who had just had their first ride
in an aeroplane and said that it was grand and gave them a
real thrill. No one took much notice of these stories; people
seemed to live to incredibly great ages in the Balkans. It was
perhaps something in the air.

It was Sophia's private opinion that the peasants of the
Balkans could not count properly. They got in a muddle,
boasted, attracted favourable comments, and found it was too
late to retract when some more sophisticated grandchild did a
bit of reckoning, and exclaimed 'But, Grandpa, that only makes
you ninety-three, not a hundred and thirty-three.'

As for the werewolves, the roads haunted by old men who
begged for lifts in passing cars and then vanished, and the
Things that lived at the bottom of wells, no one did much
about them either.

The other mailers were about fashions in colours for finger-
nails or interviews with minor Japanese and Austrian statesmen,
and were easier to deal with.

She sometimes wondered why she kept her job, for she had
no established position in the C.N.A.; she just made herself
useful in whatever way she could, exactly filling the vague
description of an 'editorial assistant', but not doing it efficiently.

She could only take down in shorthand at eighty words or
so a minute, her typing was not neat and she forgot things.
The only gift of which she was sure was her writing. When
she was expressing a meaning in words, decoding, toning down
a mailer, or making a coherent and vigorous letter from Mr
Piper's dictation, she felt confident. Words were at once her
delights and her servants; she marshalled them and played with
them and dreamed about their meaning and history until each
word had its aura and personality, and seldom allowed herself
the luxury of thinking solemnly about 'style'.

When a young woman is told to type a five hundred word
article on 'London's Women' straight on to her machine and

given half an hour to do it in from the word Go, she has little
time to think about style. This was what occasionally happened
to Sophia when the C.N.A. was short of copy for the mailers
that went to Canada; and very good it was for her, too.

Miss Candy did most of the filing and routine work, twit-
tering about in her yellow jacket with her dark curls carefully
arranged about a small white face. She was twenty-eight, and
fond of pleasure, but a little afraid that she would never succeed
in marrying one of the minor naval, aerial and military gay
dogs with whom she ran around. Her slang was strictly Service,
and she smoked a great deal and Sophia had been distressed
to notice her smelling of cocktails one day after a lunch with
someone whom she called 'my little naval engagement'. She
was kind, gay, silly and charming. Sophia felt years older than
she, and liked her.

Then there was the manager, Mr Piper, an improbably large
Canadian with big, clear grey eyes, who called Sophia 'my
dear child' and never tried to flirt with her, gave her articles
to write which earned her extra half-guineas, and was sometimes a little drunk, which did not prevent him from being an
admirable manager, but which distressed Mr Burrows, who
decoded the cables when Mr Piper was busy with interviews
and negotiations outside the office.

Sophia was fond of Mr Piper; she would have been alarmed
had he tried to kiss her, but pleased. She would have said 'No',
but she would have liked him to try.

This is the second trace of humanity discernible in Sophia;
it will be remembered that Mr Marriot had detected another
during the reading of the will. No one had ever tried to kiss
her, and she sometimes felt surprised and a little indignant
about this, for she considered herself handsome. Stern, and
nastily dressed, but undeniably handsome.

As for Mr Burrows, he had been a subeditor on the
Evening Star for twenty-three years and had been sacked when
the *Evening Star* was eclipsed. Unlike most journalists, Mr
Burrows had saved most of his comfortable salary during the

twenty-three years, and had enough money to live quietly with
his wife in their little house at Kenton near Harrow. But no;
Mr Burrows could not bear to stop away from Fleet Street; he
resigned his membership of the National Union of Journalists,
but he nosed about unhappily until he got this job with the
C.N.A. at a small salary, which satisfied Mr Burrows because
it gave him something to grumble at and enabled him to run
a little car.

Mr Burrows took immense care never to let anyone in the
office know that he had any other means than his salary; Sophia
in particular was extremely sorry for him when she first went
to the C.N.A. She pictured his straitened, pitiful life in a mean
suburb, and imagined him living in terror of being sacked,
because he always looked so miserable. It was only after Mr
Piper, while merry, had accused Mr Burrows of running a car
and leading a double life, pounding him the while on the back
and giving vent to loud, slow shouts of laughter in front of
the whole office that she perceived Mr Burrows was not poor
at all; he was far, far richer than she was, and much safer and
more comfortable. Mr Piper, of course, knew all about Mr
Burrows, because everyone in Fleet Street always does know
all about everyone else.

As well as these three and Sophia, there was a tousled,
smelly office boy, who looked rather like a lion but who was
much liked by them all because he was a bit of a wit and had
shining red cheeks under his shock of tow hair. He lived in
Hoxton, and the extreme poverty of his parents, added to his
natural untidiness, made his clothes a source of constant worry
and embarrassment to Miss Candy and Sophia; they had all
belonged to other people at one time, and to different ones at
that; and they were always coming unbuttoned, splitting, falling
off, flying open and abruptly disintegrating.

These five people worked together in two small rooms, on
one of the many corridors of a huge block of offices and chambers, in a narrow turning off Fleet Street, close to Fountain
Court and to the little collection of courts and gardens and

old houses which is like a charming nest of legal documents
boxes lying between Fleet Street and the river.

In her lunch hour in the summer months Sophia liked to sit
on Oliver Goldsmith's tombstone near the Temple Churchyard,
under a bright green plane tree, eating a tomato sandwich
bought from Dolly's, the cooked meat shop on the corner, and
admiring the thin, vivid grass growing round the base of the
Templars' Church; or looking up at the mild silly face of the
little Lamb, with his hoof curled ineffectually round his Flag,
who stands above many old doorways there; she could dream
over the tulip tree which grows in the wide garden facing the
river, and see the leaves fall from the plane tree in Plane Tree
Court, and wonder what it must be like to look down into a
great bushy head of green as the people can do who live in the
highest rooms of the houses in that courtyard.

It was an interesting job, an officeful of nice, cheerful people,
and there were peaceful places near the office in which she
could rest and dream; but she did wish that it did not take up
so much of her time.

CHAPTER XI

As soon as the three were settled in the cottage they became, of course, householders, and no one can be this without attracting a number of satellites and pensioners. People gravitate to a household; this is probably a habit lingering from feudal days when barons kept open hall.

One Saturday morning about half past nine Sophia was sitting alone in the cottage, dipping into *Little Women and Good Wives* and eating her breakfast. She was occasionally given a Saturday morning off, and this was one of them. The cottage was sunny and quiet; Francis had gone off nearly two hours ago to his job, and Harry had just left for a rehearsal at ten o'clock.

The day was windy, or the door would have stood open, letting in more sunlight. It came in through the open window, pouring on to the disordered breakfast table, Sophia's steaming cup of tea, her bent head with the short plumes of soft fair hair falling forward on either cheek, the transparent narcissus flowers in a green ginger jar on the table. She sipped her tea, took a bite of bread and butter, smelled the narcissus, turned a page, listened to the stillness, gratifying as many of her senses as possible at the same time.

She was not sure if there had been, a second or two ago, a faint, flat, despairing sort of dab at the front door knocker.

A pause; and then it came again, a little louder but still flat and despairing.

She looked up and across at the door.

A curtain of white net hung across the upper part of the door, and at first she could not see anything through it. Then she saw what looked like a squashed black box. It was moving restlessly about. It seemed to be trying to peer through the letter box, for it bobbed down, and the letter box suddenly bent inwards. Two eyes, vaguely set in what looked like crumpled reddish-brown paper, stared at her for an instant. Then, apparently in panic, they vanished. The letter box clicked to. The squashed box reappeared, dodging about; and the dab on the knocker was repeated.

She got up and opened the door.

There, looking very ready to run away, stood the tiniest and dirtiest old woman in the world, wearing a coat and skirt so stained, ragged and filthy that it did not look like a coat and skirt any more; it looked like a part of her, and so did the squashed black box that was her hat, and her enormous broken shoes.

She was tiny as a goblin, not more than four feet and a few inches high. Two faded blue eyes, bright with the moisture of old age, shone out of her crumpled toothless face; and she smelled of ancient dirt.

Sophia, feeling sick with pity and the smell, smiled down from her tall height at the terrified old face and said:

'Good morning.'

'Good mornin', dear,' said the old woman, breaking into an amazed, watery, tremulous smile; evidently she had expected to be kicked or hit on the head.

An embarrassed pause followed.

Sophia wondered where her purse was, as the old woman had evidently come to beg. The old woman seemed to be caught in the toils of language, like many a greater soul before her. She twisted her coat in two awful little worn hands, twisted her mouth, looked piteously at Sophia and was silent.

'Can I do anything for you?' asked Sophia at last, adding quickly, 'I mean, you mustn't mind. Can I help at all? Would you' (she looked ruefully round at the breakfast table and at her pretty cups wreathed with cherries) 'would you like a cup of tea?'

She did not at all want the old woman to drink out of one of her cups. She would make it very dirty. Her appearance and smell had already, Sophia resignedly realized, put Sophia off her breakfast.

But she thought firmly about Sir Philip Sidney and Keats, and repeated loudly.

'A nice cup of tea? There's one here, all ready.'

'Thank you, dear. Thank you very much, dear. Aow, you *are* good to me. It ain't that, dear. I was just wonderin' ... Mrs Carmody, she was 'ere last summer, she give me the step to clean, see? The young lady she see me in the 'Igh Street last night, see, and she says there was someone 'ere again, so I jus' wondered if I could do the step, see? It gets very dirty, bein' so near the road. That would be a 'elp, see?'

'Of course you can!' cried Sophia, by now only too delighted at the idea of being able to help the old woman in any way. 'Twice a week – will you?'

'On Wednesdays and Sat'days,' agreed the goblin, eagerly and importantly. 'That'll keep it nice, see?'

'I'm sure it will. And how about – will one and sixpence be enough, do you think?'

'Aow, you are good to me, dear!'

'Well now, would you like a cup of tea? Do have one. It's so refreshing when – when you're tired.'

'Aow I will, dear. Thank you very much, dear. I'll do the step first, see? You give me a drop of water, and I'll soon 'ave it nice. I got me own bucket ...' and here she rummaged round the corner of the door, and produced a zinc pail with a worn scrubbing brush in it, a cloth which was chiefly shreds, and a very small piece of hearthstone. 'You juss give me the water, see, and I'll soon be done.'

Sophia drew her some in the bucket, and closing the door because she was eagerly assured that 'I can get on, dear; I'll get along fine, see,' she left the goblin to its task and tried to finish her breakfast.

But it was no use. She was clean put off it; and so she cleared it away, wondering whether a cloth which was so shreddy, such a worn brush and two such terrible little twisted hands could possibly, between them, produce a snow-white step; and whether she was to be put off her breakfast every Wednesday and Saturday morning?

There was a long pause. She went upstairs and made the beds, not daring to peer out of the window at the unsuspecting goblin for fear it should look up and see her and be hurt.

Finally, while she was prowling uneasily about in the boys' room, there came the flat knock at the door again. But this time it was more robust and cheerful.

The old woman was standing outside looking timidly at Sophia and then down at the step.

It certainly did not look very nice. It was not quite clean, and it was smeary.

'It'll dry white, dear. It's a bit of a job, see, 'cos the stone's very worn, and it don't come up so nice, and me brush is a bit old, see, and I really need a new cloth. It's the Enbury water; terribly 'ard, it is. It won't lather, see.'

Sophia was waiting for her to say that the bucket leaked and that she never could clean steps in a high wind, but her flood of excuses stopped abruptly, and she stood silently looking up at Sophia, waiting for encouragement and praise.

She was evidently not used to either, and looking at her dirtiness, her inefficiency and a certain air of most unbefitting pugnacity and determination which had showed itself in her feeble but obstinate attack on the door knocker, and her sudden production of the implements for step cleaning which she had concealed in readiness, Sophia was not surprised. Her manner combined an excess of self-pity with a certain arrogance. She was a putting-off old woman. One felt that she was going to be the most frightful nuisance all the year round. One looked into the future, and one quailed.

But in Sophia these misgivings were swallowed in immense pity, and a sense of shame that another human being should be so small, dirty and piteously unpleasant. She felt as though she were to blame for this old woman, and that she must do everything she could to atone to her for her condition.

She said enthusiastically.

'Yes, it looks *very* nice. It's drying white already. Thank you very much. Will you have your tea now?'

The old woman, proudly looking at the smeary step, said that she would; and Sophia sternly chose a clean, shining cup and saucer, made a little pot of fresh China tea, let it stand for a few moments and then handed a full cup with plenty of milk and two lumps of sugar.

'Here you are. It's nice and hot. May I know your name, please?'

'Mrs Barker. I live up Cannon's End. Got two rooms in a house there. Beetles! You ought to see the beetles we got! Thank you, dear; that'll do lovely.'

After her first sip of the tea, an expression which can only be described as reserved fell upon Mrs Barker's face. She said no more. She indicated to Sophia, with gestures, that she would not interrupt her in the housework, that she would stay outside to drink her tea, that she would put the empty cup down on the window sill when she had finished. To give point to her protestations, she began delicately to shut the door.

Sophia, who had a busy morning in front of her, was relieved. Perhaps she was not going to be such a nuisance after all. She gave her the one and sixpence, closed the door upon her, and went into the bathroom to wash stockings.

Half an hour later, swinging her shopping basket, she left the house to buy her weekend provisions.

The cup and saucer stood on the window sill, the cup tactfully turned upside down, the dirty grey step was dry, and Mrs Barker had gone.

But Sophia's eyes had the habit of reporting countless seemingly unimportant details to her brain, and they informed

her that someone had recently poured away a cup of tea in
the gutter.

Apparently Mrs Barker did not appreciate the flavour of
China tea.

Nevertheless, she became a confirmed pensioner of the
cottage, with one or two unfortunate results. For instance,
Sophia could never hope to display a snow-white step which
should be a credit to the Vale; it was always grey and smeary,
and she never dared to hint to Mrs Barker that it was not all
it should be, for fear of hurting Mrs Barker's feelings.

Then she had to buy a quarter of a pound of Lyons' second-best
tea for Mrs Barker's private use; and the effect of Mrs Barker's
age, size, dirt and misery upon Harry was the most disastrous
consequence of all, for he could never see her without turning
out his pockets and giving her all his small change, in a passion
of chivalry and embarrassment. As he usually carried anything
from one and fourpence halfpenny to three and elevenpence, Mrs
Barker did very well out of these encounters, and would station
herself at likely corners in the hope of waylaying him, lurking
outside the Tube station in the morning and mutely planting
herself in his path on his way to rehearsal.

Celia, on being told about the engagement of Mrs Barker,
remarked, 'Mother had her in to clean the kitchen when we
left the cottage but we had to give her up. She made things
dirtier after she'd finished than they were before.' And she
added thoughtfully, 'I'm rather sorry you've got her.'

The dog Taffy was another pensioner of the cottage, and so
was the dog they called Jimmy Barrell, because of his superb
chest. Jimmy Barrell belonged to the ill-tempered looking
gentleman who lived a few doors from the cottage. He was a
hearty, athletic, contemptuous sort of dog, who used to come
into the cottage as one who bustles in during a morning of
necessary civic activities to visit admiring but shiftless friends.

He, like Taffy, would sit still for a few moments, having his
chest admired, looking rather scornfully round the cottage

('he's comparing it with his own home,' said Harry) and then bundling off, full of importance.

Taffy's visits were made in a different, though an equally contemptuous spirit. His sneezings and abrupt paw-shakings, his lean, nervous lines and beautiful golden coat suggested that his was a neurotic, moody and poetic temperament. Jimmy Barrell consented to recognize the three when he met any of them in the street, but Taffy, absorbed in sniffings, inspections or in mere aimless trottings, would always cut them all dead. If Celia was with them he would caress her and sneeze over her in a pointed way, but if Sophia patted him he would stare indifferently away over the Heath, as though absorbed by the view; this annoyed Sophia, who thought him a fascinating but ungrateful dog.

Then there was Dan. He was a large woolly Airedale who lived somewhere in the Vale and went out for walks with a master who had no control over his actions at all. He would occasionally walk into the cottage, with a patronizing rather than a contemptuous air (only one of the dogs in the Vale ever showed any signs of gratitude or pleasure at being allowed in the cottage) and allow them to pat and feed him, but he was too dignified to do this often, and they usually heard or saw him only at night when he was taken out on his final run. His master liked to stop and gossip with acquaintances who were out on the same errand, and his roars of 'Dan! Come *here*, sir. *Come* here, you brute, or I'll *flay* you! *Will* you come here, confound you! Dan! leave that alone, sir! Drop it at *once*!' could be heard every night about ten o'clock, echoing all over the Vale.

Dan took no notice at all. Like a large, calm woolly dreadnought he voyaged and sniffed wherever he chose, interrupting his master's little chats by disappearing alarmingly for moments at a time, silently rushing after stray cats, walking stiffly and offensively at other and smaller dogs, and lingering over a smell while his master stood holding open the gate for him and bellowing. The children anticipated that one night he would pause, choke, and have a stroke, and it would all be Dan's fault.

The dog who did show a proper spirit of humble gratitude and affection towards the cottage and its inhabitants was a dog whom Sophia called Wodge, because she said that was what he looked like.

Wodge was large, grey, woolly and of an amorphous shape. He was also apparently dumb. No one knew where he lived or whom he belonged to, but on sunny mornings when Sophia was sweeping the sitting room floor with the front door open, Wodge would come sauntering past, and would pause at the threshold and look wistfully in. Sophia would call to him encouragingly, and in he would come, with extreme hesitation and diffidence. He would ponderously sit down exactly in the place where Sophia wished to sweep, look about him, and sigh as if in admiration. Then Sophia would pat him; and at first he showed no signs of pleasure, looking at her almost with reproach as though to ask, 'Why do you waste your caresses on so miserable a thing as myself?' But gradually his manner would change. First his stumpy tail and then his firm, fat body would begin to agitate, until he was shaking all over with rapture and looking up adoringly at Sophia.

Then, as though reminding himself that violent delights have violent ends, he would slowly get up, shake himself, and saunter soberly away. He resembled a sheepdog more than anything else, but there was also a suggestion of fabulousness about him; so may the Beast have looked to Beauty.

As Harry was to give his sister two pounds a week as soon as 'The Racket' was produced, Sophia thought that she would be justified in engaging some daily domestic help.

She accordingly gave her name and address to a domestic agency, humbly stating that she wanted a clean, reliable and honest charwoman (or 'outworker', as the agency preferred to call it, with a fine suggestion of banditry and limitless horizons) to come to the cottage for three hours a day at a salary of fifteen shillings a week.

It is certain that Miss Tessitt was clean and honest, but it is surprising how clean and honest a person can be and still be a most confounded nuisance; and as for her reliability, she could be relied upon to be almost as unsatisfactory as a woman is capable of being, and that was all.

But Sophia, who was certainly an ass in many ways, engaged Miss Tessitt because she was sorry for her, and because she was afraid, after asking one or two questions of her, to say 'Miss Tessitt, you will not suit.' It did not occur to her to say, 'I will let you know,' and then do nothing more about it.

Miss Tessitt called upon Sophia one evening when the boys were out. She arrived panting, and her first remark to Sophia was that It Was A Climb. She added that her heart was weak, and that she was not very strong. She did not look it. Her face had the fixed, red, transparent colour of those whose hearts are weak, and she was too thin. She was neatly, if bittily, dressed and her whole person breathed a dried, prim, cooing spinster-ishness which was emphasized by her thin, prunes-and-prisms voice. She pushed her sentences through a tiny pursed-up mouth shaped like an O, while her round light eyes stared at Sophia indignantly through rimless glasses.

She explained carefully that she was always called Miss Tessitt, not Tessitt or Louisa. It was 'nicer'. She told Sophia four times that she was not strong, for in addition to the weakness of her heart she suffered from high blood pressure, occasional severe headaches, and mysterious fits of dizziness, aches, inabilities of the feet, etc. The list, Sophia felt, was capable of extending indefinitely.

She could cook a little, but she did not like it. In fact, she did not care for rough work at all. Nor for washing, of course. When she was with Mrs Lacey of Priory Walk, every bit of washing was sent out every week. Every bit of it. Even bits that most ladies would have wanted done at home. Mrs Lacey had a flat. That was very convenient, because flats had no stairs, and stairs were bad for Miss Tessitt's heart, blood pressure and feet.

Sophia timidly pointed out that the cottage stairs were a
very short flight.

'But very narrow, are they not?' said Miss Tessitt looking
at them in a melancholy way. 'Very dangerous, Ay should say.
A person might easily stumble on them, might they not? One
of them is broken. Look,' and Miss Tessitt pointed unerringly
with the umbrella which she had brought out to fend off the
rigours of a clear April twilight. 'You'll 'ave that seen to, will
you not? Ay might stumble on it, and fall, and be laid up a
'elpless cripple for the rest of may life, and Ay am not yet
turned six-and-forty. Are all the floors parquet?'

Sophia confessed that they were.

'That would mean a lot of work,' remarked Miss Tessitt
impersonally, as though this fact would not concern her at all.
'Mrs Lacey only had parquet in the drorin'-room. May knees
give may a lot of trouble, may knees do. It is a small place, is
it not?' she observed, looking commiseratingly at Sophia and
then slowly round the sitting room. She added, 'But compect,
is it not? Very compect,' and Sophia felt that the cottage's
reputation was redeemed.

By a series of hints, hesitancies and avoidances of any coarse
remarks about references, Sophia and Miss Tessitt at length
arrived at the decision that Miss Tessitt should enter Sophia's
employment at the salary mentioned to the agency; and she
was to begin work on the following Monday. She did not look
at all pleased about it. Once or twice Sophia, who was already
wondering whether Miss Tessitt would be any use at all, was
alarmed to hear her give a deep sigh. However – 'It is may
indigestion,' explained Miss Tessitt graciously, laying a gloved
hand upon her bosom.

She paused on the threshold as Sophia was showing her out,
and pointed the umbrella at the steps.

'Somewen does not know how to clean steps,' she said with
playful severity. 'They do not look very nace, do they, now?'

'Oh, that's poor old Mrs Barker,' said Sophia, heartily and
rashly. 'She cleans them for one and sixpence a week.'

Miss Tessitt grew suddenly stiff all over. The umbrella remained suspended above the steps, as though frozen with horror. The round eyes widened, and stared at Sophia.

'Not old Mrs Barker of Cannon's End?'

'She does live in Cannon's End. Why?'

'Oh dear, Ay am afraid Ay could never work comfortably for a lady who had old Mrs Barker. She is a dreadful old woman. Ay often see her about. It always seems dreadful to may that a *woman* could let herself Sink So Low, does it not? Whay, the police have told her that if she does not clean 'erself up, she must leave the neighbour'ood. Oh dear, Ay hope she does not come here very often?'

'Twice a week, on Wednesdays and Saturdays,' said Sophia, looking at her. She was thinking how much nicer was old Mrs Barker than Miss Tessitt, despite the latter's honesty, realiability and cleanliness.

'Well, Ay shall not be here until long after she 'as gone, Ay 'ope. Ay shall not be able to get here until twelve o'clock. It upsets may for the rest of the day if Ay have to get up early.'

So Miss Tessitt went away, having planted her standards of living firmly on the soil of the cottage, and begun as she meant to go on.

Sophia went upstairs to her bedroom, and pulled an old padded box covered with a faded brocade to the window. She sat down on it, and leaning her elbows on the sill, stared out into the twilight.

These were the times when she most loved the cottage, when she was alone, surrounded by objects which she loved, by memories, by the thoughts of her absent brothers and friends. Her tiring day's work, and the managing and catering and washing-up which she had to do at home, were all steps which led to these short times of peace and solitary dreaming.

Lovers passed below her window, entwined and silent, or sauntering a little apart and teasing each other in the ringing jeering tone which trembles on the edge of passion and silence. The thrush was dark against the slowly darkening sky, with his

lifted head and quivering throat among the aerial buds, singing
and singing in the twilight while the clear yellow, the green
and rose of sunset fell lower in the west and threw light on
the dim white clouds in the east. Star and song, solitude and
the voices and footsteps of lovers under her window! Dreaming,
she sat there until night had come.

CHAPTER XII

A period of happiness and apparent prosperity now set in for the inhabitants of the cottage. It may be compared to that burst of radiant hot weather which precedes a thunderstorm.

'The Racket' was produced, and was such a success that even the gloomiest persons predicted that it would run through the summer slump until next Christmas. Sophia earned four guineas by writing a series of articles on 'Canadian Landmarks in London' for the C.N.A., and another half-guinea for a poem which she sent to a weekly paper. This was the first poem she had had published. The sight of it in print with her name at the bottom gave her so much joy that for days she thought about little else. Francis liked his job at Graby & Bryant's and seemed to be giving satisfaction to his superiors. Rent and wages and the bill for the milk were paid at once; and the land flowed with sausages, new gramophone records and fresh flowers.

Sophia's housekeeping methods were simple. She bought, strictly paying cash, as much food as everybody could possibly want, and cooked it. Then, whenever anyone was hungry, they could go to the larder and pick. She bought no tinned food except baked beans (they all liked baked beans heated in milk and put on buttered toast) and she never had time to learn how to make pastry, but she brought the making of stews to a fine art, putting big prunes, herbs, and cheap wine into the pot until the stews smelt paradisal and tasted ambrosial. The cottage may be said to have lived on stew, baked beans, sausages, oranges and China tea. Harry often asked for a joint on Sundays, but here Sophia struck. She liked a little peace and solitude on Sundays and she told Harry that he only wanted a joint because respectable people had joints. He could go without or cook it himself. Harry thereupon did cook a leg of mutton, so beautifully, so reverently and naturally, that he was at once established as a master. Sophia went on doing the ordinary cooking, but that was different. Whenever they had a Sunday joint, Harry cooked it.

As there was always music, much to eat, bustling gaiety or restful indolence in the cottage, it was natural that people should like going there. People popped in. They were put up on the sofa. They slept on mattresses in front of the fire. They overflowed into Celia's house, fifteen minutes away across the Heath, and exchanged stew and China tea for Lyons' cakes and grilled steak at half past ten in the morning. Nobody over twenty-five came near the cottage to point out that this way of living was shapeless, extravagant, and queer, and so everyone had a perfectly lovely time; even Sophia, who would sometimes have liked just a little more time to herself, and a pause in the flow of huge, majestic meals.

She had succeeded in keeping the relatives at bay, even though the three had been living in the cottage for nearly five weeks, but it was generally felt that this present state of affairs could not go on much longer, and that sooner or later the relatives must be invited to tea in a body.

Meanwhile, the life led at the cottage was exceedingly odd, but it was harmless. There is, after all, not the slightest reason why people should not stay in their dressing gowns until four in the afternoon and sleep on cushions in the bath and lie around all Sunday arguing about pacifism and God if none of them mind and none of them are drunk, drugged, unchaste or boring. And none of the people who came to the cottage in those first two months were any of these things.

Celia brought earnest young people from the London School of Economics, Sophia invited lazy, intelligent, charming young women with whom she had made friends at University College, Harry and Francis brought no one so far except a hearty chap or two from Northgate, because Francis had not yet acquired his girl, and Harry had not been long enough in 'The Racket' to get to know many people; Edward and Emily Sweeting were in Manchester, rehearsing for the try-out of a new Hensatt show.

But when this idyllic life had been going on for some six weeks, and it was the beginning of May, and Sophia had decided that their lives, if not orderly, were certainly delightful, and Uncle Preston had rung up five times in the fortnight to know how they were getting on, and Sophia had spent some of her article-and-poem money on some black silk and made herself a dress to wear in the evening if she were asked out to dine – a new and sinister element was introduced into life at the cottage.

This was beer.

It says much for the influence which Sophia unconsciously exerted over her brothers that so far their existence in the Vale had been a beerless one. Harry, who liked beer and had got used to it and to all kinds of alcohol on tour, used to drink whenever he felt like it at rehearsals and between them, and sometimes he would say to Sophia, 'Shall I go down to the pub and get some beer?' and Sophia would say, 'Good lord no, beastly stuff. I hate the smell of it. Besides, beer is jolly expensive,' and as Francis did not like it because he had only tasted it once when he was ten and had spat it out immediately, Harry would not bother to press his suggestion.

But when Francis had been in his job three weeks or so, Harry came down and took him out to lunch, and they had beer, and Francis decided that he liked it.

Besides, he was determined not to be melodramatic about drink, because his father had misused it so cruelly. If I never touch a drop, thought Francis, that will be putting too much importance on the stuff. Much more sensible to have it now

and then, and not make a fuss. It isn't likely that I shall become a drunkard, when I remember what Father was like. ...
This was certainly a sensible way of looking at the situation.
It resembled, in its fragile and neat logic, those nautilus shells which put out upon the black and boundless ocean.

The double pressure of Francis's and Harry's desire for beer broke down the barriers of Sophia's influence. Beer bottles were frequently seen at the cottage. Indeed, as the days went on, they were seen there too frequently to meet with the approval of Miss Tessitt, who was, of course, a total abstainer.

'Ay have always thanked Ged that never a drop 'as passed may lips since Ay was five years old and may Uncle Frank, in fun of course, gave may some port in a spoon, Ay was very sick. Ay was most unwell for days,' said Miss Tessitt, picking up the beer bottles rather as though they had been dead stoats.

Old Mrs Barker, on the other hand, liked to think of the children drinking beer. She would look pleased when she saw the empty beer bottles through the open door on Saturday mornings when she came to do the step. 'Been 'avin' a party, dear?' she would ask Sophia. 'Thass right. Enjoy yourself while you can, I say.' Mrs Barker never referred to her own feelings about beer, but Sophia judged from her appearance when encountered on Saturday nights in the High Street that she liked it.

It was just possible that Harry and Francis craved for madder music and stronger wine than the China tea and baked beans, the arguments and rather intelligent jokes, provided by the friends of Celia and Sophia. Also, Harry was tired of kissing these young women, whom he had known for some time; while Francis not only thought them unattractive but would have been afraid to kiss them even if he had; they were all too old and too clever.

None of Sophia's intelligent friends took any notice when they were proposed to by Harry; they laughed, patted him and said 'Bless you, no I won't,' while the unintelligent ones fell rather miserably in love with him and bored Sophia very much by asking her if she thought Harry Really Cared? Sophia's two stock replies to this question, given according to the seriousness of the case, were, 'I shouldn't think so for a moment' and 'Good god, of course not.'

But with the introduction of the beer and the development of that dreary festival known as a beer party, Harry and Francis got more kick out of the impromptu gatherings. Faces which Harry had known since he was twelve grew hazy, mysterious and freshly alluring when seen through a fog of beer. Francis derived much pleasure from sitting in a corner playing his quiet, sad little songs to himself on the ukulele while sipping his beer and deciding that he was a sexual maniac. No one, he felt, could have such passions and not be.

Sophia used to get rather bored at the beer parties. She did not like beer. It was a task to her to get through a glass of the stuff. She did not like kissing the earnest and talkative young men which were the chief amorous fare provided for the young women at the beer parties, nor did she want to kiss the hearties. It was true that none of them wanted to kiss her, after she had dodged away once or twice or carefully explained that she did not like being kissed, but that annoyed her, too. She would often wander out for a walk on the Heath among the buds and starlight while a beer party was in progress, wondering if she were abnormal until she forgot her boredom and her speculations in the beauty of the night sky.

'We really must have the relations to tea next Saturday,' said Sophia one evening in the middle of May. 'They keep on clamouring.'

'I've got a matinée, of course,' said Harry, very pleased.

'Need we have Angela?' implored Francis.

'Yes, we need. If we don't there'll be a fuss and she'll have to come later, and that'll be worse. Much better to polish them all off at once.'

'How long do you think they'll stay?'

'Hours, I expect. Never mind; we'll have a lovely tea with prawns and watercress and éclairs.'

'Have you had that stair seen to yet?'

'I keep on meaning to ... and the table leg, too. It really isn't safe. I'll try to remember tomorrow evening, on my way back from work.'

All the relations eagerly accepted Sophia's telephoned invitation; and Miss Tessitt, on being told that Sophia's uncles and aunts were coming to tea on Saturday and having received a hint that therefore the cottage might look extra nice, seemed quite relieved and pleased.

'Ay thought you was alone in the world like mayself,' said Miss Tessitt. 'That is to say, Ay have may married sister, but Ay do not count her. There are some people who are worse than no one, in a manner of speakin'. May sister was married very young. Mayself, I believe everyone ought to get married. It makes someone to talk to in the evenings.'

Sophia had paid the guinea to the agency in return for securing the services of Miss Tessitt, and she saw the guinea go with regret. Miss Tessitt was not slovenly, but she was extremely idle and, as she was never tired of explaining to Sophia, her bad health made it impossible for her to work quickly and hard. The result was that the cottage was kept clean, but not very clean; tidy, but not very tidy; and Miss Tessitt was constantly mentioning to Sophia tasks which she could no longer undertake because her feet, her head or blood prevented her. Sophia foresaw the day when Miss Tessitt would sit at home doing nothing at all and having fifteen shillings posted to her every week. She had what she called 'may other people,' which brought her in a further eighteen shillings, and upon this she lived; Sophia wondered if she did as little for may other people as she did for the cottage.

However, the cottage looked very nice on the Saturday afternoon of the tea party.

Sophia and Francis had hurried home from their work and eaten lunch at the Primrose Café in order not to disturb the shining purity of the cottage china and linen; and they were now anxiously cutting bread and butter and putting prawns into a green dish shaped like a vine leaf, and beautifying themselves.

At least, Francis was beautifying himself, but Sophia rather disturbed him by refusing to do anything of the sort.

'*Some* people,' said Sophia, emphatically slapping the cherry-wreathed cups on to the table, 'have time to nim around painting their faces (which heaven knows could do with it because they have no more expression than an elephant's behind) and spending hours fiddling over their clothes. Others would *like* to, but they have more important things to do. Don't worry; Angela will provide all the girlish dew this afternoon. I shall just look as large and plain and cheesy as I can.'

'Aunt Grace will say something about it.'

'Let her. Look, this prawn smells a bit queer. I shall see that she gets it.'

'Harry has all the luck, with his matinée.'

'Nonsense, you know you enjoy upsetting the relatives. Don't pose.'

Indeed, they were both rather looking forward to the party, because the cottage looked so comfortable and elegant, with its shining floor and shining silver cups and My Collection ranged fiercely round the walls, and Sophia's vases of yellow flowers, and a little fire in the grate because the day was cool and rainy. They wanted to show all this glory off.

Of course Aunt Grace and Angela were the first to arrive. 'Trust them!' muttered Francis getting up from the sofa with a charming smile of welcome and going to open the door.

Angela was already standing tiptoe on the step, peeping (she always peeped) in through the top of the door. Her eyes were wide open with excitement and she curled her fingers on either side of her ears and waggled them at Francis in greeting. She looked very pretty in a dark green suit; Sophia glanced down dryly at her own uncleaned brogues and worn tweed skirt. She felt lumpy, dowdy and superior, and wished it were time to begin on the prawns.

'Here we are – here we are, all starving hungry and longing to see the little home!' cried Aunt Grace, kissing Francis. 'Why, Sophia, dear, we haven't seen you for ages.'

'Oh, Sophia, what a *thrilling* place!' cried Angela. 'Oh, isn't it the wee'est, wee'est little house that ever was! Oh, what's that little door over the fireplace? Does it open? Is it a secret panel or something romantic like that?'

'It isn't anything,' said Francis glumly.

'But surely it must open?'

And Angela picked at it with one pink fingernail, looking over her shoulder at Francis.

'No, it doesn't. It's just nothing.'

Sophia then took Angela and Aunt Grace upstairs to take off their hats and coats, and only smiled forbearingly when Angela said that the cottage reminded her of Pooh's House; and Aunt Grace, laying her hand upon her niece's shoulder, whispered:

'Don't you think, you funny girl, you might have put on something a little lighter and prettier for your party? Your little home is so nice, dear, that you ought to want to look nice, too. We all like to see our girl looking pretty, you know.'

Sophia thought vengefully about the prawn, and made no reply beyond an enigmatic grin. It was a really frightening grin, which seemed to look out from deserts where Aunt Grace could never venture, and Sophia was quite pleased with it. Aunt Grace, somewhat alarmed, turned away to the long mirror which gave depth to Sophia's tiny bedroom and began to tidy her hair. It occurred to her that her dead brother-in-law, Sophia's father, had really been very eccentric indeed.

The arrival of Uncle Preston and Auntie Loo in a small brand-new car next created an enormous diversion and excitement. No one had known that they were even thinking of buying one.

Uncle Preston was rather worried about the car. It was either not going as fast as it could, or it knocked, or the windscreen wiper was jammed or something; Sophia, who was bored by cars, could not make out quite what was up with it, but something was. Auntie Loo sat inside, looking a little stunned by her new grandeur, but evidently pleased to be there, and carefully holding on her lap a parcel pinned up in brown paper.

Presently Aunt Maxine arrived, in a perfectly square black hat which looked quite meaningless upon her head as though it had been wafted there by a frolic wind, and a taxi. She spent a brisk four minutes having a row with the taximan in which she was worsted, and vented her feelings by giving a tremendous dab on the cottage door knocker.

She was not soothed to find that Harry was not there, and Uncle Preston's new car made her worse still.

'Shouldn't have thought a car that size would be of any use to anyone,' observed Aunt Maxine, stooping with a cigarette drooping out of her mouth, and squinting discontentedly at the inside of the car. 'I nearly bought Chris Carney's big tourer just after Christmas. It holds ten, and he was letting it go for two hundred. Pity I let it slip ... worst of these little cars, they're always going wrong.'

Sophia was in the kitchen making the tea, while everyone else was outside examining the car, and presently she was aware that someone was cautiously and patiently trying to insinuate themselves into the kitchen; it was not easy for a plump person to do this when someone else was in the kitchen and the flap table was in use.

'Auntie Loo! I'm so sorry there's such a squash – there, that's better. Do come in. Aren't you longing for your tea? I am.'

'I shall be quite ready for it, dear, when you are, but there's no hurry; they're all outside looking at our car. Look, Sophia, I've brought you this. I thought it was rather pretty, and it will last for a little while, too. Fresh flowers are so expensive, though it's nice to have them.'

'Oh, how pretty! It's lovely. Thank you very much, Auntie Loo. How kind of you.'

'And here, dear. A little coal, and some salt, and a pair of tweezers. You should always give those, you know, when you go to see someone in a new house for the first time. It's a funny old custom; I thought it might amuse you.'

Sophia was cross to find tears – those miserable, ready tears which were her bane – rising to her eyes as she bent to kiss Auntie Loo upon her soft wrinkled cheek. The little dark green plant with shining orange berries should go up in her bedroom on the dressing table; she was really pleased with it; it looked as though it had come out of an old Hindu picture.

'I'm so glad you like it, dear. It's only a tiny thing … How are you keeping? I expect you're working very hard at your office, aren't you? You must get very tired.'

'I do, rather.'

Sympathy is a dangerous drug. It suddenly occurred to Sophia, as she put the lid on the teapot, that she did work very hard and get very tired and how rarely anyone asked her if she did.

'You ought to try Mil-koko. That's very good; your uncle takes it regularly now and his nerves have been much better since he began taking it. You should try it, dear. It's only one and threepence for quite a large tin, and it's very economical in use.'

'Yes, I must try it. Thanks awfully, Auntie Loo.'

And, forgetting Mil-koko as though it had never been, Sophia carried the tea into the sitting room.

Uncle Preston was asking Francis questions about the work at Graby & Bryant's, so they were having quite a conversation, but over the three females a languid silence hung. They had nothing to say to one another.

The Gardens had no general conversation. Their chief interest in life was the family and its misdoings, and when two or three of them were gathered together and one was absent, they could always criticize the absent one. But when they were all there together, one could not very well start an absorbing discussion about why on earth Grace did not send Angela to a secretarial college or how on earth Maxine managed to get through her income or what in heaven Preston and Looie wanted with a car.

Hence the silence of Maxine, Grace and Angela. Maxine was also rather jealous of Angela's slimness and curls, and Grace thought Maxine's hat was too killing for words but did not dare to try and convey this opinion by eyebrow and jerk to Angela.

As for Angela, she was always bored when she was not talking, flirting or dressing herself.

'Tea's ready,' said Sophia, setting down the teapot.

This bald announcement revived them all, and they moved towards the tea table; Aunt Maxine lingered a little to examine the panel over the fireplace, asking Sophia if it opened and receiving the reply that no it did not, it was just nothing; and then she too advanced upon the éclairs and the prawns.

The table was a small, gate-legged one, at which there was only comfortable room for three people, so Sophia, Uncle Preston and Aunt Maxine sat down to it, while the others arranged themselves as near to it as they could. Some sat on the sofa (Angela close to Francis, with many smiles and pattings of the seat next to her) and others on the hard and uncomfortable chairs.

'I hope everyone likes China tea,' observed the hostess sternly.

Everyone murmured that they did, though some of them detested it and others had never tasted it.

Sophia poured out Aunt Maxine's cup and put it down in front of her.

She raised the teapot a second time – and one side of the table collapsed, flinging prawns, éclairs and Aunt Maxine's tea all over the legs of Uncle Preston!

'Oh – oh,' wailed Angela. 'Oh, all the lovely tea! oh!'

Uncle Preston sprang to his feet like a wounded faun, dabbing wildly at his trousers and muttering 'T-t-t-t-'

'Are you scalded, dear?'

'Oh, Sophia, what a shame' – Aunt Grace was on her knees eagerly picking up the prawns. It was with a sense of frustration that Sophia, who had not said one word, observed her carefully place the doubtful prawn on the edge of the green plate in awful isolation from its fellows.

Francis had not said a word either.

The disaster was too terrible. He knew what Sophia must feel. He contented himself by exchanging with her one long, meaning look of mingled sympathy, rage and despair and then knelt down to pick up the éclairs, which were considerably bent.

Auntie Loo was mopping Uncle Preston and the carpet alternately, while Aunt Maxine slapped Sophia on the back and told her not to look so down in the mouth. Aunt Maxine thought it was rather a joke. Poor Preston's face! Never should she forget it!

'Very *odd* the table suddenly *collapsing* like that,' said Uncle Preston when the fragments were all picked up and the company was reseated round the treacherous board. 'Is one of the *legs* loose, by any chance?'

'Must be, damn good thing it wasn't the side with the cups on,' said Aunt Maxine, with her mouth full of tea and sandwich.

'Do try the prawns, dear; they are very good,' interrupted Auntie Loo, who had observed a sudden look of guilt and alarm upon Sophia's face. 'And some bread and butter ... how thin it is, Sophia. Do you use one of those saw knives?'

'I did not *see* the cause of the disaster,' pursued Uncle Preston. 'I confess I was too busy drying myself after my *bath* – heh! heh! heh! But the leg must be loose, surely? When we have finished tea, Francis, we must *inspect* it. Nothing like taking these little matters in hand *immediately*, is there, Looie? We know that at Holmedale, eh? And that reminds me ... that stair. The stair with a crack in it ... have you—'

'Do have an éclair, Uncle Preston.'

'No, thank you. No more. I never take a *large* tea; I find it does not agree with me. A large breakfast, a light lunch, *no tea* and a *good* supper; that is my rule. It has taken me over thirty years to find out what *does* suit me, but now I flatter myself that I *know*.'

'More tea, then? Do.'

'Half a cup. Half a cup, thank you; no more.'

The danger passed, the breath of the whirlwind died before it swooped; and Sophia's expression grew less strained.

(And of course no one inspected the table, so none of the relatives found out what Sophia and Francis afterwards did; that the leg was nearly detached from the pull-out flap, and heeled over drunkenly under the least pressure.

Sophia made up her mind that she would have it seen to that very next Monday.)

CHAPTER XIII

It cannot be denied that this incident cast a gloom. To begin with, there were the disagreeable damp patches on Uncle Preston's knees; there was the shock to the feelings of all, there was the damage to the éclairs, and the surreptitious inspections which everyone gave to their prawns and watercress, in search of stray carpet-hairs or bits of grit, before eating them. Fresh bread and butter must be cut; everyone must be assured several times that the incident would not recur; and though the disaster provided a topic for conversation which lasted almost to the end of the meal and gave eloquence to tongues which might otherwise have been silent, it was not a topic which Sophia, had she been given a choice, would have chosen.

She became rather silent as tea drew to a close, and the conversation grew more and more jerky and facetious; she stole a glance at the clock. It was five. They would certainly stay until six, because Harry would be home by then, but what was to be done with them until six o'clock?

She had already taken Angela and the aunts over the house on a visit of inspection and she was now apprehensive lest Uncle Preston should demand to see the furnishings of the bedrooms, and discover that the stair had not been mended.

But Uncle Preston did not want to see what had been put into the bedrooms. He knew that they were there, two of them, because he had seen them on his previous visit, and he was satisfied. He now wished to sit by the fire in the most comfortable chair, dry his knees, and digest the prawns. With these intentions in mind he sat down immediately they all rose from the table and looked about him with the peculiarly vacuous yet intent expression which the Garden family wore when it was not thinking about anything.

Auntie Loo helped Sophia to carry out the tea things into the kitchen while the others stood about in bored silence, staring at My Collection, picking up things and putting them down again and making no attempt to conceal the fact that they were in need of entertainment.

'Where's your wireless, Sophia?' asked Angela, who was practising dance steps on the parquet, with one eye on Francis.

'We haven't got one.'

'Haven't you? Aren't you absolutely lost without it? Mumsie and I would be, wouldn't we? Mumsie likes to have it in the kitchen in the morning while she's talking to the girl about the meals, and then I have it in the bathroom while I'm doing my little daily dozen, and we always have it on at lunchtime and Mumsie likes to listen to the Children's Hour just after tea. She's a great big baby, I always tell her, and then there's the dance music, of course—'

'You like the wireless, then?' said Francis, putting coal on the fire with his back to her.

Ripples of laughter from Angela and tossings of the curls.

'Sarky, aren't you, of course we do, or we shouldn't be always listening to it. We'd feel quite lonesome without our little portable, shouldn't we, Mumsie?'

'We should indeed, dear. But I expect Sophia prefers something classical. They often have really good music on the wireless, you know, Sophia. You really ought to get one, dear. It's company when you're alone.'

'Yes, I really must think about it,' said Sophia amiably, who hated the wireless, next to cockroaches, more than anything in the world. She thought, I have company when I am alone, too much. So much that I shall never find time to get it all into words, on to paper, out of my mind, so that my head feels blown clean inside as though a west wind had gone through it.

A diversion was here created by a subdued rattling at the kitchen door which was latched on the sitting room side so that it could not be opened from the kitchen, and Aunt Maxine was observed to be much amused about something, jerking her thumb at the kitchen door, laughing behind her hand, pointing, and drawing the attention of the bewildered company to what was going on.

Uncle Preston was missing.

Sophia saw immediately what had happened, and hastened to release him. He came out, trying not to look cross and self-conscious, while everyone at once burst into a roar of conversation and Francis rushed upstairs to laugh out of his bedroom window.

Uncle Preston had been to wash his prawny fingers in the bathroom, which could only be reached through the kitchen and Aunt Maxine had chosen thus delicately to draw attention, by locking the kitchen door, to his absence and his errand.

But when this incident had been relished by all, languor again descended upon the company; and it was only a quarter past five.

Suddenly Sophia pulled herself together. This just would not do.

'Let's play "Truth", she announced, more as a command than as a suggestion. 'It's very easy, and great fun. Francis, get some pencils and paper.'

'Oh dear, is it one of those brainy games?'

'Do we have to draw? I'm afraid I can't draw, dear.'

'I hope it is not a very *complicated* game; it always takes me some time to master the *rules*, and by the time I know them well enough to enjoy the game, it is time to stop *playing* – heh! heh! heh!'

'Haven't you any cards? (What is 'ome without a joker? as they say.) We might play bridge – Grace plays, don't you? And Preston – what about Angela?'

'No, we'll play Truth. It isn't at all complicated and you won't have to draw, Auntie Loo. It's quite simple. Francis, you tell them.'

'Another name for it is the Dodo Game,' began Francis.

'What a weird name! Why is it called that?' interrupted Angela.

'Oh, I'm not sure – I believe some woman in a book called Dodo used to play it – never mind that now. Well, I give each of you a piece of paper. It's got Virtues and Vices written on it – Beauty, Truthfulness, Tact, Greed, Tidiness and things like that – and the highest mark is Ten. We each have our names written at the top, but of course we don't mark our own papers, and all the marking is done anonymously, though you can confess what marks you gave if you like when the papers are read out afterwards. Then the slips are passed round and each person puts a mark against the Virtue or Vice for someone else. For instance, Aunt Maxine, if Auntie Loo deserved eight for Greed in your opinion, you would put an eight against Greed on her paper.'

'But that would be rather a high mark, dear,' protested Auntie Loo, mildly, 'and I am not really greedy. At least, I try not to be. But there! it is only a game, and one must not take it seriously, must one? Well, it sounds most amusing. I think I understand the rules. Shall we begin?'

'Just a minute, 'continued Francis. 'Then we add up everyone's marks for each quality, and the highest total score wins. For instance, if Aunt Maxine had ten for Looks, marked down on her paper six times by six people, she would have 60 for Looks and be top. Now does everyone understand? Let's begin.'

But they could not begin yet because Uncle Preston did not understand and Francis had to sit beside him and explain to him on paper. Aunt Maxine was rather scornful about a kid's game, and Aunt Grace, whose favourite pastime was talking, wanted to indulge in it.

But as soon as Sophia and Francis had succeeded in showing them that the Dodo Game was a heaven-sent way of telling each other home truths without actually signing their names to the statement, they fell upon the game with avidity.

'Flirtatiousness – oh, do put in flirtatiousness!' begged Angela, hanging over Francis as he wrote out the slips. '*I* know someone I'm going to give *ten* to, for flirtatiousness!'

'We'll put in silliness, too,' observed Francis. 'And lack of S.A., shall we?'

'Put in extravagance,' Aunt Maxine suggested, 'and fussiness.'

Sophia and Francis knew, of course, that the Dodo Game was a rash one to play with relatives who were all only too ready to take dirty cracks at one another without the help of the Dodo Game, but they had not yet learned that it is far, far wiser when playing this game, to leave out the vices and include only the virtues.

Chasms have slid open before unsuspecting feet, the trusts of a lifetime have been betrayed, the illusions of forty years gone bouncing to the twelve winds of heaven because of the Dodo Game. It might be described, among parlour games, as Public Enemy No. 1.

Sophia and Francis dimly suspected this, but alas! their suspicions only made them more eager to go ahead with it.

There was some difficulty about the choosing of the Vices and Virtues, because all the relatives except Auntie Loo wanted the list to consist entirely of Vices. Vices were more fun.

However, at length seven qualities were chosen; Looks, Greed, Sex Appeal ('not the same as Looks; nothing to do with them' explained Francis), Tidiness, Brains, Good Temper and Selfishness, as there were seven people present; and the highest score gained for any one quality was fixed at sixty marks.

Then everyone pulled in their chair to the fire, the curtains were drawn against the cool May evening as though winter had returned, the pencils were handed round, and the game began.

Francis and Sophia, of course, could not give vent to their prejudices. If they had, everyone except Auntie Loo would have got 0 for Good Temper, Looks and Brains, and 10 for

Selfishness. But as hosts they could not be candid, and they forced themselves to be pleasant, if not strictly just; and their estimates wandered round the cool regions of fives, sixes and sevens, when they were considering the Greed of Uncle Preston or the Sex Appeal of Aunt Grace.

But no such restrictions hampered the rest of the party.

It is possible, of course, to play the Dodo Game with intelligence, justice and mercy. It is also possible to use it as a gorgeous opportunity for taking whangs at people and paying off old scores. It need scarcely be said which was the method adopted by the Gardens.

Sophia, having finished a paper before her neighbour, stole a look round the circle of intent faces, bent over their problems, and felt quite alarmed.

She had never seen countenances expressing so much energy, spite and furiousness, concentrated in one small circle; the relations looked like a nineteenth-century engraving called 'The King Over The Water: a Jacobite Meeting in the Cellars of Auld Reekie.' Every now and then one of them would give a sudden, fierce, satisfied nod and slowly, cruelly inscribe a 2 or a 9 on the paper which they held. No one spoke. No one giggled. The Dodo Game had them in its grip. Even Angela seemed infected by the spirit of the meeting, and sat frowning over her paper, forgetting to snuggle up to Francis, who had just mercifully given her seven for sex appeal when he considered that she deserved one.

Sophia signalled her apprehensions to Francis, who looked pleased. He sat back luxuriously on the sofa and waited for the fun to begin.

She collected the papers, which were handed to her in a kind of drugged, stealthy hush which was far from reassuring, and shuffled them. She saw that the first one on the sheaf was Auntie Loo's; well, that was not so bad. Even if everyone had been spiteful to dear Auntie Loo, the latter would not mind very much; she was used to it, and it would put the others in a good temper to laugh at her.

'Well ...' began Sophia, a little nervously. She wanted to laugh but did not dare. 'This is Auntie Loo's paper. She gets 23 for Looks – that's made up of 7, 8, 2, 1, 3 and 2. There, Auntie Loo! Two of us think you're quite nice-looking, and four of us don't! I wonder,' said Sophia, looking thoughtfully at Angela. 'I wonder who gave you *one?*'

'Well, dear, I never was a beauty,' said Auntie Loo comfortably; she had taken out a little piece of pale blue crochet, and was working away and listening with a cheerful smile. 'What else have I got?'

'Only seventeen for Greed (so I should hope, indeed; I gave you 0) and eleven for Sex Appeal (Well, that's very rude of them, but I shouldn't mind if I were you) – oh – 50 for Tidiness – (I'm glad there's some justice in the world; you ought to be top for that), and 26 for brains—'

'More than I expected, my dear.'

'Well, I gave you nine for Brains and so did Francis,' said Sophia, recklessly.

'Then,' said Auntie Loo, crocheting busily, with her eyes on her work, 'the rest of the company gave me eight marks for Brains between them.'

Sophia hurried on—

'That's it, dear. And you get fifty for Good Temper, and 27 for Selfishness ... what a shame! Someone gave you 10 for selfishness – such nonsense.'

She turned to the next sheet. She guessed by Aunt Maxine's steady glare into the fire who had given Auntie Loo 10 for Selfishness. That was because of the new car.

She unobtrusively shuffled the papers so that Aunt Maxine's paper came next instead of last. Aunt Maxine should go through the hoop immediately.

'Aunt Maxine,' she read out clearly ...

Aunt Maxine tried not to look self-conscious. She smiled and nodded tolerantly, as though to say 'Bring on your tumbrils,' gazing meanwhile into the fire; her large legs in their silk stockings were crossed over one another and she showed a length

of clean but oddly repulsive light petticoat. In that moment
Sophia disliked her aunt extremely. Coarse good humour does
not excuse every petty vice that flourishes in a vulgar nature,
and Sophia decided that in the past she had been too tolerant
of Aunt Maxine's faults.

'Looks, 36. It would probably have been more, only two very
critical people gave you 2 and 3.'

'Still that's not so bad. It's over half marks,' retorted Aunt
Maxine, still staring into the fire with the complacent smile.
She had evidently decided not to be shaken, but at the reference
to the very critical people her smile became a little set. Angela
and Aunt Grace carefully avoided looking at each other.

'Greed, 51,' read out Sophia.

'Quite true. I do enjoy my food, I'm glad to say. I'm not like
some people who make their own lives and everyone else's a
misery with their precious digestions. Go on, Sophia. It's most
interesting.'

'But still, Maxine – *fifty-one* marks for Greed out of a possible *sixty!*' tittered Uncle Preston, at whom the dart about
digestions had been aimed. 'Why, that almost makes Greed
your *besetting sin*, does it not? heh! heh! heh!'

'Sex Appeal, 20.'

Aunt Maxine's smile had now almost vanished, but still
she stared into the fire. She made no comment on this announcement, even when Auntie Loo said soothingly, 'I gave
you seven, dear. That was for your hair and eyes,' for Auntie
Loo could never, like most of her generation, be made to realize
the difference between good looks and sex appeal. Sophia and
Francis, out of a desperate sense of chivalry, had given their
unfortunate aunt six marks each, thereby mortally perjuring
themselves; and had not mended matters for after this there
came a sullen pair of O's and a one.

'Tidiness, 13.'

'Here, I say, dammit!' cried the lioness, roused at last. 'Anyone
would think I was a slut. Thirteen, indeed! Here, let me see
– how d'you make that out?: 6 – 5 – 2 – 0 – 0 – 0. Who put

in all those 0's? A joke's a joke, but this is going a bit too far
... silly rubbish.'

'Perhaps you would rather I didn't go on?' asked Sophia
coolly. Odd that the slander on her neatness should have roused
Aunt Maxine when the really unjust figures about her supposed
greed did not! One never knew people ...

'Oh, go on, by all means. It's damned interesting. At least
I know where I stand with some of you.'

The lioness was now in the open, roused and dangerous,
and the rest of the party was rather embarrassed but full of
a fearful joy.

'Brains, 19.'

'I gave you nine for brains, dear. I always think you're so
good at those crossword puzzles,' said Auntie Loo.

'Thank you very much, Looie; very kind of you, I'm sure,'
was Aunt Maxine's reply, awful with sarcasm.

'Good Temper, 12,' read Sophia quickly.

'How many? Twenty?'

'No ... twelve.'

'Twelve? Here ... let me see. $5 - 5 - 0 - 2 - 0 - 0$. Well,
that's candid, I must say. That's straight from the shoulder. And
who was good enough to give me two, I should like to know?'

'Me, dear,' replied Auntie Loo, unmoved. 'You have a very
quick temper, you know. Just like poor Grandpapa, and poor
Oliver, and Hartley. I've often thought what a trial it must be
to you; such a nasty thing to have. Never mind, everyone makes
excuses for hasty people; it's only the mild-spoken ones who
are never allowed to fly out.'

And Auntie Loo agitated her ball of crochet cotton, which
rolled on to the floor and was picked up by Francis.

'Well, go on, go on. There's Selfishness to come yet, isn't
there? I suppose I've got sixty for selfishness. Well, this has
been a revelation to me. It's opened my eyes in a way I shan't
forget in a hurry. Don't misunderstand me, Sophia. I'm not
sorry I came here this afternoon. I wouldn't have missed it for
anything. There's nothing like knowing where you stand, after

all; if you don't, you may make a fool of yourself by doing some little act of kindness to people who don't deserve it. Well, go on, Sophia. What are you waiting for? Selfishness, 60.'

'No, 50,' said Sophia, in the midst of a hush which was certainly disagreeable.

'I told you so,' exclaimed Aunt Maxine triumphantly, though she had told them nothing of the kind. 'I knew it. Let me see − 7 − 6 − 10 − 10 − 9 − 8. Everyone goes as high as they dare, you see, and two people − and I can make a pretty good guess who they are − go the whole hog. Well, it doesn't matter. It's only a game, after all.' (A fact which Aunt Maxine seemed to have forgotten; she might have been coping with the retreat from Moscow.) 'Just amusement. It's funny. The whole thing's funny, really, if one looks at it as a give-away of certain people's characters. Well ... I shall know what to do now, anyway,' and she crumpled the paper into a ball and threw it into the fire. 'Who comes next?'

'Uncle Preston.'

'Ah!' said Uncle Preston, leaning forward eagerly. 'Now may we have *all* the details of this one, please, *slowly* and clearly. It should be *most* interesting.'

Sophia, looking apprehensively at the paper, had few doubts about that. An expression of spiteful triumph had replaced the sullen rage on Aunt Maxine's face and one of long-suffering wisdom adorned Aunt Grace's; evidently they had been doing their duty.

'Looks, 17 ...' began Sophia faintly.

Uncle Preston started as though stung. A bitter smile passed over his face. He glanced sharply at Aunt Maxine, but she was staring at the mantelpiece; Aunt Grace was staring at her toes.

'The total, I think you said, is sixty?' asked Uncle Preston.

'Yes, Uncle Preston.'

'And I have been awarded seventeen marks for Looks out of a total of sixty.'

'Yes, Uncle Preston.'

'May I ask you to read out the details of the total?'

'6 – 5 – 1 – 2 – 1 – 2,' said Sophia dutifully, not daring to look up.

'That is very curious, Sophia. Very strange indeed. I am not usually spoken of as an *ugly* man. Of course, I do not pretend to be an Adonis, heh! nor even a *film star*, heh! heh! But I certainly should not describe myself as *ugly*. Well, well, go on.'

'Greed,' went on his niece, even more faintly, '53.'

There was a frightful pause.

'May I ask you to repeat the total?' asked Uncle Preston, with a politeness more terrible than any wrath.

'Fifty-three, Uncle Preston.'

'Out of a total of sixty marks?'

'Yes, Uncle Preston, I'm afraid so.'

'And how,' demanded Uncle Preston, swelling, 'and how is the total made up?'

'10 – 10 – 8 – 10 – 7 – 8.'

'So three of the persons present gave me ten marks for Greed. And one gave me *seven*, which is perhaps worse. I put those three tens down to malice. Ignorant, blind malice. But the seven ... no, there was *cunning* behind that blow.'

'That was me, dear, who gave you seven,' said Auntie Loo, pulling out the scallops of her crochet. 'You are rather greedy sometimes, you know. Especially with treacle tart and roast pork and any kind of cake. Now aren't you?'

Uncle Preston did not reply, but motioned to Sophia to continue. Everyone felt that the sooner the end of his paper was reached, the better, and Sophia hastened on—

'Sex Appeal – 9.'

'Oh well, that is a joke, of course,' said Uncle Preston, laughing heartily with a most disagreeable effect. 'I hope I can appreciate a *joke* as well as anyone. And how is *that* total made up?'

'6 – 3 – 0 – 0 – 0 – 0.'

'And what hand did you have in *that*, Looie, since you seem to know your own mind so well when it comes to estimating my character?'

'I gave you the six, dear. You were very attractive as a young man, you know,' quietly replied Auntie Loo. And she looked affectionately across at him with her kind eyes; Sophia, who had not been able to bring herself to give Uncle Preston more than three, while Francis ruthlessly gave him 0, wondered how she could.

Fortunately Uncle Preston was a little soothed by receiving 48 for Tidiness, a virtue which even spite must grant him, and 50 for Brains, for Aunt Maxine and Aunt Grace and Angela considered that Uncle Preston must naturally be clever, because he was a man. Besides, he ran a business. But Sophia only gave him four for Brains; she considered him unintelligent, even if he was a man.

But the family got into their stride again with Good Temper, for which Uncle Preston received the awful total of 14. This flung him into considerable agitation, and the game was held up for some ten minutes while Uncle Preston debated whether the occasional firmness which he was unfortunately compelled to display could really be counted as bad temper; and Auntie Loo delivered another death blow by saying that certainly it could and adding that she had given him two for Good Temper because it was all he deserved. With the final cheering announcement that Uncle Preston had received 56 marks for Selfishness, the game of Dodo came to an abrupt and welcome end, for Harry's key was heard in the door, and all turned with the greatest pleasure and relief to welcome him.

'You look much older, Harry. What have you been doing to yourself?' said Aunt Grace, when the general clamour of greeting had died down.

She said what all the relatives were thinking. Harry, who was not yet twenty-one, had always an air of extreme self-possession and gay calm which made him seem older than he was; and now he had obtained his first part in a West End show, he was daily drinking gin-and-its with elaborately lacquered young women and double whiskies with cynical yet surprisingly easily-taken-in elderly men, and usually pretending, for the sake of conformity and politeness, to be much more enthusiastic about the state of being alive than he actually felt. Most persons who are on the stage demand such yea-saying; when this over-vivacious, emphatic, egoistic atmosphere is lacking, they become suspicious.

Harry enjoyed the gin-and-its, double whiskies and young women, but he found the yea-saying a strain. The experiences of his childhood had disposed him more towards nay-saying; and the effort of pretending to be constantly on top of life made him look a little fine-drawn and older.

'Late nights, I expect, isn't it, dear?' said Auntie Loo. 'Don't you get rather tired, doing the same thing every evening? I should, I'm sure.'

'Oh well, Auntie Loo, I don't have much to do, you know. The stage managing is quite hard work, but the acting is really nothing; I don't come on until the last act, and then all I say is 'You betta come clean, Spike'.'

"You betta come clean, Spike',' murmured Auntie Loo. 'That seems quite easy to remember. 'You betta come clean, Spike.' And who is Spike, dear? The villain?'

'One of them. There are four. But you'll see who everybody is when you come next week, I hope. I've got two seats for you and Uncle Preston, for next Tuesday evening, and later on I'll get two for you if you like, Aunt Grace.'

This put everyone in such a good humour (even Aunt Maxine, who had already seen 'The Racket' from seats in the dress circle with Miss Van Veek, and who naturally enjoyed feeling herself superior to those who were getting their seats for nothing) that the rest of the visit passed off in the greatest cheerfulness and comfort.

Harry's beauty, charm and obvious wish to please contrasted favourably with the grim, this-is-my-duty-so-I'm-doing-it air of Sophia and the specious smiles of Francis; all the poor relatives, who had really had rather a nasty afternoon, expanded with pathetic gratitude in the sunlight of his attentive, friendly manner and felt, not for the first time, that he was the nicest of the three.

Sophia and Francis, exchanging relieved grins as they saw the relations off, wondered sardonically how he had the patience to do it.

'And it isn't as though you liked them any better than we do,' said Sophia, when everyone had gone and the three were lying about the sitting room in attitudes of exhaustion.

'Good god, no. But I'm sorry for them. They're so awful. And besides, poor old weasels, they won't any of them be here for long ...'

'Angela will,' said Francis gloomily.

' ... so one may as well be decent to them. I don't mind them, really, as long as they don't try to run me. That *does* make me see red, if you like. Look here, Sophia, will you get in some beer? I met a marvellous girl today – god! she's marvellous, she's got better legs than Marlene – and I want to bring her back here after the show tonight. I've told her what a marvellous place we've got and she's awfully keen to see it. She's living in digs, you see, and she hates it because she's awfully domesticated, really. And I may bring another girl, as well. Girl called June Dawne, who's in "Fifty Grand".'

'Oh ... well, I'll get some when I go out. Would you like me to wait up?'

'Not unless you want to. Do if you like, of course. I don't expect they'll stay long. We shall just have a cheery half-hour and we shall have a drink or two, and they'll see the place.'

'Well, that will be very nice, darling. I don't think I will wait up, if you don't mind, because it will make it rather late and ...'

She did not finish her sentence; she was going to say that she never knew what to say to marvellous girls, but she substituted instead 'The Deedle can stay up, if he likes.'

'I was going to anyway,' said Francis mildly.

And, as Sophia was not looking at them, the brothers exchanged a glance.

It said much. It said that sisters, even the nicest of them, and Sophia was certainly a very good sort, were sometimes best in bed; it said that chaps must be catered for, chaps must have a good time and live their own lives; it said that legs which were better than Marlene's were more attractive than wit, education and baked beans on toast. It said that Harry and Francis were beginning to realize, though as yet through a glass darkly, the potentialities of the cottage.

CHAPTER XIV

Francis's opinion of Mr Graby never had a chance to blossom
normally, because after his first interview with Mr Graby he
never again saw the latter as a human being.

The instant that Francis became an Employee, Mr Graby
became the Employer; otherwise the Old Man, Laughing
Gravy, Gravy Soup, or, when mentioned in conjunction with
Mr Bryant, Gravy and Potato. He became a kind of inscrutable,
capricious and all-powerful ogre whose arrival made everyone
work a little faster and whose departure made everyone sit
back, relax their muscles and begin to rag their neighbour in
sheer relief. This is the usual defect of an employer's arrival
and departure, despite the protestations to the contrary which
are occasionally loyally lilted from a column in *The Times*.

The personnel and routine of the offices of Graby, Bryant
& Co. Ltd. resembled, like the personnel and routine of most
offices, a comic opera in full blast.

When a building and some hundred persons is devoted to
furthering the solemn and religious ends of Commerce, cheerfulness will keep breaking through; just as in a theatre where
a company of actors is devoting itself to producing gaiety and
illusion, a grim devotion to duty and disregard of personal
discomforts will develop.

But it was not until Francis had been employed there for
nearly a fortnight that he perceived the comic opera analogy,

and began to tell funny stories about what happened at work. During his first fortnight there he was too much in earnest about his work to see any person or situation in the impersonal way which perceives humour. He was afraid of being late, of being lazy, of being inefficient, of being sacked. All he wanted was to be the best and most efficient office boy that Graby & Bryant had ever had; and also the most interesting one (but this ambition was subconscious and did not begin to express itself until his first nervousness had died down.)

He certainly succeeded, in his first day at Graby & Bryant's, in establishing himself as the most unusual and interesting office boy the firm had ever had.

By lunch time on that first Monday morning the question 'Seen what the cat's brought in, down in Ulick's?' was all over the building; and everyone was making excuses to go through the typists' room (otherwise called Ulick's, because it was under the control of Miss Ulick, Mr Graby's personal secretary) in order to look at Francis.

This would have been very bad for Francis if he had known it, but fortunately he was so painfully absorbed by his small, fiddling but necessary tasks that he never thought about whether people were noticing him. He usually thought about this a great deal, but today all his energies were turned on to doing up parcels, stamping letters and going out to post them, running messages and memorizing names, faces, and official positions.

He never once thought that it was degrading that he, the son of a doctor and educated at a good second-class Public School should be an office boy. Snobbery was not one of the vices which the Garden children had acquired. Francis was arrogant, with a great sense of personal dignity and of his own entity, but he had no pride of class. He had his own private, vivid life, shut away from everyone; and licking labels and calling ill-bred men 'Sir' naturally did not affect this private dignity.

This advantage was one of the few which the three children had gained from their shapeless and traditionless upbringing. They slipped easily from world to world, carried by this lack of conventional ideas and their own tough middle-class stock; and did not waste a lot of valuable energy in deploring the fact that A was not a lady and B was not virtuous.

As Sophia would meditatively say, 'I am not always worrying because a tortoise isn't a guinea pig and wanting it to be. I say, "Praise be to Allah for the diversity of his creatures."' And so far as it were possible, the three applied this outlook to human beings.

So Francis was spared the agonies of snobbery in the offices of Graby & Bryant; and had more energy for making tea and answering the telephone; and by Monday evening the five typists had decided he was quite crackers and as fresh as they make them, but rather – at least, he would have been if he had not been a kid and an office boy at that – rather attractive.

Of course they did not betray this opinion to Francis. They all, from Lily Spain, aged seventeen and three-quarters, to Miss Ulick, aged thirty-eight and a half, at first set out to snub him.

Lily Spain received the full shock of Francis's personality when she arrived on that first Monday morning at a quarter to nine. Miss Ulick, acting on instructions from Mr Graby, insisted on Miss Spain getting there a quarter of an hour earlier than the other four. This was because Miss Spain was a junior typist. There was no other reason. She was made to do it because there is a wholesome instinct in the elderly to make the young do what they do not like doing. This is supposed, though no one has ever given satisfying reasons for the supposition, to be good for them.

This extra fifteen minutes added on to her working day was a source of the bitterest grievance to Miss Spain. She thought about it a great deal. She bored her friends by talking about it. 'Oh, shut up, do, misery!' was a familiar cry in her ears and so was 'Put a sock in it, girl, for pity's sake!'

During the weekends, when she had quite a nice time, she almost forgot about that beastly quarter to nine business, but on Sunday night the full injustice of it struck her afresh, added to the horrible certainty that tomorrow would be Monday morning; and as a result she walked into the office, where Francis was diligently polishing the brass rim of the fireguard with a duster, in an extremely bad temper.

Girl ... flashed over Francis, as he looked up and met her dark, sulky, surprised eyes with his own fierce light-blue ones. He did not stop polishing the fender, but smiled at her with his teeth shut together (an odd habit of his when he was nervous) and said 'Good morning.'

Miss Spain did not reply. If this was the new office boy, looking like a duke and grinning at her as though he had known her all his life, she would show him where he got off. If he was not an office boy – and certainly he did not look like one – what business had he in their room?

Curiosity began to mingle with her sulkiness, but she would not indulge it by asking him his name or who he was. She began her elaborate face toilet in front of the mirror (it had been polished; that was Little Sunshine at work, she supposed), and Francis, passing a last satisfied glance over the newly filled inkpots, the uncovered and dusted typewriters, the chairs in position, the mirror, and the type erasers neatly arranged beside each machine, opened the string canister to make sure that it held an ample supply for the day's demands.

He took no more notice of Lily Spain. He had sized her up; and knew exactly how to treat her. Plenty of contempt, with occasional flashes of sympathy, was the diet that would bring Miss Spain to heel.

Not that he wanted her at his heel particularly, but she was a girl, and therefore she must be subdued; she would do to practise on while he was looking for a girl he liked better. He admired her slender ankles displayed by very high heeled shoes, her bright dark eyes and dark curls, but her complexion was not good and – poor Miss Spain – she did not look very clean, in spite of her varnished nails. Her white collar was grubby and there were unsightly stains on the bosom of her red dress.

Had she good teeth? Impossible to say; she had not yet
smiled. Much would depend upon her teeth; he could not even
bother to subdue a girl who had bad teeth.

His silence, industry and new suit soon produced the effect
he wanted.

Miss Spain said sneeringly:

'Busy, aren't you?'

'I've been here since eight,' said he with disarming mildness.
'There was quite a lot to do. Your last chap doesn't seem to
have been very efficient.'

'He was all right,' retorted Lily, defending the grime, pimples,
cheek and laziness of one Wally, who had been her deadly foe
during his time there, and her curiosity, which was now overwhelming, made her add, 'Are you the new office boy, then?'

Francis repressed a natural desire to reply, 'No, I'm Clark
Gable,' and said simply, 'Yes.'

And he added, with an old-fashioned courtesy which made
Lily want to giggle and yet impressed her, 'My name's Garden
– Francis Garden. May I know yours?'

'Miss Spain,' she muttered, staring at him. 'Will you do all
Wally's work, then?'

'Of course.'

'Make the tea and go down to the wharf and everything?'

'I shall do whatever Wally – whoever Wally may have been
– did. Only I shall do it better.'

This was a false move. Lily did not like boys who were
conceited; and this one was only an office boy, even if he was
very well dressed. She was haughtily turning away towards
her typewriter when Francis said:

'What time do the others get here?'

'What others?'

'The other type – wom – young ladies?'

'Nine o'clock,' said she bitterly. 'And it's five past now. *I* have
to get here at a quarter to, and I do, too.'

Francis stared at her. He saw exactly what was needed to
make her his firm ally. He advanced upon her until he was

standing above her, looking down into her surprised and rather
spotty little face.

'I say,' said Francis, in a low, serious voice, 'What a rotten
shame.'

And just then Miss Ulick came in, furling her wet umbrella
and followed by Miss Bates, Miss Cannard, and Miss Forbes;
and the day had begun.

But Francis's aim was achieved. He had made a friend. He
had no more sulks and hauteur from Lily Spain; instead he
had admiration and the liveliest interest in all he said and did,
and frequent and rather unintelligent laughter at his jokes.
She tried to make an alliance with him against the four older
women, who were inclined to snub her, but he was too wise
to take up such an attitude. Besides, her teeth were not good.

The other typists soon got to like him, and became used
to the lack of subservience in his manner. He could not bring
himself to call any of them 'Miss'. He gave them their full name
or just said 'you'; and at first this outraged Miss Ulick, Miss
Bates, Miss Cannard and Miss Forbes. But his manner was so
polite, if unconventional, and he made the tea so deftly and
always chose such nice cakes with the five pence which they
gave him to lay out on their behalf, and he was so intelligent
when he answered the telephone (far more intelligent than
poor Lily Spain, whose task this had been before his arrival),
and he never bungled a message.

He was a wit, too, in a mad and rather shocking way. They
were used to humour of the 'You're another' or the 'A word in
thine ear, fair maid' variety. Francis introduced them to irony
and exaggeration; he drew absurd imaginary verbal pictures for
them, in which he described Mr Graby's home life until they
were all choking with laughter, for he had some of that wild,
high-piled fantastic humour which Sophia loved to exercise.

Of course he had more prejudices to conquer than the one
against his un-office boyish appearance and manner. There
was some resentment because he looked like a comfortably-off
youth, and yet filled one of the lowest jobs in the building at a

pound a week. The typists and some of the junior clerks said (on behalf of the three office boys in the other departments who would certainly never have thought of such a grievance for themselves) that he was taking the pound out of other prospective office boys' mouths. They said that it was a damned shame that Laughing Gravy should push one of his little pets who wanted a spot of pocket money into a soft job; and Francis's own arrogant, faintly ironical and fantastic manner did not make them see his position in a more charitable light.

But presently these antagonisms died away. Francis proved a first-rate, if eccentric, office boy, and Miss Ulick reported as much to Mr Graby, who grunted. His common sense would have preferred that the pale, flashy, stuck-up boy should have proved a failure, but another part of his nature was pleased. He told Uncle Preston that his nephew was getting on well; and Uncle Preston was very surprised.

Had he not told Auntie Loo, Aunt Maxine and Aunt Grace that Francis, poor boy, had no sticking power (just like his unhappy father) and would probably be sacked at the end of the first week?

The unspoken but calm acceptance of Francis by Mr Graby and Miss Ulick gradually percolated throughout the building, and made the small fry also accept him, without bitterness. The large fry, of course, never came in contact with him. Then it was observed by the sharp eyes of Miss Beryl Cannard that Francis's overcoat was not so smart as the famous suit: it was a schoolboy's overcoat, rough and worn and shapeless, and though Francis wore it with a dark red silk scarf and an air, it made him look much younger and less cocksure. He was not so well off, then, as it had at first appeared!

And presently, without affectation or pathos, he told Miss Ulick that he had no father and mother, that they had been unhappy together, and had both died less than a year ago. This statement, which was made simply enough in the course of a gossip over tea one afternoon, moved Miss Ulick, and she asked him if he had been left badly off, and Francis, who was not a money snob either, told her exactly how much money he and Sophia and Harry had.

True, he boasted a little about the three thousand pounds, but Miss Ulick, a sensible woman, saw that this was as yet fairy gold and was not impressed. As soon as she knew that it was really necessary for Francis to earn his own living and found that he was ambitious, she became very fond of him and her attitude affected that of Miss Bates, Miss Cannard and Miss Forbes. They were all much kinder to him.

They found his story strangely pathetic; the idea of the three young orphans living together in their little house fascinated the typists. They kept on telling Francis how sad it was, which made Francis extremely angry, as in his opinion he and Sophia and Harry were having the time of their lives. It was not sad to be an orphan when you were much happier than when your parents had been alive.

Anything, even death (he tried to explain to the shocked typists) was preferable to the kind of family life which he had endured in those last years before his parents died. He had, he told them, an awful sort of feeling left over from his youth (this was the word he used), a feeling as though he could never go back and try to make things better for his father and mother, a feeling of shock and bitterness; and he still missed his mother very much, and his father too, in a queer way. But he was not unhappy because they were dead. If he could bring them back ... he hesitated. Well, certainly he would not want his father back, and his mother would not be happy without his father, and anyway, they were dead and nothing could bring them back. Things were as they were; and that was all there was to it.

But Miss Ulick, Miss Bates, Miss Cannard and Miss Forbes still thought of the three young Gardens as tragic figures, and were kinder to Francis than ever.

So he was happy in his job, and could therefore forget about it when he was not there and devote all his spare time and energy to finding the girl, the adoring and quiescent girl with perfect teeth.

For he had not yet found her. But he was not in so forlorn and girl-less a state as he had been two months ago, because Harry was steadily collecting a posse or charm of girls, young actresses who did crowd work and occasional small parts at Elstree and Twickenham, whom he asked back to the cottage after the show, in twos and threes (but three was not a popular number, somehow) and Francis came in for some of their favours.

He kissed them, for instance. He was surprised to find how easy it was to kiss them, and how alike they all tasted. They looked like brilliantly enamelled and exotic little flowers, so fragile that a kiss would probably blur their bloom, as the sheen on a petal can be spoiled by a breath, and they seemed as unapproachable as queens because of their beauty. But Francis took no notice of these impressions reported by his eyes and his youthful inexperience. He made straight for the exotic flower queens, quietly and masterfully, and kissed them. They liked it; and when Harry told them with laughter that Francis was not quite seventeen, they looked at Francis with respect, not with shame because they had allowed a kid just out of school to get fresh with them. From the superior peak of their eighteen, nineteen or twenty years, the flower queens looked kindly upon Francis and prophesied that he would do well.

All this was rather deplorable. It is possible that Francis was a horrid boy. But his upbringing had not taught him to be afraid of kissing young women. He had been familiar with the idea of doing so from an early age, just as Harry had; they had heard jokes from their father, and had there not been the incident with Miss Leadlay which Sophia had seen through the sitting room window and reported to her brothers? It was really impossible for the Garden boys to look upon young women as unbodied angels and fear to approach them. Their upbringing had made them, so far as one can be in extreme youth, realists.

But Francis dreamed, nevertheless, of love. So did Harry, in a different way. Francis soon became bored by the little flower queens. 'Nice kid but dumb,' Francis would say of some gorgeous girl. 'God, isn't she marvellous!' Harry would retort, in a dazed voice like that of a man who wades slowly through swathes of flowers with bells of blue and yellow dragging their showers of dizzying pollen over his eyelids and lips. On he went, lifting a petal here, a tendril there, and seeking for perfect love, ultimate romance.

'I want a little girl, with perfect teeth. One I can have jokes with, who won't talk when I want to be quiet,' thought Francis in his turn. 'These girls are too expensive for me, and too excitable.' And though he did not put the thought clearly to himself, he was also a little afraid that these young women, in whose natures so little of childishness remained, might laugh at My Collection, his admiration for Rider Haggard's stories, and other things which were dear to him.

What did Sophia think, as she lay upstairs late at night in bed with her severe young face dutifully cold-creamed against the ravages of weather and the calm assault of Time?

It would be half past twelve, perhaps, when the taxi would wake her up, stopping, of course, just under her window.

'Jeez! where's the beer? June, you dumb-bell, you're responsible. Harry darling, where are you? I can't see. Is this the cottage? Jeez! isn't it cute?'

Then Francis, opening the front door and standing on the threshold with his legs a little apart, looking rather dramatic and impressive and not saying anything:

'Hullo, old cock!'

'Jeez! where's my bag? June, you had it. You borrowed my lipstick ...'

'*Sh-h-h*—'

'Sh-h-h yourself. I can do that, too. Why should I sh-h-h, anyway?'

'You'll wake my sister.'

'Oh, god, a million pardons, I'm sure. Got the beer? Come on, June ...'

Whispers, sudden bursts of laughter, somebody stumbles over a chair, the sound of the electric light switch, the sound of beer being opened, the murmur of voices, silence, the switch again ... silence.

Sophia, lying awake in the dark, would tell herself that after all, it was only the third time this had happened and that it was all quite harmless. They were only drinking two bottles of beer and kissing a little in the dark, and being very quiet. It would be easy for her to drop off to sleep again; nice of them to try not to wake her. There was no doubt that her brothers loved her and considered her feelings; and that was all the more reason why she should not show signs of disapproval over their way of enjoying themselves. After all, they had never had any fun as children. It was perfectly natural now that the cork, so to speak, was removed, that the champagne of youth should foam out of the bottle.

Whatever happened, at all costs she must never kill their affection for her by making herself a tiresome, fussing elder sister, a sort of female Uncle Preston.

Any amount of Junes and beer and kisses would be better than that.

All the same, Junes and beer scarcely fitted in with her first noble conception of 'orderly lives'. Something would have to go overboard; and as she turned upon her side, feeling suddenly lonely and shut away in her little room from the warmth and kisses in the room below, she decided that it would probably have to be the orderly lives.

But not without a fight, thought Sophia firmly, digging her nose into the pillow. When things got worse — if things did, but probably they wouldn't — if beer-and-Junes began to have a definitely bad effect upon life at the cottage and the characters of Harry and Francis, then Sophia would put up her tactful and cautious fight under the standard of Orderly Lives for Garden Orphans.

But fortunately the time had not yet come to think of making anything so uncomfortable as a decision.

CHAPTER XV

The part about his job which Francis liked best was going down to the Docks.

This happened on an average every ten days or so; but the most delightful thing about it was that he never knew when the order would be given him; and thus every morning he would go down to the City thinking 'Perhaps I may go down to the Docks today,' and his whole routine would be coloured by this pleasant feeling of excitement and anticipation.

On a blue soft day towards the end of May when London was full of drifting cloud shadows and the stone of its buildings looked very white, he was sent down to the Docks to collect some samples of silica.

He rode off on the top of his 142 bus feeling as exhilarated as though he were in a racing car, with the wind rushing through his hair and the interesting map of the City's streets rolling out on either side of the bus. While the houses were still tall and decorated with gold lettering he saw two exciting cartloads; one of stiff hides, splaying out to every point of the compass with a bored-looking boy sitting on the top of them; and one of curly iron filings. It was oddly pleasant to see so many iron filings at once – goodness and mankind's peculiar make-up alone knew why. 'Coo! what a lot of iron filings!' one thought, hanging over the side of the bus like everybody else, and staring; and one felt pleased.

But soon the tall, sinister warehouses with their red flaps
began to dwindle as the bus moved down into Rotherhithe.
Here the thrilling little houses began; thrilling in that old and
finer sense of the word, which means a *frisson*, a strange chord
struck suddenly upon the harp of the imagination. Goblins
might live in these little houses of two low storeys, which
were covered with dark yellow plaster of perhaps a hundred
and twenty years old; the tremendous bright sky which swept
over them dwarfed them still more. One had a door knocker
like a hand grasping a wreath of iron flowers; some had little
spaces of bright coarse grass in front, with the sturdy flowers
that grow in cities; some had miniature Ionic columns on each
side of their sooty front doors. Smaller they grew, until the
bus towered over them as it thundered by. There were dates
on some of them. 'Liverpool Lawn, 1811', 'Waterloo Square,
1817'. Back into the past went the motor bus under the towering
sky, until the clouds seemed to rise and rise, the little houses
to cower and dwindle; and one saw in fancy the figure of a
man on horseback across the heavens, and realized that the
little goblin-houses had been built when the mighty shade of
Napoleon lay over Europe.

At the Surrey Docks Station Francis got down, and hesitated
for a moment, wondering whether he should take a bus across
the three bridges to Tartar Lane, or walk. Whether he walked
or rode, he might be held up for half an hour while a string of
barges or a tug went under any one of the three swing bridges,
which cut across the route to Tartar Lane. Down in the Docks,
the river rules the road traffic. The Thames has no power at
all in New Bond Street, but near Tartar Lane, roads running
close to the Docks are liable to be split suddenly in half while
a ship sails through the middle of them, and the passengers
sit resignedly in the motor buses, getting very friendly while
they wait to be released.

Francis decided to take a motor bus because he liked being
held up in one. Last time he came down to Tartar Lane he
was held up for over half an hour, and an old man who was

sitting next to him alternately showed him wonderful green and red dragons tattooed on his legs and talked very fiercely against these 'ere Fasheests, who, he thought, would land us in a mess if we wasn't careful.

So he got into a bus, hoping for the best, and it set off along an ordinary dusty white London road running between wooden fences, above which showed long piles of bright gold planks; and they safely passed the first bridge, and everyone looked hopeful.

But when they got to the second bridge, by which stood a neat old yellow house with a bush of lilac blowing sideways in its garden and making it look, not like a house in the country, but like exactly what it was, a cottage in the heart of London, that reef of linked and submerged villages – when the bus got there it slowed down in a resigned manner, and stopped.

The engine's noise died to a gentle throbbing. The driver twisted himself in his seat, exchanged a short, bored panto-mime through the glass of his window with the conductor, and unfolded a Lunch Edition of the *Standard*. The conductor, who apparently had nothing to read, looked away aloofly at the lilac bush. The passengers were silent, and a siren sounded close by.

Francis had been looking at his fellow travellers, wondering if any of them would prove as interesting as the old man with the red dragons on his legs, and had decided that none of them possibly could, except a dark blue hat, a rim of fair shining curls, and the back of a white neck which was provokingly turned towards him.

He was sitting on one of the two long seats near the en-trance; the girl with the white neck was sitting halfway down on the same side, but on one of the short transverse seats. She was alone, and she was carrying a brown paper parcel and a bunch of wallflowers and purple tulips carefully wrapped in blue tissue paper, the kind that some laundries slip between people's shirts with that capacity for fussing over unimportant details and failure to practise attention to the larger virtues like punc-tuality, reliability, etc., which distinguishes laundries as a whole.

Francis was much taken by that little hat, the roll of shining curls and especially the tender whiteness of her neck. He could see nothing more of her except the shoulders of her coat, because she was sitting on the same side as he was. He could just see the flowers and the parcel because she was holding them on her knees, so that they stuck out a little into the centre aisle of the bus.

How he wished that she would turn round!

And suddenly she did; she jumped up energetically as though her patience were at an end, and came quickly towards the door. The conductor turned to stare at her. Everybody stared at her, with lustreless, vaguely disapproving eyes. Francis stared at her, too, because her own large eyes, which should have been blue and vague, were dark brown and looked so angry, and in her small, fair face they were so surprising that they took his breath away.

That's my girl, said a tiny, clear voice in Francis's mind. There she is. I shall call her Toby. There she is. She's got perfect teeth (for she had parted her lips to speak to the conductor) and she's the prettiest girl I've ever seen, prettier than Sylvia Sydney or Ginger Rogers.

'Here,' said Toby in a clear voice, just coloured by Cockney, 'how much longer are we goin' to be here? I got to get down to my grandma, and I'm late now.'

'Well, it ain't my fault,' said the conductor. 'I didn't arst to be put on this route, I can tell you. It's the same fer all of you. Yer grandma'll 'ave to wait.'

'Can't I get out and walk round somehow?'

'No, you carn't get out and walk round some'ow, or that's what we'd all be doin', isn't it? 'Ere we are, and 'ere we stay.'

'Well, how long's it likely to be? She'll be worryin'. She's ninety, my grandma is, and it's her birthday. She's havin' a party.'

'Well, if she's lived to be all that old she carn't be the worrying sort,' soothed the conductor. 'She'd a bin killed orf years ago with the air-raids and everything. You just sit down and wait. I carn't say how long it's likely to be. Might be five minutes, might be twenty-five, might be a hour. Might be two hours, come to that.'

'That's right. So it might. It gets stuck sometimes,' said a large woman in a little round hat the colour of mud, nodding gloomily, 'and they 'as a regular job with it.'

'All right, be cheerful!' said Toby, sitting down suddenly opposite Francis with a flounce, but also with a brilliant smile which took in the whole bus.

The large woman in the little hat glanced at her as though her youth, and the interesting situation of her being on the way to her grandmother's ninetieth birthday party, called for some matronly comment. But there was an air of confidence, of gay bounce, about Toby which did not encourage matrons to be patronizing and inquisitive. If Toby had not looked so neat and been so obviously a good gel, her natural manner and those eyes would have led most matrons to call her a Piece, or even a Faggot.

But Francis was enchanted. He could not stop staring at her. He knew that this was bad strategy, but he could not stop. To hell with strategy, if it came to that. And yet, no ... this was obviously no case for simple grovelling. A girl like that would only laugh if one grovelled. Probably she was always laughing at young men, crowds of them, hordes of them, some of them with motorcycles, earning two or three pounds a week, men of twenty, even of twenty-three or four, perhaps. Anyone, no matter how old, would be only too thankful to get a girl like that. And at any moment the bus might start, and there would be no excuse at all for speaking to her, and she would get up and leave the bus and he would never see her again.

A frightful pang shook him at the thought.

But here the large woman in the little hat the colour of mud said something which gave him an opportunity that seemed to fall straight from heaven.

'Aren't you afraid, dear, coming down 'ere all by yourself?' said the large woman ghoulishly to Toby. 'I should be if I was you.'

'Afraid what of?'

'Narsty men,' said the large woman, lowering her voice so that the conductor should not hear. 'There's some very rough characters round 'ere, they say. I'm a stranger 'ere meself; I live up Aldgate. Oo, I wouldn't come down 'ere at night not for anythink, I wouldn't.'

'*You* needn't worry,' said the conductor, suddenly winking at Francis. 'She'd be all right, wouldn't she, son?'

The large woman pretended not to hear him.

'I shan't be down here very late,' said Toby practically, 'so why worry? I'm all right. I can look after meself. 'Sides, me cousin Stan is goin' to be there, most likely. He'll take me home on his motorbike.'

Francis, who had made up his mind to offer her his protection to her grandmother's front door, became miserably jealous.

'Oh, so long as you got somebody ...' said the large woman disappointedly. 'That's all right, then.'

'Even if I hadn't,' said Toby valiantly, 'I'd be all right.'

And she directed a bright, not at all bashful look at Francis. It could not be called an encouraging look. It seemed to say yes, I know you admire me, but I'm not having any, thank you. It was not exactly a haughty look; it recognized his existence but it warned him that there was nothing doing.

But Francis was not easily snubbed by young women, even ones as delicious as this one was. He had been looking for her for nearly a year, and he was certainly not going to lose her without a struggle. His experiences, too, with the flowerqueens had proved to him that even the most outwardly intimidating young girls were often secretly yielding and gracious. He would not insult Toby by comparing her with the flowerqueens, but there was just a chance that she might turn out to be kinder than she seemed.

The bus stopped.

'Tartar Lane,' said the conductor confidentially to Francis, jerking his thumb.

Toby was standing up, too; it was just as well, for Francis had made up his mind to stay in the bus with her until she got out.

He got out, and she followed him, and the bus rolled off. Everyone in it was looking with interest at Toby and Francis; the conductor even gave Francis a powerful wink, which distorted all one side of his face and expressed almost everything; at least, everything of importance.

The street was dusty, mean, quiet, with a little pub called The Guardsman at the corner of Tartar Lane, small houses whose doors stood open, and one or two noisy playing children. For a second, which gave Francis his chance, Toby hesitated over which way to turn, and he was on her like a hawk. He felt a cad, he felt terrified, but he did not care.

'May I walk with you, please, to your grandmother's house?' he said, standing over her with his hat in his hand. 'I'm sure you can take care of yourself, but it would give me such great pleasure if you would let me.'

'Well I never,' observed Toby thoughtfully, after a not indignant survey of his face and person which lasted for quite four awful seconds. She added, as though appealing to those hidden powers of impartial justice which are presumed to rule the universe, 'Can you beat it?'

Francis stood still, smiling steadily. He had never felt such a fool, so helpless. His jaws ached with the effort of trying to smile naturally.

'May I?' he said at last. And instinct made him abandon his polite, rather affected manner and say with all the earnestness which he felt at that moment and of which he was capable: 'Please don't be angry. I don't mean to be a nuisance. Please just let me walk with you. You're so pretty; you're simply lovely. You're the prettiest girl I've ever seen, I mean,' he ended rather wildly.

Toby neither blushed nor looked self-conscious; she seemed to take her prettiness for granted, as a bird takes its song. She continued to stare at him soberly, but a faint expression of pleasure had come into her eyes. No young woman could hear unmoved the sentence Francis had just uttered.

'It's only a short way,' she said severely at last, 'and they'll all be lookin' out of the window, I expect. What'll they say, I should like to know?'

'I'll go just before we get to the house. Honour bright I will. Truly. If you'll just let me come. Here ... may I carry the parcel?'

'Be careful you don't drop it; it's bath salts,' she said amiably, giving it him; and lightly, as though their mutual youth had put out a finger and steered them into place, they fell into step together.

Anyone who has dreamed with intensity of walking beside a beloved person, and lived through their dream in actuality, will know how Francis felt. Here am I, here is she. I can look down and see the texture of her gloves and look up and see how her eyes change when she laughs at me. This is more real than anything that has ever happened to me, and yet it is quite unreal. Already, while I live it, I am thinking how I shall have it to remember after it is ended.

'Bath salts?' he repeated foolishly.

'Yes. Well, that's a funny present for an old lady of ninety, you may say, but my grandma likes them, so why shouldn't she have them? Verbena. That was my idea. All the others was takin' her shawls and comforters and hot water bottles' (she made the catalogue sound immensely boring and dreary by drawling the words contemptuously). 'Well, I says to Mum, 'I'm goin' to be different. Must be different,' I said. And I took her the bath salts. She *was* pleased! 'Course, she doesn't put them in her bath. She just keeps them by her, to smell.'

'What a good idea,' said Francis, half of his mind enjoying her conversation and half of it wildly casting about for means to prolong the walk, ask her name, beg that he might see her again.

'You live round this way?' asked Toby, looking at him with calm, friendly eyes. She seemed to feel that she had done her duty by saying 'Well I never' and 'Can you beat it' and was now free to be as friendly as her nature directed her to be. She took him for granted in a way which he found at once sweet and painful. In just the same way she steered a route round a very small child who was playing in her path, saying to it 'Up-se-daisy, sis; make way for the Lord Mayor.' He had never seen a calmer girl. She looked as though nothing could surprise her.

'Me? Oh no. I live in Enbury Heath. I'm just down here on a job, for my firm.'

A faint, far reverberation, a warning quiver as though from an immense distance, sounded in his mind. The firm. Graby, Bryant & Co. Ltd. He was stealing this enchanted walk out of the firm's time.

He dismissed the warning quiver; he forgot it.

'That's a nice part. I live in Highbury. My dad's a fireman. Like the song, you know. 'My son Jim's a fireman, what do you think of that?''

'By Jove, is he?' said Francis. He was so young that this piece of news gave him a feeling of envy. A fireman! That was a job worth having. He wondered if, when he went to call on Toby, he would be allowed to crawl all over the fire engine; he should like that.

'Yes, *by Jove*, he is. You said that so funnily! Do it again.'

'By Jove,' muttered Francis, grinning with delight.

'*By Jove*. I never heard anyone say it before, except on the pictures. You hate yourself, don't you? Have a few flowers.'

And she held the pale purple tulips and wallflowers just under his nose. Any other girl would have clumsily jammed them into his face, but Toby put them up delicately, half withdrawing the bouquet even as she offered it. All her movements were like that; neat, self-confident, poised to the verge of grace.

'I say, my name's Francis Garden. May I know yours?'

'Mae Kellett. Mae with an *e*. Don't say it!'

'Don't say what?' demanded he, much startled, in his present exalted condition, by her vigorous tone.

"Come up and see me some time.' Honest, I spelled it that way long before I'd seen the film. I like it better that way. Must be different again, you see.'

'Like the bath salts?'

'That's the idea. Well, we're nearly there. Look, that's Grandma's, at the end of the row ... and there she is, lookin' out of the window, and young Stan and Auntie Cissie, and Uncle Ben. I expect they're waitin' tea for me. I must fly. Don't you come no further. You pop off, there's a good little boy. Thanks for the beautiful flowers.'

She held out her hand for the bath salts.

'But please ... I must see you again. Please. Won't you give me your address and let me write to you? You can't just go off like this and leave me—'

'Oh, can't I?' said Mae with an e, sparkling.

'No, you can't. I shan't let you. I *will* see you again. I must. Do, please, give me your address.'

'I don't see the good of it, but you can have my 'phone number at work if you like. Heythrop 4775. It's Rozanne's the hairdresser's in Milton Street, near Warren Street Station.'

'Heythrop 4775.' He was writing it down. 'And may I ring you up?'

'I wouldn't if I was you. Miss Pilkington (that's Rozanne) she's very down on us girls having private calls.'

'But why do you give it me, if I mustn't ring you up?'

'Well, you asked for it. Anything to keep the baby quiet, I say. You can ring up one lunch time, between two and three. She's out then. I don't say I'll be there, but I might be. Anyway, if at first you don't succeed, try, try again. Goodbye.'

Her look was always, he was to learn, far kinder than her words; she must have been the original person for whom the phrase about barks and bites was invented. Now, as she hurried away, she left him with the loveliest warm, friendly smile as though he and she were old friends.

Against her wishes he lingered there until he saw young Stan, Auntie Cissie and Uncle Ben come pouring out of the little house and engulf her, while at the window the head of Grandma bobbed approvingly up and down.

They all went inside; and the door was shut.

He turned slowly away. He had no idea where he was. This was a street of small, neat cottages which were of a better type and class than most of those lying round the Docks; it was called China Walk but he did not know how it lay in relation to Tartar Lane, because he had not noticed where they were going while he walked with Toby.

He stopped a young man and asked him the way there, turned back on his steps, and soon found Tartar Lane.

As once before when he had carried his father's will, his fingers kept finding his inner pocket to make sure that a piece of paper was safe. As soon as he had collected the specimen of silica, he proposed to find a telephone box and look up Rozanne and see if there really was such a woman in Milton Street; for Toby, he felt sure, was quite capable of giving him a false address and number, and telling Stan, Auntie Cissie, Uncle Ben and Grandma, as an exquisite joke, all about him and his By Jove and what an ass she had made of him. She looked such a kind girl! but so sure of herself and gay, like one of those crisp, nutty sweets which are hard to bite when once the eighth of an inch of soft chocolate which coats them is dissolved.

He was glad that she worked in a humble hairdressing place off Tottenham Court Road. That meant she would only earn about thirty-five shillings a week, and he could just afford, if he borrowed judiciously from Harry, to take her out in the way she was used to, or perhaps a little more luxuriously.

Then he thought of Stan and his motorcycle, and felt miserable. He growled at himself. He hated feeling miserable and humble about a girl, and girls hated it too. Harry had told him that. 'Don't crawl, my dear chap. Never crawl. They hate it. They try to get you to do it and they hate it when you do. I do it rather too much, I'm afraid. It's a thing I've got to get out of.'

Fortunately for Harry's masculine pride his girls usually began the crawling before he did, and bored him; then he could abandon them with a light heart.

It was difficult for Francis to remember what he had to ask for at the warehouse. He still felt slightly drunk. The narrow streets roofed with soft, pure blue sky looked beautiful. The tall warehouse, white with millions of grains of talc, chalk, milk powder and cement looked peaceful as a country mill, and there was the voice of water knocking musically near, hidden behind a wall, and freshening the air with its mysterious life.

Francis climbed to the second floor to find Mr Cartwright, who was in charge of the warehouse; and went down a narrow lane between sacks of milk powder piled ten feet high on either side of him. His shoulders were already patched with white and his shoes showed black creases across their dust.

This annoyed him, but he liked the warehouse. When he came to the end of the lane there was half the side of the building knocked away and through it glittered the sparkling freshness of the river, all over flat scales of gold, but blue as a dragonfly, and on it floated five barges piled high with the brightest gold planks, which ran their dazzling ladders of yellow reflection for fifteen feet across the blue water. All the white clouds sailed and ran, the far shore was dim with brown wharves and the green bushy trees of Greenwich and the snaky heads of cranes. One red funnel stood up in the smoke of the distance. The blue and gold and movement ran into the senses like a delicious smell, mixing with the dry faint one of chalk, and that of newly cut wood, the hidden mud and weeds and moving water.

Confused by love and hope, his eyes dazzled with the dance of blue, Francis soberly and with immense precision asked for, and obtained, his specimen of silica.

CHAPTER XVI

He got back to the cottage feeling happier, for he had looked up Rozanne in the telephone book and found that her number was Heythrop 4775 and her shop was at 43 Milton Street, as Toby had said. He had also realized that today was Thursday, which explained why Toby could be away from the shop during working hours; the hairdressers outside the West End close on Thursday afternoons like most suburban shops, and stay open late on Saturdays. Evidently Toby's shop did not come within the glittering circle known as 'up West'.

He found Sophia making preparations for a party which was to begin at ten o'clock that night, and also getting the supper. There was rather a lot to do, because neither Francis nor Harry considered a meal was a proper meal unless it included potatoes in some solid form.

Potatoes called 'crisps', which were thin as paper and could be conveniently bought ready cooked for twopence a bag, were not recognized by her brothers as potatoes. Nothing was said, but when Sophia served this variety of potato with beef or stew, an air of dignified regret hovered about Francis and Harry, rather as if Sophia had committed some error of taste.

So potatoes had to be peeled and boiled or mashed; and Sophia was now busy with them; for of course she could not ask Miss Tessitt to peel half a dozen potatoes and leave them ready to be boiled by Sophia on the latter's return from town.

Miss Tessitt would have called that Cooking, and she had not been engaged to cook.

The front door was open and Francis walked slowly in, swinging his hat. The little house felt cool and pleasant after the noise and dust of the London he had left in the valley, and there was a good smell of sausages frying. He inhaled the smell with pleasure, for he was not one of those dreary persons who dislike a smell of cooking, and thought that he would have a bath after supper, before the guests came. He lay down on the sofa and, putting his feet up, closed his eyes. He was exceedingly tired. It was surprising how the stamping of letters and the tying up of parcels, the making of tea and going down to the Docks and back could exhaust one. He had to be up every morning at six to be at work by eight o'clock, and the climb up the hill to the tube, and the long journey to the Monument took energy from him. He was still growing very fast and was doing a day's hard work, in the full pressure of the harsh economic claw, when most boys of his age and class were developing in the sheltered world of school.

'Is that you, darling?'

'Yes.'

'Tired?'

'Dead.'

'There'll be some supper in about twenty minutes. Oh, I do wish there wasn't this party tonight.'

'Who's coming besides us and Celia?'

'Edward and Emily, and they're bringing a girl. I don't know her name. And George and Wiggins and Jane. And probably Celia's young man, Capel.'

'Can't stand him.'

'He is a bit serious.'

Silence. Sophia was hidden from him, busy with her sausages and potatoes in the kitchen behind the little glass-panelled door; and as she said no more, he fell asleep.

He was still asleep when she came in ten minutes later to set the cloth; and she stopped short at the sight of him, subduing her movements.

She had never seen anything looking so like a white, beaky, exhausted young bird. He was sprawling on the sofa with his head back and his mouth open; he had taken off his spectacles and his childishly thick eyelashes lay closely on his pale cheeks. He was alarmingly thin. The famous suit was beginning to hang on him in folds.

Sophia looked very like him as she stood staring down at him, her face heavy with worry. She too was pale and grimy from her day's work, and her blue linen dress unbecomingly showed her large bones. She was not, in fact, so unhappy as she looked, because her natural expression was severe and a little worried, but if their mother could have seen Sophia and Francis at that moment she would have been very unhappy about them.

Three months of life in the cottage might have been delightful, but they had not been able to put fat on the bones of Sophia and Francis, nor make them look less fierce and tired. It was rather unfortunate (thought Sophia, taking out knives and forks from the cupboard as quietly as she could) that an unusually tiring childhood should be succeeded by an unusually tiring youth. By the time we are about thirty, thought Sophia, to whom that age seemed so remote as to be incredible, we shall all three be very tired indeed.

The fact was, what with the necessity for earning their own livings and for having as much fun as possible in the intervals of so doing, there was no peace.

No peace, she thought, pouring water on to the tea. But that isn't our fault. In order to have peace you need a stable background and money coming in which doesn't have to be worked for quite so desperately hard, and you need kind, sensible older people to turn to sometimes. The relatives aren't kind or sensible, though presumably they mean to be, and that's very tiring, too. And then I suppose we can't expect to forget the misery of Father and Mother in three months, even if we have been able to do as we like and enjoy ourselves; you can't forget twenty years in a quarter of a year.

Everything conspires in fact to make Francis and me tired, and Harry a rackety-pot. I can see it all quite calmly and sensibly but that doesn't make things any less worrying.

I don't really think it's my fault that there isn't much peace here, she decided, as she put the butter into a little dish of red glass. I like peace but the boys don't seem to like it, though they may *need* it. It's very difficult to make people accept what they need but don't like. I might stop having so many people here, but then the boys do so enjoy showing the place off, and we could never do that when we lived at home, because things were so awful.

It does seem rough luck if they can't have a little fun now.

Even if I did stop the parties, we should still have to work for our livings and be likely to be sacked at any moment, all of us. I suppose everyone has to work, or almost everyone, but surely other people whose fathers were doctors don't have to work quite so hard, when they're quite so young, without any feeling of security at all?

And she wondered for the thousandth time what would become of the three of them? She supposed that the relatives and Celia would never see any of them starve to death, but it would be very disagreeable to have to ask Uncle Preston for help.

In old-fashioned books young people who had to battle with life were often depicted as rushing at it, so to speak, with rosy cheeks and yelps of belligerent pleasure, rather as though they were taking part in a mixed hockey match. But then they had ambitions, and they believed in God, and they were so extremely sure about what was right and what was wrong. That must be a great help; the young Gardens were not at all sure about any of these matters, for they had not been brought up to be.

Sophia had not so far enjoyed battling with life, but a dry, dour feeling of satisfaction peered out sometimes from among her emotions when she wrote a poem which satisfied her or when she took a step towards peace and security. She had this feeling when they secured the cottage, when Francis and Harry got their jobs, when her first poem appeared in print.

We're getting on, she thought cautiously on these occasions.
She had long ago decided that, finally, there was no power
which cared whether human beings were exquisitely happy or
cruelly miserable. Something might create human creatures
for a hidden purpose, but it did not care what they felt like.

Meanwhile, the world was a beautiful place, full of varied and
exciting experiences. With luck, eighty years might be passed
in it; and eighty years was a terrifyingly short time, though
thirty seemed so far away. Why! only yesterday, it seemed, she
had been seventeen and now she was nearly twenty-two. Her
aim was to wrest order, beauty and happiness from life; and
every time she wrested a little piece she smiled mockingly
in the face of that lack of interest manifested by the creative
power, and she thought, Done you again!

She was quite intelligent enough to know that this was a
shallow, melodramatic attitude, but she had too much to do at
the moment; she had no time to worry over her philosophy.

But she was worried about money.

It was not that they had not enough money. They seemed
to have plenty. Sophia had three pounds a week, Harry had
five, Francis had one. Mr Marriot stood in the background and
could advance money from the practice and from its prospective
sale, if they ran short. In theory, the three should have had a
comfortable feeling about their finances, but Sophia was worried
because they spent so much and saved nothing.

The rent of the cottage, the wages of Miss Tessitt, and the
food they ate absorbed frighteningly large sums. Sophia found it
impossible to save a halfpenny. Light, the electric power which
heated the daily bath of Francis and Harry, fares, lunches in
town, clothes, cleaning materials, to say nothing at all of parties
which flowed with port, sherry, gin and beer, sucked in money
like blotting paper.

Sophia knew that she was not what is called a good manager.
She did not waste money; it was spent on food, and other
necessities, but she was lavish. She could not bear to think that
anyone living beneath her roof had not more than enough to

eat, and she liked the house to shine with rosy lights, and with
a fire on a grey evening. Her days in the country cost money,
and so did the concerts to which she now treated herself, and
the presents she gave her friends. She loved to give, and to
buy flowers as they marched in delicate procession round the
curve of the year.

She did not get into debt; but that was her only piece of
prudence. Otherwise, she spent carelessly and royally, but not
gaily. She worried.

They had not yet asked Mr Marriot for a second advance
from the practice's takings; money was being saved for them,
and it was her only pleasant thought. But so far no one had
offered a high enough price for the practice, and, as Uncle
Preston told her when he talked to her on the telephone, its
value was growing less every week, because its numbers were
going down.

Then he would ask her how much she and Harry and Francis
put into the bank each week, and though she did not plainly
answer this question, he often sent her little brochures about
Home Safes, and National Savings Certificates and even, as a
humble last effort, Stamp Deposit slips. In his telephone talk
with her only yesterday evening he had said that he supposed
she must be quite a rich woman by now, heh! heh! heh!

Poor Sophia did not scorn Home Safes and all the parapher-
nalia of security. She wanted them, but she could not see her way
to getting them.

She thought of the future. Harry and Francis were enjoying
life too much at present to think of more than a few months
ahead, but she thought often and sadly about their middle
age and their old age, and wondered if Francis would die of
consumption and Harry take to gambling.

This anxiety was her inheritance from the Gardens. They
cut her out of their wills, but they left her other, invisible
legacies. They passed on to her their dark weights of the spirit
and their nervous fears, and she suffered but could not escape.

As she put the dish of sausages on the table Francis woke up.

'Hullo. Been asleep,' said he, moving his lips uncertainly as a baby does when it awakes.

'That will do you good, darling. It's a sign of greatness to be able to go to sleep anywhere. Napoleon could.'

It is also a sign of nervous exhaustion, but she did not think it necessary to tell him this; and, having washed themselves sternly in cold water, they sat down and ate their supper in comfortable silence. Harry had a matinée today, and usually took a sandwich in town between the shows on such days, so he did not come in. He would be back about twelve o'clock when the party, heaven help all concerned, was at its height. It was his party in fact, given in honour of Emily and Edward, whose new show was being a success. It was really Mr Hensatt's show, but the Gardens always called it Edward's show.

After supper Francis retired into the bathroom with his ukulele. His bath would take about an hour and a half, and would be punctuated by songs in his pleasant tenor, while Sophia was cutting sandwiches and wishing she could go for a walk on the Heath instead of having the party, for the may trees were in bloom and the moon was rising.

The food for this party was rather nasty, but Sophia did not care. It was Thursday evening, which meant that none of the three had much money because it was the end of the week, and also that the shops were shut when Sophia tried to buy things on her return to Enbury Heath about six o'clock. The sandwiches were made with fish paste from Eddie-Creab-the-Notorious-Gangster whose shop, of course, was open. It was bright pink and it cost fourpence halfpenny a pot. It had no name. It was just called Fish Paste, as though it were made of all kinds of fishes, as no doubt it was. Sophia rather liked it. She kept eating the sandwich crusts, as she cut them off, with thick dabs of the Fish Paste on them.

There were two pounds of chocolate biscuits, sardine sandwiches, a jar of barley sugar and half a large, dark rich cake made by Celia's charwoman, who cooked admirably.

And that was all. It was certainly rather miserable food. Sophia felt half ashamed of it, and half that she did not care if it was horrid; and if people did not like it, they could go without. Anyway, the drink would cheer up the provisions.

She had admitted to herself that she did not enjoy these parties, and now felt more resigned to them. Her method of dealing with the parties was to play a passive part; handing food and drink, dancing when asked, drinking as little as possible and avoiding embraces.

This attitude may have satisfied her; it annoyed Harry and even called out mild expressions of disapproval from Francis. It was certainly damping. The presence of one Christian, according to those works of fiction describing the trials of the Early Church in Rome, could take all the kick out of an orgy; and this was rather the effect which Sophia's passive resistance had upon the revellers at the cottage.

'She makes me think,' complained Harry to Francis, 'of some beastly vicar's wife being all broad-minded at a night-club.'

It was certainly not the impression which a hostess would wish to give, but Sophia was unconscious that she gave it. She thought that no one noticed her attitude.

By nine the sandwiches were all cut and arranged on the kitchen table with an old damped shirt of Harry's wrapped round them (the cottage owned no table napkins) to keep them fresh. Francis came out of the bathroom dressed in white flannels, feeling romantic and much restored, and sat on the sofa with the ukulele, to stare out of the open door at a little white and red may tree in flower, strum, and think about Toby.

Sophia went into the bathroom, which was disagreeably moist and full of wet towels, and made a discovery.

'Oh god, have you fused the geyser?'

'I'm afraid I may have. Something snapped in a queer way with a blue spark. I'm terribly sorry, my dear. I'll pay for it.'

'It's not that, but I *do* wish you'd be more careful. It's too sickening, Francis. This is the second time in three months.

And it takes days to get it mended and costs fifteen and six and now I can't have a hot wash and I'm coal-black.'

'I'll put a kettle on for you,' and he obligingly did.

'Thank you. I'm sorry I was cross, but I do wish you would turn it off in the order it *says* – first two turns to the left, *then* the water, and then the last turn to the right. You *will* do it all at once, and then turn on the water. That's what fuses it.'

'Nonsense. It doesn't make any difference.'

'Yes it does. The man said so when he came to repair it.'

'After you asked him if it did, I suppose.'

Sophia was silent. She felt too cross, too tired, too worried about Francis's thinness and Harry's increasing passion for parties and beer, and the uncertainty of their future, to go on with their argument.

Oh, why was it not possible to live from day to day, taking life as it came, without anticipating misfortunes which might never arrive? Why was it not possible to pray, and put her burdens into the hands of God? Some people did, but she could not. She had been taught her prayers as a little girl by her mother, but she had stopped praying when she was sixteen for what had seemed to her good reasons, and now she was alone. She must go on, and manage everything by herself.

But after she had washed in the kettleful of hot water and gone upstairs to her bedroom and leaned out of the window to stare at the deepening evening, she felt better.

She looked into the may tree, which so strangely had one branch of white flowers amid its red ones, and her spirit lifted gently, exactly as though she had sighed with relief.

It was untrue to say that she was alone, when the sight of a star or a tree could give her such peace; and she believed that nothing could ever take this comfort away from her.

She decided to cheer herself up by putting on her new black silk dress, with a delicate breadth of white lace round the low neck, and it looked surprisingly well. The piece of lace was real; there was a yard of it and it had cost seventeen and sixpence of the article money.

Then she combed her straight fair fringe and the hair which just came below her ears, and tucked the hair and some lavender water behind those same ears, and went rustling downstairs, rather pleased with herself.

'Hullo. You look nice,' observed Francis, with that accent of surprise which is not flattering.

'Do I? Good.'

His compliments were not frequent, and this one soothed her still more. It, and her dress, and the may tree, almost succeeded in banishing her sadness, and when the first guests arrived, Sophia announced that she was quite looking forward to the party.

Celia said that she was, too, but her young man said nothing. He was rather good at doing that; Sophia used to say that she could never decide whether she preferred him to imply his disapproval by silence or by some burst of the stunning candour with which he thought it necessary to dynamite his way through the effete thickets of social life. He was a very serious young man of twenty-three, who was taking a degree in Economics at the same school as Celia. It was generally supposed, even by Celia, that he was in love with her, but he had the oddest ways of showing it. He did not seem to like her very much, which distressed her, for she was a simple and tender person and ready to be happy, when her young men allowed her to be. But she had an unfortunate capacity for attracting young men who suffered with their souls; or who allowed their bodies to get entangled with their souls while their intellects danced ring-a-roses round the barbed entanglements; and in these circumstances it is not easy for a love affair to be happy.

Celia conveyed the information to Sophia that Capel was not feeling party-ish this evening.

'He nearly didn't come, poor dear,' breathed Celia, carefully not looking at Capel while she chose a chocolate biscuit, 'we had rather a scene.'

'Strange – strange!' retorted Sophia, who found Capel a trial. 'What's the matter with him?'

'Oh ... me. He says I've got such a strong personality that I subconsciously want to dominate him, and he feels it subconsciously, but *consciously* I give way to him, and that isn't really what I want to do, and he knows it. And part of *his* nature wants to give way, too; but the subconscious part resents it. It's his masculine pride, you see. And if he gives way, I don't really like it. At least, he says I don't, but he never does give way, so I can't really tell whether I like it or not, can I?'

'He's a selfish little beast, and he pokes about in his own mind too much. That's all that's the matter with him, and for two pins I'd tell him so.'

'Oh no, Sophia. It isn't as simple as that, really. Poor dear, he's still rather adolescent in some ways, I'm afraid. Only I do wish he wouldn't make scenes. I do so hate them.'

Sophia glanced across at the large, square face of Capel. It was such a serious face; beside it the elegant young hawkish face of Francis looked ten years older in experience, in gaiety, in decisiveness. Capel's very complexities were only simplicities which he had allowed from a false sense of their importance to get into a muddle.

'He's so easily hurt,' continued Celia.

'And what about you?'

'Oh well ... he can't bear hurting me, poor dear, only he doesn't always know when he is, you see.'

'You aren't in love with him, are you, for mercy's sake?'

'Oh no. But I'm very fond of him, poor dear. He's very sweet, really. He's got marvellous qualities, you know. He could be a very fine man.'

'Well, he won't be, if he isn't careful. He talks too much and he reads too much and he doesn't think.'

'He's *always* thinking!'

'Not thinking. Only brooding. And he's so fearfully intelligent he gives me a pain. There's nothing more awful than a natural ass who's read too much.'

Celia was uncomfortably convinced of the truth of some of these sweeping remarks and hastened to return to the object

of them, who had pinned Francis into a corner and was slowly
and ruthlessly extracting from him a history of the development of the French chalk trade in the British Isles during the
last hundred years. Francis did not mind; he rather enjoyed
showing how much he knew about his job.

Celia came and stood gracefully, in silence, by Capel's
shoulder. She felt so sorry for him! She, and she alone, knew
how young, how bewildered and earnest he was beneath that
hard heavy manner, and how remorselessly he submitted every
emotion he experienced to the judgment of a not very good
brain, which had been battered into a most peculiar state by
the study of Lawrence, Gide, Hemingway, Spengler, Pound,
Joyce, Eliot and other contemporary prophets.

For the first half of the evening the party had an intellectual cast which pleased Sophia; it was more like a salon, she
thought, than a party.

Jane and George, who were married and whose youth only
displayed itself in the awful seriousness of their minds, and
whose cleverness only burst out harmlessly in difficult games
with pencil and paper, played peacefully in a corner with Celia
and Capel. Wiggins, who was a friend of Harry and Francis
from Northgate, sat and wound the gramophone and played,
at Sophia's request, music by Haydn while he told her about
a Rugby football match in which he had played a bold and
decisive part and hurt himself considerably, much to his satisfaction. Francis, in the intervals of the Haydn, sang some of his
little songs, accompanying himself on the ukulele and looking
so earnest and wistful that Sophia and Celia decided that he
must be in love at last and wondered who on earth it could
be and hoped to heaven that she would not be too frightful.
Everyone was quietly enjoying the party, even Capel, but there
was a general feeling of anticipation and expectation in the air;
and when, at nearly twelve o'clock, a car was heard coming
down the road into the Vale there was a stir in the salon, and
murmurs of 'Here they are!'

Francis hurried the bottles of drink into a more notice-
able position, Sophia (not without misgivings) brought out the
remains of the Fish Paste sandwiches, which looked even less
appetising now that they were lying languidly all over the dish.

Francis opened the door and the blue sky glimmering with
soft stars, a breath of sweet night air and solemnity floated in;
and in, too, floated four beautiful young people who shone like
candles, because their natural vitality was a little heightened
by drink. They eclipsed the salon completely. The Footlights
swept everything before them.

'Hullo! Hullo, Francis!'

'Hul-lo, Sophia! How are you, my dear!'

'Oh Harry, what a *darling* place! isn't it *sweet*!'

'My god, you've got a fug on in here, haven't you? Leave
the door open for a bit. Emily, have some gin, my sweet. What
have you all been doing? You were very quiet as we came up
– not a sound.'

'Ah-ha!'

Someone put a hot record on the gramophone; and gaiety
began to pump up into the rather stagnant air. Emily stood
with one elbow on the mantelpiece, talking to Sophia, who
never tired of looking at her red curls, her white skin and
large clear green eyes. She was a beautiful young woman, who
heightened her loveliness by nothing more artificial than clothes
that fitted her perfectly proportioned body, and a collection of
rich, loose fur coats with big collars which made her little face
look even more exotic than it was. On looking at Emily, one
first thought, 'But this cannot be real,' and then one looked
again and thought, 'But it is, ye gods!'

The same could not be said for the young person who was
sitting on Harry's knee and patting his face.

Sophia and Celia, in discussing this person afterwards, agreed
that it was not the Paint nor was it the Being Drunk, nor the
Pawing Harry. No; it was the air of contemptuous amusement
which this young person, who was aged about seventeen and

whose beauty suggested a ripe damson, carefully painted, turned upon the cottage, its furnishings and its inhabitants.

'Who's that?' cautiously enquired Sophia of Edward, who had joined his wife and his hostess at the mantelpiece.

Edward's dark face, as attractive in its more severe masculine lines as Emily's, became indignant. He was an extremely kind young man with good manners which even a little too much gin could not drown.

'Hasn't Harry introduced you? He is the extent. Harry, you old fool, come here a minute.'

'No, darling. Stay with me,' said the damson, embracing Harry. And it added in a piercing whisper, which alcohol made more shrill than was intended, 'Your shister doeshn't like me.'

In this there was no more than the truth, for Sophia, who certainly was a prig, had taken umbrage at the poor little damson, and refused even to look at it.

'Yesh she doesh. Don't be silly. You're 'magining things, my sweet. Of coursh she liksh you. Sophia! Sally thinks you don't like her. Come here a minute.'

But Sophia had gone into the kitchen to fetch a glass of water for Emily, who drank little alcohol because it was bad for her complexion, and would not hear.

'No she doesn't. I can shee. She won't look at me. Doesn't like me. You like me, don't you, darling?'

'Of course I do my sweet. Sophia!'

'She thinksh I'm drunk. But I'm not.'

Harry kissed her glowing little face and whispered into her neck where dark bright curls clustered.

Fortunately she took it into her head to dance, and forgot about Sophia while she circled in Harry's arms. Francis took Jane, Emily was too tired, after an evening's dancing which was extremely hard work, to want to dance again, but everyone else danced cheerfully in a haze of smoke and the smell of a good many different kinds of alcohol. The party was decorous enough. Except for the presence of the little damson-creature, even Uncle Preston could not have called the party wild.

'She's one of the chorus from "Fifty Grand,"' said Edward. 'Nice kid, but being spoiled. She's been taken up by Lukass. He's the sort of swine who'd spoil anyone.'

'I wonder she bothers to come here, when she could be at the Savoy or somewhere with Lukass,' muttered Sophia, who knew the things that were said about the Brooklands ace.

'She's not so bad. Only got swollen head.'

'Isn't there any champagne?' suddenly demanded Sally. 'It makes me feel shick. I feel shick. It's all your fault, darling. Oh, god, I feel so sick. It was that sandwish I had. It was a fish sandwish. Nasty.'

'It wasn't the sandwich at all; she was tight when she came in, little fool,' observed Edward, who went to so many wild and rich parties during the week that he enjoyed a quiet and rather dowdy one, where he could relax, for a change. He liked leaning amiably on the sofa, watching people. Like Harry, he usually had to be in top gear. He enjoyed being in top, but god! it was a relief sometimes to slip into third. His tastes were simple.

Sally annoyed him; throwing her silly little weight about and insulting Sophia's food. He wished she would shut up. He and Emily merely wanted to be quiet, drink a little gin for friendship's sake, and go home. Why did Harry have to bring her?

'Horrid, it was. Fish. Ugh! Made me feel sho shick.'

'I really don't think it could have been the sandwich,' said Sophia judicially. 'None of the rest of us feel sick, and we've been eating them all the evening.' Her stark honesty compelled her to add, 'Though I'm afraid they're not very nice.'

Edward at once gallantly ate a sandwich and pronounced it very good. But it happened to be a sardine one.

Harry, with the incalculability of one who is rather tight, abruptly forsook Sally at the end of the dance and bore down upon Jane, who was much amused by his attentions; but Sally began to cry.

'Feel so sick,' moaned Sally. 'Going to *be* sick.' Harry took no notice.

Francis's chivalry was roused. He went over to her and took her arm with grave politeness.

'I'll take you to the bathroom,' said he, steering her between the revellers. She did not attract him, because for the moment he could think of no girl beside Toby, but he felt it his duty as a host to see that people had somewhere to be sick in if they wanted to be.

He glanced reproachfully at Sophia as he passed her. Surely this was her job. But Sophia and Celia were carefully not looking at Sally; and he had to take her into the bathroom and sit her miserably on the edge of the bath, with a chiffon handkerchief which smelled sweet held up to her mouth. Her large dark eyes, round which the lashes stood out in stiff rays, looked moistly up at him, her cheeks were crimson with youth, health, excitement rouge and gin. It was not easy to believe that she felt sick.

'Feel bad. Not drunk. It was that nasty sand-wish.'

'I'm sure it was,' he soothed her politely. 'Now you just stay quietly here in the cool, and you'll feel better.'

'Want Harry. Where's Harry? He's a swine, going off and leaving me when I feel sho bad. Feel so bad. Want Harry.'

'I'll try and get him,' promised Francis, who was bored with the situation. How tiresome women could be. He went back along the corridor which isolated the bathroom from the rest of the cottage, and approached Sophia.

'She's sitting on the bath. She keeps on asking for Harry. I think it's just a try-on to get him into the bathroom; she's no more sick than I am.'

'Leave her alone; she'll get over it,' advised Edward. A wail came from the bathroom, so loud that it sounded above that of Mr Bing Crosby intoning 'Stormy Weather.'

'WANT HARRY. FEEL SICK. Oh, I feel SO BAD.'

'Damned little bore,' murmured Edward, interrupting his own crooning of 'Stormy Weather'. 'Harry,' he called, 'you're wanted in the bathroom.'

Harry, who was kissing Jane, waved him away impatiently.

'Harry. Come here. Be a sport. Want to tell you shomething. Important.'

Sophia had gone to the large cupboard on the right of the mantelpiece, and was taking from it a tin of Eno's Fruit Salts.

'Perhaps,' remarked Sophia to Celia, 'she really does feel sick. I think we had better go in to her.'

And Sally, who had looked up hopefully at the sound of footsteps coming along the corridor, was horrified to behold two severe young women dressed in black, the tall one holding aloft a tin of Eno's and the short one a glass of water with a spoon in it.

'We have brought you some Eno's,' said Harry's sister politely. 'I am sorry you feel ill.'

'Shorry to be a nuisance, darling,' said Sally, with her dazzling and lovely smile. 'It was that nasty sandwish. Fish.'

'Perhaps,' suggested Celia, looking at her with thoughtful curiosity, 'it is something you ate before you came here. Or drank.'

'Nothing but champagne. Only half a glash. Nasty fish. Feel better now.'

'Good,' said the two black-robed figures.

'Quite better. Funny, wasn't it?'

'Very,' they agreed.

'Not sick any more. Shorry, darling,' and she got up and fled down the corridor back to the sitting room.

'And don't call me darling, damn you,' said Sophia softly, laughing. 'That must be the quickest cure on record. Nothing like Eno and cold water.'

Unfortunately Sally's attack of sickness, like other ailments, had its after-effects. Soon after her return to the sitting room the party broke up, for it was now after one o'clock and Edward had to drive back to Taplow, and he and Emily were working so hard just now in the Hensatt revue that they did not want to have too many late parties. Sally, still murmuring at intervals that she knew Harry's sister did not like her, was put at the back of Edward's car and told by him to shut up, which at last she did, and went to sleep.

It was a rather flat end to the party, which had not been a good one. Sophia stood at the door sh-sh-ing everyone and still more subduing their already subdued spirits, because every sound they made could be heard all over the crowded hollow of the Vale; and Capel, who was escorting Celia home across the Heath, was gloomy and silent because she had twice danced with Harry and talked for fifteen minutes with George, while the others were sleepy and thinking about how to get themselves home.

Sophia was profoundly depressed; two of a set of green drinking glasses had been broken, the cottage was scattered with cigarette ash and broken meats, and when she got home tomorrow evening Miss Tessitt, who stayed late on Friday to receive her wages, would say, 'Ay see you hed another little party last night. May! You are gay! There was quate a lot of washin' up, and did you know two of them teen glasses is broken. How did *that* happen, Ay says to mayself? Ay haven't done much to the place today. There was such a lot of crocks; Ay was quaite worn out when Ay had finished them all. There is a lot to do 'ere for such a small place, is there not?'

When everyone had gone, and the footsteps and voices and the sound of Edward's car had died in the mild and beautiful stillness of the night, she turned back into the cottage.

Francis could be heard in the bathroom, vigorously cleaning his teeth. Harry was sitting on the sofa, leaning forward with his head bent and his hands clasped between his knees. All the light and gaiety had gone out of his face. He looked tired, sulky, lost in sad thoughts. He did not look up as his sister came in.

His stillness and the sulky, resentful look on his face annoyed her. She said:

'You seem very fed up.'

'I am.'

'Why? I thought you were enjoying it.'

'Well, I wasn't. It was a bloody party. I was ashamed for Edward and Emily to meet awful people like that friend of

Celia's. God, he was wet. And the food was awful, too. I was nearly sick. No wonder it made Sally ill, poor darling.'

'She wasn't ill, she was only pretending.'

'No she wasn't, it was that filthy fish paste.'

'Well, I don't care if it poisons her, little beast. Coming here half-drunk and sneering at us and our food and our friends.'

'Your friends, you mean. Mine are all right.'

'Mine weren't drunk, anyway.'

'No, they were damned dull, which is worse. It was all your fault. You're always the same – asking a lot of highbrows who spoil everything. They don't know how to enjoy themselves. They make me sick. And why couldn't you get some decent food?

'I ran out of money. And besides, the shops were all shut. I did my best. At least, that's not quite true – I could have got some food in town and brought it in, but I was tired and didn't bother.'

'And what did you want to sneer at Sally for, making her cry, poor little sweet? She's a grand kid. Do you know she keeps her mother on her salary?'

'Who says so?'

'She does – and it's true.'

'Well, I don't believe it' (but, having a tender heart she did, and remorse made her feel angrier than ever). 'And even if she does, that's no excuse for getting drunk.'

'Oh you're perfect, of course. Pity you don't get drunk sometimes; it would do you good.'

She turned away to hide her tears, and was going slowly up to bed in silence when Francis appeared, breathing toothpaste and satisfaction. He was not depressed. He was going to ring up Toby tomorrow.

He saw at once what had happened, and competently set himself to smooth matters. He was used to being a buffer state between Sophia and Harry; he was so like the one in nature, and loved the other so dearly, that he knew how each one felt when Sophia's principles and Harry's tastes came into combat.

He said nothing, but kissed Sophia 'goodnight' tenderly and squeezed her shoulders and sent her up to bed with the feeling that somebody loved her, and then gently led Harry into reciting his woes in a low and grizzling monotone which greatly relieved his feelings. For nearly an hour Francis, lying in his bed beside Harry's, listened to rhetorical questions, self-justifications, grievances, legitimate and otherwise, and never once vehemently agreed with nor contradicted his brother. He was used to this rôle; he had been doing it since he was five years old.

In her room, Sophia lay listening to the rise and fall of voices in the darkness. She was not feeling hurt any more. Harry had not meant what he said; he never did. Tomorrow, when the fumes of the party had worn off, he would be sorry.

But just after three o'clock struck from the tower of Enbury Church, high above the Vale on its hill, she heard the light switched on in the next room. Someone got out of bed.

Her door opened gently.

'Sophia,' whispered a voice, 'are you awake, dear?'

'Yes. What is it?'

'It's me. I'm sorry I was a beast.'

'Oh darling, so am I. Sorry I was one, I mean. It's all right,' and they kissed and forgave one another.

CHAPTER XVII

During June Uncle Preston was disturbed by a number of incidents which agitated the Garden family and which he had to put right, but he found time to suspect that all was not as it should be at the cottage.

He suspected that Things Went On there. There were cocktails, he suspected, and what he vaguely but disapprovingly thought of as Jazz. He did not know that cocktails cost too much for the cottage to make a habit of buying them. Like the editors of newspapers he had only to mutter 'Cocktails' to himself to see an awful symbol, an alcoholic Scarlet Woman whose number was 666, instead of a joyless and nasty drink which costs from 1/6 to 3/- a small glass.

Dissipation was only what he had expected from poor Hartley's children. Still, it distressed him. Sooner or later he would have to Speak to the children about these goings-on; when he had put matters straight between Maxine and Grace, who had had a dreadful row about Miss Van Veek.

Miss Van Veek had had a good innings; she had been Aunt Maxine's bosom friend for six months. She had shared Aunt Maxine's flat and the attentions of her latest horrid cat, who was named Juley; she had been driven with Aunt Maxine by numerous red, hard, prosperous men down to Brighton and out to roadhouses and to Maidenhead and the Hog's Back, roaring, and stopping at pubs on the way, and returning to play bridge in the evenings. Aunt Maxine had taken her to theatres and to cinemas, to lunches and teas.

And how did she repay all this kindness? She stole the venal affections of Juley (who rushed to welcome her whenever she appeared, and ignored Aunt Maxine, except at meal times, in her absence) and she criticized Aunt Maxine at great length and in detail to Grace, to whom Aunt Maxine had introduced her and with whom she saw fit to go secretly to tea one wet Saturday afternoon.

Of course Aunt Grace thought it her duty to warn Aunt Maxine against Miss Van Veek, and Aunt Maxine, in the course of two telephone conversations, which lasted respectively fifteen and twenty-seven minutes, had it out with her sister-in-law and her friend. Up and down the flat she tramped, kicking at tuffets, swearing, scattering ash all over the carpet and terrifying Juley, who hid under the sofa pretending that she was out; and casting Miss Van Veek from her bosom.

Uncle Preston heard all about this, even down to the treachery of Juley, from Auntie Loo, who happened to be lunching with Aunt Grace when Aunt Maxine telephoned. Auntie Loo did not want to tell him, but she knew that if she did not, Aunt Maxine would, so she got in first with her version, which put both parties in the light of silly women with not enough to do.

Uncle Preston did not see it like that at all.

Gardens were quarrelling, the solidity of the family was threatened. He must put matters right. Aunt Grace, of course, was only a Garden by marriage, but she was the mother of a Garden's daughter, and had imbibed, during her marriage to Oliver, enough silliness and seriousness to entitle her to being considered a Garden. Of course she and Maxine must make it up.

Getting them to do so took him nearly a fortnight, and then he had a slight accident with the car, which had to be repaired, and the insurance company refused to allow his claim, and that meant more bother. Auntie Loo developed a stye upon the lid of her right eye; such an odd thing to get in the summer. So tiresome. And finally Mr Marriot wrote to tell him the good news that a doctor was considering buying the practice for two thousand pounds, and added that he would like an opportunity, if Mr Garden could spare him half an hour one afternoon, of discussing the financial affairs of Miss Garden and her brothers.

It appeared that Mr H. Garden had applied to Mr Marriot for a sum of twenty-two pounds to settle a tailor's bill for that amount. Mr Marriot would like to know whether Mr Garden would like him to advance this sum to Mr Harry Garden.

He had had a telephone conversation with Miss Garden which he would also like to discuss.

It was this letter which convinced Uncle Preston that his fears about life at the cottage were well founded; and even his relief at hearing that a doctor wanted to buy the practice was tainted by worry and apprehension of woes to come.

Mr Marriot told him, in the course of their interview, that Miss Garden had telephoned to ask him how much money they had.

That was the phrase she used. How much money have we got, if you don't mind my asking and if it is all right for you to tell me.

'She meant, I gather,' explained Mr Marriot, 'that she did not wish to press her question unless I were within my legal rights in answering it.'

'What did she want to know for?' demanded Uncle Preston fretfully. He was much alarmed. Had Hartley's children been getting into debt?

'I gathered that she was concerned about the lack of stability in their finances. I understood from her that they are living right up to their income, that she finds it impossible, at the rate they are living at present, to save money, and that she is somewhat concerned about their future.'

'Not saving *money*? But she said ... I asked her ... that is, I understood that they were all putting something away each week,' stammered Uncle Preston.

This was a lie, but like most lies told by the Gardens, it was not recognized by the speaker as one. Uncle Preston meant that he wanted to understand that the children were all putting away money each week. His strong desire to believe this comforting fact, coupled with Sophia's refusal to tell him anything definite about their savings, produced the illusion.

'Well, I am afraid they are not.'

'Not in debt, are they, eh? Dear, dear, dear, dear! Just like poor Hartley. He never could save a farthing ...'

'There is only this bill for twenty-one pounds, so far as I know, about which I have already told you.'

'So far as you *know*, eh? Do you suspect that there may be other debts that we don't know about?'

'Miss Garden did not mention any others, and I think that she would have done so, had there been any. She seemed rather distressed.'

'And how much have they got?' asked Uncle Preston, who had been dreading to ask this question.

'There is some forty-six pounds in hand from the practice. And I have great hopes of Dr Cameron. He really seems,' said Mr Marriot in a tone of musing wonder, 'eager to purchase the practice and take over the house.'

'That would mean some two thousand pounds, I think you said?'

'Yes. Though of course the bargain is not yet concluded.'

'Come, that's not so bad, though,' murmured Uncle Preston, reassured. 'Of course, it is not *handsome*, and there is the *future* to think of, but they need not *starve* just yet.'

'So I told Miss Garden. Nevertheless, I appreciate her anxiety, and I may say that I respect it.'

And Mr Marriot, who knew what a small sum of money two thousand pounds is, tied up some documents with pink tape, looking dryly the while at Uncle Preston's silly worried face.

The man had all a fool's respect for money in the lump; such men mentally kept money in an old stocking, though actually they might keep it in a bank. They never saw it as a sharp gleaming weapon, nor as a silent golden god moving about the world and shaping history.

'Of course. Of course.'

'I think we may hope for two thousand pounds,' the lawyer went on. 'Of course, the practice has dropped considerably in numbers since your brother's death, and when the poverty of the neighbourhood is taken into consideration, and the inconvenience of the house, and the lack of amenities, to say nothing of the hard and disagreeable work involved, I think two thousand pounds will be a very handsome price. I consider,' he confessed, 'that I was over-optimistic when I estimated the probable value at three thousand pounds some months ago. Still, I have, as I say, great hopes of Dr Cameron.'

But Uncle Preston's mind had gone straying. He did not take in the sense of what Mr Marriot said; he was staring at the tip of his shoe with a surprised expression.

'Extraordinary,' he murmured. 'You actually mean that people preferred to be attended by my brother? I should have thought that they would have welcomed Dr Casey as a new broom.'

'So should I,' said Mr Marriot dryly, 'but people seldom behave as one would expect them to. There is not the slightest doubt that Dr Garden was very popular in Enbury Fields. I might almost go so far as to say that he was loved. Your brother, Mr Garden, was a most unusual personality and a very handsome man, and he had that gift of mixing with all classes of people which makes a man popular. Oh, there is no doubt that they liked him.'

'But his life! All that ... well, well, it is not pleasant to discuss it. I confess that it *bewilders* me.'

Mr Marriot made no reply. So many things bewildered Uncle Preston, who suffered from a permanent sense of grievance because events and persons would not fit into the frame through which he looked at life.

Uncle Preston strongly advised the lawyer to refuse Harry the twenty-one pounds. Let him save it out of his salary. If Harry insisted, he must have it, his uncle supposed, but he would much rather that Harry didn't. After all, the boy was still under age. Even if no guardians had been legally appointed, he, Preston Garden, was the tiresome lad's natural guardian; and Harry must recognize the fact.

Mr Marriot promised to let him know immediately there was any more news from the agents about the sale of the practice; and so the talk ended.

Uncle Preston was lost in a fit of gloomy musing as he rode home to Forest Hill (the car was still having things done to it).

Like all Gardens, and most human beings, for that matter, he seldom saw his life as a whole. He only worked doggedly from day to day to make it *safe* and to keep free from *annoyances*, just as Aunt Maxine instinctively worked to get as much coarse enjoyment as possible, and the dead Hartley had clutched at beauty, passion and excitement, and the dead Oliver had turned to drink and to some dark, vague satisfaction in his own mind which had always escaped him.

There was No Peace, thought Uncle Preston, staring unseeingly out of the railway carriage window at the miles of grey houses running past under the pure sky of a summer evening. There was Always Something. Rows, styes on people's eyes, asthma, debts. Surely, when a man was always taking pains to keep worry at bay, worry ought to recognize the fact, and stay at bay? But worry seemed to haunt him, like a wasp.

And he got up still gloomily as the train drew into Forest Hill Station, with the problem unsolved; and went soberly homewards, swinging his quite unnecessary umbrella. With him, safely lodged in his skull, went the Garden nervousness and craving for excitement which was responsible for all his worryings; which welcomed the rows, asthma, even the styes on people's eyes, because these incidents fed its restless activity. Neither he nor any of his brothers or his sister had ever heard the beautiful and appalling saying, 'Mine was a nature which dreaded storms, but it needed them.' Yet how true it was of them.

*

Harry and Francis, meanwhile, were obtaining their ration of natural excitement in a healthy manner through a little too much to drink and through love.

Francis's affair with Toby had opened out with the ease of a flower in the sunlight; and they now spent most of their non-working hours together, making jokes and love.

He had pursued her with such singleness of mind that he had awed her into submission.

All his fears had been realized. She occasionally did go out with men of twenty-three. One, who owned a small sports car, wanted to marry her. She was pursued by boys of all shapes and sizes, at all hours and wherever she went.

But Mum, like a blessed tower of propriety and strength, stood in the way of all these suitors and fobbed them off. Toby had been brought up on the most severe Victorian rules; and this training had combined with her natural dancing gaiety and vitality, instead of fighting with it, and the result was such a combination of common sense and sweet warmth as intoxicated Francis.

One reads sometimes of women who manage their lives and their love with what can only be called sweet reasonableness; and more rarely one meets them. They will yield naturally to a lover, yet keep the relationship orderly and full of happiness. The lucky lover usually has the sense to marry his love.

Sophia suspected that Toby belonged in this rare class, though Francis never spoke of his relationship with her and she knew nothing definite about their feelings for one another. Sophia knew that, on the face of it, it was most unlikely that Toby should belong to this type. Her class and upbringing made it unlikely. Yet such charmers flourish calmly, and get what they want and give what they desire to give, in the most unfavourable circumstances. Sophia believed that Toby had simply absorbed her mother's warnings about Keeping Oneself to Oneself, Having Everything Nice, and Not Being Rough or Fast, and Respecting Your Elders, and quietly arranged her secret life as she pleased.

All these imaginings upon Sophia's part were vague, and she asked no questions to test their truth. She saw that Francis and Toby were cheerfully happy; she told herself that her brother's life was his own to manage. His relations with Toby, like most other circumstances at the cottage, appeared to be unconventional, but they only worried Sophia as a part of the general lack of plan and order.

The increasing disorderliness of life at the cottage troubled her deeply.

'You'll go to parties, yes, lots of parties,' prophesies the song and adds defiantly, 'So will I, so will I.' The singer appears to derive some comfort from the prospect; Sophia did not. There was a party at the cottage every weekend, with much port and sherry and noise. The port and sherry made the party more expensive; people seemed to enjoy it more, too.

And every Friday morning Harry had to borrow half-a-crown from Sophia to pay his fare down to the theatre. Only Providence and the bars round Leicester Square knew what he spent his money on. Sophia took two pounds of it, feeling unkind, but justified, and the rest melted.

Much of it seemed to go on what was vaguely known as a cheery evening with old Edward. From this exercise Sophia, who liked results, saw none.

She could not blame Harry for not knowing where his money went, for her own melted in the same mysterious manner.

She did try for a month to keep accounts, but she never could make what she had spent balance with what she had had, and this depressed her exceedingly. And she was always losing the little penny notebooks which she bought to keep her accounts in and having to buy new ones, and forgetting to put items down and worrying about where that elevenpence halfpenny had gone.

She was also handicapped by a strong secret feeling that it did not really matter a hoot where the elevenpence halfpenny had gone, when once it had gone. She *persuaded* herself that it mattered, but this was very different from having a fervent *feeling* that it mattered.

As Freud triumphantly says, 'There are no mistakes' – by which the good old man presumably means that if one forgets to do one's teeth, one does not wish to do one's teeth. So it was with Sophia and the penny notebooks. She forgot them because she did not want to remember them; and the same reasoning applied to the elevenpence halfpenny.

But her bad management still did not lead her into debt. It merely meant that she had a continual sensation, which was so strong as to be almost physical, of anxiety, confusion and distress about the lack of orderliness and prudence in the life they were leading. This was not shared by her brothers. They were agreeably lulled by the fact that there was always money coming in and parties being given. They did not seem to realize the awful fragility of the economic structure upon which their pleasures rested.

'We might all starve. Easily. All of us,' Sophia would sometimes say.

'Oh nonsense. People don't. You're getting melodramatic and Garden-y,' said Harry. 'Marriot wouldn't let us starve. Besides, we shall have the practice money soon.'

'We haven't got it yet, and when we have, it won't last for ever. What about when we're old?'

'Well, we aren't old.' He made a calculation. 'We're only about sixty years old between the three of us.'

'Nonsense!'

'Yes we are. Count up and see.'

She was much cheered by this piece of arithmetic; though she did not quite know why.

Apart from the disagreeable feeling of anxiety and insecurity about the future, and her apprehensions about Francis's delicate health and Harry's increasing love of gaiety, she was enjoying the summer.

It was delicious to return each evening to the quiet little valley amid the gorgeous summer spaces of the Heath. She knew every tree and path, and had some memory hovering about each.

There was the tree whose thick bough hung over a pool of
dark water, in the hollow near the famous fir trees painted by
Constable; the very same bough from which Harry had dipped
the screaming Celia into the pond, when they were both eight
years old. There was the excitingly dark and smelly pipe which
conducted the waters of a little stream in the valley near the
viaduct. The pipe was big enough for a child to walk through,
if the child did not mind stooping, darkness, smells, echoes
and mud, and here on a never-to-be-forgotten morning had
Sophia, Francis, Harry and Celia bravely clambered through
the pipe, encouraging each other with shrieks, and remaining
for the rest of the day slightly drunk with their own daring.
They still reminded one another of it with complacency, now
that they were grown up.

There was one of Sophia's favourite trees (she had twelve
or so), a little white hawthorn twisted into a shape suggesting
a true-lover's knot; here was her tall queen-beech overlooking
the square white dignity of Wrenwood House standing on its
hillside; and here the first one to put on leaves every year of
all the trees on the Heath; a big chestnut standing in one of
the gardens in the Vale.

There were the two chains of ponds, with their attendant
swans, ducks, purple water plants, and gulls in the winter;
their swimming dogs and fishing boys, and boys with boats
in the summer.

There was the big silver willow tree which Sophia called
to herself the Mandarin; it stood alone in a hollow amid wide
spaces of short grass, and its leaves lingered until far into the
winter. She had seen them hanging with twisted tips in the
dull light of a December day.

She and Celia took much pride in Enbury Village and the
Heath. They often went for walks together, on which they
would survey the landscape and clutch at one another, gasp,
make sounds of dismay and even enquire of workmen whether
they were going to cut down that old elm, or build flats on the
site where a Queen Anne or Regency house had stood.

They had been particularly upset by the conversion into flats of one of the most beautiful and superbly situated houses in Enbury Heath.

This was the Judge's House, which stood next to the Turpin Arms on the airy summit, in a walled garden. It was called the Judge's House because, though it was only some hundred and fifty years old, another house had once stood upon its site whence the local authorities of that day were said to have administered justice during the Great Plague.

The Judge's House was too big, alas, for one person to wish to make it a home.

Its rooms were large, and beautifully shaped as a theme by Mozart, and they looked out upon an old garden full of solitude and shade, but they were not convenient. The house had been built when Enbury Village was as quiet as a village in Herefordshire; but now motorcycles roared past it and persons parked their cars outside it in order to be close to the Turpin Arms, beer and gaiety, and it could not be described as quiet. Also, it was not in good repair and, as in the case of most old houses, bits frequently fell off it.

Nothing outrageous had been done to it. The house was allowed to stand. It was redecorated, and central heating was installed, and three oddly shaped but distinctive and expensive flats were constructed from its rooms.

Sophia and Celia were indignant about this, but had to admit that they could think of no other satisfactory fate for the beautiful Judge's House, which had lingered too long on the surface of the earth, and must now earn a living in its extreme old age or give back its site to Progress, and die.

'You wouldn't want it to be a museum,' pointed out Sophia, 'or a tea shop. I hate it being made into flats, too, but a house has got to work. It can't just be a sort of frightful coy parasite, like all those forges and mills in Sussex that used to shoe horses and make bread, and now they sell expensive home-made cakes and are too ghastly refined and artistic for words.'

'I should like a nice family to live in it.'

'No nice family would. It's too noisy. But three nasty rich families might, and I hope they will. I expect the people who built it were what we should call vulgarly rich. It's queer ... nowadays one reads about people's publicity stunts and private aeroplanes and aimless travel and one thinks 'How vulgar.' But when one reads about people building enormous great Follies in the eighteenth century, like that one at High Wycombe with the gold ball on the top, it only seems like interesting eccentricity, and one talks about the decay of the Character or Worthy in contemporary English Life.'

'I don't.'

'No, you don't, because all you're interested in is your boring Communism and India for the Indians and all the rest of it. If you're not careful you'll get so international that you'll fade away, and there won't be anything left of you except a sort of frightful Standard Woman, full of breathy enthusiasms about Work and Leisure and Culture and the Masses. Like boiled water, you'll be.

'I don't care, so long as I'm intelligent.'

'You're welcome. I regard your Communism and Internationalism as profoundly anti-poetic, and that's enough for me.'

One evening at the end of June Sophia came home by Tube, instead of by bus as she usually did in the summer, and slowly climbed the High Street to the summit of the Heath.

She paused to look down at London before she took the path down into the Vale; it rolled away terrifyingly on every side, far below, endlessly grey and delicate in the distance like some complex growth of the deep sea.

She was thinking, as she stared down at the city, of Keats's cry 'Oh, for a life of sensation rather than thought.'

It was impossible for her to come to any decision about the political and economic questions which were tearing at the world, let alone moral and social ones, and symptoms of mismanagement in the economic system like old Mrs Barker. The mere effort to decide made her mind feel bruised and whirling. Yet one could not ignore the misery on the earth; the North of England in the frost of industrial decline, violence and starvation in Europe, America staggering like a wounded golden giant.

Keats had known that the plunder of the senses could not be enjoyed in selfish peace.

> *'None can usurp this height,' returned that shade,*
> *'But those to whom the miseries of the world*
> *Are misery, and will not let them rest.'*

and

> *'Thou art a dreaming thing,*
> *A fever of thyself: think of the Earth.'*

Dear me, we are getting on, thought Sophia. We are comparing ourselves with Keats now.

She moved forward to take the path into the valley, but was stopped. A young man was standing in front of her, smiling.

It was an embarrassed smile. She stared at him, puzzled. He had a white bull terrier on a leash, and just behind him stood an elegant dark young girl dressed in pale blue.

'I say, you aren't going to hit me this time, are you? Do you remember me? I'm the chap you had the fight with by the pond. I say, by Jove, we were in a temper, weren't we? I was jolly angry, I can tell you. I went straight home and told my sister all about it. Here she is. This is my sister, Belinha' (he called it Belinya) 'and here's Brandy. Brandy, you old fool, where's the little bird, eh? Fetch him! Where's the little bird the naughty doggie killed? Naughty dog! Bad dog, sir!'

While he was saying all this in school-boy English and a foreign, accent, and with an air of extreme heartiness and what Sophia at once described as *stupidness*, he was looking at her with much embarrassment. He made her think of a certain kind of dog (not the kind in the Vale) which is always pleading.

Brandy had much more reserve; and the girl Belinha had silent and effortless dignity.

'I'm sorry I got in such a rage,' said Sophia amiably. 'I'm sure Brandy didn't do it again.'

'Oh yes he did, didn't you, old chap? Coo! I had a jolly fine business with him, I can tell you. He chased a sheep and worried him, and the keeper was furious. Coo! he was wild!'

'I can imagine it,' said Sophia.

'I've often seen you about. Once when I was in the car I saw you with two chaps.'

'Oh yes, my brothers.'

'I say, where were they at school?'

'Northgate.'

'Oh, a jolly awful place! We often played Northgate at footer. Awful blighters, we always thought they were. I was at Handall's for two years. My name's Juan Morales.'

Sophia could find nothing to reply but 'Indeed.' She wondered why Handall's, an expensive new school in Uxbridge, had not cured his foreign accent. He seemed a stupid but friendly person. She looked shyly past him at the girl, who smiled at her, and then turned away to gaze at the city in the valley.

'I say, I wonder if I ever came across your brothers?'

'You may have. The eldest played goal for the first eleven.'

'Harry Garden?'

'Yes.'

'By Jove, I remember him quite well. A jolly handsome chap.'

'I'll tell him you said so.'

'Ha! ha! I say, that's jolly good! Yes, do tell him I said so. But I say, won't you and your brothers come in for a cocktail this evening? Do come. It would be awfully jolly. I'd like to see old Harry Garden again, and meet your younger brother.'

'Thank you very much, but—'

'Oh, I say, you must come. We only live just across the road, at Judge Court.'

'The Judge's House?'

'Is that what they used to call it? Coo! it's a queer old place, isn't it? My aunt likes it, but I'd sooner be in one of those topping new places in St. John's Wood.'

I'm sure you would, she thought, bored at the idea of the cocktails but wishing very much to see the inside of The Judge's House.

Her wish won; she told him that she would come at nine o'clock if she could get Francis; Harry would be playing, of course.

He said hospitably that Harry must drop in after the show. He and Belinha never went to bed early.

I seem to be the only person in London who ever wants to, thought Sophia, going slowly down the hill when these arrangements were made.

Harry and Francis were at home. Harry was sitting at the table working out with pencil and paper how many glasses of alcohol each guest could count upon at the next party if one bottle of gin, one of whisky and two each of sherry and port were provided. Francis was, as usual, in the bath.

Sophia felt disillusioned. The cottage looked shabby; the parquet ill-polished, the flowers faded, the furniture too worn for comfort. No shabbiness could destroy the cheerful charm of the little house, but it was undoubtedly beginning to look very battered.

'Hullo darling.'

'Hullo. Do you remember a boy named Juan Morales? He says he remembers you. He was at Handall's.'

'Oh yes. A bit of an ass but quite decent. An enthusiastic sort of chap, very young for his age. How did you come across him?'

'Nearly had a fight with him on the Heath, months ago. He was setting his dog on the ducks. I met him just now, on the Mile, and he spoke to me. He wants us to go in for cocktails tonight about nine. They're living in The Judge's House. You can come on after the show, he says.'

'All right, I will. Very friendly, was he?'

'Was he not! I shouldn't think he's got a friend in the world.'

'He was always like that. They're Argentinians and very rich. The chaps used to rag him frightfully. He never minded. He's an ass, but not bad.'

Sophia, climbing wearily to her bedroom, called down to him:

'He's got a sister, too.'

'Ah-ha! What like?'

'About the most beautiful girl I've ever seen.'

Harry thought so too when he walked into the drawing room of the Morales' flat at twelve that night.

The white room was full of smoke and the noise of dance music. Sophia, in her best black, was sitting in a squat chair covered with white vellum, looking glum and sleepy and listening to Juan telling her of some dull experience in the Argentine, whence he had just returned.

Belinha, in a silver dress with a red rose stuck in her breast, was dancing lazily with Francis. She was a little girl with smooth black hair and large blue eyes. She was groomed so exquisitely that she did not look real.

She was a silent girl. Harry went straight for her and they danced together, hardly saying a word, while Juan shouted boring reminiscences about Handall's and Northgate to Harry, addressing him as 'man.'

'I like this room,' muttered Francis to Sophia as he handed her some sherry. He looked with simple admiration at the leopard-skin seats of the chairs, the sheepskin pouffes and a painting by Chirico of two splendid heavy horses which reared over the built-in electric fire. The room glittered with money and newness. Francis had never seen a place like this.

'Don't you?' he added.

'Mercy, no. I like the horses, but not, oh not in a house like this!'

'Why not?'

'It's all wrong. Like playing a theme from the Fifth Symphony and syncopating it.'

'Well, I like it.'

Better than the cottage, thought his sister bitterly. She was in a bad mood. It distressed her to see the rooms of The Judge's House furnished without individuality, like rooms in a fashionable hotel. The room was beautiful, but it was clear that some of our leading decorators had done their most chic with it. Not so should a house of character be furnished.

But Harry and Francis seemed to like it.

Poor lambs, she thought, watching her brothers. Luxury's so utterly new to them; we've never had even a sniff of it. No wonder they enjoy it.

CHAPTER XVIII

They were granted many sniffs of it for the next month or so.

Juan took a great liking to both the boys. This was not a compliment, because Juan liked everyone except his Aunt Maria, an extremely small, brown, silent, smiling person who glided into the room when the children were being entertained at The Judge's House, bowed, made a sound like 'Pleece' and glided out again.

For some time Sophia believed her to be dumb, but did not dare to ask Juan if this were so; the question would be so indelicate if she were not, or, for that matter, if she were.

Francis had no such scruples.

'I say, Juan, is your aunt dumb?' he demanded one day, after the aunt had said her piece and made her exit.

'Man, of course not! She can say enough when she wants to. She's always on at me about driving too fast, and jawing Belinha about flirting. Coo! she's an old cow, I can tell you.'

Sophia found it hard to believe that the aunt was an old cow, but she wondered very much what went on in her head, as she wondered about everyone.

Juan shared his car and much of his leisure with his new friends. He was to be in England for two years, learning banking and getting acquainted with English life. He would finally take a post in a large Argentinian bank which was largely controlled by an uncle, not the husband of the old cow, but another uncle, who was her brother and Juan's guardian. His parents were dead.

The weekends were their nicest times. In the week, as Harry was playing, they could only have impromptu parties after the show, which sent Harry and Francis carolling home to bed at half past two in the morning, but at weekends Juan would drive the two Gardens and Belinha out to a roadhouse, where they danced and swam and spent a great deal of money.

Once they took Toby, but that evening had not been a success.

Juan and Belinha were not snobs, they did not know much about the English class system, and Toby's manners were as pretty as they were unconventional, so they took her for granted and treated her as one of the family, but Toby was embarrassed and awed by the lavishness of the Morales' appointments. She also disapproved of Francis staying up until three in the morning, and borrowing money from Harry to pay for drinks.

'It isn't right,' said Toby obstinately and rather sullenly. 'It's soppy ... you being an office boy all day and then chasin' round like Lord Knows Who all night. Besides, you need your beauty sleep. You work so hard all day, dear, you need plenty of rest.'

For Toby, like Sophia, was burdened by a maternal instinct.

Francis saw the common sense of this remark, but he could not resist the delights offered by Juan. So far he had only seen the sordid side of dissipation. There was no attraction for him in playing cards until four in the morning with coarse fools, as his unhappy father had done, or in solitary drinking. But there was ecstasy in flying along in Juan's car on an empty moonlit road at three in the morning, just drunk enough to be divinely careless, his head back and his senses swimming in streams of cool wind, and all the stars in heaven flying above him!

He borrowed money from Harry to buy a dinner jacket; one could not go to the Monastery and the Queen of Clubs unless one was properly dressed.

The car made a great difference to their lives.

'I can't think how we ever did without one,' said Francis complacently.

'God, no. It's marvellous.'

Francis continued to take Toby out twice a week, and to enjoy her society and the sharp little bouquet of her personality, and he still loved her. He was not attracted by the girls he met at the roadhouses or at Juan's parties. He always returned to Toby with a feeling of peace and pleasure. She was the bread-and-butter of his odd topsy-turvy life, and even at seventeen he knew that, if man does not live by bread alone, he is most ill-nourished without it.

Yet he would not allow Toby to influence him; nor would he promise to spend less and go to bed earlier.

'I do my best with him. It's no use,' said Toby sadly to Sophia, one evening when they were washing-up in the tiny kitchen.

Toby had been to supper at the cottage, and was looking forward to a peaceful evening playing Old Maid and Snap! (two games at which she excelled) when Juan rang up to ask if Francis could come to The Judge's House for an hour. He had a nice chap he wanted him to meet; and Francis, making excuses, had gone ... just for an hour, he said.

There was a pause. Sophia was vigorously wiping the last two cherry teacups. The other four had been smashed in four collapses of the table leg.

At last—

'Neither can I,' she said in a low voice. She liked Toby, and did not mind her knowing that she was failing to make an orderly life at the cottage. Toby understood and was sorry.

'It's them being so near, isn't it?' said Toby. 'They can pop in any time.'

'They do. It's awful. And they *are* so boring. I really believe Belinha isn't all there.'

'Soppy thing,' said Toby, viciously wiping a jug. 'Never says a word. I do hate that sort; you never know what they're thinking about. Sly, Mum calls them.'

'She's very beautiful,' said Sophia, anxious to be fair.

'So is auntie's old cat,' retorted Toby, who produced this imaginary feline as an illustration whenever she wished to imply that she disagreed with a remark, but was too polite to say so.

'Don't you think she is?'

'Anyone can be beautiful if they've got enough money,' said Toby with truth.

'Harry thinks she is, anyway.'

Harry was so much in love with the silent Belinha that he could talk of nothing else. He was lost in a romantic thicket of red roses, music, nightingales. He had no idea what she thought of him, and he lived on hope and dreams. Belinha might not be all there, but she had at least learned that when a girl is as beautiful as she was, she need only be silent, and a lover's imagination will do the rest.

'Well, there's one comfort; she and the Aunt don't talk too much,' said Sophia, carrying plates across to the cupboard. 'If they both talked as much as Juan, I don't know what I'd do.'

'Puts you in mind of the parrot house at the Zoo, doesn't he,' agreed Toby. She put her arm round Sophia's waist and said coaxingly, 'Listen, dear, won't you come down to Rozanne's tomorrow afternoon and let me wave your hair nicely? It *would* make such a difference, you don't know.'

Sophia laughed. She thought that it probably would, but did not say so.

'And pluck your eyebrows. Will you? Do! I'll be ever so careful.'

'Toby dear, it's sweet of you, but I don't think I will. I should feel so unlike me.'

'A nice, soft, deep wave!'

'Some day, perhaps. We'll see.'

At ten o'clock the dog Taffy came scrabbling at the door for his drink of water, and stayed for a few moments, staring disdainfully into the empty grate. Dan the Airedale went past on his nightly walk, accompanied by his master and the usual roars of 'Dan! Come here, sir, confound you!' The Vale did all the usual things which it did every evening before it went to bed; but half past ten struck from the church tower on the hill; and Francis had not come.

Saying crisply that she wouldn't half give him the rounds of the kitchen when he rang up tomorrow, Toby kissed Sophia good night, and went home.

Sophia knew that Harry and Francis did not go about with Juan only because he had a car and helped them to have a good time. They said that they liked him; and he was likeable ... if one did not mind his insensitiveness and the fact that he talked too much. She decided that he had achieved the life of 'sensation rather than thought'; and as he had no nerves he was a restful companion for her nervous and over-sensitive brothers. He was good natured, and an emphatic yea-sayer; and the society of such people can be most stimulating and pleasant.

He was not so reckless that he made more sober people feel disagreeably responsible when they were with him, and yet he was reckless enough, because of the confidence given him by his money, to convey a delightful 'doesn't matter' element into his pastimes.

Until she knew Juan, Sophia had not realized that an imagination can become, like the grasshopper, a burden.

Belinha was stupid. Sophia suspected that she was also affectionate and gentle, but never had a chance to find out because Belinha hardly ever spoke about anything, let alone herself. Probably she never thought about herself, either. Her senses lay close to the surface of her nature, like the rosy purple roots exposed in soil after rain, and she was guided by them to make the very most of her beautiful appearance, to smile, to be divinely silent, but her mind was like a bud that will never open.

There would be fewer unmarried ones, Sophia decided, if women would learn to talk less.

Juan's good nature and Belinha's beauty gave ample excuse to the Garden boys, should they ever have to justify this new friendship, and added to these attractions there was the important one of tastes in common.

Juan's tastes were certainly common. He enjoyed, as nine people out of ten enjoy or would enjoy if they could, getting rather drunk, kissing, going very fast in an expensive car, dancing, swimming, laughing. He would still be enjoying these pastimes when he was fifty, and as he was wealthy, he would be able to have them when he was fifty. Francis and Harry enjoyed them now at the ages of seventeen and twenty-one; but as they were poor, it seemed unlikely that they would be able to have them at the age of fifty. All the more reason therefore to taste these gorgeous joys now; to drink the gin, and kiss the girl, and dance solemnly to the incantations of the snow music, and go at seventy miles an hour.

All their own nervous vitality, and the appetite for strong and deeply coloured pleasures which they had inherited from their father conspired to drive them at these natural joys like wild young horses; and if their prospects and background had been rosier and more solid, Sophia would have realized that such foragings were inevitable, and she would not have been quite so worried.

But dismal things happened to poor young men who acquired expensive tastes which ravened to be fed. Sophia, walking across the Heath intoxicated by the smell of young leaves and the steady fall of the sunlight on her face, thanked her stars that her own desires were fed by objects which did not cost much money. She painfully, priggishly tried to understand why the boys enjoyed kissing young women whom they did not know, and all the other pastimes of which seemingly they could not have enough; and could not understand at all, and made herself extremely irritating to her brothers by trying.

The month of July was a dull, unhappy one for her. The interest and pleasure which her brothers had first taken in the cottage had dwindled. They took their home for granted. It was a useful place to have parties in when old Juan's aunt had said that they must have no more in The Judge's House for some time, and they still felt its charm when they mentioned it to new acquaintances, but its novelty had departed. They used it, Sophia bitterly thought, like an hotel; and she was the chief muck-and-bottle washer.

She never knew when they would be in to supper or to meals at the weekends. The domestic evenings with My Collection and the baked beans had vanished into the happier past. My Collection was never cleaned; and Francis had sold half of his dear Rider Haggard books when he was quite without money one Saturday morning, and he proposed (though not without regret) soon to sell the other half. He also sold gramophone records and the two sword sticks.

The three knew all about selling things, because they used to help their mother to do this when she was being kept particularly short of money by her husband; the knowledge was one of the useful legacies left them by their upbringing.

Of course Sophia did not like selling books and sword sticks. Irritating girl! she liked hardly anything her brothers did at this time. She was always protesting, gently arguing, trying to be tactful, trying not to be like Uncle Preston, and yet avoid being like Aunt Maxine, trying to crush her own boring love of law and order, trying to save some money to go for a week's holiday in France at the end of August. She had a fortnight's holiday, but could only afford to go away for a week. Nevertheless, as she had never been abroad she was looking forward very much to the journey, the new smells and sounds and sights.

It was the one touch of happiness in a wretched month.

She managed, somehow, to keep the state of affairs from the relatives.

Uncle Preston was often in touch with her at this time, because he had to let Harry know how the negotiations with Dr Cameron were going, and as Harry was seldom in, Sophia had to take messages for him.

'And how are things with you all?' Uncle Preston would ask, scenting decay from afar with that devilish sixth sense possessed by one's relations. 'All *well*? All *prosperous*? All *happy*?'

'Yes, thank you, Uncle Preston.'

'Your Aunt Maxine and I are always ready, you know, to help you out of any little difficulty. Yes.'

'Yes, I know, Uncle Preston. Thanks most awfully.'

'I do not mean *money* difficulties, heh! heh! heh! We are not *millionaires*. By the way, I understand that Harry has written to Mr Marriot asking for *all* the money which has been collecting from the practice during the last two months. Is that so?'

'I'm afraid I don't know.'

'Well ... I *strongly* advised Marriot not to let him have it. What can he want it for? What does he spend his money on?'

'I don't know,' said his niece, truthfully this time.

'Well, it is all most annoying. Most worrying. ... Yes.'

It is that, thought Sophia as she hung up the receiver. And how much worse it would be when the state of affairs at the cottage could no longer be hidden from the relatives, and they had to know that she and Harry and Francis had failed to make a home together!

That was what she minded so dreadfully.

They were no longer enough for each other. Three was company no more. All her plans for an orderly happy life together had collapsed, and they lived in a state of scrappy confusion and continuous efforts not to quarrel.

She knew that she was boring, elder-sisterish, tiresome and a spoilsport. She did not really blame the boys for being angry with her. But what other attitude could she take, when she thought she saw her brothers, the two people she loved best in the world, beginning the journey along that road which their father had taken?

Yet if she spoke out strongly, and reminded them of his example and fate, Francis said, 'Oh rot. We should never get like Father did; we've seen too much of that sort of thing,' and Harry said, 'Oh rot. It'll be all right. Don't worry. You're getting just like Uncle Preston.'

This accusation could always silence her.

Miss Tessitt was another thorn. Miss Tessitt, of course, knew what was going on, and derived much pleasure from disapproving.

'I see your brothers in that car last naight with that girl. May! they was goin' a pace! Well, Ay says to may friend, sooner them than *may*, Ay says. Always out, aren't they? Not at all what you might call home birds, are they? Ay shouldn't laike to keep house for them, Ay must say.'

And old Mrs Barker, timidly yet tenaciously coming every Wednesday and Saturday morning to maltreat the doorstep and pocket her one and sixpence, would say:

'You had a party lars night didn't you, dear? Always 'avin' parties, aren't you? I come pars about eleven o'clock, an' 'eard the wireless.'

'The gramophone,' corrected Sophia glumly.

Why should she be accused of having a wireless in the cottage? Had she not enough to bear without that?

'Gramophone, was it? 'Aven't you got no wireless?'

'No, Mrs Barker.'

'Aow, what a shame.'

Sophia contented herself with smiling at Mrs Barker, handed her a cup of her special Indian tea, and firmly closed the door on her.

What a lot of pensioners would go down when ...

When the cottage went down ... when they separated ... but they couldn't! They mustn't separate!

Oh, how horribly quickly the idea had come into her head, and was now enthroned there, driving all other thoughts into the background. She tried not to think of it. She told herself that this state of affairs would not last. Harry and Francis would get tired of Juan, and then the three could make a fresh start.

During the third week in August 'The Racket' came off, much to everyone's surprise.

This was serious. At a blow it docked the Gardens' income of five pounds a week, and flung them on Sophia's salary and Francis's. Harry had not saved a penny and neither had Sophia, and in the circumstances Harry felt that he was morally entitled to call upon Mr Marriot.

Mr Marriot listened in silence to his rather halting remarks
and then quietly told him that Dr Cameron and his partner had
agreed only that morning to buy the practice for two thousand
pounds.

This news completely drove all thoughts of 'The Racket's'
fate and the practice's paltry takings out of Harry's head. It
came at exactly the right moment, as events so seldom do. And
in a week he would be twenty-one.

'I presume,' said Mr Marriot, 'that you will wish to invest
this money. Invested in a safe security at five per cent, it would
bring you in a hundred pounds a year. A very useful sum. Small,
but useful. It would mean that you could not starve.'

'Couldn't live on it,' said Harry.

'Not in comfort, certainly, or for long, but it would tide you
over a time like the present, for example, when you are out
of work.'

Harry was silent.

Tiresome young cub, thought Mr Marriot, looking at his
charming obstinate face. He knew perfectly well that Harry
planned to secure the two thousand pounds and spend it. He
knew it as well as though Harry had said so. And the lawyer
had only a fortnight in which to persuade him to invest it. On
September the first Harry would be twenty-one, and he could
demand his money, and would have to have it; the law (confound
it) would stand behind him and support his claim in face of all
the sober advice of Mr Marriot and Uncle Preston. The law
was like that, always magnificently sacrificing the particular
on the altar of the general.

'Would you like me to send you a list of suitable stocks in
which the money might be invested?'

'Thanks awfully. That would be a good idea, wouldn't it?'

'And, if I may say so, I advise you to get matters in hand
quickly. Money has a habit of draining away before you know
where you are.'

Harry agreed heartily with this remark.

He finally went away, however, with a cheque for twenty pounds in his pocket. It came from the proceeds of the faithful practice, not from the sacred two thousand pounds, but even so Mr Marriot felt a pang at giving it. He quite saw that Harry must have money to live on while he was looking for another job, but in what manner would he live? Lavishly, thought Mr Marriot gloomily. He found himself taking a personal interest in these three unusual young people, just as Mr Graby and the typists did in Francis. He still disapproved of them, but his imagination played about their youth and their forlorn state. He wished that they would all be sensible. But who ever was? And why should they be, with an heredity and an upbringing like theirs?

He sighed; and told his secretary to look out a list of safe, steady stocks and post it to Mr Harry Garden with an explanatory letter.

Harry took a bus home because he only had a shilling, and a cheque for twenty pounds which no taxi driver would cash.

The longed-for thing had happened. The practice was sold, and in a fortnight he would have two thousand pounds. For have it he would, and spend it, and damn old Marriot and Uncle Preston.

He could not analyse his feelings clearly, but he knew that he hated this money and wanted to get rid of it.

It was tainted by those dark frightening times he had known as a little boy, when he would hide under the kitchen table with the cloth pulled down to make a tent, and tremble with terror at the noise of his father's angry shouts upstairs and the slamming doors; and with those awful, helpless moments in which he had seen his mother, the source of all comfort and peace, crying as he cried when he hurt himself, and he had been held close to her warm, wet cheeks so that he was shaken by her crying.

It was all beastly, all the past; miserable and damned boring, and when he thought of how his father had worked for this same money, he wanted even more to chuck it away and buy a good time with it. The work which had made it, amongst dirt and disease and pain, had helped to kill his father whom he had loved. Father knew how to spend, he never saved money like a damned old maid, and I'm going to do the same, decided Harry.

He telephoned Sophia at the C.N.A. when he got home and told her the news.

'Oh. Good,' said Sophia without enthusiasm. She did not feel any.

Now that this fairy-tale event had happened, which they had talked about with such anticipatory pleasure six months ago, it seemed oddly flat. It did not seem to be real money, like the fifteen pound notes which were in her handbag and would pay for her holiday in France. It was still phantasmal, as it had been six months ago.

About four o'clock, when the office boy was making the tea, Sophia drearily realized that the two thousand pounds would probably lead to new troubles. Harry would want to spend it. The elders of the tribe would want him to invest it. It would mean even more expensive dissipations with Juan and temporarily remove all sense of proportion and responsibility from Harry's mind.

She looked so worried and unhappy that Miss Candy noticed it.

'Something on the old mind?'

'Have I not! My eldest brother's just got hold of two thousand pounds.'

Even thus she felt a gloomy pride in the largeness of the sum.

'*Honestly*, my dear? I mean, did he come by it honest?'

'Oh yes. It's the money for the practice. You remember ... I told you.'

'Of course. But, my dear, how too wizard! You'll be able to have *the* most marvellous time while it lasts, and mind you get a hundred or two out of him for yourself. You enjoy yourself while you're young. One isn't young for long. Up to twenty-five it's marvellous and then everything goes phut and the old wrinkles begin a massed attack, so to speak.'

'I do enjoy myself in my own way, but I can't when I know this money will be chucked about like water, and none of it saved for our old age.'

Miss Candy shook her head. The thought of old age, which seldom left her mind, was like a cold ghost lurking among the butterflies of her philosophy.

'You take life too seriously. My advice to you is – take the cash in hand and blow everything else or whatever it is the poet-wallah says.'

'I can't.'

But on the following Saturday morning, when she climbed the hill from the Vale among the quivering blue and green shades of a summer day, on the first stage of her journey to France, she could not help feeling cheerful.

She carried one small suit case and a heavy rucksack on her back. This latter gave her a burdened yet pilgrimish and adventurous feeling which was very pleasant, and she enjoyed the look of her worn heavy brogues; they had gone with her through many tangled thickets and over cushiony turf and she was fond of them.

She found that she could easily, too easily, forget to worry about money, Harry, Juan, the cottage and Miss Tessitt. All these were washed away by a wave of delightful excitement and loneliness. 'I was lonely,' says someone; and one feels pity. 'I was alone,' says another, in such a tone of happiness calmly remembered that one feels envy. Sophia's solitude was of the last kind.

The cottage put out one last reminder to her as she was leaving the Heath for the road down to the Tube.

Mrs Barker, a tiny figure, suddenly emerged from behind the thick trunk of a chestnut tree, seeming blacker and smaller than ever in the glowing green cave made by the branches and the rich fresh grass.

She appeared as usual, about to cry; but when she saw Sophia she gave the watery, amazed, grateful smile which she saved for the three young Gardens.

Oh lord, thought Sophia, wondering if she had any small change. She remembered that it was Saturday; Mrs Barker must be on her way to smear the cottage doorstep. She was swinging a battered bucket.

' 'Ullo, dear.'

'Hullo, Mrs Barker. You just off to do the step?'

'That's right, dear. You goin' away, dear?'

'Yes, for a week to France. It's all right,' she added hastily. 'My eldest brother will be there on Wednesday and Saturday to give you your tea and everything.'

Mrs Barker's face, which had begun to express bottomless despair mingled with indignation, became more peaceful.

'Well, I'm glad you're 'avin' a 'oliday, dear. That's right. You enjoy yerself. One day you'll be gettin' married and then you won't be able to go off for holidays and enjoy yerself. It ain't the same,' said Mrs Barker broodingly, 'when a gel's married.'

'But I don't particularly want to get married, thanks. At least not yet,' she added with her scrupulous honesty.

'Don't yer, dear?' shrilled Mrs Barker in the liveliest surprise and much disapproval. 'Not get married? Aow, every gel ought to get married.'

Sophia was tempted to say, 'Why?' but refrained. It was no use. Mrs Barker was but Aunt Grace writ small, so to speak. Neither, it appeared, had derived benefit from the married state, and both realized it, yet both loyally upheld the Juggernaut which had crushed them. It was confoundedly irritating and illogical, but there was no sense in arguing with them. In doing so, energy was used which might be more profitably employed.

'Well, I'm off,' said she soothingly. 'Goodbye, Mrs Barker.'

'Goo'-bye, dear. 'Ope you 'ave nice weather.'

Sophia walked away under the trees, her shoulders stretching pleasantly to the weight of the rucksack.

CHAPTER XIX

The night of September the first chanced to be unusually beautiful. There was a moon, a soft wandering wind, slow clouds and all the dim silver points of the stars.

It would not be strictly true to say that this night was never forgotten in the Vale, but it was remembered for a long time.

Motionless upon the landing of the second floor of 1 The Walk stood Miss Belper. It was nearly three in the morning. Miss Belper was looking out of the landing window, and by her side stood Mrs Amsett, who occupied the flat downstairs. Both ladies wore dressing gowns and looked extremely sleepy and angry.

'If *only* the Colonel were at home!' exclaimed Mrs Amsett, for the sixth time. 'So unfortunate that he should have chosen this very weekend to go to Aldershot!'

'I expect he, at least, is getting a proper night's rest,' said Miss Belper tartly. 'Besides, even if he were here, what could he do?'

'He could speak to them. He could go over and rap on the door. They would be bound to take some notice, surely.'

'I don't expect they could hear,' said Miss Belper, yawning miserably. She added darkly, 'Probably they are *too far gone by now* to hear *anything*.'

They returned to their gazing from the window.

'I wonder the police haven't interfered!' suddenly and violently exclaimed Miss Belper.

Much the same thing was being said at Myrtle Cottage, The Hollies, 3 Vale Street, and most of the other houses in the luckless hamlet. Old Mr Pell, of Myrtle Cottage, had got so far as unchaining Jimmy Barrell, who was extremely pleased and excited at the prospect of a moonlight walk and began to bark loudly and cheerfully and had to be rushed back into his kennel and told to lie down, sir. Old Mr Pell went back to bed and put cotton wool in his ears.

Taffy, who lived in the house next door to the cottage, was awake too. Occasionally he did a bout of barking, and Dan the Airedale at 4 The Hollies joined in with eager pleasure. Other dogs (perhaps Wodge, whose sleeping quarters were wrapped in mystery, was among them) joined the chorus from time to time.

The little house from which came the furious racket of music, shouts and confused sounds blazed with light like a troll's cave. All the Vale was moonlit, shadowy, still, surrounded by the wide grassy acres of the Heath where huge trees dreamed in the silver-green moonlight; and in contrast the cottage looked furiously glittering and alive.

'It's like a witch's sabbath,' said the sleepy, but inclined-to-be-sympathetic young husband at 5 The Walk, to his wife. He was twenty-four and liked parties.

'I was thinking it looked like that advertisement for health-food – "sleepless in a sleeping world."'

'The sister's away. I saw her go off on Saturday.'

'That accounts for it.'

'Old Pell will probably send her one of his notes when she comes back.'

'Sure to. He's too fond of notes.'

'No, but really. It's a bit too much of a good thing ...'

At four o'clock the Vale had gone back to its beds to get what sleep it could. The noise in the cottage had subsided to what may be described as a dull red glow with occasional flickers. By five o'clock, when a lovely morning was coming into the east, there was an exhausted silence which was not broken until just before eleven, when the gramophone started again and shameless figures in dressing gowns and shirtsleeves and pyjamas came out, yawning and dancing, to take in the milk.

When Sophia got back to England on the afternoon of September the third, which was a Saturday, she was pleased to find that the autumn had begun. The trees were turning, and subtlety had come into the light. She had enjoyed her holiday very much, though it had only been spent wandering in Boulogne and over the sand dunes just outside it. She approached Boulogne with respect as a town, not as a cross between a joke and a place where Channel boats stopped, and it rewarded her with an atmosphere, a history and the strangeness of a foreign place.

Celia met her, and they treated themselves to a taxi back to the cottage.

Celia was rather silent. Sophia suspected some fresh bogglement with Capel, and tactfully said nothing about the silence; she asked whether Celia had seen anything of the boys.

Celia started out of a dream.

'Not much ... no.'

'Did you go to Harry's party? I sent a wire. Bless him.'

'I just looked in.'

'Was it a good one? Where did they have it?'

'At the cottage.'

'I thought they were having it at The Judge's House?'

'The aunt wouldn't let them.'

'Oh lord, then I suppose they had it at the cottage.'

'Yes.'

'Was it a good one?'

'Pretty good. I can't stick Juan, you know. He *is* so intellectually lazy.'

'Celia, what's the matter? Was it a *ghastly* party?'

'No ... it was all right. I didn't stay till the end.'

Sophia asked no more questions. A foreboding began to chill her. What, oh what, had Harry and Francis been up to? She felt aggrieved, She had not been three hours in England and already something awful was looming over her. It was too bad. The delightful lazy peace of her holiday was already receding like a dream.

At home she found two notes awaiting her.

'Dear Miss Garden,

I have been bad with my legs the doctor says I am to rest them so I have taken a few days of the hill would be sure to make them worse so if the place is a bit dusty you will now Sincerely, L. Tessitt.'

'Mr C. J. P. Pell would be grateful if Miss Garden could spare him a minute on her return. Mr Pell has a matter of importance to discuss with Miss Garden.'

Sophia looked round the forlorn, dusty, untidy cottage, and then at Celia, and then at Francis, who was sitting on the sofa (whose springs, Sophia noticed, were giving way) looking depressed, and then back at the two notes in her hand.

'Who is C. J. P. Pell?' she asked robustly; more robustly than she felt.

'He lives at Myrtle Cottage,' explained Celia.

'He's an old sissy,' growled Francis.

'Any idea what he wants to see me about?'

Francis was silent.

'Where's Harry?'

'Motoring with Juan. They've been out all day.'

Sophia went into the kitchen, where dirty cups and plates were piled in the sink, and put on a kettle for tea. She was trying hard not to feel depressed, but she could not help thinking that never had the poor little cottage seemed less attractive. Its native charm and air of happiness was almost lost under dust, bits, dirty crockery, dead flowers and a smell of stale tobacco smoke. It's high time I came home, she thought grimly.

Celia had to go off almost immediately; and when she had gone, Francis came into the kitchen and leaned against the wall in silence, watching the kettle.

'I'm sorry it's all so beastly for you to come back to, my dear,' he said at last.

'Never mind. We'll soon have it nice again. What a curse old Tessitt is. You seem very depressed. Is anything the matter?'

'Nothing much.'

'But something is? Do tell me. I can't bear having things hanging over my head.'

'It's nothing much, really.'

'*Francis!* For mercy's *sake!*'

'Well ... it's Toby's mother.'

'Toby's mother? What on earth do you mean? Is she kicking up a fuss about your seeing Toby?'

'Not yet; she may, though. She says she's thinking about stopping us seeing each other.'

'But why, in heaven's name? What have you been up to?'

'Oh nothing ... nothing anyone normal would make a song about. It's only that I wrote to Toby when I was frightfully fed up and used the word 'bloody,' and Toby's mother found the letter and was awfully shocked, and now she says she doesn't think I'm a fit person for Toby to go about with.'

'Oh ...' Sophia was relieved. 'Well, she'll come round. You give her time. I thought it was something awful, from your face.'

'That's just it; she won't come round. She won't see me and let me explain. She says she must see you.'

'*What?*'

'To talk it over, she says. Yes, I know it's sickening for you. I'm frightfully sorry, dear. But she's got it into her head that if she could see you, and you would tell her that I was really all right and respectable and everything, then she would believe it. She's heard a lot about you: Toby's told her, and she'd take your word, you see. I'm awfully sorry to have to ask you, my dear, but Toby and I would be eternally grateful if you could go and see her, and just explain.'

'But, Francis, how can I explain? If you wrote bloody, you wrote it, and that's all there is to it. Incidentally, what a silly thing to do. You know those people—'

She stopped, and wiped a dish with care. She had been going to say that working-class people were always easily shocked, but that was snobbish and it might hurt Francis's feelings. And anyway, bloody was an ugly word; it was a pity that other classes were not shocked by it.

'It's seeing it written, I suppose?' she amended.

'I suppose so. Anyway, it's a most sickening bore. Will you go, darling? Do. It won't be so awful, really. Toby's mother is very nice when you get to know her.'

'Is she frightening?'

'Well, just a bit at first, perhaps. She's got a rather severe manner.'

'*Oh!*' exploded Sophia, dashing down her dishcloth, 'it's *too* sickening! I come back from the first peaceful holiday I've ever had, and here are all these awful things waiting for me. You know I loathe rows and explanations and fusses and things. It's too bad of you to let me in for this. Curse Toby's mother, I say. And what's this note about from X. Y. Z. Pell or whoever he is? You've been up to something, I suppose. What was it? The twenty-first party? What happened? I suppose it was frightfully rowdy. You may as well tell me.'

'Well it was, rather. You see, Juan would have champagne.'

'Oh, he would, would he? And who paid for it?'

'He and Harry went halves.'

'How much did it come to?'

'Oh … rather a lot, Sophia. But it's all right. Harry's got plenty of money. You see he asked old Marriot for the two thousand pounds, and he got it, too!'

'Francis!' She stared at his half-ashamed, half-triumphant face. 'He *didn't*. Oh, what *shall* I do? What shall I *do*? How could Marriot let him have it?'

'He had to. It's Harry's.'

'But Uncle Preston … didn't he do anything? He must have been in an awful state …'

'Oh, as soon as Marriot told him he began telephoning. We answered the 'phone once, and then Harry rang off because Uncle Preston kept on blethering so, and he wouldn't answer the telephone again. It kept on ringing all the evening. We stuffed the bell up at last.'

Sophia looked at the bell. It was muffled by one of Harry's socks.

'When did this happen?'

'Yesterday evening. We were having a party.'

Sophia sat down on the step which led into the kitchen, and looked up at him. He looked at her with the steady, fixed smile which she knew meant that he was both angry with her and ashamed of himself.

'Another rowdy one?'

'Pretty rowdy. June came, and that little Sally-object, and Juan and Edward ...'

'How long did it go on?'

'Finished at four this morning. I didn't go to work. Harry 'phoned to say I was ill. I felt it, too. Champagne and gin is a bit too much for me.'

He was boasting to hide his discomfort at the sight of her stricken face. She said nothing. She got up, and took a dirty glass off the flap and began to wash it carefully.

'It's all right, Sophia. For god's sake don't take it so seriously. You're as bad as Uncle Preston. It's only natural that we should want a bit of a burst now we've got the money. Harry was afraid you'd mind. He's bought you a lovely bottle of scent. It's upstairs on your dressing table. Would you like me to get it?'

She began to cry.

The thought of Harry buying scent for her was too much. She was wretched because he thought of her as a person who must be soothed by bottles of scent, and touched by his thought for her in the midst of his junketings, and dreadfully reminded by his kindness of the early days at the cottage when they were all peaceful and happy and hopeful together.

'Shall I get it, dear?'

'Oh, no – I'll look at it myself later. Please leave me alone. I'm all right.'

'And will you see Toby's mother, darling?'

'Oh, I suppose so. Do go away. Do leave me alone, can't you?'

He retired into the bathroom with the ukulele; whence he came out half an hour later to meet Toby.

The evening was passed pleasantly by Sophia between Mr Pell and Uncle Preston.

After Francis had gone she cried herself sick; then she made some tea and got into a temper.

The boys might behave badly, but she was not going to rush into the bosoms of Uncle Preston and Mr Pell and admit that they had.

She would stand up for them to these old gentlemen, whose business it was not, however she and her brothers chose to behave.

She found a telephone number on Mr Pell's notepaper, rang him up and told a female voice that she would see Mr Pell at half past eight that evening. At the cottage. Her cottage. The female voice went away and came back and said reprovingly that Mr Pell had a cold, and did not wish to venture out, and would prefer that Miss Garden came to Myrtle Cottage.

Sophia said politely that she had one, too, and that she did not want to venture out either, and so would Mr Pell come to her. The voice came back and said, outraged, that Mr Pell would.

As soon as Sophia had hung up the receiver the muffled bell rang; and there was Uncle Preston.

With a voluptuous inhalation of the breath he hailed his niece's return. At last – at last – he could have a long, detailed, deliciously chewy discussion about the unspeakably frightful behaviour of Francis and Harry.

It appeared that the whole family was seething like a rookery.

No one had been able to get in touch with the boys for the past three days.

Some twenty-first birthday presents and messages for Harry (including a silk muffler crocheted by Auntie Loo with some difficulty and pain because of the stye on her eye) had not been acknowledged; and when Aunt Maxine was motored over by a friend on the afternoon of the birthday itself, she found the cottage shut up and all the curtains drawn, and though she suspected that somebody was at home (for she swore that she heard sounds within) no one would answer her knocks and whistles.

And one evening while Sophia was away, Harry had driven over to Aunt Grace's in a car with another young man and a girl, and they had taken Angela out to some dreadful night-club and brought her home at three in the morning *the worse for liquor.*

Sophia was reluctantly compelled to grin at this picture.

'Aunt Grace shouldn't have let her go. She ought to have known what would happen.'

'Your aunt *naturally* assumed that Harry would be *responsible* for his cousin.'

But then my aunt is an ass, thought Sophia while the tide of words flowed over her. She could imagine silly Aunt Grace's excitement at the arrival of the two lordly young gods in the car, and Angela hurrying into a bright pink frock and repeating how thrilled she was, and Aunt Grace watching them drive off with all kinds of fond and foolish hopes. It was silly but it was also sad. And whether Angela had enjoyed her evening or no, they ought not to have let her get drunk, because there was heredity, in the shape of Uncle Oliver, to remember. There was no harm in Harry showing himself off to the relations if he could not resist so doing, but he ought to remember heredity ...

'And apparently this young man, this Gorales or whatever his name is, *insulted* Angela.'

'How?'

'He ... I understand that he kissed her. Not at all in a nice way, Sophia. Yes.'

I'll bet she liked it though, thought Sophia. All Gardens (except, apparently, herself) liked kissing and its inevitable developments. They pretended to be shocked by it, but they liked it all the same. Too much.

But the Angela scandal, though very important and shocking, was as nothing beside the two thousand pounds scandal; and altogether Uncle Preston was on the telephone for nearly three-quarters of an hour. Sophia refused to discuss it. She would only say 'Yes' and 'No' and make non-committal statements; and in the midst of one of these came a precise knock at the front door, and there was Mr Pell, punctual to the second.

Sophia hastily abandoned Uncle Preston, but not before he had made her promise to go and see him on Sunday, the following day, to discuss matters.

Mr Pell was large, square, and owlish. He had made the mistake of bringing Jimmy Barrell with him, who, to Sophia's great surprise and pleasure, rose to the occasion and greeted her as a friend. This did not soothe Mr Pell.

'The dog knows you, I see,' he said with the gloomiest suspicion in his voice as he stepped over the threshold. He implied that Jimmy Barrell had often chased Sophia over the Heath with strings of stolen sausages.

'Yes,' said Sophia crisply. 'Do sit down, won't you. What do you want to see me about?'

Now Mr Pell chiefly wanted to see Sophia and the inside of the cottage because curiosity was the breath of his nostrils and the reason why he disapproved of everybody's goings-on. Disapproval gave you a right to poke and interfere and find out; it gave these actions the lustre of duty rather than the meretricious glitter of pleasure. But of course he could not say so. Indeed, he did not himself know what his true motives were. He thought that they were a sense of duty and the desire to assist his neighbours.

He was also handicapped by a strong desire to stare round the cottage and to ask Sophia all about herself and the two young men she lived with. He did not like the look of any of them. He deplored their behaviour. He suspected the worst – in many forms. But he did want to know.

'There have been complaints,' he began.

'Who from?'

'Myself, for one. And many other people living in the Vale. About the noise. Night after night. Until the small hours of the morning. When we should all be getting our rest. Including those who make the noise. Last night it was the same thing over again. Over and over again. The gramophone. And people running up and down stairs. You should tell your two gentlemen friends ...'

'My brothers.'

Mr Pell looked disappointed.

'Your brothers. Two of them?'

'Yes.'

'Your brothers, then,' he repeated in a tone of flat disbelief, 'that it causes annoyance. You, I believe, have been away ...'

'Yes.'

'You were away a week, I think. Did you go far? A holiday, was it?'

It was, thought Sophia bitterly. She quoted to herself: 'This is a holiday, that was.'

'I went to France.'

Mr Pell's face brightened. This was better. This fitted in with what he had suspected.

'Ah. *To Paris?*'

'No. To Boulogne.'

Well, that was more likely than England, anyway. All French places were the same. Gay. Full of licence. Dissipation at home and licence abroad. He glanced stealthily round the cottage in search of empty bottles, and his glance was not unrewarded; Sophia had left them there on purpose.

'We all feel very strongly about it. A peaceful little community. A village, so to speak. Each dependent upon the other. For peace. For quiet. For mutual benefit.'

'Yes.'

'One discordant element, and all suffer. Have you got this house on a long lease?'

'I don't know.'

'You don't know? But surely ...'

'No. My brother Antony,' said Sophia with cold recklessness, 'arranged all that before he went to prison.'

Mr Pell's face positively shone. So! He knew it! Licence, dissipation, crime ... He had suspected it all, and here it was.

'Dear, dear, dear ... May I ask *what for?*

'Forgery. And my sister Helen. Both of them got ten years. Oh, and a bit extra for blackmail. Eighteen months, I think it was.'

But she had gone too far. Even Mr Pell heard something odd in the ring of her last words. He drew back, looking at her very queerly. He longed to believe, but something warned him not to. Probably the girl was lying ... and that in itself was black enough. He coughed loudly, and delicately blew his nose, with one eye turned towards Sophia.

'I may take it, then, that they will stop?'

'Who? Helen and Antony? Oh, I'm afraid so ...'

'The parties — the parties,' said Mr Pell hastily.' The noise. The gramophone.'

'We'll do our best,' she promised. And because she was a good citizen and secretly suffering shame at the social nuisance caused by the cottage, she added, 'I'm sorry we've been a bother.'

She was careful to say 'we'.

'Ah,' muttered Mr Pell.

He testily recalled Jimmy Barrell, who had gone into the kitchen, and Sophia opened the front door for him. She patted Jimmy, who wagged his tail, and the two went off together. Mr Pell's back was bristling with gossip. It was fortunate (but Sophia had closed the door and could not see) that he should meet Colonel and Mrs Amsett, who had strolled out to post a letter, just outside Myrtle Cottage. The three stood talking for some time.

CHAPTER XX

No practical results came from Sophia's visit to Uncle Preston the next day.

She went in a mood of sullen obstinacy and repelled all his accusations and questions with a polite cold vagueness.

She refused to discuss her brother's actions.

The most she would do was to agree that it might be wiser if the two thousand pounds was invested; she promised to ask Harry to do this. Uncle Preston did not get from her the detailed, earnest and melodramatic discussion for which he longed. 'She seems to take no interest,' he said to Auntie Loo, fretfully, when she had gone. 'She is a very *hard* girl, Looie. Very *modern.*'

Auntie Loo looked at him; and bounced her ball of wool so that it fell on the floor.

And despite a one-sidedly jocular conversation between Sophia and Aunt Maxine, and a one-sidedly indignant telephone conversation with Aunt Grace, who was waiting for that very wild but very rich boy to telephone Angela and ask her to go out again, which she most *certainly* would not do unless he promised to behave properly, and a brief visit to Mr Marriot, in which he advised her, with real concern, to persuade Harry to invest ... nothing could be done.

Nothing. Harry was well away, like a graceful colt over a prairie of spring grass, the faithful Francis and Juan galloping and neighing at his side.

He was hardly ever at home, but when he did pop in, he usually had a box of chocolates or a bunch of carnations for Sophia, and she was always rather afraid of tackling him about anything, because it was so easy to hurt his feelings. She did not mind going for Francis because he could stand up for himself, but she felt that Harry could not.

And he was enjoying the spell of gaiety so much! He liked being out of a job and not having to look for one, planning parties, dashing about in Juan's car, and kissing Belinha, who seemed to like it, and him. Now that he did not have to pretend enthusiasms, he felt them naturally. He revelled in the unsophisticated and cheerful company he kept, and it would have taken an extremely strong-minded sister to tackle him and pin him to earth and investments.

So, though Sophia was increasingly wretched and worried, she said very little. He and she avoided the topic of the two thousand pounds. It lay between them like Banquo's ghost but neither would mention it. It was realized by all that this unnatural silence must soon be broken, but the three dreaded the inevitable moment.

There were no more parties at the cottage; they were held at The Judge's House instead, and were therefore presumably more decorous. Sophia did not know. She was not asked to any of them and would not have gone if she had been. There was a week of her poor little holiday left to her, and in it she had plenty to do.

She had humbly offered to call on Toby's mother at any time and on any day which should be convenient to her. Toby's mother, replying with dignity through a letter from Toby, chose Thursday afternoon at half past three.

Sophia felt really despairing when she heard the hour. Its awful earliness suggested that Toby's mother was going to make an afternoon of it. Francis and Toby were extremely grateful to her, but she felt too miserable and frightened to be soothed by this. It was a horrid situation, she felt: she could not even see any humour in it. She had to confront an angry, shocked stranger and justify her brother's action ...

It occurred to her, not for the first time in the last ten wretched days, that she was always justifying her brothers' actions to somebody. She seemed, as the poem says, born for naught else.

So on Thursday afternoon, dressed with dismal care in a frock of grey silk, a snowy collar, and her large black artist's hat to give her courage, for it was becoming, Sophia set out for Highbury.

Of course she felt sick with nervousness and her stomach churned about miserably and her heart banged. She sat in the Tube and wished that she were dead, while Harry, Francis, the cottage, the two thousand pounds, Juan and Francis's letter went round in her head in an exhausting whirl. Her holiday seemed years away. She felt as tired as though she had never had one.

Suddenly she thought, I can't stand much more of this. We'll have to separate. It's no use. I'd better face it. They'll be happier without me, and I can't do anything for them. It's awful, it's horrible, I can hardly bear to think about it, but it's got to happen.

As soon as the thought had come into the foreground of her mind she felt more calm. She pushed it away again until she could have time to get used to its sadness, but she no longer resisted it, trying desperately to cling to the hope that matters would come right. They could not come right.

She could not change her nature and cease to disapprove of wild parties, extravagance and irresponsibility, and her brothers would not cease – at least, for a long time they would not cease – to want these things. In such circumstances it was mere stupidity to hope for an adjustment. No one had any influence with Harry and Francis except their sister, and she had failed to bring to them a sense of sobriety and purpose.

The forces of heredity and early environment had proved too strong for her, just as the accumulated forces of twenty years had defeated her when she had tried to rescue her mother from cruelty and drudgery.

I give in, thought Sophia. I ought to be grateful that the boys still love me, anyway. For there was no doubt that they did, with their ludicrous bottles of scent and their relyings upon her when anything went wrong and their pleasure in her company, even when she had been disapproving and elder-sisterly and boring. It was something that they loved her, even if she had failed in her duty and let them begin on the road to ruin.

When she got to the fire station where Toby's father lived, she became interested in the novelty of her situation, and in trying to get a glimpse of the fire engine as she climbed the iron steps leading to the firemen's quarters, and her unhappiness and worry went away into the back of her mind.

The men were doing something to the fire engine in its garage immediately below the stairway, so the doors were open, and she had a good stare at its gallant scarlet and glitter. A fire engine is a terrifying, powerful object. It is more like a dragon than any other contemporary machine, and there comes from it a heartening emanation of peril and bravery. It is a fitting object with which to quell the awful power of Fire; and the sight of it made her feel ashamed of her fear of what life might bring, and her unhappiness.

Heartened by the fire engine, she knocked at the third door along the row at the top; and it was at once opened by Toby looking properly subdued. She gave a vehement wink, however, and muttered:

'Isn't it awful! You are a dear to come. Do come in. Mum's here.'

Half past three struck somewhere.

Sophia's first impression of Mrs Kellett's parlour was that she had stepped inside the fire engine. It was very small, and everything seemed to be bright red and glittering, or green.

Some things glowed, the moss-green carpet, the red plush chairs, the emerald-green tablecloth; and some glittered, the mantel mirror and the fire irons and numerous little boxes and frames; and some had a frosty white glimmer, the lace curtains draped at the windows and a tea cloth put half across the table, and Mrs Kellett's own white apron. Every object shone with cleanliness. There was a fresh smell of furniture polish and the pleasant but indefinable one of clean linen. Sophia thought of the state into which Miss Tessitt's ailments and her own worries had allowed the cottage to sink, and she felt ashamed for the second time.

'Mum, this is Sophia.'

'Very pleased to meet you, I'm sure.'

'It's very nice of you to let me come ...' mumbled Sophia. She had never seen a more intimidating woman than Mrs Kellett. She looked like one's idea of a Roman goddess. She was nearly six feet tall, and very big, and her handsome head was crowned with more fair hair than Sophia had thought existed in this niggardly life. It was coiled, looped, twisted, coroneted, and plaited in an inconceivably intricate device, and her large severe grey eyes looked at one with awesome honesty and dignity. Here was a woman who looked as though she knew what she wanted and had always known, who looked chaste, strong, simple. Sophia was awed. She felt herself to be in the presence of a natural force like the Niagara Falls. She forgot to be nervous about the letter. She was afraid of Mrs Kellett, but too interested in her to be very afraid.

There was no awkwardness about the conversation. Mrs Kellett was never embarrassed.

'Please sit down, Sophia. You don't mind me calling you Sophia, do you' (she announced it; she did not enquire). 'You see, me and Dad have heard such a lot about you from Maysie here. Is this the first time you've ever been over a fire station?'

It was not likely to be anything else, but Sophia supposed that most of Mrs Kellett's friends (if the goddess had any) were always hopping about from one fire station to another as their husbands moved from district to district.

'Yes. It's very interesting. I'd no idea people lived up here.'

'It's very small. Only two rooms and a kitchen, but we make do,' said Mrs Kellett, looking round the bright, gay little place with serious pride. 'Dad and me are in the next room, and Maysie and Babs in here. That couch you're sitting on pulls down and makes a nice bed for them, doesn't it, girls.'

'I don't like sleepin' with our Maysie,' said a dispassionate voice from a corner. Sophia started and stared. A tiny sallow little girl, with two brown pigtails and a cotton overall over a drill tunic, was sitting there, a book on her knees. She was exactly like a mouse. Toby put out her tongue at her.

'Girls!' said Mrs Kellett, but placidly. 'Always on at each other, they are,' she explained. 'I hope you like a fire, Sophia. Myself, I always like to begin fires about the middle of September. It's our first today, you see.'

Her guest was indeed grateful for the little fire on which the black kettle steamed. Her hands were cold with apprehension, for she had just seen, on the high old-fashioned mantelpiece, an envelope addressed in a writing which she knew.

It was the letter.

Oh, if Mrs Kellett would only get it over.

But Mrs Kellett seemed to have a sense of the importance of ritual which was Japanese in its meticulousness. For half an hour exactly conversation was made about fire engines, the weather, home-made dresses, the pictures, and young girls going out to work. The topic of brothers was avoided by all. Then, as four o'clock struck, Mrs Kellett announced, 'We'll have our tea now,' and Toby went into the kitchen and came back with a tray of cups and a large brown teapot and other things, among them a glass dish in which were a lettuce and some tomatoes, looking very bright because there were so many other green and red objects in the room.

'Maysie said you liked green food, and I remembered and got these for you,' said Mrs Kellett, lightening her awfulness by a kind and friendly smile.

Sophia was touched; but this little attention was going to make her task more difficult than ever, she felt. She tried hard not to look at the letter. No one looked at it. Even the mouse, who must have been well drilled for she seemed the sort of child who would take a relish in embarrassing people, did not look at it; and tea was taken with dignity and more conversation.

'Maysie tells me you write poetry,' said Mrs Kellett. 'Do have another tomato.'

'Yes,' murmured Sophia. 'No, thank you.'

'That's very clever,' said Mrs Kellett, rather as a missionary might congratulate an aborigine on his skill in throwing the boomerang.

'Not clever. It's like having lovely hair,' said Sophia audaciously. 'Natural, that's all.'

Mrs Kellett laughed for the first time, and put up her hand a little shyly to the edifice.

'I never do anything to it. Just Sunlight soap and water,' she said; Sophia could see, in the smile and gesture, what she must have looked like when she was eighteen years old. But oh! when was she going to get on to the letter? This silence, this avoidance, the ritual feast and ceremonial remarks, were beginning to make the victim feel hysterical.

At last, when tea had been finished and taken away and the time was a quarter to five, Sophia observed, as she was making a remark to Toby, Mrs Kellett motion the mouse into the next room. The mouse gave her mother an imploring look (it was evident that the mouse was a favourite), but was sent scurrying by an imperial frown; and when she had gone Mrs Kellett stood up, turned her back on the two girls, on whom an alarmed hush had fallen, and took down the letter.

She slowly turned round.

Two very pale faces, with very large solemn eyes, looked up at her.

'Well,' pronounced Mrs Kellett, 'I don't think we'll say any more about this, shall we?' and, removing the kettle, she dropped the letter into the heart of the fire.

'Oh ... thank you very much ... I'm sure he didn't ...'

'We'll say no more about it.'

And so the incident closed.

No well-bred woman could have managed the matter with more dignity, generosity and tact. Sophia felt really awed. For the first time in her life she saw, in the person of a fireman's wife who lived in two rooms, the magnificent antique virtues upon which great nations are founded. She went down the iron staircase, after a firm handshake from Mrs Kellett and a grateful hug from Toby, feeling very small, very contemporary and very weak-minded.

A slender man with dark eyes was crossing the yard as she went out. This might be Dad; this was where Toby got her eyes and a certain warmth which the goddess lacked. The goddess, Sophia surmised, either kept Dad well in order or had to forgive him now and then.

Though the affair had ended so well she felt exhausted by the strain of the afternoon's happenings, and angry with Francis as she rode homewards.

It was too bad. He ought not to have let her in for such an interview; he should firmly have made it plain that she could not go. The interview might have been very unpleasant indeed; for all Francis knew, it would be. He had let her in for it too easily, and she was angry with him.

The boys were making a habit of behaving rashly and then leaving Sophia to face Mr Pell and the Vale, Uncle Preston and Mrs Kellett, and soothe them, and make explanations. It was too sickening, and even at the risk of behaving like Uncle Preston, she would have to tell them that it must stop.

CHAPTER XXI

There was no one at home when she finally got back after her journey and some household shopping and she was glad. She felt that she must have peace and quiet immediately or she would have a nerve storm instead.

It was seven o'clock on a mild autumnal evening whose shadows filled the Vale and the cottage with peace and a faint sense of chill. Hardly a leaf had fallen, but a long way off the breath of winter could be felt. Sophia stood at her window for some time, thinking dreamily about the cold that was coming from the mysterious plains of the North, swinging snow and bare trees across Europe, and gradually her mood grew more tranquil and even hopeful.

With immense relief she decided that she would not leave her brothers. She would stand by them in this difficult period, and help them to weather the storm, as the three had weathered their father's storms of rage when they were children. If she left them now, it was likely that they would get into serious trouble. The existing wildish parties and drinking could not be called serious trouble. They were foolish, and they set up tastes which later might cause misery, but so far no real harm had been done. And it was her business and responsibility to see that it was not done.

Nothing mattered, she decided, so long as they did not all stop loving one another and liking to be together. While she still had her brothers' love she was not powerless, and if she remembered to be tactful she could do much to influence them.

So, resolved to be very tactful and to do her duty, however nasty it might be, and to stand by the erring Harry and Francis unto the last ditch, she went soberly but cheerfully downstairs to prepare her supper, and looked round the cottage with a disapproving eye. It was dusty. A film appeared to have settled over it; a sort of Tessitt-film, languid, and just not quite clean. She would have to speak to Miss Tessitt.

As usual she felt at once braced and soothed because she had made a decision; and she hummed a tune as she set out her supper. She turned on the light, neatly stacked three copies of the *Daily Express* and one of *Razzle*, threw away dead flowers, wound the silent clock, made some tea, took down the *Decline and Fall of the Roman Empire*, opened it at the excessively dull bit about the system of governing the Empire under Constantine, and began to eat an egg and to read sternly.

This peaceful scene was interrupted by Harry and Francis, who arrived in the taxi in which Harry had fetched Francis from the offices of the long-suffering Graby & Bryant.

Sophia, bent on being tactful, looked up with a pleasant smile as the door opened, trying not to wonder how much the taxi had cost.

Harry and Francis blew in. That was just what they did. Everyone admits the transfiguring force of Love; that of Money is equally great. Six months ago the two had had a slightly defiant air; their native charm was part of their defence against life, which they assumed was going to hit them. Now their charm and youth lay like a delightful gloss upon their happiness. They felt secure. They had pounds and pounds and pounds, and it would last for months. Uncle Preston and Mr Marriot might as well have tried to stop the sun from shining as stop these two young men from doing what they wanted to do.

'Hul-lo, darling!'

'I say, did you see her?'

'Yes, it's all right. Francis, *what* a woman! She's like a goddess. But she's really grand. I'm glad I met her.'

'You're sure it's all right? What did she say?'

Sophia briefly told what had happened that afternoon, and Francis was very greatly relieved. He kissed Sophia affectionately, and thanked her several times, and she almost felt that this repaid her for the afternoon. It was delightful to help people and to feel that one was a brave, tactful, unselfish and reliable person. No wonder people got so keen about being good; it certainly was a very pleasant sensation. She went on with her supper and her book, glowing smugly and thinking that after all it would not be so difficult to be tactful and do her duty.

But in a little while she became aware through the pleasant atmosphere which filled the cottage that there was something wrong.

This familiar sensation refused to go away. She read the same paragraph three times, she ate another fresh fig with relish, but it would not go. And then she realized that Harry and Francis were not behaving as they usually did. They were wandering about, glancing at *Razzle* and tossing it down, fiddling with things and keeping silent.

At last she looked up and said amiably: 'You going out?'

'Old Juan's going to' phone about nine. We may go down to Buzzy's.' (Buzzy, whose status and sex never became clarified in Sophia's mind, had a flat in a mews off Berkeley Square.)

'Oh.'

She went back to her book. The uneasy feeling persisted.

'Sophia,' said Harry at last.

She looked up, and across at him with a feeling of dread, of actual dread. The silence had become like that before an explosion, and had stolen her feeling of peace and happiness while she tried to read and to ignore its menace. All her black anxieties returned.

'Yes? Is anything up?'

'Look here. I know it's pretty rotten coming on the top of seeing Toby's mother, but the fact is, Juan's aunt wants to have a talk with you. She's fed up with Juan and Belinha and us, silly old fool, and she wants to talk things over with you – you being the respectable member of the family.'

'What sort of things?'

'Well—' He paused, and fiddled maddeningly with a match-box. Francis had gone into the bathroom.

'Well, look here, don't be too fed up, will you? We've put off telling you as long as possible, because we thought you'd be upset. The fact is, old Juan wants the Deedle and me to share a flat with him.'

'For good, you mean?'

'For the next two years, anyway. You see, the aunt's taking Belinha to Paris for six months, so they won't keep their flat open just for Juan. It's too expensive. And Buzzy knows a woman who's got a marvellous furnished flat to let somewhere near Buzzy's place. Only three quid a week. Marvellous. So old Juan thought it would be a good idea if we all clubbed together. It wouldn't be so expensive. It's in a mews, and there's a garage underneath for the car, and a marvellous pub at one end. It used to be an old coaching sort of pub, where the Regency bucks used to go. Marvellous. So old Juan thought it would be a good idea.'

His voice tailed off nervously. Francis came back, whistling carefully and drying his hands and not looking at Sophia, who was staring at Harry.

She could not find any words. Her thoughts flew round and round in her head, driven by an awful sinking feeling of dismay.

'I hope you don't mind about it too much, darling. We thought you'd like a little peace and quiet, as you don't like parties. It'll be all right, we'll still see lots of each other, and you'll have more time for writing poetry and everything. Marvellous. Only if you just would see the old cow and tell her it's all right. She's afraid we'll get into messes. Silly old trout. It'll be too marvellous. If you could just soothe her down ...'

She burst out so violently that they both jumped—

'I won't. I won't soothe her down. I've had enough of soothing people down for you. I won't do any more of it. What do you think I am, a sort of doormat or a buffer or something? I've been wanting to tell you this for a long time, and I'm glad I can. I'm damned sick of clearing up your messes ...'

A fluttering pause. They said nothing; both looked sulky and dangerous.

'And as for your living with Juan, I think it's insane. You must both be crazy. You'll get into the most frightful holes, and into debt, and land yourselves in some ghastly mess or other. I agree with Juan's aunt. I'm glad she's got some sense, at least. You'll do nothing but have parties and drink. I know. And I'm going to move heaven and earth to stop you doing it!'

They stirred at this. Harry lowered his head and stared across at her with his chin stuck out. She stared back at him. Just so had she seen her father look in one of his rages. It was an almost animal look, piteously touched by weakness. It was her father's very gesture. Francis's lips were tightly compressed and he was very white, with a ghost of a jaunty smile.

'What'll you do? You can't do anything. We can do as we like,' said Harry slowly, staring.

'Can't I, by god? I can, and I will. I'll get the whole family on to this, you see, and I'll cable to Juan's uncle in South America, too. Uncle Preston and Mr Marriot can stop the Deedle going, he's under age. You shan't go. I won't sit down and see you mucking up your whole lives and going the way Father did. *I won't.* I can't bear it. You must both be mad. You know what his life was like, and how ghastly miserable he made us all for years and years, and killed Mother, and *in spite* of knowing all that, and knowing he was a drunkard and neurotic and so miserable that he used to say he was in hell now, and so he didn't care if he burned in hell after he was dead – *in spite* of all that you want to start living the same kind of life that he did.'

She stopped, the tears running down, and stared from one to the other. Francis moved uneasily and said in a conciliatory tone—

'Oh rot. You're just being melodramatic, like Uncle Preston. You take things much too seriously. It's just because Father never had a good time when he was young that he got in such an awful state when he was old. We shan't be like that. We're going to get it out of our systems while we're young. As for Uncle Preston, i he added fiercely, 'if he tries to stop me doing anything, I'll—' he paused. A mantle of icy dignity fell upon him. 'I shall ignore the poor old swine,' he ended gently.

'Old Marriot can't do anything either,' said Harry. 'I'm of age. I've got my money. He can't do a thing legally.'

'They can make themselves beastly unpleasant. They can telephone and come round here and be a damned nuisance.'

'Let them try. There's nothing I'd like better than putting the police on to Uncle Preston.'

'Oh, don't be so bloody silly, Harry. You make me sick.'

'And so do you make me sick, trying to interfere with our lives and run us. *God*,' he clenched his fists and gritted his teeth – 'god, the rage I get in when anyone tries to run me. I'm like Father—'

'Yes, you are like Father. You both are. You can't run yourselves and you won't let other people, who are better balanced, run you either.'

'We won't let *you* run us, anyway, so get that quite dear.'

'I don't want to run you.'

'Yes, you do. Like Uncle Preston and the whole rotten, melodramatic, nosy crew. I hate them.'

'Oh Harry ... I'm not like Uncle Preston!'

'Yes you are. You're too virginal and priggish for words, always being shocked and hating being kissed and trying to stop people leading normal lives. You're just like Uncle Preston.'

'I'm not – I'm not!'

'You are a bit, Sophia,' said Francis, judicially. 'Especially about parties.'

'Well, then, if I am, you're like Aunt Maxine; she's coarse and selfish, and so are you. Pity you and Aunt Maxine aren't a bit more virginal. Besides, I'm not virginal. I can't help it if drink and being pawed about bores me. I've *tried* to like it, god knows.'

'There you are! *Trying* to like it! You make me sick. And anyway if you don't like it, you needn't stop other people.'

'Yes, I need, when it's bad for them.'

'It isn't bad for us – just as though we were kids! It's natural and good for us.'

'For other people, not for us, because we've got an awful heredity. We ought to be frightfully careful about drink and sex because of Father.'

Francis shook his head.

'Much better to get it out of our systems.'

'You silly little fools,' said Sophia coldly and patiently. 'Can't you see that you're only driving it *into* your systems, as you call them, and getting a taste for it, instead of controlling yourselves and sublimating it?'

'Oh, and collecting stamps, I suppose, or pressing seaweed, like Uncle Preston used to?'

'There *are* other things to do. I thought when we came here you'd have hobbies and things,' she began to cry again at the memory, 'and live orderly lives—'

'God! Hobbies!'

'Yes, I did. I tried to make it nice for you,' she was crying so much that the words were almost inaudible, 'and make everything comfortable so that you wouldn't want the things Father wanted.'

'Well, you had a funny way of making things nice, being virginal about our friends and getting in a damned inefficient old tart like Tessitt who couldn't keep the place clean, and never having a joint on Sundays ...'

'We did ... Oh Harry, we *did* have a joint on Sundays sometimes!'

'Only if I cooked it.'

'I tried ... I did try!'

'It was nice at first, Harry,' said Francis, reluctantly, looking down at his sobbing sister. 'Only things went to bits, somehow.'

'We none of us like the same things, that's the trouble,' he added moodily.

'You and I do. We like having a marvellous time and not being melodramatic. God' – he clenched his fists and gritted his teeth again – 'how I *loathe* melodrama! Anyway, we shan't have scenes with Juan. He's not a Garden, thank god. He's a normal, sensible chap,'

'*You're not going with Juan.*'

'I tell you we *are*. You'd better shut up. We're going the week after next when the aunt goes off to Paris. It's all fixed up. Juan's twenty-one and he's got his own money and so am I and I've got mine—'

'Not much of it left, I should think, by now ... oh, oh! and I did so hope you'd want to invest it ...'

'Catch me. Filthy stuff; I want to get rid of it as soon as I can.' His angry young face grew sad for a second.

'And I'm coming too,' said Francis.' I only hope the old fools will try to stop me. I should enjoy it. I should just tell Uncle Preston exactly what I think of him. I should tell him ...'

'Never mind that now,' said Harry, who, like many gentle people, easily took command of a situation when he was roused. 'You won't see Juan's aunt, then, Sophia?'

'*No, I won't.* I'm damned if I will. I'm going to telephone Uncle Preston this very night and tell him all about it and ask his advice ...'

'Flopping on the blasted relations now!'

'Who else can I flop on? There's no one to help me or to be sensible ...'

'Sneaking and sucking up!'

'I'm not ... I'm not ... but I must do something ...'

'Letting us down ...'

'*Harry!* It's for your own good.'

'You're a filthy little traitor.'

'Oh, how dare you say that! How *can* you! I'm going to telephone Uncle Preston now, this minute, and tell him ...'

She got up clumsily, sobbing and stumbling, and went to the telephone. Harry let her pick it up, then seized it and they struggled for a second, Harry trying to tear her hands away. Francis, shocked, started forward, but even as he did so Harry wrenched the telephone away, it fell on the floor, and the mouthpiece smashed.

'Oh – Oh!' cried Sophia.

She turned, darted to the door, flung it open and ran out into the street.

The door slowly swung to behind her, and closed with a click.

'She'll get over it,' muttered Harry, picking up the telephone. Francis said nothing. He had taken little part in the row, beyond supporting Harry, but his legs trembled and he felt sick.

The telephone, restored to the shelf, at once began to ring. Harry glanced at the clock; it said nine.

Five minutes later the cottage was empty.

CHAPTER XXII

A week later Aunt Maxine was superintending the preparations for an evening of bridge at her flat. The preparations consisted of a lot of whisky, gin, sherry and port and a few olives; the olives were, so to speak, an excuse. Aunt Maxine was absorbed in her activities, bustling about in a red velvet evening dress which was too tight, and bullying her daily maid, who was being paid extra to stay on for the evening and give tone to the festivities. Like the olives, she would not be noticed much, but she would supply an atmosphere.

The telephone bell rang.

'Blast, who's that; I'll take it, Kate. Hope it isn't someone saying they can't come.'

'Hullo. Is that Maxine? It is I, Preston. Preston. Yes. I thought it would be as well to telephone you and let you know about the children.'

'Up to something again, are they? Well, you're only young once. I've been expecting it for some time. Harry got someone into trouble?'

'Bless my soul, I hope not. I hope not. If that were so, on top of everything else. ... No. No. It is only that they have decided, I understand, not to live together any more.'

'I'm not surprised. Never did think it would work. Did you?'

'No ... no. I cannot say that I did. Poor Hartley's children. No. One did not expect that they would make a success of sharing a home. They are all too much like their unfortunate father. But the extraordinary thing is, Maxine, that I only found out this by accident ...'

'Keeping it dark, were they?'

'Apparently. Very *odd* I consider it. Very *secretive*, when we all take such an interest in them. It appears that Angela rang up Francis at his place of business (a most unnecessary thing to do, I consider, but then Grace has brought Angela up, as we all know, in a *peculiar way*, and she seems to have no control over her at all ... and Francis, too, in such a *very* minor position, almost an *office boy*, heh! heh! heh! they must have thought it very *odd* for him to receive a telephone call from a *young lady*) yes, well, Francis told Angela that he and Harry are going off next week with this young Morales.'

'The devil they are. To live with him, d'you mean?'

'I gathered so from *Grace*, who of course rang me up and told me all she knew the moment she heard of it from Angela. Why, I asked myself immediately, why had Sophia not *informed* me of this? and I rang up her office at once. At once. But she was out. After some delay, I was told that she was out. Yes.'

'Well, Harry and Francis ought to have a damn good time coming to them. The boy's rich. What's Sophia going to do? I'll bet she's laughing on the other side of her face.'

'I cannot say at all, Maxine. I am completely in the dark. I must say that I think it is too bad of the children not to have informed me of this decision. I should naturally have liked to talk it over with *Marriot*, and to have given it *every consideration*. And then, of course, there is the question of *money* ...'

'Harry seems to be running through his pretty rapidly. I don't blame him, mind you.'

Uncle Preston gave a kind of exhalation of the breath which expressed worry, reproof, distress and a few more emotions, and was preparing for a comfortable discussion of Harry and money when Aunt Maxine's first guest arrived, and he was most reluctantly obliged to ring off.

Aunt Maxine, after a brief prophetic glance into the future in which she saw Harry and Francis in the dock and Sophia on a corner in Piccadilly (for Aunt Maxine's views on women were sturdy and old-fashioned) went out to slap her guest on the back. As she did so, she admired her own reflection in a mirror, and it struck her that Sophia would probably not make a success of Piccadilly. Too thin.

As Uncle Preston replaced the receiver and turned to go back to his *Evening News*, Auntie Loo came into the hall in her coat and hat.

'Are you going out, Looie? Cannot the girl fetch what is necessary?' said Uncle Preston, fretfully. He liked to know that Auntie Loo was in the house when he was. He might not want her for anything, but then again, he might.

'Just for a few minutes, dear. I won't be long.'

She had gone before he realized that she had not said where she was going. Where was she going? 'Looie!' called Uncle Preston, opening the front door. The autumn drifted in, and he shut the door quickly. He could ask her when she came back. Auntie Loo, meanwhile, with a very sober look on her little round face, had trotted to a telephone kiosk which was just round the corner. She dialled a number, and waited.

'Hullo,' said a young and rather impatient voice.

'Sophia, is that you, dear?'

'Oh, Auntie Loo. I'm so sorry; I thought you were some ghastly person.'

'I'm sorry to disturb you, dear, but I only heard your news this evening from your uncle, and I wanted to tell you how very sorry I am, dear. I'm speaking from a call box, not from home. I came out specially, just to tell you.'

'Oh, Auntie Loo, you are a lamb. It's all right, really, don't worry.'

'What are you going to do, dear? You mustn't mind my asking. Don't tell me if you'd rather not.'

'Well, I've got a rather nice room in Fitzjames's Avenue. It isn't on the Heath, of course, but it's quite near, and I shall move in one evening next week. I can't stay on here. It's too expensive for one person. Celia's mother is coming back next month, and she and Celia are going to let the house Celia's in now, and live in the cottage for a bit.'

'Is it really a nice room, dear?'

'Oh very. Two big windows, and lime trees outside, and I shall paint the floor green. Oh, and Auntie Loo, what do you think, this really is rather nice. An owl lives in the back garden.'

'An owl, dear?'

'Yes. I went in last night to leave some of my things, because I'm moving in by degrees, and it was nearly dark, and the moon was coming up. And when I went over to the window to look out, there was something big and white sitting on a branch just under the window and two huge eyes looking up at me. We stared at each other for quite a long time, and then he suddenly floated off like a shadow. It was lovely.'

'He will keep the mice away for you, dear. Well, I hope you will get moved in comfortably. That's all, dear. I just wanted to tell you.'

'Thank you very much, Auntie Loo. It's awfully kind of you. You are a pet. Goodbye.'

'Goodbye, dear.'

Sophia put the receiver back with a warm feeling for Auntie Loo in her heart and a disagreeable consciousness that the news of their break-up was by now all over the family.

Silly Francis, who had to boast to silly little Angela and give everything away! She, Sophia, had exercised self-control after her one wretched outburst of a week ago, and had spoken to no one about their decision, except Celia, with whom she had spent the night of the row. She had scarcely seen her brothers, but when she did they were all careful to be extra kind and thoughtful of one another's feelings.

They all felt ashamed of the quarrel. The things which had been said during it had to be said. They were the fruits of secret discontents and serious differences in opinion; they had to have vent. But now that they were out and had done their hurtful work, everyone was sorry they had been said. The air might be clear, as a result of the row, but it was only the mournful clarity which comes before rain.

Sophia was defeated, and acknowledged it. Her threats had done no good. Both she and her brothers knew that she could never execute them. Three was company still, in spite of everything; and she could not betray her brothers to the relations. She was helpless. She had done her best, hampered as she was by the fear of losing her brothers' love, her doubts as to her own wisdom and her fear of becoming like Uncle Preston: and could do no more.

Fortunately her last days at the cottage were so filled with activity that she did not have time to feel wretched. She had had to find a room, with Celia's help, and buy a bed and other things, and this had to be done after her day's work, so her evenings were occupied as well as her days.

But when she had time for thought she felt profoundly lonely and sad.

It hurt her deeply not to be on terms of the friendliest intimacy with her brothers and she was also extremely worried about their future. She seemed to feel the spirit of their father lingering in the background of their lives, and imagined his influence growing in the natures of his sons like a stain. He could not be ignored nor forgotten. He was dead, but his influence lay on his children like the shade of a dark tree, as their mother's influence was like the sunlight beyond it.

Harry and Francis were also extremely occupied, signing documents and flying about in Juan's car. They did not discuss their plans with Sophia; this was not because they were still angry with her, but because they did not want to hurt her feelings. A barrier stood between the three, despite their careful politeness to each other. The last ten days at the cottage were most unhappy ones. Everyone was looking forward to the Saturday evening which was to be their last one in the Vale.

One disagreeable task which fell to Sophia was the dismissal of the cottage's pensioners. She dreaded telling Mrs Barker that they were going, because Mrs Barker seemed to rely heavily upon the cottage, her one-and-sixpence, and her two cups of Indian tea and Harry's periodical bursts of small change.

'I suppose you couldn't take her on when we're gone?' said Sophia to Celia, not hopefully.

'Darling, we had her once, you know, and she was too awful. Honestly, things were dirtier when she'd finished than when she began. Besides, she's an awful old whiner. She's got more than she says she has. She rather imposes on you.'

'I don't mind. I feel responsible for her. Couldn't you have her if I paid you the one and sixpence every week?'

'I'll ask Mother, but I'm sure she never will.'

So Sophia had to break the news to Mrs Barker.

'*Aoaw!!*' wailed Mrs Barker, her face contorting into the best mask of watery grief, amazement and indignation that it had yet achieved. 'You aren't ALL going away, are yer, dear?'

'I'm afraid so, Mrs Barker.'

'*Aoaw!* you '*ave* been so good to me, and now you're all going away and I do count on the steps so. They 'elp. It all 'elps. Not gettin' married, are you, dear?'

'No, I'm certainly not.'

'Oo's comin' 'ere then?' asked Mrs Barker, shrewdly.

'Mrs Carmody,' said Sophia without thinking, and then saw what she had done.

A more peaceful look, with a suggestion of bodeful planning, came over Mrs Barker's face.

'Aoaw, then that's all right, dear. I know Mrs Carmody, see. I worked for 'er before. She'll 'ave me do the step, see. It'll be all right. Why didn't you tell me before, dear?'

'I expect I forgot,' said Sophia ruefully, who was wondering why she had told her now.

'When's she comin', dear?'

'I don't know.'

'Well, I'll be down 'ere every mornin' after you gone, see, dear, and I'll catch 'er, see.'

I'm sure you will, thought Sophia, watching Mrs Barker's tiny goblin figure bobbing away with its bucket, after it had made a watery goodbye.

She was spared a scene of this kind from Miss Tessitt. She had the pleasure of sacking Miss Tessitt without letting her know they were leaving the cottage. She considered that Miss Tessitt had played quite a large part in the collapse of their ménage. She had idled shockingly, scamped her duties and let the cottage get dirty and unattractive, imposed shamefully upon Sophia's youth and inexperience and taken advantage of the fact that she was away from home all day. It was true that Sophia should have taken her firmly in hand and made her work, but that did not excuse Miss Tessitt's behaviour. Sophia would have liked to tell her that Mr Harry had called her an inefficient old tart. She imagined that the noun would give more offence than the adjective, though it did not describe Miss Tessitt with accuracy, and the adjective did.

So when she came home one evening, a few days before they were to leave the cottage, the usually peaceful Sophia was pleased to find a cause for complaint in the logbook of the laundry which she was about to check and put away. Miss Tessitt was waiting to receive her fifteen shillings. Sophia gave it her; and then said: 'Miss Tessitt, I see that two kitchen cloths were sent to the laundry last week.'

Miss Tessit made a bird-like inclination of her head over the laundry book.

'So there was,' remarked Miss Tessitt impersonally. She implied that the cloths had gravitated to the laundry of their own will.

'Who sent them?'

'Well, Ay did. They was very dirty. Ay says to mayself, "May! they *are* dirty, Ay says." So Ay slipped them into the basket just as it was leavin' with the man.'

'I should think you might have washed them out at home, or boiled them. It wouldn't have taken you five minutes.'

'Ay was not engaged to do washin',' said Miss Tessitt, going a bright brick-red.

'You can hardly call that "washing", surely – a couple of kitchen cloths.'

'It all means puttin' the 'ands in water,' said Miss Tessitt with dignity, 'May 'ands easily get chapped. Ay 'ave a very sensitive skin, and the Enbury water is very 'ard. When Ay was with Mrs Wertheimer of West End Lane, the kitchen cloths was all sent to the laundry every week. Ten of them. Regular. Ay 'ardly ever 'ad may 'ands in water while Ay was there, except to wash before a meal. But then Mrs Wertheimer 'ad a regular establishment, as you might say. Two in family and faive kep'.'

'Then I think you'd better go back there,' said Sophia, losing her temper.

'Pardon?'

'Make some other arrangement, I mean. I think I'd better get someone who isn't afraid of washing a couple of teacloths.'

'Just as you wish, of course,' said Miss Tessitt, going an even brighter shade of red. 'Ay take it you would wish may to come in next week?'

'I don't think you need bother, thanks. I'll manage.'

'Then Ay will wish you good evening,' said Miss Tessitt, with increasing dignity. 'There was nothin said, Ay think, about givin' a month's notice on either side?'

'Nothing, so far as I remember.'

'Then Ay will wish you good evenin',' said Miss Tessitt again, breathing very fast by now and very red in the face indeed. Sophia loftily inclined her own head, and Miss Tessitt made a slow and dignified exit, punctuated by heavy breathing and semi-bows.

There would be no question of the dogs in the Vale missing the three. Wodge, in his dim mind, might possibly miss Sophia a little, but Jimmy Barrell and Dan and Taffy would not miss the children at all; Celia was coming to the cottage, and all the dogs, especially Taffy, liked Celia better than they did Sophia,

and so long as the cottage door stood open sometimes, and
so long as they could bundle in and be patted and admired, it
would be all right. Like heartless, witless nature in Professor
Housman's poem, they would neither care nor know.

So the end of September drew near, and the autumn deepened with misty moonlight and falling leaves; it came to the
day before they were to leave the cottage.

Sophia came home by bus that evening and got out at the
stop by the Dominican Priory because she had to buy some
bread for breakfast, and she was late, and all the shops by the
tram terminus would be shut except this little dairy which she
knew, hidden in a dimly lit side street.

She was feeling tired and unhappy, depressed by the chilly
autumn dusk over Enbury Fields and the clanging of the
trams and the tiny squalid shops with their humble lights, the
display of tinned food, and the drab people who hurried in like
gnomes to buy.

She saw the shadow of the economic claw lying across the
world, slowly contracting and relaxing, and there seemed no
regal power or proud beauty left; only odd goblins, pathetic
gleams of prettiness, humble little cosinesses which people made
for themselves in the shadow of the claw, and the courage of their
ironic laughter. And she was very miserable about her brothers.

She bought her bread in the dairy, and stepped outside into
the twilight, lingering a moment to look in the window of a
dirty, feebly lit secondhand shop which was full of small junk;
chipped vases, paste combs with stones missing, soiled books,
broken strings of beads.

And suddenly the sky above the dim, dirty street seemed
to grow as blue as deep water, and the long superb line of the
Wrenwood beech trees, which hung on the horizon at the end
of the street, seemed to grow until it filled all heaven with
murmuring shade and beauty.

In the middle of the dirty window she saw the painting she
called 'Nydia', which Mrs North had bought from the sale at
the surgery six months ago.

There she was, in her dress the colour of yellow roses bordered with the red key pattern, her dark eyes looking a little beyond Sophia's gaze, holding out her apple of tranquil wisdom for the tired world to eat.

'Nydia,' muttered Sophia. 'It can't be true.'

But it was. There was even a white scratch in one corner of the painting; it seemed that Nydia, like Sophia, had been roughly handled.

Sophia went into the shop.

The man who came out of a den at the back saw by the young lady's look that she had taken a fancy to the picture, and he had the sense, in spite of being newly roused from a frowsy sleep, to ask five shillings for it, which he got.

But the young lady reached over and took the picture out of the middle of the window, and was off before he could say, that on second thoughts it was a nice little thing and worth seven and sixpence. Taking it out of the window like that – he never see such a thing. He was half a mind to go after her, but he was still sleepy, so he went back to the den instead.

Sophia went home with the bread in one hand and Nydia in the other. She could not believe that she had got her. She stared and stared at her, and her head chimed with memories of beautiful places and things that she had seen, and she thought of the poems she hoped to write, and the tram came to anchor at the edge of Enbury Heath.

Blind I must have been, thought Sophia, stepping out again into the mystery of the evening. Blind, and a coward, but now I've got Nydia again and poetry, and I don't care. I'm not afraid or blind any more.

So when the next night came, and the three were in the cottage together for the last time, waiting for Juan's car to fetch the boys, and for Mr Cross's van to carry off Sophia and her few possessions to her new room, she was not so miserable as she had feared to be.

Nydia was on the mantelpiece in a shrine of yellow roses and dark red carnations which Harry had brought for Sophia, and she stood for so much that every time Sophia glanced at her, she felt happier.

The boys were pleased to see Nydia again.

'Hullo! there's Nydia,' said Francis interestedly, speaking to Sophia without constraint for the first time in ten days. 'Where did you get her?'

'At a little second-hand shop in Elizabeth Street, for five bob.'

'North must have sold her,' said Harry, coming downstairs with his two battered suitcases, and carefully not treading on the broken stair, which, of course, they had never had mended. He was rather pensive because Belinha had gone that morning to Paris; but his heart was far from being broken.

'I expect she did. I'm sure she only bought her to spite me. Father knew I liked Nydia, and he must have told North, and the old cow sold her again as soon as she'd bought her, I expect. Talking of old cows,' she added, 'how's Juan's aunt taking it?'

Harry and Francis looked relieved at this sign of returning interest and cheerfulness on the part of their sister. Harry said with animation, 'Oh, old Juan had a ghastly row with her and told her where she got off. She howled for hours, he said.'

Sophia said nothing.

Harry glanced at Francis.

'My dear,' said Francis, putting his hands on her shoulders, 'you don't mind awfully, do you? Things are just the same, you know. It won't make any difference to our caring about each other because we aren't all living together, and we'll see each other very often, and ring each other up, and have parties – nice gatherings, I mean' (Sophia had begun to laugh) 'and everything will be all right.'

'Oh, if only it would!' she said longingly.

'Well, I'm sure it will – that is, if the old fools will only keep their noses out of it, curse them.'

'Aunt Grace,' said Harry, 'rang up this morning to know if we still loved each other.'

'God, she *didn't!*'

'She did.'

'She's the worst of the lot, you know.'

'Oh, I don't know. Uncle Preston is the worst, I think. He *enjoys* it all so.'

'I think Aunt Maxine is the worst,' said Sophia pensively, twiddling a rose.

'And yet one can't help feeling sorry for them.'

'I know. They've never had a chance somehow, have they?'

'That's what's so sickening – disliking them *and* feeling sorry for them.'

'I hope our nephews and nieces won't feel like that about us,' said Sophia.

'I shan't have any children. They cost a lot,' said Francis at once. 'Repairing their ruddy little boots, and all the rest of it. I shall send all mine, if I do have any, to Dr Barnardo's.'

'You'll probably have to, anyway,' observed Harry. 'It'll be the cheapest way of running them.'

'I keep on expecting one of the old fools to ring up,' said Sophia. 'Do they know we're clearing out tonight?'

'Yes, but I told them the telephone was being disconnected. It isn't really, of course. Mrs Carmody wants it.'

In the pause that followed, the lordly sound of Juan's car could be heard coming down the hill. It was half past eight.

'There's Juan!'

'Will you stay and see him, Sophia?' asked Harry, a little timidly. 'The old chap feels rather bad about breaking up the home, you know.'

'He needn't,' said Sophia at once, and meant it. 'He was just the last straw, so to speak. If it hadn't been him it would have been something else.'

'Well, thank goodness we can be candid about having different ideas, and talk things out and still be good friends,' said Harry. 'If we were typical Gardens we should have been cantering round, foaming at the hocks and saying we would never mention each other's names again or some such blah.'

The car drew up outside.

Francis went to open the door, and Sophia took pains to welcome Juan with an easy cordial manner, just touched with mischief, which at once soothed him; he was looking very nervous when he came in.

The suitcases were piled into the car, the floor of the; cottage was stacked with boxes and rolled-up cushions and bundles of books.

'What's the time ... nearly nine,' said Harry. 'What time will your van be here, darling?'

'Oh, I don't know. It might be nearly ten; Mr Cross's young man can't get here until the shop shuts, and it's late on Saturdays of course.'

'Well, will you promise something?'

She looked alarmed.

'What is it?'

'Don't look so frightened ... it's only that we want you to stay here until the post gets in.'

'Why – are you expecting a letter?'

'No ... we just want you to promise, that's all.'

'All right, I will if you like. That will be about half past nine. I'll wait. What is it? One of your heavy jokes?'

'Just a mood, darling. The beloved old figure in the shabby dressing-gown must have its whims gratified; it won't be with us for long.'

'Well, man, shall we be hareing along,' suggested Juan,' Got everything? Coo! doesn't the place look dismal!'

Francis, whose opinion of Juan's tact was low, raised his eyebrows at Sophia, who agreed that the place did, indeed, look dismal. She suggested that it might possibly be because it was dismantled, and there was no fire, and Juan heartily agreed with this point of view.

They moved towards the door.

Two warm kisses on her lips, the pressure of Francis's hands on her shoulders, a warm hug from Harry, wavings, shouts, laughter – 'Promise you'll stay till the post comes, Sophia!' and her own reply, 'I will, but heaven knows why' – they had gone.

She turned back into the cottage.

It was silent. The sound of the engine died away (going much too fast, she thought) and she closed the door.

There was the tick of the clock for company, the silent glowing presences of the roses and carnations and the gracious figure of Nydia, bowered among her flowers. Sophia leaned her elbows on the mantelpiece and stared down into the fireless grate, and was surprised that the tears did not come.

After all, she had only lost some of their time and company, not their love. They all three cared as much for one another as ever; more, perhaps, because they had been through this battle together, and come out of it knowing one another better, and more able to make allowances. She would see them often, very often ... and it would certainly be pleasant to have a little time for writing poetry sometimes in the evenings, for reading and dreaming and walks. And she was not like Uncle Preston after all; Harry had said that of course she wasn't. It was a rotten thing to say, and she must forgive him. She had at least avoided that danger.

A letter suddenly landed on the mat; and she started. The post was early tonight; she heard the postman's steps receding down the Vale, and Jimmy Barrell dutifully barking at him.

She picked up the letter.

It was addressed to her, in Harry's writing.

She opened it, with shaking knees and a dry mouth, and unfolded a cheque for two hundred pounds made out to herself and signed by Harry. And there was a little note saying that this was for her with his love, to do just as she liked with.

She had not lifted her eyes from it when the telephone bell rang. Aunt Grace ... Aunt Maxine ... Uncle Preston ... it must be one of the old fools.

But Francis's voice hailed her—

'Hullo, my sweet. Has the post come yet?'

'Oh Francis, I should think it has! It's lovely ... I've never dreamed of having so much money. Where's Harry ... Where are you? Can I speak to him? Surely you aren't there yet! You must have done eighty the whole way ...'

'No, we're in Tottenham Court road. I'm speaking from a call box. The fact is, that ass Juan ran into something. There's being a bit of a fuss. Quite a crowd. Can you hear it? I'll open the door.'

In the pause she heard a very different sound from the one she expected. It came from outside her own front door.

It was the thrilling and mysterious sound of the first flight of autumn leaves, driven by the rising wind over the pavements. Adventure, lonely places, love, all the power and promise of the huge earth seemed to open in front of her as she listened, and realized that she had perhaps fifty years in which to follow the promise of that sound.

'Can you hear it? Here come the police ... I must fly.'

'Francis, was anyone hurt?'

'Lord, no, it's only a laundry van ... shirts all over the road. You never saw such a mess. God only knows what time we'll get to the flat ... Juan's talking ten to the dozen and Harry's trying his famous charm on the driver. The beloved old figure in the shabby dressing gown doesn't seem to be doing so well ... I must go and help. We'll 'phone you tomorrow. Goodbye, dear.'

'Goodbye ... *do* be careful, Francis ...'

He had gone.

It's very queer, she thought. I'm all alone now; and goodness only knows what will become of the boys without me. We've got no prospects. We've got an awful heredity, and we haven't made a good start at managing our own lives. And yet in spite of all these things, I can't feel unhappy. I can only feel excited and full of courage. I've got the strongest feeling that in the long run everything will be all right.